FutureBust

No part of this book may be reproduced in any manner without prior written permission from the author, except for brief quotations embodied in critical articles or reviews

This is a work of fiction. All characters, places, and events are either fictitious, or used in a fictitious manner.

Copyright © 2008 Dell Wagner
All rights reserved.
ISBN: 1-4196-2212-9
ISBN-13: 978-1419622120

Visit www.booksurge.com to order additional copies.

DELL WAGNER

FUTUREBUST

2008

FutureBust

"Let me put it to you bluntly. In a changing world, we want more people to have control over your life."—George W. Bush

FUTUREBUST1.0

A.D. 2015

Surrounded by groves of towering pine, spruce, and aspen, Larry Wilcox eased back in his lawn chair and relaxed, enjoying the warm, gentle breezes of summer next to a pristine lake. With eyes closed in concentration, he listened to the calls of songbirds, flittering through the forest canopy. Sunglasses rested comfortably, though precariously askew on his nose, which always made the kids laugh. It was the first vacation the family had taken since the twins were born. A couple weeks of R&R, then they'd head home to the grind of Washington DC.

The sound of waves sloshing against the shoreline was hypnotic. Fishing was in the works once the sun eased its way down through a cloudless sky. The walleye and bass liked to bite at that time, as loons sent mystical calls across calm evening waters. In a sense, it all seemed too good to be true. Larry's thoughts scrolled back across the long, difficult half-decade. Even while on vacation, the turmoil was never far from his mind.

An economic depression always gets people's attention, especially when it's much worse then the 1930s. To historians, that created a dilemma. It sounded silly to label current difficulties as the Greater Depression. And God help us when the Greatest Depression washes up on the beach. It would destroy the country. In hopes of avoiding that scenario, reclassifying and downgrading the relatively minor economic problems of the 1930s into the *Great Recession* solved the problem. Current difficulties could then be labeled the Great Depression, which they truly were.

More than half of the population didn't have a job, considerably worse than eight decades previous. The old-timers thought they were suffering with twenty-five percent unemployment. By modern standards, that was a piece-of-cake. Even the most hopeful forecasts predicted a moderating downward spiral over the next five years. And the *optimism* emanated from the same government economists who once claimed the national debt was a relatively minor concern, best swept under the rug and forgotten. With the unemployment rate at fifty-two percent and climbing, most felt lucky to know someone with a job they could mooch off.

The Great Recession of the 1930s had been difficult, despite America being more rural and willing to make sacrifices. The accepted standard of living was then much lower. Most people worked hard, clung to life by the skin of their teeth, and made do as best they could until a world war on the horizon created an economic upswing.

But modern times differed. It started innocently enough during the early 1980s. Tax cuts and loopholes for the rich bit heavily into government revenues. The formula was simple. If the top five percent income bracket didn't get sixty to seventy percent of the benefits from a tax reduction, the bill probably needed to be reworked. Follow with increased, wasteful spending, and it reignited an old nemesis: burgeoning deficits and a malignant national debt. Just twelve years later, the red ink had quadrupled.

Around the turn of the century, hundreds of major US corporations went offshore, avoiding taxes by claiming their corporate headquarters was a mailbox in the Caribbean. These huge companies had lots of friends in Washington DC. Congress refused to rein in the farce and the United States treasury lost $175 billion a year. If lucrative government contracts were to be had, the same corporations would hand out campaign cash in exchange for a no-bid consideration. Obviously, an element of hypocrisy and unethical opportunism existed, but no one in Congress seemed concerned. Append $200 billion a year in uncollected taxes along with another $225 billion in corporate welfare, and the lost revenue started to add up.

Attach energy problems created by America's Big Car Lifestyle—5000-pound gas-guzzling behemoths used to carry one passenger—and the cards were stacked against sustainable economic growth and prosperity. Congress failed to grasp why four percent of the world's population shouldn't be allowed to guzzle one quarter of the oil, six times its fair share. The rest of the world should be damn thankful the good people of the United States didn't use ten times their fair share, or just simplify the process and take it all. Talk about an impetus for terrorism!

Next came inflation, spurred on by the medical profession. Combine fifteen percent annual increases in the cost of medicine, exasperated by an unhealthy lifestyle, and America's aging population sagged and morphed into a healthcare nightmare. Medicare showed signs of thrombosis. The medical profession was heading for intensive care with a monetary blockage and impending cardiac arrest. Along with a collapsing dollar, the frightening implications caused a stock market panic in late 2013. Four months later after a slight upturn, it crashed a second time and hit eighty-year lows. Times were tough. Only doctors and plumbers could afford medical insurance.

Not used to living in the shadow of poverty, a law enforcement nightmare developed as roving, heavily-armed bands of rightwing fanatics (militia groups) began robbing and plundering—taking anything they could get their hands on; i.e. living off the fat of the land. These same people had fought tenaciously to maintain a right to bear arms. Turns out what such freedom-loving, law-abiding citizens really wanted was to turn their arsenals on others once things went south economically. If you had it and they wanted it, get used to looking down the business end of an assault rifle. It was their way of grabbing *fair share*, a pernicious euphemism bandied around at the time. Law enforcement budgets needed to be tripled but the money simply wasn't available.

As the worldwide decline deepened, many people became more self-centered, self-absorbed, thoughtless, and greedy—precisely the attitudes that created the problems in the first place. Others, however, reacted the opposite, giving back all they could in an attempt to build a new paradigm. It's a matter of personal philosophy and moral character. The cold, hard reality is that most are driven by the basic instinct of self-preservation, even when their impulses are not in the best interests of humankind as a whole.

It all seemed elementary when distilled to an even simpler absurdity. The economy was built on sand. The political system—a house of cards. And humanity greedily played Russian roulette with the environment. Any moron with the skill and technical expertise to operate glue or duct tape could have predicted the results. America had built up too much vulnerability.

The writing was on the wall, spray-painted in graffiti a half-wit could grasp. But Congress was still working on that. Besides, their time is too valuable to be wasted on solving pressing problems, or fretting about the survival of the-world-as-we-know-it. An election cycle loomed, with a campaign to worry about. No time to lose! They'd hit the fundraising circuit immediately after returning from an exhausting taxpayer financed fact-finding junket to Honolulu, whose beaches need methodical federal oversight.

The inevitable result of severe economic travails is substance abuse—alcohol in particular—a drug known by its fluid aliases: Liquid Courage, or Christmas in a bottle. Others just called it grog and guzzled to block out the pain. Hard times necessitate hard liquor so it's no surprise that prohibition became a hot political issue.

As such, ninety-seven percent of the nations around the globe reluctantly came to terms with reality and committed to a systematic, coordinated effort to combat the problem. Drug addiction became so pervasive during the teens that no feasible alternative existed. Some old, forgotten four-star general once coined a phrase that pretty much summed it up. To solve the problem, *first you cut it off, then kill it.* That method is direct and to-the-point. It also works for unwanted facial hair.

As a world leader (drug abuse is no exception), the United States embarked on a nonstop drinking binge. Families were torn apart and lives destroyed. Countless hopeful futures sank agonizingly into oblivion. Other hopeful futures were obliterated in a split second—when the drunk driver hit. Alcohol isn't particular in how it shatters life or whose goes to waste. As an equal opportunity annihilator, traffic fatalities tripled in just five years.

Substance abuse had to be handled creatively or the cost to society would be unprecedented. With a myriad of social and economic problems to confront, such self-defeating addictions created an unnecessary burden on resources—slowing social progress to a crawl, or more correctly, stomping it into the ground. The solution was simple if not elegant: ban drugs and ban them now. Outlaw the substances. Cut them off and kill them. No looking back. No second-guessing. No mercy! Unfortunately, lawyers and diet book writers weren't included, but one can't expect to get everything perfect on the first try.

Officer Larry Wilcox was about to start a career at the newly created *Drug Enforcement Service*. The DES was a selfless attempt by cash-strapped bureaucracies to consolidate resources—vital in a depression economy. No longer would countless little fiefdoms of jurisdiction compete in pursuit of the same goal. Drug Enforcement united under one roof. The umbrella incorporated drug interdiction and social work, helping the afflicted with their problems. *No mercy* was temporarily on hold.

Law officers wouldn't force self-righteous drug eradication policies down the throats of addicted people who'd lost control of their lives. Addicts could opt for counseling, thus bypassing the courts and prison. There'd be ample opportunity to satisfy the get-tough crowd in later years. And, oddly, the law was devoid of hypocrisy, which had made a mockery of a previous anti-drug effort known as *WoD*, or War on Drugs.

Larry was on vacation—two budget-conscious weeks with the family before starting his career at DES. The best and brightest from various agencies were recruited. He was apprehensive about his new position, yet glad to have a job providing a genuine paycheck redeemable for currency at most locations. Cash-money is a good thing to have during a depression. One also needs common sense. Don't spend money you don't possess. Avoid debt. Live simply and think positive, uplifting thoughts. Eventually the mother-in-law will get her own place. Conditions will surely improve. Unfortunately, few grasped the full, long-term impact of the economic uncertainty. If they had, even a stiff drink wouldn't have helped.

The transition was two weeks away. Right now—vacation time. On a personal level, things were looking up. The mother-in-law? She'd take care of the kids when everyone was busy. That's the positive-thinking part. She's also a fine cook, thus will make the best of any food that's scrounged up.

The depression aside, things had changed in a big way. Alcohol was illegal—banned—being just too destructive. People realized that booze costs money. Hard liquor—hard currency. The major commercial-industrial breweries and distilleries struggled to convert to productive products like ethanol.

Many feared a rebellion against prohibition, but it hadn't materialized. Pockets of resistance (right-wing extremists and beer-guzzling militias) were rounded up by the National Guard and sent to rehab. Of course the drug dependent corporate interests weren't too happy. Financially, alcoholic industries such as breweries and distilleries were plastered. The tobacco stocks got smoked. All were in the middle of a difficult economic struggle trying to convert to some productive business. The wine industry was guilty of sour grapes. Even before the ban on alcohol, climate change ruined the harvest. Things weren't the same. The growers couldn't deal with temperamental weather patterns.

Fortunately for connoisseurs, a determined industry chemist invented synthetic, nonalcoholic wine. Low-and-behold (big surprise), it was better than the real stuff. What did you expect? The guy had a Ph.D. from a prestigious Massachusetts university. The innovation, however, was a financial disaster because the new, drug-free libation lacked sufficient snob appeal and high-society acceptance—a necessary requisite for success.

Wine historians, outraged by the synthetic upstart, graciously volunteered their services to prove the newcomer a fraud. However in blindfolded taste tests, the experts were often fooled. Of course these eminently qualified aficionados huffed and puffed and sputtered with excuses when the labels were removed, revealing Brand X actually had more aroma and body than some fancy-pants imported Chardonnay sporting an exclusive French name. It proved one thing. High-class wines like Chateau de Blasé had been a mischievous, profitable fraud all along—nothing more than glorified *Rotgut*.

This gave one energetic entrepreneur an idea: bottle the inexpensive synthetic behind a counterfeit, pretentious, stuck-up label and sell it on the black market at a premium. He made a fortune, then escaped to TobagoBago, an offshore tax haven in the Caribbean. It all became immaterial after drug prohibition. Drink nonalcoholic or don't drink at all. For law-abiding guzzlers, *O'DOUL'S* was all the rage. The smart money purchased stock in that company when it broke away from its struggling parent corporation.

Concerning the legality issue, the grace period was the reason for a successful transition. Alcohol and tobacco were illegal, but individuals were allowed personal possession in small amounts, essentially a *get out of jail free* card. The grace period continued for two years. Then on January 2, 2017, c'est fini—addictions conquered or it meant time in the cooler (not the one holding the beer). New Years Day was twenty-four hours past the deadline, but the government gave everyone a freebee. After that, jail time was ramped up. A tobacco violation would get thirty days. By 2020—two years. Same with alcohol and Hippie Lettuce. Repeat violations meant stiffer sentences: twenty years or more for traffickers and violent offenders. But the heavy hand of the law had been put on ice until people overcame addictions in a stress-free setting.

Larry's law enforcement experience brought to mind another fact as he relaxed on the dock in the bright, summer sun. Dollars were transferred from pork barrel prison programs into rehabilitation with astonishing results. Research into anti-addiction drugs expanded. Irony? Success quelled the laughter. As always, the pharmaceutical stocks got high on profits. Cautiously rising expectations blossomed within law enforcement. More cost-effective than prison, prevention became the focus, getting people to look inward where drug problems originate. But this inspirational reverie was squelched as the twins dumped a bucket of cool lake water over their father's head.

FUTUREBUST1.19

Time passed quickly in vacationland. The girls complained it was too early to go home, and Larry wholeheartedly agreed. DC is a difficult city. Living costs are high; social pressures push hard on the psyche, creating stress. He knew where he'd retire: the northwoods, and the endless chains of blue lakes. The religiously inclined called it God's country.

In the meantime, it was off to the East Coast. Folks lived harder, drove faster, and rushed around willy-nilly. The nation's capital had unique problems: confused individuals lacking focus and direction, needing special help and encouragement. But the new Congress would pull through, one way or another.

FUTUREBUST1.2

The initial years at DES were productive and fulfilling. Larry worked with his new colleagues, each having strengths and weaknesses, faults and strong points. In his first days on duty he met a fellow who was six-foot-six, weighing in at two-forty—essentially one tough hombre. This man often referred to his coworkers as Little Fella, Small Fry, or Junior Midget if you happened to be short. Other monikers included Sonny Boy, Punkin' Head if you were a rookie, or worst of all: Mama's Little Helper if you happened to be a wimp. Larry was glad that title didn't apply to him. Buck wasn't a mean, insensitive guy. He just had a knack for giving everyone a nickname, many of which were funny. The problem? You accepted what was given. Buck was adamant about that. Larry earned the nickname…well, maybe we shouldn't go there. It'll save for another time.

FUTUREBUST

Buck had a manner, a persona making him dominant, though not domineering. He was not only big, but also fast, due to years of Marshal Arts training. Skilled in the art of *Jeet Kune Do*, Buck could wipe out the entire neighborhood in a fight. He'd taken it up as a boy after seeing a movie about a Kung Fu master. But in the early days at DES, no one knew of his fighting skill. They would find out later.

One day a *Punkin' Head* just out of college and eager to earn a meager paycheck, asked Buck what his real name was. The big man didn't particularly like the question. "We needn't get into that," he replied gently. "It's not healthy." Close observation revealed annoyance; the rookie flirting with no small amount of Whoop-Ass Potential (WAP)! But the subject inadvertently revived sometime later.

"Why do they call you Buck?" Lieutenant Jackson asked casually. "That can't be your real name, yet it's listed in your employment file. You came from upstate New York. Nobody names their kid Buck unless they come from Texas."

"I don't want to talk about it," Buck replied ominously. He left the room. Eyebrows raised, Lieutenant Jackson understood the implications. The matter didn't resurface until months later when Buck earned a commendation for saving a DC policeman's life. Armed perpetrators had overpowered an officer, who surprised them during a convenience store robbery. Buck was walking home at midnight when he noticed something not quite right up the block. He ran to the scene as closest available backup. Three men with broken bones were taken into custody. Their donnybrook with Buck lasted ten seconds.

He was given the award in a ceremony attended by DES officers and members of the DC police force. Buck walked to the podium to receive his honor. The mayor shook his hand, then unknowingly asked the dreaded question. "Buck is an unusual name for a man from this part of the country. I'm wondering what your given name is? I hate to use a nickname during such an important occasion."

This is a bad position to be in—a professionally important event with a large crowd of curious onlookers present. Buck swallowed hard, knowing he couldn't threaten WAP on the entire audience present to honor him. Everyone waited with question marks scrolled across their faces. The room went stone-cold silent. He could conceal the truth no longer! "*Robin*," Buck replied in a timid voice. Extraneous chuckles were silenced with a stern glance. WAP isn't entirely useless at large gatherings.

The mayor continued, oblivious to Buck's sensitivity. "This commendation for bravery and incredible fighting skills is presented to Robin Klassen, for going above and beyond the call of duty in saving a police officer's life." The mayor seemed like a nice guy, but had a little twitch in his arm. He was definitely in the middle of an extended withdrawal, just like everyone else in the country—nothing to be ashamed of.

No one talked about the incident, though three years later it became irrelevant with Buck's promotion to Sergeant. For about fifteen seconds he was known as Buck Sergeant, but an angry stare…(WAP yet again). After that everyone called him Sarge.

Buck and Larry busted their share of perps, but at the most critical time the two ever faced, they were separated. It was a couple years after joining the DES—Autumn 2017.

FUTUREBUST1.3

Larry and Buck were on patrol in the early morning hours of June 25, looking out for anything suspicious. Their beat: the entire DC area at night—not an easy task considering how many devious lawmaker-types ran around loose and unsupervised. But someone had to step up to the plate, take responsibility, and keep an eye on those shysters.

In the best traditions of cops everywhere, the two stopped at a *24-hour* (donut shop) for a break. It'd been a quiet, uneventful shift, unearthing no persons of dubious character. After crawling out from under rocks, such ethically challenged individuals often leech off the various branches of government as lobbyists and consultants. Most reside out near the beltway, Interstate 495, thus are known as the Beltway Bandits. They come into town only when free money is available.

Buck purchased a donut with pink icing and multicolored sparkles. "Don't tell anyone I bought this sissy-looking thing," he cautioned, "or I'll be breaking bones."

"I might be persuaded to keep quiet." Larry placed his hand out, palm up.

"Blackmail is not a viable option," Buck warned. "You don't want to make a Whoop-Ass issue out of this, do you?"

"Probably not," Larry conceded. "In that case, I'll have the same." It was the only time the two men ever discussed WAP. Both sat at a table and enjoyed the moment. Some would call it male bonding, but not in front of Buck—not if wanting to avoid WAP! "So why did you go in for the DES?" Larry asked out of the blue.

"Years ago, I lived next door to an alcoholic," Buck replied. "The guy terrorized his family and beat his wife. The kids, one being my best friend at the time, were deeply affected. It was such a waste to watch him go downhill. I tried to interest him in Marshal Arts, to get him on a positive path but it didn't work. His self-image remained negative. I never saw him after he moved away, but he did contact me once; said he was struggling with the same problems his father had. Alcoholism spread to him like a disease." Buck hesitated, deep in thought. "There's no good reason to have that stuff around. Besides, my body's a temple." Larry smiled at Buck's biblical assessment of his physical being. The big man continued. "Getting beat up by a more qualified fighter, that's okay. But never abuse yourself."

"So you're a clean-cut, all-American boy?"

"Pretty much," Buck laughed. "Except for my long hair, leather jacket, earring, tattoo, the hardtail Harley Davidson I park in the living room right next to the TV, and that really big boat I'd like to own someday when the economy gets better, I'd say you pigeonholed me perfectly. How about yourself? What do you think about all this drug controversy?"

Larry shrugged. "The boys I ran with used to have guzzling races to see who could down the most beer without taking a breath. It was a lot of fun until a friend didn't make it home from the pizza parlor one night. Too much alcohol made him drive into a tree. Some of us gave it up after that happened. I quit and never looked back." Larry paused, sorrow evident in his voice. "You'd think we'd have figured it out before something like that happened, but we were just stupid kids, not yet legally old enough to drink."

Both men sat quietly for a time. After that night, Buck never called Larry...Oh, we didn't get to that nickname, did we? Maybe we'll let it ride. From then on, Buck referred to his partner by his given name. Their careers would run parallel for the next thirty years.

A few hours on patrol and the shift ended. Larry dropped Buck at his doorstep at 5 A.M. Living back across town in a section more suitable for families, he decided to cruise past the Capitol and admire its majesty. Not too distant from the solemn and stately symbol of legislative power, he noticed a small cube van pulling away from the entrance to a large underground facility housing the logistical supplies needed to keep government running efficiently. Warehoused were items from floor wax to typing paper to big screen TVs, all necessary for a smoothly functioning democracy, at least in the eyes of Congress.

Also available underground were other necessities of life for hard-working legislators, including a workout gym; an Olympic-sized pool which could be reserved for special occasions; squash courts; facilities for tennis and bowling; a Congressional parking area and car wash (yes, paid for by taxpayers); barber shops and shoeshining stations; a subsidized travel agency where airline and train tickets to anywhere they wanted to go on official (yuk yuk) business were a bargain; and even a department store. With living costs high in DC and Congress so underpaid, the lawmakers saw no reason why they shouldn't have subsidized shopping.

And building the vast, underground complex created jobs, a good thing in tough economic times. Who could resist it? A lot of ground was dug up between Constitution, and Independence Avenues. The park-like surroundings were efficiently excavated, stuffed with perks and privilege, then backfilled before anybody realized what had happened. Once completed, you couldn't even tell. All that wonderful subsidization was covered over with fresh grass and hidden from public view—underground as it were. Only current members of Congress and families were permitted in. And the whole complex was connected right to the Capitol Building basement via a tunnel. They could walk from one to the other without being seen, creating plenty of incentive to get reelected. Cost overruns were well within working parameters, only four times the original bid.

Larry contemplated his current situation. Even by governmental standards, it was unusual for a vehicle to be pulling away from an underground loading dock at 5 A.M. Logistics were handled symbolically during the daylight hours. After all, democracy is supposed to be operated aboveboard, out in the open—by and for the people. Why would anyone want to keep secrets? The truck had a government license plate and twelve-digit vehicle ID. It sped into the darkness, running with headlights off for a block.

Larry continued home and put the anomaly out of his mind, but was unable to rest. Something (more than the lack of headlights) seemed out of place. He'd once seen a similar truck near the House of Representatives Office Building at an ungodly hour of the night, and at the General Accounting Office the morning before a farewell party for a half-dozen retiring bigwigs. It was also spotted leaving the Federal Reserve at 2:30 A.M. He finally fell asleep for a full hour before his five-year-old twin daughters jumped on the bed.

Buck came over on the hardtail that afternoon. "What's on your mind?" the big man asked. "The kids wake you again? You've got bags under your eyes."

"I saw a US Marines truck unloading something near the Capitol early this morning after I dropped you off. The vehicle was definitely suspicious."

"Did you get the license number?"

"I was too far away," Larry recalled. "It just seemed unusual to me. I've seen it before. We'll keep an eye out from now on. If we see it, let's tag it."

"Sounds good," Buck replied. "Sometimes it's best to trust instincts. You may be on to something." He hesitated. "It wasn't the same little truck we saw at the Supreme Court a few months back, just before the new Justice was sworn in, was it?"

FUTUREBUST1.4

Weeks flew by and summer turned to fall in the capital city. Buck and Larry made some drug busts, though nothing out of the ordinary. Organized gangs of disheveled, unemployed tobacco executives tried to sell contraband cigarettes from their overcoats, mostly to junior high kids. The longstanding policy to addict them while young was still in force. DES kept a close eye on the schools. Lurking former tobacco execs were easily identified by the barefaced lies they carried around as sales tools.

It just so happened that Congress was back in session, making laws, and spending the (employed) taxpayer's hard-earned cash. The economy was struggling, up to fifty-five percent unemployment at times, so the boys and girls at the Capitol crowded around the public trough, trying desperately to funnel money to their districts. There was more oinking, squealing, and grunting, than usual. The slop, no matter how useless or disgusting, was quickly lapped up by one group of Congressional porkers or another.

MAMA, the Military Aircraft Manufactures Association (with two well-connected members) wanted to build a new strategic bomber, the B4 LOAD or Low Orbit Atomic Destructor. Still in the initial stages of development, components and parts for the aircraft would be produced in just about every state in the union—the exception being Puerto Rico, which didn't have much of a Military-Industrial Complex up and running. The fifty-second state was more interested in tourism.

Once deployed, the B4 would be a technological marvel, flying to the edge of space—over twenty-five miles high—at speeds of Mach 12 or greater. Within three hours, the stealthy space-plane could reach any part of the globe from a proposed base in Topeka, Kansas. The cost—$161 billion for twenty-eight planes, a bargain at only $5.75 billion apiece.

Congress leapt at the chance to do its patriotic duty, and hijacked cash from the Social Security trust fund. The flag-wavers were everywhere, thus lawmaker's patriotism was gauged by how much they'd allow the Pentagon to squander. There's no way the plane could justify its cost unless the pigs squealed and hogs grunted. Not surprisingly, the debate resembled a livestock-calling contest at the state fair. True, an ICBM with MIRV warhead could more accurately reach the target in one/sixth the time—thus a considerably cheaper way to destroy the world. But that wasn't the point. Congress sought to replace the aging B1B and the technologically backward B2. Worse yet, the B3 went beyond useless to counterproductive. Four of the first seven crashed while in the testing phase.

All had been mind-numbing financial boondoggles. But bygones are bygones. The country needed a bomber to mop up after the final war concluded. "Armageddon won't be a pretty sight," the chairman of the Senate Armed Services Committee blustered, "but by God, we're going to do it right and finish what we started!" Hand it to strategic planners. They're awfully creative when it comes to destruction.

After the money was allocated, cost-conscious legislators complained the only thing the B4 could do was to bounce the rubble created by ICBMs. But pork-barrelers dismissed these criticisms as lovey-dovey, twinkle-toes objections because some districts didn't rake in as many Iron Triangle dollars as hoped. And besides, if saving money is the goal, they can always cut back on school lunch programs for undernourished toddlers, veteran's benefits, or maybe pollution control enforcement for air and water, which isn't cost-effective anyway. The national defense comes first. Without the B4, there's a *Window of Vulnerability* due to the continued failure of the $216 billion Missile Defense Shield!

One conscientious senator claimed that the B4 was a totally useless waste of money, but late night talk show hosts quickly rebuffed such criticisms. They pointed out that the phrase *useless waste* is a double negative, making the B4 a pressing, vital necessity. What did the senator want; a *useful* waste? Another talk show host opined that even the Pentagon had not yet devised a platform that was totally useless. The B4, as worthless strategically as the B1, B2, and B3 had been, would make a fine addition to the Postal Service for speeding up overseas mail delivery. The jokes continued for weeks until an angry four-star general, tired of all the comedic abuse, was overheard at a social event loudly proclaiming the fact that the Air Force didn't even want the damn aircraft anyway. It was the politicians funneling money to their districts with no regard for the best interests of the armed forces or the country as a whole. Two days later the general publicly apologized for his unfortunate off-the-cuff remark, picked up by a DC newspaper reporter. The politicians put the squeeze on him. Either get with the program or take a hike. When confronted by the media, the general caustically admitted that "it'll be thirty years before the B4 proves its *uselessness*". He'd caved in, but days later came to his senses, sucked in his gut, and again publicly denounced the aircraft as nothing but welfare for the aerospace industry. His resignation was accepted with little sympathy. Flag-wavers accused him of being a turncoat. But more thoughtful, budget-responsive members of Congress saw him for what he was, a true patriot, sacrificing his career for his country.

Though not a milestone in itself, the B4 is indicative of the changes that had taken place over the decades. Gone are the days when the Pentagon wasted money in the thousands or millions, on $234 hammers or $2091 hex nuts or

FUTUREBUST

$471 toilet seats. Such chump change stimulates fond memories for budget cutters. But they're no longer relevant when it comes to military expenditures. Only the big spenders have clout. In the modern world, waste is in the hundreds of billions, and cumulatively in the trillions if compounding interest on the national debt. Some experts consider half the weapons budget as pork. But that's an unpatriotic thing to say. It's safer to keep quiet and drape oneself in the flag.

FUTUREBUST1.5

Back in the real world, Buck and Larry were on duty one warm night in October. It was the usual: patrol then donuts then patrol. Larry got a kick out of Buck's pink frosting with sprinkles; the ones he ordered at the 24-hour. Donuts were his partner's only vice, yet it didn't show. Buck was superbly conditioned. He'd recently won a regional Marshal Arts tournament featuring various fighting disciplines—multifarious weaponless warriors displaying their *Art*. It didn't take more than sixty seconds to dispatch each of his opponents. Buck was invited to a national competition in Los Angeles a couple weeks hence. There was talk of a movie contract if he did well.

At about 3 A.M. they drove past the Capitol. That little green truck was parked down in an underground entrance ramp, illuminated only by distant streetlights. The patrol car rolled by as if nothing was happening. Buck nudged his partner. "Is that it?"

"That's the one," Larry replied. "Think we have any hope of tagging it?"

"I didn't see any guards, and the lights inside the facility weren't on."

Both men looked at each other. Larry had driven a block past. He stopped the car. "No guards near an entry to the Capitol Complex! That's got to be considered somewhat out-of-the-ordinary, even by governmental standards." Larry's joke didn't mask the seriousness of the matter. "Let's go back and tag that vehicle!"

Both officers exited the patrol car. Buck grabbed the tagging kit containing a tiny GPS homing device no bigger than a thumbtack, and a tube of Stick'um used to paste the tag on the object of surveillance. Rubber gloves were included. The glue was so strong (claimed the manufacturer) it'd take dynamite to dislodge the device. Once activated, GPS could track it anywhere in the world via satellite. Larry entered the serial number into the cruiser's onboard computer.

Avoiding the streetlights, they jogged to the sunken entrance and observed two men—neither resembling a Marine—not unless jarheads are into permed hairdos. "What do you think about getting a look inside?" Larry whispered.

They were only fifty feet from the truck, backed against the doorway. All lights were off.

"We may have to split up," Buck whispered, then stepped from hiding and stealthily reached the front of the truck where he glued the tiny GPS device on the cab. He hopped on the passenger-side running board and stayed very still. Buck was dressed in a black shirt and pants so he disappeared into the darkness as Larry watched. The driver of the truck prepared to leave. Larry slipped around behind and got as close to the entry as possible. Buck remained with the truck, holding onto the passenger-side door handle, kneeling down on the running board as it drove up the ramp to the surface, then away into the night. The driver ran dark for three blocks.

As Larry approached the unlit entrance, he could see the shadow of a man inside the storage area. He slipped through the door and crouched behind some barrels of floor scrub. The man grabbed a clipboard, then returned to the entrance and punched a button. The garage door closed and the lights came on.

Larry stayed invisible. He was now in the Capitol Building's underground storage complex, still a block or more from the building proper, watching some guy load cardboard boxes onto a four-wheel cart. The man lifted a box and placed it carefully, then began stacking more. Clearly they were fragile, probably holding bottles filled with...Larry had a good idea what. A two-way (radio) suddenly came to life.

"Dieter?" it squawked.

"Go ahead," Dieter replied, pulling the handheld from his belt clip.

"Remember that car we saw driving by when we were offloading?"

"Yeah, sure." Dieter spoke with a slight German accent.

"It's DES, parked near the corner of Independence. There was no one in it when I drove by." Larry could hear the radio conversation between the two men. Despite being well hidden, he knew he was in trouble.

"Got'cha," Dieter replied sharply as his mood darkened. He switched channels. "We may have a problem. Krueger spotted a cop car. You better get some men out here now!"

"On our way!" came the angry reply. "Don't let anyone get near that shipment!"

Larry held his breath as five men ran into the storage facility from a set of double doors that led further into the underground complex and all the way to the Capitol Building proper. They looked like something out of a Hollywood movie. Two had ponytails; one a crew cut. The others sported permed hairdos with glittery sparkles throughout. Larry rolled his eyes. Besides being neatly dressed and unusually large, they were clearly upset.

"Günter, Dolf, the dock area!" one man barked. "Thor, check outside!

Find that cop!" They scurried like rats. "Get this shipment out of here. Lars, help Dieter!"

Two guys hastily stacked the jingling boxes until the cart was overloaded. Dieter pushed the four-wheeler towards a door that led further into the complex, slowing only enough to give Lars time to open it. As he negotiated a turn just beyond the threshold, one cardboard box fell hard. The glass contents broke, spilling liquid onto the cement floor. Larry knew it wasn't aftershave.

"Sorry Ulrick." Dieter was disgusted with himself. "I'll clean it up now."

The leader became incensed with the spill. "Get it the hell out of here! Dolf, help them with the cart!" Larry silently chuckled. Ulrick, Dolf, Günter, Thor, Krueger, Lars, and Dieter. Who'd have guessed. Then one of the big guys grabbed him from behind and lifted him right off his knees.

"I've got him!" Günter's two-foot long ponytail swished back and forth.

To struggle was Buck's forte, but he was gone. Three guys surrounded Larry, including a newcomer wearing a nametag on his lapel—Igor, scrolled in red.

"Bring him here!" Ulrick ordered impatiently. First or last name? It really didn't matter at this point. Larry was hustled to the middle of the room with two guys firmly holding his arms. Another grabbed him by the hair. All three were at least six inches taller, and clearly PO'd. "Check him!" Ulrick ordered. Then, over his radio, "We've got him, sir."

Larry was aggressively frisked. They took his wallet and concealed firearm. Then his hands were secured behind his back with a plastic strap. The guy pulled it very tight, cutting into his wrist. Thor rummaged through the wallet, confiscating two twenties and a ten. "He's DES alright. Officer Larry Wilcox."

Ulrick was furious, kicking a box of paper towels off a nearby shelf. "I don't need this right now! How the hell did a DES officer get in here? How'd they find out about this?" He kicked another box containing cleanser. In a rage, he stomped a little cardboard canister into the floor. White powder exploded into the air. Ulrick shouted into his radio. "He knows what we're doing here. We've got to get rid of him!"

"No," came the calm voice over the radio. "Bring him here."

Ulrick looked startled, but obeyed. "Take him!" Then he picked up another canister and threw it against the wall. They exited the storage area through the double doors, leaving an expanding cloud of cleanser dust floating aimlessly toward the ceiling. Ulrick was so disheveled from his outburst, he had to straighten his coat and tie. Two more guys appeared in the hallway. Both had nametags: Urnst and Hanz. Hanz even spelled his name with a *Z* instead of an *S*. It looked more *Hollywood* that way.

Larry was surrounded by five big guys, all of them PO'd and hoping to bury their fist into his midsection. Big trouble. These men had no morals.

They were drug dealers, probably working for a cartel or syndicate right in the Capitol complex. He was hustled through a long, poorly lit hallway, then into an office and forcibly shoved into a wooden chair. His sense of direction told him he was directly under the Capitol Building in the basement. Ulrick entered and slapped him across the back of the head.

FUTUREBUST1.6

Larry sat with hands secured behind his back, facing a gray-haired man seated in a black leather chair. A desk constructed of teak separated them. The man was composed, yet a dubious smirk underpinned his naturally sour expression. "Untie him," he ordered, looking puzzled. "How did DES find out about our little enterprise?" His tone, though not aggressive, wasn't to be taken lightly.

"Lots of background work!" Larry rubbed his wrists.

The boss chuckled. "Where is your backup? You've done all this background work and decided to bust us by yourself?" Larry remained silent. No point in saying anything. The guy was enjoying himself and didn't need an answer. "No," the man shook his head, "there was no background work." He rubbed his hands after applying hand lotion from a convenient bottle. "You stumbled on us all by yourself, didn't you?"

A large man entered the room and handed over a piece of paper. His nametag said 'Phill' (another Hollywood spelling). The boss read quietly, then glanced at his prisoner. He spoke slowly, condescendingly, as if Larry was mentally deficient. It was irritating as hell.

"Larry, it says here that you've been with DES since its inception. You've done lots of fine work for them, I'm sure." The old fellow remained silent for a few seconds, then ordered his men to leave. The last one, with a braided ponytail, closed the door. "My name is LeRoy. The boys sometimes call me Uncle Roy. I work at the Capitol as a facilitator, keeping things shipshape, since you once spent time in the Navy."

"By providing dangerous drugs to Congress?"

"Larry," LeRoy's sadistic smile belied his gentle words. "You've got to let go of this hostility. I'm no criminal. I deal with reality, not some fantasy world you dream about in your sleep. People here play hardball, political cutthroat, dog-eat-dog. Take my boys for instance. They're butchers. They dress so fine in three-piece suits and fancy hairdos, but underneath they're animals with no feelings for anybody. They do what I say and are paid accordingly. In fact, if I hadn't been in the office so early this morning…" LeRoy spoke as if not caring one way or the other, "I shudder to think how much pain you'd have endured."

Larry shook his head in disbelief. He'd heard all the arguments before. "Larry," Uncle Roy protested gently, "let me explain something. Here in DC, things are a little different from other localities. Washington's lifeblood is power. The men and women who work here worship it. They chase after power like jewels and gold because to them it is."

Larry interrupted his lesson in human nature. "You're CIA, aren't you?"

Uncle Roy tolerated the question. "If I tell you the truth, what will you do with that information? You know, I could have my boys make you forget you ever existed as a human being. It's entertainment to them."

Larry glared at the elderly gentleman. His question had been answered so he asked another. "Why is it so important to supply drugs to Congress?"

"It's not just Congress," Uncle Roy volunteered a surprising bit of information. "And it's not just alcohol." He reached into his desk and pulled out an expertly hand-rolled Cuban, neatly encased in a protective, clear plastic tube—probably worth a pretty penny on the black market, for the big-shot corporate types who still had that kind of (shareholder) money to squander. "We supply every Cabinet Department and bureaucracy here in Washington. Think about this for a minute. What do the people of DC have in common?"

"They want to work in government," Larry replied ambiguously, hoping his newfound acquaintance would fill in the blanks.

"Well," Uncle Roy admitted, a cynical smile crossing his face, "they do aspire to work in government. But don't you think there's an ulterior motive in most, if not all of them?"

"Okay, they covet power," Larry admitted. "So what."

"And why do they desire power?"

"So they can dominate; do as they like; maintain their advantage."

"You're being simplistic," Uncle Roy replied, a look of pity on his face. "Go deeper."

"What do you want from me?" Larry demanded.

"I'd hoped you might want to join us. Working for the Firm has tremendous advantages."

"Like?" Larry pretended to be interested.

"How does an extra salary sound?" Uncle Roy enticed. "You'd keep your job at DES along with the miserably low pay, and earn three times what you now make…Oh," Uncle Roy continued in a surprised, patronizing manner, "did I forget to mention? It's tax-free. We wouldn't want the IRS to know about your clandestine activities. All you have to do is promise not to attract attention by spending it on luxury sports cars or other items that DES agents cannot afford. Essentially, you'd still have to eat corn flakes for breakfast." LeRoy laughed at his joke, something a good comic never does.

"You want me to spy on my own organization?" Larry was incredulous.

"Not spy. We're all working for the same team, pretty much. I want you to keep tabs on the DES and let us know what's going on." LeRoy grinned, as if all he'd asked was that Larry do his patriotic duty.

"I didn't know your agency was involved in domestic surveillance."

Uncle Roy sat up and clasped his hands together on the desk. "My dear boy, we keep tabs on everyone and everything, regardless of what you've heard. We have moles in the FBI, NSA, the Congress, we have them in every Cabinet Department, in the White House, we even have them at NASA, and if we thought the dog pound needed watching, we'd have them there too. The CIA has moles spying on other moles. That's just what we do."

Larry withheld criticism, as well as a joke about rodents, which wouldn't have been appreciated. "So what does all this have to do with supplying drugs to Congress?"

"Oh yes," Uncle Roy affirmed. "We never did get to the bottom of that matter, did we? Think about it for a minute. Why do people seek after power?"

"They want control," Larry admitted.

"Keep going," LeRoy prodded. "Why the control?"

"Maybe to further their interests."

"Maybe," Uncle Roy spoke as if that wasn't the end of it.

Larry obliged. "They have a need to dominate."

"Some do, but it's deeper than that." The elderly gentleman shook his head in disgust and fidgeted as he spoke, a grimace on his face. He was clearly annoyed at the lack of integrity in the representative pool known as Congress. "Why does an elected official spend most of his time chasing after money? Why has there been no substantial campaign finance reform in fifteen years, when the old reforms have been completely undermined? Why are ethics so lax that members of Congress fall completely out of touch with the rest of the country?"

"They want to raise large sums of money to get reelected," Larry admitted.

"To…"

"Maintain mastery over power," Larry shrugged, pretending ignorance.

"There's only one more step in the equation," Uncle Roy encouraged.

Larry sat perfectly still, realizing what the old gentleman was thinking. He spoke with visible surprise on his face. "Insecurity! Many elected officials are emotionally deficient, using power to cover it."

"A potent form of denial," LeRoy agreed smugly. "Congress as an institution is built on a framework of denial. Why do you think so few problems get solved? It's not that we can't correct things, but Congress doesn't want to. There are powerful special interests afraid of losing wealth, control, domination, or prestige. So they champion representatives who work to prevent needed reform. It's a vicious circle. Money buys access to power, generating a systematic advantage, which feeds the arrogance and pomposity that covers insecurity and inadequacy, creating the denial that corrupts our values. Put simply, it's a classic example of an ADS!"

"Arrest Deprivation Syndrome?" Larry was surprised by LeRoy's use of the abbreviation, and couldn't grasp the connection. "I thought only cops experienced ADS."

"I'm talking about an Active Denial System."

Now it made more sense. "I see your point. So why the alcohol?"

"Alcohol is Liquid Denial. Those people in Congress aren't totally unfeeling. Deep inside they know what they're doing is wrong. But the influence peddling keeps right on rolling. Alcohol helps them survive—gives them courage to face another day of dull, dreary, emotionally debilitating work in an unresponsive government. They're addicted to anything that will help maintain the cushion of denial. Otherwise reality is much too painful."

"And if we denied the Liquid Denial?" Larry asked expectantly. The old man's explanation was getting interesting.

"They'd still have power to cover their insecurities," LeRoy admitted. "But if those people had to face their inadequacies, really take a good look at themselves, I'm afraid they'd be down here in the storage area, sitting in the corner sucking their thumbs. Do you want to put the whole government into withdrawal and end civilization as we know it?"

"You're saying our system of government attracts maladjusted people into positions of power," Larry suggested cautiously, still keenly aware of being held captive.

"Read your history, my young friend." Uncle Roy shook his head in despair. "Political leaders often have underlying insecurity as the motivation for seeking power. And if an extremely insecure individual takes control, we end up with a tyrant." LeRoy paused for effect. "Let me give another illustration. What do you think you'd get if you rolled up all those Congressional personalities and egos into one person?"

"Why would I want to do that?" Larry wasn't following.

"To simplify our discussion," LeRoy encouraged.

He didn't think long about the question, yet took time in answering to more closely observe his captor. LeRoy waited patiently as Larry replied. "A very confused, angry, insecure person in deep denial who craves attention!" He tried not to laugh out loud.

"These people have issues!" Uncle Roy's forehead furrowed. "They need constant help, encouragement, and understanding! We're in a depression. Make a cost-benefit comparison between alcohol and taxpayer financed psychiatric help. In the final analysis, alcohol comes out cheaper. Do you see what I'm getting at?"

Larry admitted the obvious. "Congress isn't ready to face reality."

"In a nutshell," LeRoy agreed. "But there's more. You see, people who cover motives behind a veil of superiority are as a rule, rarely introspective. They are power addicts because they know of no other way to survive emotionally, and aren't even aware of their own inner turmoil. In some, it eventually eats them alive. Alcohol helps them cope, at least in the short term."

"It sounds like the medicine creates a problem worse than it cures," Larry protested, milking the situation for relevant information.

"You may be right," Uncle Roy conceded with a sigh. "But in a perverse way, it helps. Alcohol, like denial, destroys lives yet allows its victims to temporarily withstand the emotional pain and hopelessness of their slow, agonizing demise." Larry wondered if the man really empathized with the people in Congress, or was just collecting his fat, tax-free paycheck. "So what do you think of my offer?" Uncle Roy queried while absentmindedly adjusting some writing utensils on his desk.

"I've got a question," Larry announced cautiously. LeRoy nodded his approval. "How long do we cover this problem, pretending it doesn't exist? You are not currently helping the situation."

"That's a valid point," Uncle Roy admitted while leaning back in his chair. "Let me ask you a question. How long do you think it'll be before America selects leaders with the country's highest aspirations in mind, instead of their own little special interest cliques and parochial advantage? Do you have any idea how much money is spent detrimental to the national interest, just to provide useless, unproductive, make-work jobs in Congressional districts blessed with a representative who chairs a powerful committee? Some pork barrel projects for the armed forces even endanger the lives of military personnel deploying them. Those jobs benefit no one but the locals, while driving up government debt. The Military-Industrial Complex is full of such waste, and it's alive and well, here in DC!"

"The B4," Larry shrugged. Everybody knew it was a boondoggle.

"Good example." LeRoy seemed pleased. "There are a dozen high-ranking generals who don't even want the damn plane, but they can't say anything for fear of reprisals from Congress. The fastest way to end your distinguished career in the military is to complain about a new weapons platform being built in the home district of the House or Senate Armed Services Committee Chairman. And worse yet are the unsafe weapons. Do you remember the Marine Corps' tilt-rotor aircraft called the Osprey? A Secretary of Defense tried to stop the program before things got out of hand. But the porkers in Congress prevailed.

Though a good idea on paper, it should have been killed while still in the design phase!" LeRoy became visibly upset. "Any fool could see it might become unstable in flight if a malfunction occurred! Trying to maneuver or land with only one engine was questionable. The idiots didn't understand that a $25 million aircraft costing $100 million is no bargain, even if they got it to fly safely. And then, as if to add insult to injury, they proposed the Super Osprey. It will cost $240 million, and all this money is spent on an aircraft replacing $15 million helos. Plus it's classified so the public will not find out that billions were wasted. The tilt-rotor program should have remained experimental!" Larry kept silent, wondering how LeRoy knew such things. "But you didn't answer my earlier question," LeRoy reminded after calming down. "The one about quality of representation."

Larry said nothing, realizing the gray-haired gentleman was right. Parochial interests are always paramount. Denial is a well-established tradition in Congress. In the foreseeable future, there'd be big, stubborn, insecure egos seeking domination within government—the last people you'd want in positions of power.

"I'll let you in on a little secret," Uncle Roy continued, "a straight answer to your question. The Pentagon has developed a top-secret, chemical-sensing prototype more versatile than anything they've had in the past. They wanted a device to locate landmines, chemical weapons, and other dangerous substances hidden underground without jeopardizing human life—a laudable goal. The prototype failed in its objective because it couldn't penetrate the ground, but they found it could sense the presence of various chemical substances above ground, including your illegal drugs. This technology can be semi-trailered and moved to any location accessible by road. Its search radius is three hundred feet. Future advances will extend that."

"Why the top-secret classification?"

"The boys in the Pentagon savor their alcohol. They have a twenty-year supply, for the brass and government bigwigs only. By that time, I guess they figure it will be legal again."

Larry laughed at the idea of DES raiding the Pentagon. It'd be hard enough to bust Congress. "So what do you want from me?" He asked a direct question to determine his chance of survival. "Are you going to let me walk away from here?"

"I've decided to let you live." Uncle Roy's voice revealed the dichotomy of cold, insensitive graciousness. The elderly man rose from his chair and sat on the desk. "I don't even want to know what you're going to do. All the evidence in this building will be removed before you get back to your car. And I'll disappear into the mist. For all practical purposes, I don't exist. However, I'll keep tabs on you. If you raid Congress, consequences are on your head, and I'll make sure you are never considered for a promotion in law enforcement."

"I can't be your mole," Larry acknowledged.

There was a moment of silence. "That's too bad." LeRoy's disappointment quickly reverted to a cold, calculating stare. "I'd hoped for better. You seem like a fine, upstanding young man with much promise. Given the opportunity, we'd have transformed you into something worthwhile." Uncle Roy handed Larry his wallet. "I'll be watching the news later. If I hear you've raided the Capitol…" He paused and then made a surprising statement. "Sometimes it's difficult to resolve differences or dissipate conflicts in such a short timeframe. Still, it'll be business as usual for the good of the country. However, as I implied, I'll be moving this operation." Uncle Roy remained silent, gazing at the DES officer. "I've always felt the Smithsonian would make a fine hideout. It's an awfully big place."

FUTUREBUST1.8

Larry shook the man's hand before walking out the door. He made his way back through the Capitol Building storage complex without escort, aware of the early morning stillness. Dolf, Igor, Dieter, Thor, Lars, Günter, Hanz, Urnst, Ulrick, (and who could forget Phill?) were not around. Larry ran back to the patrol car—he was worried, though not overly so. Of all people, Buck could take care of himself. But finding him. Had he stayed with the cube van or been detected by the driver?

He jumped into his vehicle and switched on the GPS software. The truck was stationary, parked near the Pentagon. He fired up his brand new 2017 CV Investigator with a supercharged, sixteen valve, four-cylinder motor. Larry broke traction and left two ribbons of rubber on the capital city's deserted streets. Predawn traffic was minimal, allowing excessive speed. He buried 140 mph on I-395.

Larry crossed the Potomac and approached the Pentagon, slowing as necessary to negotiate some very sharp turns, then headed for the guardhouse next to a gate which closed off the Pentagon's newly enlarged and upgraded parking area. With Larry at the wheel, this is no understatement. It exploded into splinters and shards behind his car. The brains in planning built it out of wood instead of brick, thus much less of a deterrent to forward progress than the gate itself. That oversight could be blamed on cost-cutting liberals who were tired of Pentagon waste. The budget had to be trimmed somewhere.

The two guards that dove out of the way were not amused. They radioed for help, but too late. A volley of bullets didn't slow Larry's progress. He went through a chain-link fence, ruining the car's finish still further, then sped across acres of new blacktop. They even rerouted the access roads around the building, making the southeast side of the Pentagon more secure. Larry glanced at his computer. GPS could locate that truck to within inches. He circled in a clockwise direction towards the north side of the building. More grass had been converted to asphalt and more guards scurried behind, their tiny images disappearing in the rearview. His quarry came into sight, parked near a dumpster a short distance from the building. No one was around. He hit the brakes, putting the patrol car into a screeching, four-wheel sideways skid, coming to a halt next to the truck like in the movies, only Larry did it on the first take.

The smell of burning rubber hit his nose. Jumping from the vehicle unarmed and out of breath, he opened the back door of the truck. Buck was sitting inside, arms folded across his chest, casually whistling an old Rock & Roll tune. Three other men were slumped next to the Marshal Arts master: one was the driver of the cube van, Krueger. The other two were military police, all stacked in a neat little self-supporting pile, something that later became a trademark after he beat up a large number of people. Buck was not a clean freak, yet he held much disdain for the unkempt appearance of mayhem by leaving bodies strewn willy-nilly after a fight, which other Marshal Arts masters seemed to endorse. He stood up and jumped out. "They'll be okay. A mild headache—now let's get out of here!"

They left more rubber on the Pentagon's precious blacktop. A slow, clumsy military jeep had pulled to within seventy-five yards while they were stationary, but Larry multiplied the distance once his foot was firmly ensconced on the accelerator. The lot was empty, providing plenty of uninhibited pavement to make an escape. It wouldn't be prudent to exit through the same gate so he took out another guard station and more chain link fence on the way out, then headed up river. The crack on the windshield spread like a spider web.

Buck looked at his partner in stunned amazement. "What took you so long?" The patrol car skidded back out onto city streets, making a sharp, rubber-squealing turn. A hubcap dislodged and rolled to the side of the road just like on TV police chases. Buck grabbed hold of the armrest to maintain his position. In the rush to get away, he hadn't buckled his seat belt. As the pursuit by Pentagon police dissipated, Larry headed for DES Headquarters. Sarge looked at his partner as their speed declined to a safe level, then finished the question he was unable to ask earlier. "Where did you learn to drive" (like this)?

"I was unavoidably detained." He slowed the patrol car. "I ran into a guy named LeRoy. He works for the CIA supplying drugs to Congress. What'd you do to those guys?"

"It was past their bedtime," Buck replied with a paternal smile.

"So what'd you find out?" Larry asked, looking at the grin on his partner's face. Buck always smiled brightly when he got a chance to beat on a bunch of bad guys. "And what was that song you were whistling?"

"It's a hell-raiser tune from the last century called *Born to be Wild*," Buck replied. "And I found out plenty. The Pentagon is knee-deep in alcohol. We'll have to court-martial a bunch of the very tipsy-top brass."

"Wait until you hear what else is going on," Larry added. "They've invented a sensor machine that detects chemical substances from as much as a football field away. It apparently works on booze as well as nicotine. You can tell what's in a building without entering. It'd be great to get our hands on one, but I question whether the courts will let us apply that in civilian use."

"The wonders of modern technology," Buck's astonishment was muted, "and the legal ramifications thereof."

Larry laughed and pulled what was left of the patrol car into the parking lot next to the brand, spanking new DES building located on prime property near McMillan Reservoir and Howard University. It'd been built on land hijacked from the Veterans Administration in a turf battle, or more correctly, a battle for turf. DES won. Actually, the VA needed the money because they weren't getting it from Congress. Budgets were tight. It's a lot more exciting to waste money on useless platforms like the B4 or the Super Osprey, than care for the disabled veterans who fought our wars for us. The VA had fallen on hard times in the federal government's list of priorities.

Both men surveyed the automotive wreckage. "The lieutenant's gonna kick your butt!" Buck laughed sheepishly, knowing he was in for it too.

"My butt?" Larry objected vehemently. "I was trying to save your butt when I did this. You can at least back me up here." Larry preemptively rubbed his behind as they walked into the beautiful new National Headquarters and sat down. It was quiet—a good sign. Time to fill out reports and think up excuses.

FUTUREBUST1.9

The morning shift started at 4:30. Lieutenant Jackson was fuming. He had an angry colonel on the phone, a heavily damaged patrol car, and nothing to show for it. "Wilcox, Klassen, in my office now!" He settled down after hearing what happened. "A machine to sniff out chemical substances." Lieutenant Jackson's eyes lit up. "We could clean up all the drug abuse in DC in a couple of years, courts permitting."

Larry was out of hot water. "But what are we going to do about Congress?"

Lieutenant Jackson bellowed. "We're going to bust'em! To hell with the self-righteous bastards! The law is the law. They have to obey along with everyone else."

A colonel in charge of Pentagon security stopped in later that morning to return the missing hubcap. Larry and Buck stayed for the confrontation. The officer was furious. "Who the hell do you guys think you are, *Andy of Mayberry?*" He stormed in like a lion but left like a lamb. Lieutenant Jackson made a deal with him. The generals got to keep their heavily stocked bar hidden at the Pentagon in return for that electronic sniffer they christened NOSTRILS. SecDef (Secretary of Defense), known to imbibe herself, quietly approved the bargain.

However Congress wasn't so lucky. Sarge and Larry wouldn't have missed it for the world. DES raided the Capitol's underground storage complex but found everything had been carefully cleared out. Larry noticed the cleanser still spread over the floor. No drugs remained except for an almost imperceptible spot on the concrete where the case of whiskey had fallen off the four-wheel cart. If Ulrick had listened to Dieter and cleaned up immediately...a lab test proved it was alcoholic. Congress was busted!

Larry did manage to confiscate some evidence: the thickly padded black leather chair. He kept it in his TV room as a souvenir of the ordeal. Lieutenant Jackson still uses the teak desk as his office furniture.

All hell broke loose in the federal government—the kind of media sensation every reporter drools over—a story they knew had legs. There was talk of impeaching the House and Senate, clearly one of the more cumbersome constitutional crises ever faced. The difficulty was figuring out who'd do the honors. But just in case that problem could be resolved, the President made a preemptive strike and pardoned everyone. Rumors leaked that she'd done it for a case of beer and a hand-rolled Cuban (cigar).

As if to prove Uncle Roy's point, that everyone in Congress is not totally calloused and unfeeling, some members—mostly back-benchers (at the behest of more senior members)—performed dozens of hours of community service at the DC zoo ("We don't do manure.") in *heartfelt* penance. They even made a public promise and signed a nonbinding pledge to behave, at least in theory. They planned to display the document at the National Archives next to the Declaration of Independence. But in an oxymoronic twist, it turned up missing and was never located.

In an otherwise unselfish (and uncharacteristic) fit of contagious honesty, a few members of Congress admitted to cheating on their taxes. Conveniently for everyone, the President's pardon was of the blanket, all-forgiving variety. Despite a chronic shortage of clergy in DC, confession became all the rage, thus there was no longer any need for the Permanent Subcommittee on Investigations. Its members relocated to other more CCA (Campaign Contribution Accessible) committees. Still, a proactive Congress wasn't taking any chances. They later passed APRB, an Automatic Pardon at Retirement Bill, but the Supreme Court overruled the law, labeling it Legislative Predetermination.

Larry tried for years to locate the old gentleman from the CIA, but to no avail. As LeRoy had claimed, he did not exist. Buck failed at the national Marshal Arts tournament in Los Angeles (disqualified in the finals for accidentally breaking his opponent's leg), but later procured a movie contract. He filmed three moderately successful Kung Fu films during extended vacations. The money he made (after taxes) later bought and maintained a very large boat, even though the Great Depression was still chugging along at a good clip. Larry followed Buck to Hollywood as his friend's agent and confidant. His four-percent share of the legal tender bought a retreat on a clear blue lake in northern Minnesota, the only area of the country where the per capita number of vacation homes is still above eighty percent. In fact, any resident not having at least one lake home is looked upon as a possible communist infiltrator. Such people must register on a statewide offender listing, which is posted on the Internet, or they are subject to fines, imprisonment, and/or overseas interrogation. Out-of-staters cannot enter unless trailering a boat, or possessing a special permit explaining why not.

Lieutenant Jackson wanted to live in sunnier climes and eventually transferred to San Diego in reward for his creative bargaining efforts with the Pentagon, netting the first Drug Sniffer ever used by civilian law enforcement. He was later promoted to captain of the Los Angeles DES office.

FUTUREBUST1.98

Yes, 2017 was quite a year. It goes without saying that the populous of the United States was disappointed in their representatives. Hypocrisy has a way of sticking out like a sore thumb, once smashed with a hammer. The American people demanded the Full and Equal Participation Amendment be passed, which required elected officials to live by the same rules as the rest of the country. Talk about throwing a monkey wrench into the machinations of Congress, this Amendment stipulated that Federal employees be treated the same, thus generous Congressional medical and pension benefits were truncated. And their propensity for upwardly mobile salaries was curtailed, requiring Congressional remuneration be tied to the minimum wage, on a percentage basis. Thus, a two percent increase for the masses triggers an equal increase for Congress. The full implications of this Amendment have yet to be realized. Being that it's retroactive back to the turn of the century, over four hundred cases are pending in Federal Court, seeking reimbursement for past grievances.

Finally, in the ongoing quest to restrict drug-related music, the songs *Okie From Muscogee* by Merle Haggard, and *Cocaine* by Eric Clapton were banned—being too drug-oriented. *Margaritaville* by Jimmy Buffet barely survived scrutiny. *Tequila Sunrise* by the Eagles and *Tobacco Road* by the Everly Brothers are still under review. *Rocky Mountain High* by John Denver was pardoned. *Green Tambourine* by the Lemon Pipers was determined to be a drug song when played backwards. Though the list is too extensive to be cataloged here, previously outlawed songs include: *I Want a New Drug* by Huey Lewis and the News; *Under Moonshine* by the Moody Blues; *Mary Jane's Last Dance* by Tom Petty; *Acid Queen* and *Whiskey Man* by The Who; *Purple Haze* by Jimi Hendrix; *Smokin'* by Boston; *Sweet Cherry Wine* by Tommy James and the Shondels; *Don't Step on the Grass, Sam* by Steppenwolf; *Yellow Submarine* by The Beatles; *Light Up Or Leave Me Alone* by Traffic; the entire playlist of the Doobie Bros., except for *Jesus Is Just Alright* (Single Version); *Love Potion #9* by The Searchers; *Tiny Bubbles* by Don Ho; *Alabama Song* by The Doors; *Smokin' in the Boy's Room* by Brownsville Station; *One Toke Over The Line* by Brewer & Shipley; *Dr. Feelgood* by Motley Crue; and *Wasted on the Way* by Crosby, Stills, & Nash. A complete registration of over 23,200 banned songs is available upon request. Include $15 to cover handling costs. Terms and conditions apply. Offer ends without notice. For those interested in an extensive list of songs banned because of sexually suggestive lyrics or bad grammar, go to www.bannedsongs.gov.

FUTUREBUST1.99

"Let's try out that new drug sniffer over by the Smithsonian," Larry casually suggested one morning.

FUTUREBUST2.0

A.D. 2041, Los Angeles, South California

Jim Blackhawk was once again into his nightly routine, flying over old, familiar territory. There was a slight buffeting due to unstable air but the turbocraft automatically compensated. The stars were obscured by diffused ambient light from the city below. He gazed through the canopy at the urban landscape, shrouded in darkness and shadows, mystery and intrigue. Another kilometer passed silently beneath. A few cars and trucks on the freeway below scurried here and there. Tiny headlights pierced the night, then dissipated into unlimited darkness. Silence reigned. At 2 A.M., a small number of desperate, despairing people were still out and about, searching for a destination, a meaning or purpose—anything to suppress the restless boredom of their lonely, desolate lives.

Jim winced, his thoughts running like the first paragraphs of a B-grade mystery novel. He stared into the inky blackness of an uninhabited industrial area. Tilting his head, he listened to the muffled sound of the four turbo-thrusters keeping his vehicle aloft, feeling not the slightest out-of-place vibration that would indicate a need for maintenance. A five hundred-foot smokestack, below and off to the right, evacuated industrial exhaust from a fully automated manufacturing facility. Red obstruction lights blinked rhythmically on and off, warning Turbo-Jockeys to keep a safe distance.

Everything was going *turbo* these days. Products needing a boost in sex appeal were *turbo'd* by advertisers. He'd recently seen a TurboFrost refrigerator at the appliance store. Okay, nothing unusual there. It sounded fine. But Turbo-fried chicken? That made no sense. All that enhanced poultry-power might blow out the digestive system. Jim shrugged. Was there anybody out there who understood what *turbo* meant? A cool sounding word to be sure, it always looked good, at least on paper.

In some circles the word was in danger of becoming ubiquitous, like *pro* had years before. Jim visited a dime store recently and noticed they sold pro paperclips along with pro pencils and erasers. And don't forget to pick up an extra packet of Pro *Tiddlywinks*. He had laughed at that too. One wouldn't want to get caught using amateur Tiddlywinks. Jim grimaced. What would the neighbors say if they found out?

His attention returned to the here-and-now. Greater Los Angeles is an endlessly expanding town of twenty-four million residents—the urbanization uninterrupted up the Pacific coast to the state line, just south of Salinas. It contains as much territory as one man can realistically cover. Jim leaned forward in the captain's seat, keeping a keen eye on the sensors while also enjoying a varied view of the city. The industrial park morphed into residences: first low-class, then middle, and finally upper class homes as he progressed towards San Bernardino.

Unilaterally in the mid-teens, the world undertook a jihad on substance abuse known nationally as BADASH—Battle Against Drugs And Substance Hazards. In crude, less-cultured circles the acronym was BADASS—Battle Against Drugs And Substance Slavery. The goal: end drug abuse forever and for all time. During the worldwide economic depression that started in 2013, it became an epidemic—a plague of biblical proportions. The world's population was gripped by panic. But as time passed, clear thinking prevailed. Most nations were involved. In North and Central America, only Cuba abstained.

This night seemed just like any other—not much happening. Jim, as usual, was out on patrol in the turbocraft, a single-seater vehicle with vectored (directionally adjustable) thrust from four articulated motors. So agile and maneuverable, it could be described as a 320-kilogram mechanical hummingbird, with flight characteristics to match.

In his younger days, Jim helped test-pilot the preproduction turbocraft, a redesigned, upgraded version of turn-of-the-century VTOL (Vertical Take Off and Landing) technology. The first generation Category-one, or Cat-one was so safe, efficient, and reliable, it quickly supplanted smaller helicopters.

Next, the forty-four-year-old Lakota native entered the top-secret profession of intelligence gathering, taking part in covert operations his superiors claimed had never happened—at least in theory. Black Ops always had *plausible deniability* attached, in case of a major screw-up. An example: "Nope, it didn't happen. We don't know *nothin'* about that." This is classic denial twisted inside out. Liars! The double negative proves it.

Later, Jim sought out fresh adventures, relocating to the west coast and embarking on a career in criminology—specifically drug enforcement. In the decades since, he'd never gotten over the use of plausible deniability. It dishonored the meaning of patriotism, freedom, and the American Way. Those people didn't equate democracy with tolerance of the opposition and a commitment to the rule of law. That they once held positions of power within the government of the United States had frightening implications.

Theoretically, that's all in the past. Others in the downtown Los Angeles DES office had law-enforcement backgrounds. Larry and Sarge were old-timers. Born in the early eighties of the last century, they now approached retirement. Even so, both were tough as nails and could competently handle their respective jobs, including every cop's favorite pastime: paperwork. But if a mission went critical, they'd be out front. The two men had more experience in drug enforcement than all the others combined.

Lieutenant Bo MacKinsey commands Alpha Squad. Just five years out of Drug Enforcement School, the twenty-eight-year-old has everything going his way. Graduating at the top of his class, he's aware of every trick in the book. Nobody pulls the wool over his eyes. Bo is as sharp as a Swiss Army Knife and resourceful as an Eagle Scout.

Rounding out Alpha: slender, studious (and always impeccably dressed) Cy Bergstrom, a top-ten graduate of Stanford Law School (class of '38). Cy maintains legal standards in a technologically advanced, *get-tough* law enforcement-oriented world.

Now within the city limits of San Bernardino, Jim's turbocraft continued its preprogrammed flight, performing a standard grid-search. A Category-four first produced in 2036, its sensors could sniff out illegal drugs from one mile away. Fully automated, it would fly an entire search route unmanned, but regulations specified the use of a pilot whenever possible, and Bo preferred it that way. Jim too. It gave him a chance to break the routine of the office and clear his head. Besides, having a turbocraft flying pilotless around town with its sensitive scanning capabilities conveyed a *Big Brother* feel to the whole operation. Pilots added a much-appreciated human touch to the drug searches.

The work this night continued without incident or need for concern. Drug abuse had dropped to almost nothing, with few willing to test current technology, commonly known by the military acronym as NOSTRILS: Neutral Operations Strategic Tactical Reconnaissance Intelligence Logistical Sensors. Most of the drug-sniffing canines used in the last century would have traded their gourmet doggie meals for a fraction of NOSTRILS' capability. But such dogs now work as family pets, or are unemployed.

FUTUREBUST2.1

Back at HQ, Lieutenant Bo MacKinsey reclined with his feet on the desk, twiddling a pencil between his fingers as he gazed at the array of screens in front of him. The DES Command Center is a small office containing a workstation of inlet monitors hooked to cameras and telemetry feeds from the turbocraft. There's a workspace with cubbyholes, and a bookshelf containing much appreciated reference material. On the wall is hung a 3D (three-dimensional) DynaView screen for state-of-the-art viewing.

Out the door and to the left is the main office, with desks for Larry,

Sarge, the pilots, GPS tracking, and the all-important kitchenette with sink, refrigerator, microwave, and cabinet space. Farther on, a lounge and locker room with shower. Leaving the Command Center and turning right leads to the elevator. A few steps further, the seventh-floor hanger where air vehicles are housed and maintained. Personnel offices face the Command Center. Beyond—the media room if a news conference is in the offing.

Bo thoughtfully scratched his chin. He wore a dark blue tee shirt underneath a loosely fitting brown leather jacket, faded on the shoulders due to the harsh ultraviolet rays of the sun. His discolored blue jeans sported matching holes in the knee area, complete with short, dangling threads accentuating the missing fabric. Bo's casual appearance could graciously be described as that of an undercover cop, yet the obvious lack of fashion discipline didn't obscure his good looks. His dark, piercing eyes, framed by sharply defined eyebrows and neatly brushed, shoulder-length hair, retained a slight oriental slant. "Korean, Chinese, Vietnamese; what does it matter?" He'd answer the inevitable questions of his national origins with casual, self-deprecating humor. "We all look the same to you."

Shoulder length or longer hair became the standard for law enforcement officers. Most shorthaired cops went the way of the dinosaur and disappeared from the face of the earth back in the teens when it was discovered that men with long locks handled stress better than shorthairs or skinheads, thus were more accurate with firearms. Extensive scientific research at a prestigious Massachusetts university proved what the founding fathers had known all along. Longhaired men possess steadier nerves, make superior lovers, and have better digestion when it comes to pastry. Besides, short hair was nothing more than a hundred and thirty year aberration. If looked at on a millennial scale, butch hairstyles almost didn't happen. And don't forget, the world's saints were longhairs.

The lieutenant gazed at the array of monitors as he reclined in the downtown Los Angeles nerve center of urban drug busting operations. His eyes revealed casual, yet focused interest in the matters at hand. The turbocraft's telemetry and sensor information is beamed instantly back to DES Command. Airborne cameras give Bo a view of the vehicle's surroundings. If anything suspicious or sinister happens out in the field, he'll know before his pilot pushes the Alert Button.

In the age of subatomic scanning, or Population Surveys (the euphemized label for drug searches), there's no place to run or hide. Doing drugs means doing time. Hard drugs—hard time. The symbolism borders on the poetic.

Just west of San Bernardino, Jim continued the slow, methodical quest; his sensors quietly probing the murky, iniquitous, illegality-prone underbelly of an unseen drug culture. Tactile electronic fingers seek out unrighteous substances, and the drug abusers that inevitably accompany them. Filtering through the smallest cracks and crevices, into the dark corners of aging, dilapidated buildings, the sensors pursue drug offenders lurking in the dank, steamy shadows of illicit, counterculture society.

"Damn!" Jim muttered. "That *does* sound like a cheap, dime store mystery novel." Despite his mumbling, he retained the features of a classic Lakota warrior—strong, focused eyes that seemed to penetrate others thoughts. His face revealed the first faint signs of aging wrinkles. Jim never covered his feelings. What you saw is what you got. Long, straight black hair hung down his back, tied in a ponytail.

"Did you say something?" Bo gazed at the communications (comm.) monitor, which framed Jim's well-chiseled visage.

"I'm just thinking out loud again," the Turbo-Jockey revealed without hesitation. "You ever hear mystery novels playing in your head?"

Bo eyed the comm. suspiciously and shook his head. "I don't think that's happened to me recently." He paused. "You know, there's plenty of vacation time available." His eyes twinkled at the subtle hint his pilot might be losing it, catching what's referred to on the streets as *el loco enorme* (the very big crazy). There is a lot of it going around. Bo continued with an observation. "That turbocraft doesn't need a pilot to complete its search route. You could be considered gratuitously superfluous or even needlessly redundant."

Jim nodded but remained quiet. The idea of a pilot being unnecessary overkill didn't thrill him. He had a good thing going, cruising the city at altitude, and then collecting a decent paycheck twice a month for all his effort. Pilots vehemently resist the notion that they're expendable. As far as he's concerned, machinery will never do what a human can. Before computers take over the world, they'll have to fight it out with men like Jim, and he'll make their Artificial Intelligence suffer for such arrogance.

"Not much going on out there tonight, huh?" Bo's comment was intended to mend fences for underappreciated jokes.

"Nope." Jim shrugged. "You've got your feet on the desk again, don't you?"

"How'd you know? I don't sound bored, do I?"

"Yup," Jim insisted. "My sensors could pick up on your tedium from clear across the city. Besides, I can see shoes in my comm. They're probably yours."

Bo shook his head and smiled. "There's surely a regulation in the book that forbids bad posture. I don't need any demerits on my exemplary record, do I?"

"Nope," Jim conceded flatly as he relaxed in his seat. The turbocraft was on autopilot. "You don't violate a rule as serious as that…no sir."

"I hear you." Bo brushed his hair back with an idle left hand. "Another slow night?"

"Looks like it," Jim nodded, while cruising at fifteen hundred feet. Subtle adjustments to thrusters by the Flight Control Modules could smooth out all but the roughest turbulence, though agitated air from other vehicles, known as the *EggBeater,* might overload the system. For that reason, turbocraft stayed at least five hundred feet from each other while in slow-flight. As Jim would defiantly insist: To avoid such difficulties, you need a pilot. It's a positive, proactive thought, but not always true. Overly assertive pilots sometimes cause the worst in-flight difficulties.

The Eggbeater occurs when as many as three-dozen vehicles congregate in the same area, most frequently when media turbocraft get into a feeding frenzy trying to follow a high-speed ground chase on one of L.A.'s many freeways. When the LAPD pursues a bank robber or car thief through the streets, networks compete to show the best coverage. Chases are ratings boosters. However critics claim that media exposure often incites perps in more dangerous stunts and higher speeds. Fame is the catalyst. If a perp avoids capture for fifteen minutes, he's gotten his allotted share.

Law enforcement turbocraft occasionally become entangled in a hornet's nest of airborne media coverage. In self-defense, the pilots are schooled in IMAT, Intermediate Media Avoidance Training; or ATMAT, Advanced Tactical Media Avoidance Training. A law enforcement pilot has to avoid the mess of vehicles above any *media-worthy* event.

The conversation was going nowhere so Bo rode the crest of some past glories. He was perplexed, though non-critical. "How long has it been since we've busted a perp?"

"Long time, maybe six weeks," Jim replied wistfully. It'd been a while indeed. Days passed uneventfully, making it difficult to recall the last time anything had happened. "There's a shortage of offenders, at least in these parts."

"Great," Bo smirked. "We must be doing something right."

"Either that or we're just *incredibly* lucky." Jim leaned forward to check his instruments in the vain hope of finding a banned material or unrighteous substance that would indicate illegalities being perpetrated by an iniquitous person with substandard respect or reverence for the law. Such persons need jail time to contemplate their error.

"I really love my job." Bo exhaled long and slow as he tapped his fingers in an agitated manner on the mahogany desk. "You know, I could have made it as an actor, but chose law enforcement instead."

"The exact same thing happened to me." Jim's expression indicated he doubted the authenticity of both statements. The brief but poignant exchange ended on a dubious note.

Jim and his turbocraft continued through the darkness, with sensors sweeping and probing. He scanned one square kilometer after another, searching for anyone or anything considered part of the deleterious drug trade. Six weeks earlier, he'd unearthed a cocaine addict. Nasty little fellow, Jim mused. But the excitement of that bust had long receded into his subconscious. "Not so much as a single elevated readout or hopeful sensor spike," he whispered, making sure the lieutenant at HQ didn't hear his comment. Thinking out loud is a habit he picked up in his younger days while working for the CIA. Interesting times, those, a major influence on his life.

He did not relish rehashing old memories. They were too vivid. But sometimes when things got slow, they'd crowd in. Black Ops! You could write a book about such exploits. In fact some writers make careers of it. One high-ranking three star muckety-muck who thought he was clever, had cracked a joke about Jim's name. Jim Blackhawk became Jim BlackOps. Cute. At that time, Jim felt his occupation was *excessively* dangerous. He was put into impossible positions. "Not suicidal," the general smirked. "Just no escape." Jim flew sorties he didn't feel were prudent, and was blamed for the results. He rocked the boat and they didn't tolerate it. Senior officials want orders carried out lickety-split—no hesitation or backtalk, and definitely no *buts* of the Constitutional variety. Still, they were wrong, thus Jim stood on principle. It was one of those instances when the two CIA's—the Central Intelligence Agency, and a Certifiably Irresponsible Act—merged and overlapped. Time passed. In the here-and-now, he preferred drug busting.

The vast majority of the population supported the goal of a drug-free society. But as in all things revolutionary and progressive, there was still a tiny counterculture minority living in the past. Determined to abuse one sort of drug or another, they'd be a thorn in the backside of every law-abiding citizen until rooted out and rehabilitated. Strong words, those. Let's rephrase. Drug abuse provides Jim and the others at DES with job security. The public has little sympathy for lawbreakers. *Zero tolerance* is what the *get-tough* politicians call it. Some, like Lieutenant Bo MacKinsey and his frontline DES compatriots see it as subzero tolerance. But compassion is never a politician's forte, not even when they claim the opposite. No votes are gained by coddling criminals. Stiff sentences make lawmakers happy. For those caught, drug rehabilitation is a science, though jail time is often stiff. This brings smiles to the faces of political leaders and votes to advance careers.

Sarge, sitting at his desk in the main office, often contemplated pastry when things got slow. He was a veteran of WoD, the doomed War on Drugs. At the time, substances deemed antisocial by politicians were banned and illegal.

However, socially acceptable drugs turned out to be far more destructive. Enforcing hypocritical laws never works to society's betterment, a no-brainer that took policymakers decades to figure out. Yet some lessons were learned. Modern drug policies are enforced with vigor. Penalties are harsh, of that there's no debate. Hypocrisy? No, at least none has been detected so far. Like they said in the old days: "The law is the law". An economic depression helped make it abundantly clear. Considering the societal costs over the last century, most believed a prohibition of recreational drugs to be the only viable option.

And for more than twenty years it had stuck, with no sign of attitudes changing. The DES quietly became one of the most successful government agencies ever commissioned. It's impossible to believe that a bunch of power-grabbing politicians conceived the idea and passed legislation to make it all happen without the obligatory "What's-in-it-for-us?" consideration. Even they would admit that tough times require sacrifices.

Sarge's desk-bound stomach grumbled as he sat at his workstation and daydreamed of bakery goods, while making genuinely artistic doodles on the edge of a progress report. He was dressed in casual black pants and sweatshirt, what he labeled ninja-esque. His desk sported one of those signs that read: *The Buck Stops Here*. It's a joke, being that his nickname is Buck. The humor is questionable. "Hey Larry," the big man called over his shoulder to the desk behind. "Do you think that 24-hour across the street is open at this time of night?"

"Very funny." Larry checked his wallet, his voice subdued. "I suppose it's my turn to buy, isn't it?"

"You guessed it, partner," Sarge replied with smug satisfaction. "Remember, tough guys don't appreciate donuts with brightly colored, frilly sprinkles on top."

"Oh, I'll be sure to get he-man donuts for you," Larry quipped. "Wouldn't want you to go soft on us." Sarge didn't reply. He leaned back and patted his tummy as Larry grabbed a jacket, acknowledged the nonverbal cue with a smile, and headed for the elevator. The big man returned to his doodles.

Larry realized the cheapest alternative was to sneak down to the FBI lobby on the first floor and cop some of their donuts. But he knew they'd be getting stale so he headed across the street for fresh. The bakery had a better variety. FBI often stuck with unimaginative sugar and cinnamon varieties, never putting adequate creativity into the selection. Pretty boring. Larry wanted something adding zing to life. Sometimes donuts were the only excitement they experienced during the week, thus the good ones gave them something they could sink their teeth into. It had been weeks since they'd busted a perp.

FUTUREBUST

Boredom proliferated—boredom punctuated by paperwork, and little or nothing to do.

Jim remained vigilant, firmly ensconced over San Bernardino for the night. He'd scanned sixteen square kilometers since the shift began three hours earlier. It was a routine sweep, nothing out of the ordinary. He enjoyed the ride—better than being cooped up in the office like the others. One could always take in the scenery below, to avoid the tedium. On a clear night he'd be stargazing, admiring the wonders of the Milky Way. Still, his focus never strayed far from the console.

Jim was single—no wife or kids. He knew the kind of work he enjoyed would put too much strain on family life so he never married. But Jim liked children and spent time with the families of the other guys. He'd even take out the garbage if someone asked—just like he'd seen in a cop movie once—though a pretty please and five dollars under the table would enhance response time. It was a nice arrangement for everyone. Things cruised along smoothly at the LA DES—only the unexpected had to be worried over and that's what he had just smacked into.

FUTUREBUST2.3

Jim sat erect and scanned the console. Indicators flashed faintly, then more pronounced. Sensors were elevated. The four-engine turbocraft hovered as electronic probes initiated a pattern-sweep of the area below, narrowing the search radius to pinpoint the location of the disturbance. The readings had passed the level of tolerance. "You getting this?" his voice revealed edgy, focused concentration. "Looks like a serious violation. So much for the quiet evening." His demeanor revealed no disappointment.

"Cy!" Bo yelled to the legal office. Normally he'd use the intercom.

"The data's transmitting!" Cy jumped from his chair. "It's a confirmed go. The Online Judge has issued a warrant and clearance for a full scan!"

"Listen up everybody!" Bo exclaimed, looking out the door of the Command Center. "Sarge, fire-up the Enforcement Vehicle. Larry...where's Larry?"

"Yo." He'd just returned from the donut shop, placing a box on the lunch counter.

"Handle the preflight checklist. Looks like we're in for a hot one!" Bo impatiently returned to the comm. "Jim, any idea what we're up against?"

"Still scanning." Jim was now calm. "I'll brief you when underway."

"Stay on top of it!" Bo removed his jacket and donned a HVP (High Velocity Projectile) safety vest. "Let's go fellas. We've got a job to do!"

Cy grabbed the warrant off the *InstaPrint* and headed to the hanger with the others.

The powerful, multi-passenger Enforcement Vehicle (EV) is quick and agile, its four huge thrusters capable of producing speeds of Mach .5 or greater, approximately 375 miles per hour. It can reach any part of the L.A. megalopolis in an hour. Sarge navigated the seventh-floor hanger, then rocketed from HQ with an AATC, (Automated Air Traffic Control) priority clearance.

Sixty miles distant, Jim continued the prebust (investigation). His turbocraft is outfitted with the most advanced scanners available for civilian use, derived from the antiterrorist research of the teens and early twenties under the PATRIOT Act. Law enforcement bigwigs hung every goody onboard they could legally procure. Not only able to sniff out controlled substances from a distance of one mile; it is equipped with sensitive electronic surveillance capabilities. The X-ray-like Neutrino Camera (NC) can penetrate solids, allowing a pilot to observe activities otherwise hidden from view, though the picture possesses a green-grey tint much like old-fashioned night-vision goggles. Being able to monitor suspects without being detected gives law enforcement a much-needed advantage in the dangerous game of cat and mouse they sometimes play with drug offenders, drug abusers, and traffickers.

Bo, seated at the EV's Command and Control (C&C) behind the pilot, opened a secure channel to the stationary Cat-four turbocraft, hovering silently over a residential section of San Bernardino. "Jim, what have you got?"

"Strong alcohol signatures from a house below."

"Have you been detected?" Bo's inquiry was Standard Operating Procedure.

"Negative. I'm running silent at four-fifty" (meters). An understatement. The turbocraft is so quiet, a casual observer would have to be very observant to notice it hovering above. Jim jokingly referred to these stealthy capabilities as *Big Brother Attributes.*

"Report," Bo turned to Cy, seated next to the pilot.

"The owner of the house is named Robert Franklin, AKA Bubba Frank." Cy read from the screen. "No priors listed but his grandfather owned a bar before alcohol was banned." The computer divulged more information. "Mr. Franklin's electric bill is too high. The guy is using enough juice to power a welding shop!"

"TurboBrewery," Bo concluded. "Probably a Mark V, Model 261-A with enhanced micro-brew and accelerated Synth-aging, a patented process for flavor intensification and increased alcohol content."

"You sound like a commercial," Cy noted. "That machine brews an inexhaustible supply of illegal intoxicant. It'll make beer from rice, wheat, oats, or barley, which is far more addictive than were industrially manufactured beers back in the olden days. But the 261-A is a pricey unit, almost impossible for a middle-class guy to afford." Cy became serious. He knew from experience any additional information is sure to make for a risky bust. "The suspect was a demolition specialist during his stint in the service."

"Definitely trouble!" Bo adjusted his safety vest, making sure its shrapnel-resistant qualities were intact. "We may have a beerhead who likes to blow stuff up, including unwelcome DES officers! I'll bet he's got some fun surprises waiting!"

"Some guys get nasty when we break down their door," Sarge observed from the pilot's seat. Their speed was one-half Mach. "I've run into a few that were a couple of fries short of a *Happy Meal.*" Cy smiled at the analogy; implying someone operating with a side order of intellect, thus a palatable example of *el loco enorme.*

Bo grabbed a stun-gun from a compartment next to the seat. "Remember, taking him alive creates less (paperwork) of my favorite pastime."

"You take the fun out of everything," Sarge interjected in mock frustration. "It's more exciting if we haul them out in a body bag." A normal stress releaser, the big man's bravado drew hushed laughter. All things being equal, Sarge was a nice guy.

"If you boys have no objections, I'm in first." Larry voiced his preference. He'd been sitting quietly next to Bo in the back seat.

"Forget that!" Sarge vocalized. "I outrank you with several minutes of seniority. I'm on point. You can follow!"

Bo responded calmly. "The field commander makes those decisions."

"Yeah, but I'm the one who loaned you my boat last weekend when you wanted to go fishing." Sarge was pulling out all the stops.

"Interesting argument," Bo replied thoughtfully, eyebrows raised as he holstered his weapon. "I owe you for that one."

"Objection," Cy interrupted in lawyerly fashion from the EV's front seat. "You've all gone in before me on the last few busts. This one's custom-made for an impeccably dressed attorney with brilliant white teeth."

"You're good-looking also." Larry leaned forward and patted Cy on the shoulder. "But didn't you *juice* the suspect last time on point?"

"I did," Cy admitted hesitantly, looking back at Larry. "But that beerhead was armed and drunk as a skunk. He got better than he deserved! Pushers don't warrant sympathy."

"He was a trafficker," Sarge agreed. "The voltage probably did him some good. What'd they figure he was dealing, up to six kegs a week?"

"Something like that," Bo winced as he recalled the case. "Yeah, he definitely deserved worse. You did okay on that one, Cy. Maybe lawyers are good for something after all." The lieutenant spoke with mild sarcasm, though none was directed at Cy. Bo had plenty of respect for the young attorney's abilities, both legal and otherwise. It's all the other lawyers out there in the world causing problems for everybody. Labels like *scumsucker* and *slimeball* are not thrown around willy-nilly. They have to be earned.

The Enforcement Vehicle sped through the night at one-half Mach towards a rendezvous with Jim's turbocraft. The men fell silent, knowing the danger awaiting them. Beerheads are violent; a few even suicidal, thinking of themselves as martyrs for the cause of *Individual Rights*. Others have no qualms about fighting for an idea they label *Freedom of Choice*. Both are legitimate concepts, just not when combined with illegal drugs. That's the distinction. Society had come to terms with this. An insignificant loss of personal freedom is a small price to pay for the greatly enhanced quality-of-life everyone now enjoyed, especially poignant after suffering through the tough economic times of the recent past. In the days when those decisions were made, there'd hardly been a choice. The survival of the civilized world was at stake. And truthfully, the idea of personal freedom, individual rights, or freedom of choice, somehow, in some strange, unfathomable, incomprehensible way, contradicts the reality of drug addiction, which destroys the very essence of free will.

The cost of social drinking alone would boggle the mind. And there were numerous drug choices other than alcohol, though that one insatiably hazardous substance had taken a heavy toll on the fabric of society, especially during hard economic times when dependence increased. The number of people adversely affected, with lives ruined by alcohol will probably never be known, though the word *incalculable* comes to mind.

Sarge, the pilot and most experienced member of the team, slowed the EV as it neared the rendezvous point. Always gung-ho on a bust, still, in the back of his mind he longed for the good 'ole days when the worst one ran into was a heroin junkie or crack addict. But those busts are *a walk in the park* compared to a beerhead. Always doped up on alcohol and heavily armed, beerheads aren't interested in a drug-free society. Sarge was thankful his will was current. Busts like this are never forgotten—they remain vivid the rest of one's life. Maybe, if everything went well, he'd tell his grandkids about it someday—*if everything went well*. "You got an LZ (Landing Zone) picked out?" The big man's voice hinted at trepidation.

"A hundred yards from the target dwelling." Jim was on the ball as usual. "Just follow the tracking signal in."

"Any dogs? I don't want to wake the neighbors or alert the perp."

"Just one," Jim replied, "I put the *BEAM* on him. He's temporarily freeze-dried and immobile. You're cleared to set down, but go in easy. There's a flowerbed near the LZ. Surveillance is showing snapdragons and you know how much I love them, especially the dwarf varieties. It'd be positively uncool to disturb the neighbor's plantings." Jim really did like snapdragons, but that's a story for another time when everyone is less preoccupied.

"I'd hear about that for sure." Bo tapped Sarge on the shoulder. "No collateral damage. It's a federal directive. Compliance is mandatory."

"We'll put'er down nice and easy, as if it was my own backyard."

Larry released the hatch-lock as the hum of the motors died into the stillness of night. Dew formed on the grass. "I'll tell you one thing. I wish we could put the *BEAM* on perps before we arrest them!" Larry spoke the word with a mysterious inflection, common anytime the *BEAM* is mentioned in polite company.

"Civil Rights violation," Cy informed sympathetically, showing his perfect teeth in a smile. "But it would be nice."

The others unfastened safety harnesses and evacuated the four-passenger vehicle. They knelt on the grass in a vacant field where kids play soccer during the weekend. It's all business from here on in.

"You with us, Jim?" Bo checked the person-to-person comm. while watching the barely visible Cat-four turbocraft. "What defenses are we up against?"

Still hovering 450 meters above the target dwelling, Jim leaned over his console while pouring a cup of decaf. "Moderately sophisticated," he replied with an unconcerned shrug. "Sensors indicate motion detectors, a couple surveillance cams, plus explosive booby traps at the front and back entrances. It'll be a piece of cake. There are no landmines in the yard, but I'm picking up gunpowder, as in guns and bullets aimed in our direction. This guy's a typical beerhead—armed and dangerous! Don't think we want to knock on his door. I recommend the Neutrino Camera."

Bo nixed the idea. Jim shrugged reluctantly as the lieutenant explained. "What we need is more excitement in our lives. That camera creates paperwork. I'll inform the firearms boys after the bust. I doubt Bubba is part of a well-regulated militia."

"From up here you're cleared to go." Jim's voice was acquiescent.

"Okay, here's the game plan." Bo was at his best when giving orders. "Sarge, you're dressed for stealth, suppress those booby traps with blast retardant. No need for one of them to go off inadvertently while we deal with this clown. This is a *No Knock* warrant so Larry, the Puff Charges are all yours. No one blows a door better than you. Try not to send the thing into the next county. Leave it in one piece."

"You've got it." Larry was already on his feet, quietly pulling a container holding the binary (two part) explosive from the storage compartment near the front of the EV. Sarge grabbed a tool pouch that slung over his shoulder and strapped securely to his chest.

"Jim," Bo adjusted his comm., "neutralize those motion detectors and digitize false images into the surveillance cams."

"We're ready." This was not his first bust. He knew what to do.

Bo stood up and patted Larry consolingly on the shoulder. "Cy, it's your lucky day. You and your lovely smile will be the first thing Bubba Franklin sees. Oh, one more item. Remember, there's alcoholic beer in there. Don't get any on you, not even on your clothes if you can avoid it. You guys have to pass a mandatory drug screening next week. It's a sensitive test so be alert. I do not relish going before the Enforcement Review Board to explain how you got friendly with a controlled substance." That went without saying. "As always, secure the suspect, then the evidence." Everyone checked his comm. and gave thumbs up. Bo continued. "Cy, take position after Sarge gives the all clear. Larry, the door stays on the property, got it? Jim, anesthetize perimeter defenses."

"They're comatose," Jim assured. "The show is about to begin. I've got the whole area under scan. If a chipmunk so much as hiccups, I'll let you know."

"Let's do it." Bo gave the customary launch order. They walked quietly towards the suspect's house. The next few minutes would be intense and dangerous. As they say in the movies: *It's show time!* That, of course, is a really dumb statement. If you're at the movies, it better be show time or you might as well grab your popcorn and go watch cable at home.

Sarge crept through unmowed grass to the back door. The big man was dressed in his usual black pants and pullover sweatshirt, perfect for a cool, early-morning takedown. "Advise, Jim," he whispered, then took a deep breath and adjusted his headset.

"You've got blasting caps located in the wall with a trigger connected to the door. Fairly primitive, but effective."

"The guy's real creative." Sarge observed sarcastically, shaking his head in disgust. His annoyance mirrored when he spoke of politicians, bureaucrats, and gunrunners.

"Drill a hole eighteen inches under the doorbell. That will give you plenty of leeway. Bubba's welcoming surprise shouldn't be a problem unless you pry open the screen door."

Sarge grabbed a cordless from his tool pouch and drilled as instructed. He poked the nozzle of his blast retardant spray foam into the hole and gave it a squirt. *Explosive Retardants*, or ERs, were developed earlier in the century by an ingenious chemist (from a prestigious Massachusetts university) interested in finding a safer way to defuse landmines and terrorist bombs. Working through a chemical process, ERs dissipate volatile energy, leaving the device harmless— or at the very least reduced to a less dramatic potential. If used correctly and in sufficient quantities, they'll convert the "BAM!" of an explosive to a pop or fizz accompanied by a flash of light.

Despite a fierce lobbying effort by the munitions industry to ban research in blast retardants, science prevailed with a Congressional endorsement that has saved thousands of military and civilian lives. ERs are nontoxic and can be purchased as a liquid, powder, spray foam, or ointment. There's no mess, no fuss. They're effective on everything from gunpowder to high explosives like C4, TATP, CAV, and Protex. Not surprisingly, political contributions from disaffected ordnance manufacturers abruptly ceased. Congress had actually voted in the country's best interest over its own.

Sarge finished at the back door. "Give me the bad news," he whispered as he circled to the front. "At least there are no pungi sticks in the yard."

"Stay clear of the porch steps," Jim enlightened. "There's a pressure-sensitive device under the deck. Anyone as big as you could set it off!"

"Very funny," Sarge whispered. "Are you implying I need to lose weight?"

"You've got approximately fifteen grams of Protex to deal with." Jim, out of physical necessity, ignored the question. Sarge was one tough hombre.

"He's real serious about his drinking, isn't he?" the big man observed. "If the little old lady next door stopped in to borrow a cup of sugar, she'd be blown through the roof!"

"It's probably rigged to detonate with the approximate weight of three determined DES cops." Jim informed prophetically. "An LOL wouldn't set it off. Douse it good." Sarge removed the wooden obstruction and slid on his back until reaching the booby trap, wired to the joists. He smothered it with ER foam. "You can take it home for your kids to play with," Jim suggested as he watched the explosive go lifeless on his monitor. "It's silly-putty now."

With a tiny flashlight between his teeth, Sarge neutralized the trigger. He wiped perspiration from his forehead using a small cloth towel included in the tool kit, then retreated from the dank surroundings, the device securely in his grasp. "My kids are all grown up. I'll save it for the grandchildren next time they come over. We're all clear."

"Okay Grandpa." Bo was relieved the explosives were null and void.

"I'd like to once again advise that we use the Neutrino Camera against this guy," Jim suggested. "We've had enough excitement for one night. NOSTRILS indicates gunpowder in the house, in what is probably the living room. Also, when the door is blown, I'll make sure no one is nearby." Jim lightened the mood. "And besides, Larry's been known to enhance his Puff Charge binary mixture with too much explosive and not enough activator."

Bo looked at Larry, who exhibited nonverbal protest. But the advice had to be considered, paperwork be damned. Bo knew his pilot was right.

The Neutrino Camera tipped the scales to law enforcement's favor. Besides, gunpowder in the living room didn't quite add up. "Okay. What's the suspect doing in there?"

Jim activated the monitor hooked to the X-ray-like NC. The green-grey picture was sharp and clear. He adjusted depth of field and focal length, then made his report. "Looks like he's watching a rodeo on 3DTV and drinking the evidence we'll need to convict. There's a half-gallon pitcher on the table beside him, but I'm picking up faint alcohol signatures elsewhere in the house. He has more, possibly hidden under sensor-defeating material. There's also tobacco products nearby, but he is not smoking."

"Anybody helping him consume the home-brewed aqua vitae?"

Jim's eyebrows furrowed at the Latin. "He's alone. A semiautomatic handgun is on the couch. Sensors indicate more gunpowder located in the crawlspace. This guy's armed and dangerous!"

"Larry, you're up. Cy, into position!"

Cy quietly climbed the porch steps, grateful for Sarge's diligent work minutes earlier. Larry assiduously combined the Puff Charge, a high-tech, low concussive explosive safe to transport and detonate in civilian proximity. As advertised, Puff Charges can gently blow the hell out of softer materials without the racket, fuss, and flying debris normally associated with high explosives. Developed at a celebrated technical institute located not too far from the aforementioned prestigious Massachusetts university, Puff Charges have become the industry standard.

Kneeling on the grass, Larry finished mixing a golf ball-sized clump. The door did not appear heavy, thus a small amount would suffice. He tossed the compact clay-like package to the DES attorney, who divided and placed one-third near the doorknob and the rest over the keyhole of the dead bolt. Cy was careful not to jar the door, thereby tipping off the perp. He finished by inserting a detonating receiver in each clump, followed by a tiny blast deflector, which gave the effect of a shaped charge. Cy moved two steps to the right. Larry smiled, as if to say: What's wrong, afraid of a little low-cuss explosion?

Bubba's living room window had the curtains drawn; his attention focused—maybe a little too focused—on a popular TV genre. Pro rodeo rated third behind Pro Wrestling, and the number one television pastime, Debate. "What's the perp doing in there?" Cy's legal language couldn't hide his annoyance. Only Sarge was fearless around explosives.

"Still watching TV," Jim reassured. "He has no idea you're outside. When Larry blows the door, take two steps and turn sixty degrees to your left. Don't give him time to grab that firearm!" Sarge remained off to the side of the porch for safety in case of a low-cuss backfire (extra activator, not enough explosive, the opposite Larry is accused of).

Larry stood up and nodded. "On the count of 3, 2, 1"—and he hit the fire-control button on a small remote. There was a hushed, low frequency PUFF or pffffft sound accompanied by a gentle shockwave that blew the door slightly open. Despite being a lawyer, Cy was instantly through, with Sarge and Bo a step or two back.

"Freeze, Bubba!" (The universal cop greeting for anyone caught in the commission of a crime rarely does much good. Most perps react the opposite. But it *is* a tradition.) Cy grabbed the firearm. "Drug Enforcement, we gotta warrant!" Bubba Franklin was so startled, he spilled turbo-brewed alcoholic beer over his sweatshirt and pants.

"On the floor, partner!" Sarge demanded as he holstered his firearm. Bubba had no intention of complying. Grabbing the suspect by the arms, Sarge muscled him to the floor. Bubba struggled but was quickly subdued by Sarge's overpowering physical advantage.

Cy put the firearm in a sterile Zip-lock-type plastic bag, then removed his latex gloves as Bo threw on the cuffs. Bubba kicked violently, trying to free himself from Sarge's grasp. "He's a squirmer. Cuff his ankles." It was quickly accomplished.

"Go to hell!" the suspect fumed, struggling on the floor. At thirty-two years of age, five-foot-ten, two hundred pounds, Bubba had short red hair and a protruding belly—evidence his favorite pastime involved an addictive, controlled substance and gateway drug.

"Silence is golden. You know that from watching cop shows."

"Go to hell!" the perp defied Cy's legal advice.

Bo eased the tension. "He's got a limited vocabulary and bad attitude."

The suspect squirmed. Sarge lifted him gently off the floor and placed him in the seated position on the beer-soaked couch. Bubba was tense, searching for an avenue of escape. He let his feelings be known in no uncertain terms. "You guy's planted that pitcher of beer on me! I'm innocent! This is a frame-up!"

"Pipe down." Sarge smiled at the perp's accusations.

"Bad news," Jim interrupted over the comm. "Sensors indicate a small amount of alcoholic beer residue on Sarge's arm."

"Great!" Sarge checked his sleeve. "I got it on me wrestling Mr. Franklin to the floor."

"Well," Bo was sympathetic, "let me worry about that. I'll get you through the Drug Enforcement Review. That's what I'm paid the big bucks for." He spoke with a shrug. "In the meantime, take sonic showers and use TurboSoap. All the alcoholic residue will eventually come off, but you're still going to fail that drug screening next week."

"It won't be the first time." Sarge replied with resigned annoyance. "But those bureaucrats are always a pain."

Bo was back to giving orders. "Larry, grab the EV. Park it on the driveway. And nice work with that door." Larry exited the front entrance where a solid, fully-functioning door had been only minutes earlier. The wood core was neatly shredded around the doorknob and deadbolt. The hardware remained undamaged, but no longer intact. Low-cuss blew the wood fibers, but was useless on brass. Bo shook his head at the suspect, seated with hands behind his back on the sofa. "Read him his rights, Cy."

"I want a lawyer," Bubba demanded.

"You'll get a lawyer," Cy assured, before reading his rights as set forth under International Drug Law.

Bubba was riled up. "I have the God-given right to drink in the privacy of my own home. You guys are a bunch of leftwing Nazis! This bust is unconstitutional!"

"Leftwing Nazis, huh?" Cy was amused. "That's a combination I hadn't thought about before. And God never granted a divine right to consume illegal substances. Save some complaining for the judge. That beer has turned your brain into scrambled eggs. Now exercise your right to remain silent!"

"Go to hell!" Bubba blurted. "And get a haircut! It's medicinal beer. I need it for health reasons. I can get a doctor's prescription. Beer is a vital part of the American psyche!" If he'd been a cartoon character, steam would have spurted from his ears.

"Nice try," Cy informed the suspect calmly, "but alcohol is a Schedule One Controlled Substance with no known therapeutic uses and it's not legal for an MD or psychiatrist to prescribe. There's no such thing as medicinal alcohol and there never will be. All those health theories pushed by the industry were laid to rest decades ago. Besides, if your cholesterol is a problem, eat oatmeal. It isn't illegal, at least not yet. And none of us are going to get a haircut. We don't want to look like communists!" Bubba squirmed. "Now, please remain silent so you don't incriminate yourself further."

"Go to hell," Bubba angrily re-verbalized his taunt, though less adamantly than before. It appeared he was tiring of cop insults.

"You certainly have hostility and anger pent up inside," Sarge chided.

Bubba grumbled as Cy placed the warrant on his lap, including a copy of his rights, in layman's language with the part about remaining silent highlighted. "Read the warrant," Cy demanded. "It'll explain we did nothing unconstitutional."

"Okay, secure the evidence and fire up the PortaSniff," Bo ordered. "Let's see what else we can find. I'll inform the FBI weapons dudes and ICROG. Good work everyone! Don't forget to test Bubba's blood-alcohol level. And confiscate that sweatshirt he's wearing. Anything that claims *Beer is the Purpose of Life* could be drug paraphernalia."

FUTUREBUST

"I hope you don't get a hanging judge." Cy shook his head in disbelief.

FUTUREBUST2.6

Bo headed outside as the EV settled on the driveway. The sun wouldn't rise for another hour. Larry jumped out and headed for the storage compartment to unpack the PortaSniff, a less powerful, more focused, portable mini-version of NOSTRILS. "Let's keep things quiet," Bo reminded with a whisper. "We don't want to wake the neighbors."

Larry nodded affirmatively, carrying the vacuum cleaner-sized drug sniffer up the porch steps. Bo climbed into the EV and sat down. He closed his eyes and exhaled, relieved no one had been hurt. A negative influence on the children in the neighborhood had just been removed. Alcohol never produces positive results, except in massage parlors and race cars.

The investigation commenced. The field commander had to prevent mistakes that might permit Bubba's release on a cunning, lawyer-crafted technicality. He sat up in working mode and gazed at his pilot's face on the monitor to his left. "Jim, everything's under control. You may as well finish your search route, then head to HQ."

"Will do," Jim nodded. "It's all recorded. If Mr. Franklin tries the unconstitutional argument in court, he'll have to convince the judge we fabricated everything."

"I wouldn't worry about it. We have enough to convict and Larry hasn't even fired up the PortaSniff. Sensors indicated more drugs hidden somewhere. Plus Bubba's beer belly is self-incriminating evidence outside the jurisdiction of the Fifth Amendment."

"He might even be a trafficker," Jim added. "Nothing ever gets past the PortaSniff. If it's there, Larry will find it."

"That'll do it then." Bo sounded pleased. "Notify the mechanics when you return to the hanger. All that hovering probably clogged things up. It'll need a little hammer and chisel work to maintain top condition. And don't forget to thaw out that dog."

"I wasn't about to forget our canine friend," Jim assured. "The pooch will be good as new in an hour. I've filed the e-doc (electronic documentation) via satellite." Jim ended the transmission, quietly pulled out of hover, and resumed his scan of the San Bernardino area. It's unlikely he'd run across more drug abuse. Two busts in a month would be an epidemic. Two in one night—a world's record.

Bo listened as the turbocraft exited the area. It was eerily quiet. He made a call to HQ to get help with the investigation, then returned to the house. Drug and firearm charges are always federal jurisdiction.

Lieutenant Dolly Griffin, the affable, outgoing (required to meet quotas) female DES officer was already at HQ making preparations. She worked days, but was on call 24/7. The moment the Alert Buzzer sounded, her alarm at home went off. At 2:45 A.M. it probably wasn't appreciated, but that's the price of being plugged into a *wired*, though drug-free world.

Back inside, Larry activated the PortaSniff, switching to a molecular scan. Bubba looked nervous and annoyed. Notwithstanding, he was in a foul mood. "What's that for?" the suspect demanded. His freckles made him appear unusually hostile.

"It's a PortaSniff," Larry answered calmly. "If you've got controlled substances in the house, I'll find 'em. It electronically analyzes down to the subatomic level. I've switched to a molecular scan because there's an existing warrant and I want to restrict the parameters."

"The warrant states we can search for controlled substances," Cy informed. "We are limited to those parameters. If you have any stolen diamonds or artwork in here, they are currently of no interest to us."

Bubba squirmed. "You have no right to search my molecules. You guys are challenging the constitutionality of the Fourth Amendment!"

Cy looked at Bubba questionably, finally realizing what he was getting at. "I see what you're saying. Truth is, we can search at the atomic level without a warrant, and at the molecular level with a warrant. It's true that the Fourth Amendment protects your molecules, but not atoms. The Supreme Court said so in Gonzalez vs. FBI, 2019."

"Who owns my atoms?"

"The government." Cy answered with a facetious oversimplification of the law.

Bubba grimaced. The precedents deciding such issues are taught in elementary school jurisprudence and everyone understands them. The suspect tried another tact. "You'd be out of work if the present Supreme Court overturned those cases!"

"I'm a lawyer," Cy made a frank admission and commenced the rebuttal as he sat down on the uncontaminated side of the sofa. "I could turn to swindling old ladies out of their pensions." His humor fell on deaf ears. "But you're right. Many decisions have been reviewed by subsequent Courts and overturned. The ruling that decided the presidential election of 2000 over the votes of the American people was overturned twenty-four years later."

"So you are harassing me." Bubba continued his fruitless efforts to pull from the cuffs securing his hands. "I'm not hurting anybody by drinking in the privacy of my own home! Besides, beer is food."

"That argument's been tried in court and failed. Beer is a gateway drug. And your house—the law's going to confiscate it!"

Bubba looked pale and worried. He settled back on the couch and fell silent while Larry began a focused scan of the room. Spilled beer on the perp's sweatshirt had mixed ominously with perspiration. Cy wrinkled his nose in protest but the ethereal odor gave Bubba impetus to reignite. "You guys are the *thought* police!" His urge to complain was contrary to *best practices* in such circumstances.

Cy smiled at the baseless accusation and rebutted. "The DES is not into thought control, but only because we haven't figured out how to do that yet. For now, contemplate alcohol all you want, just don't drink it."

The search continued. Bubba grimaced as Larry probed the hall leading to a bedroom. "What are you doing over there? There's nothing over there!"

"He's simply searching your molecular structure, looking for nothing in particular." Cy appeared suspicious of Bubba's ranting. "Alcohol is a dangerous combination of atomic material. Its consumption is strongly frowned on. I hope you don't have more hidden in this house." The DES attorney had given up on impressing the right-to-remain-silent idea into Bubba's brain. "Now you want to tell me why you keep guns on the premises?"

"I have to protect my alcohol." Bubba explained the obvious.

"That's why alcohol is the most dangerous drug," Cy nodded. "Illegal firearms and booze are always in the same general vicinity."

The PortaSniff began to beep faster. Some do-it-yourself homeowner repairs were patched into the plaster. "I'll bet we find a hollow space hidden behind." Larry spoke with confidence born of experience. "Get out the sledge."

"No wait," Bo insisted. "There's got to be a way in. The less damage we do, the more value at auction. Sarge, the crawlspace." Bubba squirmed, not being all that comfortable in his soggy, odiferous sweatshirt.

Bo waited for the search results. Experience taught him what to expect. Sarge soon returned and spoke bluntly. "A couple automatic rifles and ammo, plus a Mark V, 261-B TurboBrewery with optional Froth Enhancer, the *BMW* of the species."

"That would explain the high electric bill." Bo's eyebrows curled. He shook his head. "The Froth Enhancer is new—maybe that's why they classify it as a 261-B. Keep scanning. The suspect is a recreational brewmeister. No telling what we'll find here."

Cy, in an exploratory mood, strolled toward the kitchen to check out the refrigerator, a device previously used for the cool, frosty storage of now illegal alcoholic beverages. His jaw dropped after opening the door. He understood what Bubba meant when he spoke of protecting his alcohol. Inside Cy beheld a rare, incomprehensible vision of beerhead nirvana. It was definitely a *hallelujah* experience. In sheer disbelief the DES attorney exclaimed, "Get in here and take a look at this!"

Bo joined Cy in the kitchen. The Latin he'd used earlier understated the significance. Both men stared. The refrigerator almost shone with a divine, beer-guzzling halo. "That's the best collection I've ever seen!" Bo spoke with reverence, as if the cosmic sound of OM emanated from within. "There's hardly room for food in here. Check this out, Sarge."

Bubba turned beet red in anger. "Stay put!" the big man demanded as he joined the others. Sarge's expression was beyond the realm of ordinary language, at least earthly words. Ecstasy, rapture, utopia; all fall far short. "Well I'll be a..." He didn't finish his sentence. "They must be worth thousands!"

"Each," Cy added. "I've never seen antiques like these!"

"Shut off the PortaSniff and take a look at this, Larry!" Bo ordered.

"Leave them cans alone!" Bubba shouted as he squirmed. "Those are priceless! This is police brutality!"

"We'll have to confiscate them," Cy insisted, looking towards the living room where Bubba sat. "Priceless or not, they're evidence." Compassion was called for. This was no ordinary drug bust and Bubba—no ordinary perp. He was a millionaire incognito!

"This is cruel and unusual punishment," Bubba protested. "You can't take them cans! They're a retirement investment."

Cy returned to the sofa. He spoke in lawyerly fashion. "You'll not need a nest egg where you're headed. Where'd you get them anyway?"

"They're family heirlooms." Bubba's shoulders drooped, his voice subdued and dejected. "My grandfather gave them to me." The suspect was visibly upset at the prospect of losing his treasured unopened beer cans—more valuable than his domicile. Bubba was getting burned twice in the same bust. The cans also explained how this normal, everyday guy could afford a Mark V, Model 261-B with Froth Enhancer, a pricey, upper-crust, high-tone, 100% top-drawer unit. As Jim had suspected earlier, the collection was covered with a layer of sensor absorbing material that defeated NOSTRILS to some degree, and explained why they hadn't found it in earlier Population Surveys.

Larry restarted the PortaSniff while Sarge went for a camera. A second EV landed with Lieutenant Dolly Griffin, FBI dudes, and ICROG, the International Civil Rights Oversight Group in tow. "Take a look inside," Sarge advised as she exited the vehicle. "You won't believe what we've found."

"Been busy, huh?" Dolly was cheerful as usual. She looked around outside, noticing the unmowed grass, then went in with the others. "Congratulations. Looks like you've bagged yourselves a live one." Dolly's irrepressible enthusiasm was always welcome, though Bubba could have used a little less optimism.

"Name's Bubba," Bo informed. "He's sensitive so go easy on him."

"Well how you doing, Bubba?" Her question drew no response other than a grimace. "It appears you're in a heap of trouble. Beer, huh? A genuine BWB."

"A BWB?" Sarge looked puzzled as he reentered the house. "You want to tell us what that stands for?"

"It's an abbreviation once used by military police. It stood for *Bubba with a Beer*, but referred to any intoxicated and obstinate military personnel on their way to the brig for Drunk and Disorderly or resisting arrest." Her nose wrinkled. "Whew! I can smell it. He has it all over him. Don't anyone touch the suspect! He's contaminated."

"There are weapons in the crawlspace, plus a turbo-brewery," Bo informed the Feds, who were distinguishable from DES because their hair was too short; hardly even down to their shoulders. One had a ponytail, the Fed's EV pilot.

The newcomers under Lieutenant Griffin's command went right to work. The ICROG man took notes and interviewed Bubba. Bo motioned towards the refrigerator. Dolly stared in stunned silence. "Those cans are unopened. They must go back twenty-five years. I haven't seen anything like this in decades! Get a close-up, Sarge, then the whole refrigerator. We'll print them off poster-size to hang on the wall at HQ."

"Can you imagine their value on the black market?" Sarge queried.

"I don't even want to know." Dolly shook her head. "Look at the brand names. Those industrial breweries either converted to ethanol or were dismantled and scrapped years ago. Maybe we should contact the Smithsonian. It might be better than destroying them. If the media gets this, we'll be overrun."

Bo looked pale. "They'll be coming in from all over the globe."

"I'll make that call to DC." She went outside. Sarge snapped his photos using an old-fashioned film camera. ICROG required film because it was harder to digitally manipulate and therefore protected the defendant's rights.

The detectives continued their investigation. Larry shut off the PortaSniff and set it beside the damaged front door. He held an unopened pack of cigarettes in his hand, found under Bubba's mattress. "The rest of the house is clean. Wow, what a night!"

"I'll be telling my grandkids about this one," Sarge announced proudly. He handed the film over to the ICROG fellow. "Maybe I'll take them to meet Bubba at rehab."

"You're not going to rehabilitate me!" Bubba's combative verbiage reignited. "I haven't done anything illegal. Beer is a creation from God. You're infringing on my religious rights!"

"That's also been tried in court," Cy informed the suspect. "The religious argument's been used with alcohol, tobacco, and marijuana. However you might convince the judge you're a collector of antiquities, or maybe just trying to preserve the traditions of your ancestors. He may fall for it." Bubba contemplated the possibilities. "Forget it," Cy continued. "They've been tried also. Resign yourself to the fact you're living an unhealthy lifestyle that's no longer permitted. A few years in rehab and you'll be as good as new."

"No chance," Bubba replied obstinately, the pitch of his voice rising. "I'm going to rot in there and it will be your fault! Think of all the money wasted to incarcerate me. I'm a productive member of society. You guys are full of it! The government's full of it! This whole drug free society can shove it up...!"

"We've got company," the ICROG guy interrupted Bubba's ranting. "Looks like the neighbors are awake. The media can't be far behind now."

A small crowd of people gathered outside. The first job: keep them calm. "Everything's under control. There's nothing to worry about. Please return to your homes."

"Is Mr. Franklin in some sort of trouble, officer?" a frail looking little old lady asked. "I live next door. We didn't know he was a criminal. He never talked to anyone—just kept to himself. I wish he'd mow his lawn. The grass grows so fast in the springtime."

"It certainly does. Here," Cy took her by the hand, "I'll help you back to your house."

"Everyone, please return to your yards." Bo was sympathetic to their concerns. People milled around, conversed, and then stood in robes and slippers, making furtive glances towards the Franklin residence.

The first glimmer of dawn was apparent through the stately hybrid elms, just starting to leaf out, though it would not be a good morning for Bubba. Some early-rising birds blithely pre-announced the sunrise. Sounding much too cheery and upbeat, they were not appreciated by Bubba either. Lieutenants Bo and Dolly confronted the perp, sulking under Sarge's watchful eye. "Those cans are going to a museum. You'll be a star in rehab."

"I ought to get a suspended sentence for my charity," Bubba insisted. "You know it burns my butt that tax dollars are paying your salary. I should get a permanent tax break."

"That's not going to happen either," Cy informed as he returned from his errand. "Tax dollars have always paid for drug enforcement. Now, I think it's time we get you downtown for booking and arraignment. It also looks like you get to meet the captain."

A chauffeur-driven SkyLimo dropped slowly with the early morning dew. "You mind your manners, Bubba," Cy warned. "You're in enough trouble as it is. Give him grief and he's liable to tack on a few extra charges. The captain has a creative imagination, despite the fact that he's an old-time shorthair like you."

Bubba wasn't a happy camper. The detectives brought his German-engineered 261-B out from the crawlspace and carefully set it on the floor. It was an expensive model with plenty of options—illegally imported. The Mark V represented years of pay for a guy like Bubba. After the trial, it'd be dismantled—its valuable electronic parts used to build cruise missiles or spy satellites. One indisputable fact—it manufactured beer in a hurry, almost as fast as an alcoholic like Bubba could drink it. There was also another sensor-absorbing blanket.

The captain disembarked. Dressed in street clothes, he was average height and weight, a pleasant face with sixty-nine-year-old features and moderately gray, kinky hair. Being thorough and observant in nature, he continued his inspection, then wandered inside. "Fine job you've done here, everyone. We're looking good with the mayor. The national media has the story so stay sharp. We'll have a press conference at noon to display all this booty. Is this the suspect?" The captain shook his head. "My goodness son, you knew that stuff was illegal didn't you? It's such a shame. Now show me those cans. It's been decades since I've held a cold one in my hand!" He stepped gingerly past the 261-B and headed for the kitchen.

"Not a word," Cy whispered, patting Bubba gently on the uncontaminated shoulder. "Keep quiet and things will be a whole lot better in the long run." Bubba wisely took the free legal advice and sulked.

Sarge opened the refrigerator door slowly, as if to accentuate the ethereal contents. The captain's eyes lit up. "Would you look at those cans!" He put his hand to his heart. "This is a religious experience for an old-timer like me! That boy's sitting on a fortune." He stared as if mesmerized, enthralled, spellbound, and dumbfounded. His pulse quickened and breath grew shallow. "Let me have one."

Sarge handed him a can. The senior officer grasped, nay caressed with visible enthusiasm, passion, and fervor—feeling the cold on his skin. Lost in reverie, he wiped the can across his brow and sighed as if sitting on a sandy, uninhabited beach on a hot, lazy, sun-soaked afternoon. Memories flooded his consciousness.

"You're not going to open it, are you sir?" Bo's expression was uneasy.

The captain continued his little charade. "Who me? No of course not. But back in the old days we did all the time. If I'd known they'd become so valuable, I might have buried a few six-packs in my own yard. Of course with the sensors we have nowadays..." his voice trailed off. The others reacted in disbelief to the captain's mood. He pretended not to notice. "This stuff used to be real popular. Take the whole refrigerator as a display case. The media is going to eat this up! Here, you better put this one back with the others, Sarge. I might be tempted to take it home." Captain Jackson caught a whiff of alcohol in the air and spoke to Sarge with disapproval. "You've got beer on your clothes, don't you? You're sure to fail that mandatory drug test next week."

Sarge didn't need reminding of the fact that he'd soon face a bevy of pencil-pushing bureaucrats to explain his alcoholic corruption. The tests are extremely sensitive. Minimal exposure on the skin will set off the alarm bells, even weeks after contamination.

Bo brought their attention back to matters at hand. "Okay, listen up. Let's wrap this investigation and get out of here. FBI dudes will close off the front door when they're done. The transport is on its way to pick up the evidence. I don't want anyone talking to the media. Is that clear?"

The captain strolled out to his SkyLimo and turned to speak. He seemed like a man who'd suddenly regained his youth. "Fine job. I'll see you at the conference." He walked toward his ride, then turned to face the others, a look of amusement on his face. "You know, I could have made it as an actor, but chose law enforcement instead."

The lieutenants shook their heads as the luxurious chauffeur-driven vehicle lifted off. Bo watched silently as it disappeared into the predawn sky. Knowing they'd been had, he spoke philosophically. "I'll be riding in one of those someday. Just wait and see."

"With this bust it might be sooner than you think," Dolly agreed. "That old fart's due to retire soon." They smiled and turned to go back inside just as the transport came into sight. Right behind were three vehicles. "Damn!" Dolly was confounded. "It's getting crowded. The media followed us in."

"Cy," Bo shouted. "Keep the press at bay while we finish up! And don't let them land on the neighbors' lawns. Sarge, get the suspect on the transport. Larry, help Delta load all this stuff. In fifteen minutes we should be out of here."

Everyone scrambled to finish before the media set up their equipment. They packed the EV for the return trip to HQ. The FBI dudes stayed behind. Sarge had to ride with the suspect in the transport so Larry sat in Alpha's pilot seat. He punched in their destination and hit autopilot. Powerful thrusters brought the vehicle to life. Slowly lifting up over the neighborhood, they hovered, taking it all in for the last time while Larry held the EV on pause. "That's one I'll never forget. Wait until Jim hears about the beer cans. He won't believe it."

"You're right about that," Bo agreed. "He probably hasn't seen a beer can since he was a teenager, except in a museum."

"We used to love beer," Larry admitted. "You weren't considered a man until you guzzled a pitcher without stopping to take a breath. Everyone I hung with succeeded before we were legally old enough to drink."

Cy winced. "I read that in school. It was considered a rite of passage. Many died of alcohol poisoning on the first birthday they were legal."

FUTUREBUST2.9

The EV sped towards HQ at three hundred miles per hour. Larry parked where it had been earlier. Jim was waiting. "Unopened beer cans." Bo slapped his pilot on the shoulder. "You found priceless artifacts from bygone days."

"You're kidding!" Jim's usually unflappable expression showed moderate excitement. "Is that what the sensors picked up elsewhere in the house?"

"Cy located them in the refrigerator," Larry informed.

"This might be a top-ten bust, street value-wise. By the way, where's Sarge? I'll bet he reeks of beer, plus he's going to fail the mandatory drug screening next week. Too bad for him." The transport parked close to the loading dock. Sarge led Bubba to booking. "So that's the suspect." Jim wondered out loud. "How long do you figure he'll be in rehab?"

"Long time," Cy assured. "He's an ornery sucker. When he gets out, he'll have to start from scratch, maybe mowing lawns for his neighbors."

The evidence guys unloaded the transport, handling the refrigerator with extra caution. It was headed for the conference room where the media could drool over the contents and take pictures, but no samples. Everyone strolled into the office and sat down. Donuts were passed around while they relaxed. The previous month of boredom was long forgotten. Sarge soon returned from booking and grabbed a donut. "Bubba's giving them hell down there." The big man shook his head in disbelief. "He refused to allow a DNA scan. Says it's a violation of his privacy rights. I had to quote from PATRIOT I, Section 215, where it stipulates we have access to his genetic data. The Supreme Court overturned it long ago, but I figured Bubba didn't know that. The fellow's in one foul mood."

"That's the little pro wrestler dwelling deep down inside of him, coming up full-fury," Dolly observed with a psychologically enhanced smile.

"Are you sure it's not just his inner child acting out?" Cy questioned.

"Same thing in some people," she shrugged. "Bubba's inner child is dressed in tights, a cape and mask, and carries a pouch of fake blood to use whenever the ref is distracted."

"That subconscious introspective psychology mumbo-jumbo stuff is interesting," Sarge admitted. "But I'm going to take a shower and get this smell off me."

"When you get a chance," Bo advised, "better write a report explaining your current state of contamination. You'll need it next week for the Enforcement Review Board."

"I'm on it," Sarge replied as he shuffled off toward the locker room, then backtracked. "I'll admit one thing. I prefer an inebriated BWB to an angry and determined LOL any day." Dolly laughed as Sarge headed for the combo-shower. Soothing sonic waves would eliminate any chance of physical contamination remaining after he was done. It will not, however, help in the upcoming drug screening. A forgone conclusion, alcohol had been absorbed through the pores and subatomic patterns are easily detectable a week later.

"What do you think the street value of our haul will be?" Larry inquired.

"No way to know," Dolly replied. "But whatever they come up with, it will be inflated by double. After the Rascone bust in northern L.A. last year, they street-valued that minivan load of cigarettes at over four million dollars. It wasn't worth one-and-a-half!"

"Inflating the value of contraband has precedent behind it," Cy admitted. "There's a longstanding tradition going back to the last century, allowing law enforcement substantial leeway when calculating a bust's actual worth. It created the illusion of progress with the problem of drug abuse. Isn't that an ADS?"

"That's deep psychological insight for a lawyer," Dolly mused as she motioned for another donut. "But you're right. It's a form of self-delusion, an Active Denial System. That's one of the reasons WoD failed."

Bo gazed cautiously at his donut, unsure of the pretty sprinkles. "We're doing things better today. By the way," Bo turned his attention toward Cy, "I heard you talking to Bubba about the Supreme Court overturning a decision."

"That was the case deciding the Presidential election of 2000," Cy nodded.

"So what's the point?" Bo shrugged. "It won't change anything or right the wrong. The damage to the democratic process had already been done."

"True," Cy agreed. "But it admits a mistake and makes sure the decision never becomes precedent. That ruling was one of the worst the court ever made, right up there with Dred Scot and Plessy Ferguson. A subsequent court had to overturn, just to show we had advanced as a nation and still believe in the rule of law. It was an example of raw judicial abuse." Cy contemplated, then continued. "Truthfully, such decisions almost gutted the Constitution. But if one looks at things over the long haul, most Americans, minus a handful of Supreme Court justices, along with an occasional attorney general and a few presidents, have understood, honored, and respected the sanctity of the Constitution."

Bo nodded, then looked longingly towards the lounge. With nothing left to do, it was time for a nap. He stood up and advised the others. "Wake me after that blasted news conference is over, not before."

All agreed. "By the way, Lieutenant," Jim questioned, "who's on patrol this morning?"

"That'd be the new kid, Lance. I know, I know," Dolly insisted with upraised hands, "you guys think he's trouble. Just give me a chance to work with him and we'll see."

"But how much damage will he do in the meantime?" Larry inquired half-jokingly. "He's awful rambunctious."

"Downright cocky," Bo added. "He used to be a race driver, right?"

"He drove formula one cars," Dolly informed. "His sponsor raced at Indy last year."

"So why'd he quit?" Cy asked with suspicion evident in his voice.

"He said he wanted to do something worthwhile with his life," Dolly replied. "Come on, lighten up. Give me a couple months and I'll turn him into one of the best."

"I'll bet it was our glamorous recruiting posters," Cy quipped.

"I'm glad he's Delta's responsibility." Bo shook his head, unsure of what to think. "Keep a close eye on him while he's in diapers. If he makes a mess, we'll be cleaning it up."

"Thanks for all the support." She pointed a finger. "But don't forget, that's what they said when you first started, fresh out of Command School with no experience. Now get some rest. You guys need your beauty sleep. I'll wake you for the conference."

"Is that really what you guys said about me?" Bo inquired a half-hour later, just as the others began to relax.

Sarge laughed, his hair still wet from the shower. "She must have us mixed-up with someone else."

"That's right." Larry backed his longtime partner and best buddy. "She's definitely got us mixed-up with someone else. That's our story and we're sticking to it."

"Uh huh." The field commander nodded. "I'll bet."

Cy laughed. Not tired, he grabbed a book and lost himself in its pages.

Dolly strolled to the conference room to observe the preparations for the upcoming media event. No doubt they'd have to listen to speeches from the mayor and other dignitaries. There'd be congratulatory slaps on the back for everyone. The contraband would be on display along with those ever-present, inflated street values, and they'd announce the eventual confiscation of Bubba's property. The global media was gearing up to make a major event out of one man's refusal to seek treatment for his addiction. Bubba would be sent to the stockade, but never conform. As one of a tiny minority of hardcore fanatics, he'd spend years in the pokey, refusing to acknowledge society's prerogative. For a brief moment on the six o'clock news, he'd become an unwilling international symbol of social edification, then fade into oblivion, never to be heard from again. Though Bubba might have other ideas, that's pretty much how it always works out.

FUTUREBUST3.0

"Are you coming?" Lieutenant Dolly Griffin tapped Jim on the shoulder. "Thirty minutes to the news conference." The pilot was out in the hanger sitting on a barrel, gazing at the inner workings of his turbocraft as Big Al tinkered with the compressors. The chief mechanic had an assortment of specialized tools spread on the floor next to his feet, including the obligatory hammer and chisel, in case a stubborn part refused less vigorous promptings.

"Thanks for the warning." Jim grinned mischievously. "Tell the guys I'll meet them at the donut shop across the street." Big Al smiled.

"That's not going to happen this time!" Her warning was stern, knowing she had to exhibit plenty of toughness or the Alpha boys would do just as Jim hinted. They'd done it before—running away when required to appear at a special function. Jim patted Big Al on the shoulder and followed the lieutenant back into the office.

"A half-hour," Dolly informed as she passed Larry, sitting at his desk in the main office. He was entering Bubba's arrest report into the computer.

"A half-hour," Jim, who was right behind, mimicked.

"A half-hour," Larry affirmed enthusiastically. "Donut shop."

Dolly frowned, then headed to the lounge where the remainder of Alpha relaxed. Sarge was intent on a spiral notebook where he'd obediently scribbled some notes for his upcoming confrontation with the dreaded ERB, the Enforcement Review Board. No, he hadn't failed the drug test yet. That will happen next week. Though still in the future, failure is assured due to the fact that he'd commingled his physical essence with the illegal intoxicant soaked in Bubba's sweatshirt. The drug screenings are extremely sensitive, taken at the atomic level. Exposure within one or two weeks of a test, even briefly on the skin, will raise the proverbial red flag. Sarge had also drawn the requisite number of highly artistic doodles along the margins.

Cy was reading, something he claimed he hadn't had time to do much of in his youth. A telescoping lamp illuminated the pages with light. He didn't look up, remaining immersed in text as Dolly entered. Lieutenant Bo MacKinsey was stretched out on the sofa with headphones over his ears. The DES field commander had grabbed a combat nap, being that he'd just worked a (not uncommon) thirty-hour shift. Dolly carefully removed the sound suppression.

"Better wake up, sleeping beauty. Only thirty minutes to the conference. You guys are all going to be stars."

"No," Bo grumbled and rubbed his eyes. "You were supposed to wake me after the conference, not before. Now I have to go out in front of all those nosey media types and explain everything that happened this morning." He yawned and stretched. "And who are you calling sleeping beauty?"

"No sarcasm intended," she countered with a laugh.

"I hope not," Sarge interjected, looking up from his writing project. "On a good day, he's at least as pretty as you, maybe even prettier."

"Damn right." Bo agreed sleepily as he sat up.

"Come on everybody," she encouraged quietly. "Time to face your adoring fans. Guess who just flew in from DC to help reap all the adulation?"

"Not Congressman Scranton again," Sarge protested, folding his notebook. "That guy's a glory hog and he's not even up for reelection until late next year."

"Get rid of him!" Cy insisted as he closed his book. "He'll be asking for campaign contributions, as if we can afford to finance his reelection on cop salaries. Besides, I've got expensive clothes to buy or my persona suffers from an image-challenged inferiority complex."

Dolly smiled. The guys were at their best when joking around. At least it made work tolerable, chasing the boredom away. "Nope it's not your favorite congressman. It's Senator Mackelroy, chairman of the Special Committee Responsible for Overseeing Drug Eradication Measures. He flew all the way from DC and wants to meet you."

"Boy are we honored," Sarge chided. "I'll get my tux."

Larry entered the lounge with Bubba's arrest report, which he handed off to Dolly. "No beer stains." He questioned with a rhetorical wink. "We wouldn't want to offend the big-shot senator, would we?"

"Very funny," Sarge grumbled. "Don't hassle me about my latest problem with alcoholic beer. It's bad enough I'll have to deal with the Enforcement Review Board weenies next week!" Sarge frowned, scratching out some of the doodles he didn't like.

"I'll see you guys out there," Dolly informed as she left the room, raising her voice ever so slightly. "Don't be late and don't try to sneak across the street to the donut shop. That's the first place we'll be looking if you don't show."

The five Alphas reluctantly came to terms with their fate. An hour with the press and some media-savvy politicians was survivable. They'd all been in worse predicaments in their lives. For Larry; combat. He'd done a stint in the Navy. Sarge got bullied and picked on as a child. Rigorous Marshal Arts training solved that problem. And Cy's childhood growing up on the mean streets of Beverly Hills—remember, there was a depression on. Bo lost his best friends in an accident. And Jim often compared media events with turbocraft crashes, yet he favored the latter as less of a headache. Alpha intended to comply with orders, but only because they had no choice.

Each man gathered his wits, bundled them tightly, and started the inevitable grooming process. They wanted to look nice for the cameras, but not like Hollywood stars. Bo, as usual, wasn't overly concerned with his outward appearance. More substance-oriented, he'd never been an *image* guy. Dressing like an undercover cop, most were surprised he commanded Alpha. Sure, he'd brush his shoulder-length hair and put on a clean shirt, but that's as far as it went. Anyone not liking his leather jacket or torn pants—tough! He wasn't going out there to meet the King, though Bo had often proclaimed loud and clear he wouldn't dress up for His Majesty either.

At the other extreme, Cy wore a tailored, three-piece suit. The certainties of life are death and taxes. Qualify that—permanent death and really high taxes! In the same vein, nobody respects a legal professional who doesn't maintain his appearance. "Half of being a successful lawyer is flimflam, the other half—good looks and charm," Cy once commented. Politicians will confirm this. That's right. The public is a sucker for image. For those who don't already know it, society is flawed.

With noon only minutes away, it was time to face the inevitable. They looked at each other, shrugged, took a deep collective breath, and headed for the conference room. Bo led the way. Passing near the elevator, he stopped to contemplate the possibilities. His expression revealed intense, mischievous deliberation and mental calculations. The donut shop was only seven floors down and a hop, skip, and jump across the street. Should they make a run for it? There's a little booth in the corner—lonely, vacant, just waiting for them, with row upon row of delightful baked delicacies in the display case, vying for their attention. They'd get a cup of coffee, talk about their morning exploits, and enjoy each other's company. The Dainty Donut Shop is one of the finest bakeries in the city, located directly across Commercial Street from the Federal Law Enforcement Building where a battalion of FBI Feds work, along with an NSA Office, Homeland Security, the Secret Service, the NTSB, the ERB, a US Treasury Office, and quite a few others including a group of diligent tax collectors known as the Internal Revenue Service Instant Response Strike Force. Those guys are up on the sixty-fifth floor. With multifarious enforcement agencies close by, the standards for pastry are lofty. *Cop-Tested and Certified*, that's what the bakery claims. Located in the proximity of so many law officers, the assertion has to be true or they'd not stayed in business so long. As such, Bo MacKinsey considered the consequences as he gazed at the elevator. If they ran for the donut shop, they'd surely get dragged kicking and screaming back to the media conference.

Or how about grabbing a bite at the law enforcement cafeteria on the seventieth floor with its beautiful revolving view of downtown Los Angeles? It might be enough to keep the hounds from picking up their scent—a doable alternative. The restaurant on the top floor is pricey, almost too much for the average cop to afford. But if it gets them out of the conference…Prudence. Bo and the others knew there's little chance of success with so few possibilities to confuse the chase. They'd get caught, they'd get reprimanded, and they'd look cowardly in front of everybody in the building for running from a cop's most disheartening duty. Talking to the media is considered worse than paperwork. Sarge, standing right behind the young lieutenant, grasped him by the shoulder, gave a gentle shake followed by a fatherly pat, and encouraged him forward. It's not pleasant or fun; and it's definitely not the best way to spend an early afternoon when the backyard pool beckons. But it is necessary. Time to face the music. Still, it'd be preferable listening to a ten-year-old play the violin.

Bo continued towards the conference room, deciding to confront Lieutenant Dolly Griffin face-to-face to show his displeasure. "I *am* prettier than you." He spoke smugly as he passed her in the hall. She didn't argue with his unusual reverse self-deprecating humor, because on a good day he just might be right. Bo's damn good-looking, and a fine, upstanding American—as are all the DES officers in attendance.

They entered the conference room where news crews had set up shop. The first order of business would be to brief the media jackals—Sarge's label—on the circumstances surrounding this morning's drug bust. Then the captain will introduce Alpha.

With fatherly authority, Captain Jackson took the podium. The mayor and Senator Mackelroy sat near a display of Bubba's Mark V, refrigerator, and a table with his firearms neatly arranged (clips removed). A department store mannequin modeled Bubba's sweatshirt, the one claiming "Beer is the Purpose of Life". The visiting politicians picked their seats carefully, to be seen as well as heard. A picture taken without them in it is a wasted opportunity. Six chairs next to the guests indicated where Jim, Larry, Cy, Sarge, Bo, and the captain would sit.

Dolly wanted no part of the formalities, staying in the Command Center to observe the turbocraft monitors. At this stage of the game, it's best to keep Lance on a short leash. He'd be okay in time, but for now she'd watch him like a hawk while keeping an eye on the proceedings from a safe distance, using the DynaView monitor. Any closer and there's a chance of getting sucked in. She knew the media was looking for red meat; something juicy to ratchet the ratings up a notch or two during the slow, midday soap opera doldrums.

FUTUREBUST

Without a high-speed police pursuit, or a standoff with a desperate criminal coming in over the satellite feed, they'd have to be satisfied with a drug bust.

The five men took their seats on a slightly elevated stage, with Cy sitting next to Senator Mackelroy, acting as a safety buffer for the others. He was as good at schmoozing as any politician. Captain Jackson stood at the podium looking like he'd burst if things didn't start on time. He rubbed his stubby, gray hair. The senior officer still had the close-cut archaic hairstyle of a man who'd been in law enforcement in olden times when short hair was the norm. But it seemed like bogus nostalgia to the others. The captain used rank to resist peer pressure.

At sixty-nine and nearing retirement, he exuded fatherly dignity, with decades of dedicated law enforcement service tucked safely under his belt. Captain Jackson is the kind of leader a newcomer should gain experience under.

"Good afternoon." He initiated the conference with the usual pleasantries. "We at the DES are proud to announce the arrest of an individual who, while not trafficking in contraband, was involved in illegal manufacture for personal use. His name will be withheld until the indictment is complete." There were groans from the audience, but this is SOP (Standard Operating Procedure) with drug charges. "The suspect, who works as a physical therapist at a clinic near his home, was an explosives specialist in the Army. He's in his early thirties and is being charged with several counts: including the consumption of a controlled substance; the use of an apparatus applied in illicit manufacture; the possession of ingredients with intent (to brew); a tobacco violation; storage of a controlled substance in a residence; possession of drug paraphernalia; plus weapons and explosives violations. He will be arraigned later today in district court, then incarcerated until trial. As usual, there is no bail for drug offenses.

"The arrest was the work of Alpha Squad, commanded by Lieutenant Bo MacKinsey. It took place during a sector grid search last night. After the discovery of alcohol in the domicile, Alpha subdued the suspect and conducted a restricted search of the premises. What you see on display was confiscated. It includes a Mark V, 261-B TurboBrewery with Froth Enhancer, capable of producing a half-gallon of medium quality, alcoholic beer an hour; a pitcher and mug which held the controlled substance; some illegal firearms; and a fine example of drug paraphernalia—this sweatshirt the suspect was wearing at the time of arrest which claims 'Beer is the Purpose of Life'. We also confiscated his refrigerator containing rare unopened beer cans from a bygone era when such dangerous substances were legal."

Captain Jackson stepped over to the refrigerator and opened the door. A loud gasp erupted from the reporters and camera operators. Most were too young to have ever seen such a fine collection of aluminum. A feeding frenzy commenced. The clicking of cameras was so pronounced, you'd think a big fancy Hollywood celebrity-type movie star actor had just entered the room. Captain Jackson stood proudly by the refrigerator, and in doing so, preempted the mayor from many of the pictures. He hadn't voted for her. She was conservative, self-righteous, and definitely too full of herself at social events. Even at a news conference she wore a string of pearls.

Sarge looked over at Bo and winked as the mayor squirmed—her free publicity squelched by a senior cop at least four steps down in the political food chain. If she ever got the chance for retribution…The feeding frenzy was now in high gear. A dozen reporters raised their hands with questions, and they were the polite ones.

"Are those cans authentic?" one reporter shouted in utter astonishment.

"Captain, a quick question," another interrupted. There was a general chorus of unintelligible vocalizations as the excitement rose.

Captain Jackson raised his hands to calm the crowd. "I'll answer your questions in a minute," he shouted, attempting to regain control. "First I want to inform you that these cans are at least twenty-five years old, and because of their rarity and value, are being donated to the Smithsonian Institute in Washington D.C. later this afternoon. Senator Mackelroy here…"

"Excuse me Captain, if I may interrupt," a television correspondent insisted, "aren't those cans evidence against the suspect?"

"Sir," another reporter questioned, "was Alpha Squad flying a Cat-four turbocraft when they discovered the suspect's deviant behavior?" Pandemonium broke loose as questions were shouted, making it difficult to distinguish one from another.

"What's the street value of this bust?" a reporter yelled.

"Is it true the suspect violently resisted arrest?" one hoped to sensationalize.

Another interrupted with: "Is that refrigerator lined with sensor absorbing material?"

Another. "Does the suspect belong to an extremist militia group?"

Bo nudged Cy in protest, shaking his head in disgust. "Batten down the hatch."

"Please calm down!" The captain slowly regained control, shouting over the clamor. He motioned everyone to relax. "We'll answer all your questions in a minute. As I was saying, because of the rarity of these cans, they are headed to DC. Being unopened, we have decided not to press charges against the suspect for their possession. This may be a stretch, but a district court magistrate has agreed to the transfer. We have plenty of evidence to use at trial. Later, Senator Mackelroy will bring you up to date on this matter."

"Could you turn the sweatshirt, sir," a determined female reporter interrupted, "so we can see it better?"

Back in the Command Center, Dolly winced as she watched it all unfold. Captain Jackson moved the mannequin as requested in hopes of keeping some semblance of order. She got a call. "Lieutenant?" Lance queried from 250 miles north-northwest of HQ.

"What have you got, Junior?" The comm. showed Lance's concern.

"I'm not sure, ma'am. It looks like faint nicotine signatures but I can't get a lock."

"No directional?" She scanned the monitors. "It could be nothing more than an old cigarette butt lodged in the sewer system. It doesn't happen much anymore, but when the Cat-threes came out eleven years ago, the sensor upgrades were so finely tuned, we homed in on discarded tobacco products from previous decades still decaying in the city dumps. I don't think you have anything to worry about."

"I don't know, ma'am," Lance continued. "It could be traffickers hiding contraband under a sensor absorbing blanket. I'm flying over a small commercial district."

"Unlikely, Lance," she argued. "You'd have faint signatures but be able to locate them. Stop your grid pattern and search in concentric circles. Then we'll take another look."

"Okay ma'am, I'll give it a try." Lance pulled the turbocraft out of its preprogrammed search and flew manually.

Dolly focused on the ruckus in the conference room. Captain Jackson was about to introduce the mayor of Los Angeles. That meant there'd be a boring speech from the old windbag, as she was referred to at HQ. The captain sat down as Madam Mayor took the podium. Dolly pressed the mute button. "Those poor guys," she mused, though a broad smile belied her words. "They must be going crazy in there." She couldn't help enjoying the moment. Her friend and colleague, Lieutenant Bo MacKinsey, disliked the formalities sometimes required of him. He was patient, respectful, resourceful, and truth be told, damn good-looking. Out of necessity, Bo had to endure. He did so stoically, with cautiously repressed indignation.

Sarge didn't like politicians and wasn't afraid to show it. In fact, Sarge wasn't afraid of anything, at least on the surface. Most people have a healthy aversion to unexploded ordnance but he takes it all in stride, having diffused so many beerhead devices over the years. Sarge is an *hombre duro*, something even non-Spanish speaking Angelinos understand.

Larry has a knack for causing trouble when things get dull, including the derivatives of chaos or mayhem. He's a prankster—thoroughly enjoying a practical joke as long as no one's seriously hurt or permanently disabled. He often takes as much as he dishes out.

A T-type (thrill-seeker), Jim hates boredom, and will stare at the ceiling, twiddle his thumbs, or surreptitiously mimic the speaker at the podium, complete with facial expressions and hand gestures. It's often difficult for the others to suppress full-blown laughter—not a good thing at a formal press briefing.

Cy will answer the legal questions. Publicity is part of his job, offering an opportunity to show off expensive clothing. The DES attorney has even considered running for political office sometime in the future. The others have warned him that if he's going to take a stab at politics, might as well shoot it a couple times for good measure. Then gather the carcass and throw it on the fire. Make sure it's burnt to a crisp! The possibility exists that politicians aren't highly regarded at HQ.

Back in the Command Center, Dolly scrutinized the monitors, showing telemetry and video from Lance's turbocraft. The senior field commander glanced at the DynaView from time to time. The mayor would praise the work of Alpha Squad, while also pointing out that she's closely involved with and mostly responsible for their success. She'd been an advocate of total drug prohibition before it became fashionable, but that's decades-old news. However, like all good politicians, she'd stumbled over a golden opportunity and now milked it for all the political pelf it's worth.

And if that isn't enough, Senator Mackelroy chomped at the bit, waiting for a chance to grab more than his share of the publicity pie as soon as he can commandeer the podium. What a spectacle to have them both on the same stage together. "Whew," Dolly winced, "this isn't funny. Those guys are really suffering!" She checked on her recruit.

"Nothing much to report," Lance replied dejectedly, his face showing mild concern. "I still have faint readings but can't pinpoint them to closer than a square kilometer. It's awful suspicious! There could be sophisticated jamming going on here."

"We'll get a second opinion," the lieutenant replied. "Sit tight and I'll be right back." She headed for the conference room. The mayor's uncharacteristically short speech was finished—the chairman of the Senate anti-drug committee outranked her. The captain took the podium to introduce Senator Mackelroy.

"Excuse me sir," Dolly whispered, putting her hand over the mic. "We've just homed in on some faint nicotine signatures. Lance is piloting."

"The new boy," Captain Jackson replied.

"Yes sir. He thinks he's found something so we may have to take a closer look. It might be a good idea to get experienced people out there."

"You could be right. Okay lieutenant, take Alpha since they're sitting right here. Better safe than sorry. But I want a full report. Keep me informed as this develops."

"Understood." She stepped over to where the Alphas were seated, then crouched in front of them. "We've got a problem." All listened, including one very interested U.S. Senator, craning his neck to hear what was going on. There was nothing else for him to do, being he'd so far been denied the podium. "Lance is on to something and may need help. You guys have just volunteered."

No one said a word. The five men obediently queued from the conference room behind her. As they left, the ruckus flared. Questions were tossed, hurled, and lobbed from all corners of the room, even from those whom up until now had been respectfully quiet. "Where are they going?" a cameraman shouted. "I've got a job to do. We haven't taken any good pictures!"

"Yeah!" another reporter yelled. "Which one's the pilot?"

Pandemonium ignited. Questions were vociferated in unfathomable numbers but it all sounded unintelligible. For the escapees, there was exhilaration.

"Whew! That was close!" Jim proclaimed.

"Good work Lieutenant," Larry congratulated. "You saved our butts!"

"I've got to admit, you were brilliant," Cy agreed. "I couldn't take much more of that political mishmash and I have a greater tolerance than most. Did you see Senator Mackelroy being denied the glory-spotlight by the mayor? I question how long he'd go without a blowup. That'd be a news event in itself."

"Don't jump to conclusions," Dolly laughed. "I wasn't joking. Check the monitors."

"Are you telling me that he actually found something?" Sarge still wasn't convinced, yet his expression exuded curiosity. "I've got to see this!"

Everyone entered the Command Center to check the screens. Sensors were ever so tenuously elevated, indicating NOSTRILS' delicate little electronic nose hairs had been minutely stimulated at the subatomic level.

"Well that's a kick in the heinie," Bo agreed. "A slightly animated nicotine readout. The kid is on to something. I thought you were making it up to get us out of that conference."

"How's it going, Junior?" Jim spoke reassuringly to the rookie after opening the secure channel. "You understand everything you're seeing?"

Lance tried to speak with some positive aspiration. His expression, visible on the comm., revealed less. "I've been circling for five minutes but can't get a fix on anything. This doesn't make sense."

"The instruments don't lie," Jim assured in fatherly fashion. "You could be picking up an antique ashtray in someone's office."

"No sir," Lance replied. "There is more here than that. It's faint, yet at the same time seems spread over a large area."

"Any junk shops in the vicinity?" Larry asked. "Some have antique spittoons."

"None that I can see," Lance replied cautiously, looking downward.

"Okay, hold on, Lance," Dolly ordered. She cut audio and looked at Bo. "Listen, I got your butts out of that conference. Now do me a favor. This is probably nothing, but Lance is new and he's going to persist. Why don't you guys get to know the kid? Make this a training mission. Find what he's locked onto and pass down knowledge and expertise."

The five Alphas were suspicious, as if something was up but they weren't quite sure what. Sarge shrugged. "That might not be a bad idea. We can give it a try. What's worse?" He pointed back towards the conference room.

"There you go," she reassured. "Teach him what you can. It'll keep all of you out of trouble." She looked at Jim. "You were about to pantomime the mayor." Jim laughed and agreed as Dolly continued. "Besides, I hate wild-goose-chases and I've got to get my nails done, or fill in the blank with whatever viable excuse works for you."

"Right," Bo mocked. "And I need my hair permed and sparkled. Come on fellows, let's go. We're not going to win. It's out of a disaster and into a fiasco."

"Thanks guys." She smiled brightly and disappeared before a course correction could be made. Sarge patted Bo on the shoulder. They'd been had, but in a nice way.

"Lance," Bo spoke into the mic, "we're heading out to give you a hand. I want you to be very conscious of your location. Don't wander up near the state line and cross into North California. That's San Francisco's jurisdiction. They get snippy when we snoop. Grab some lunch. We'll be out in forty-five minutes."

"Thanks, Lieutenant," Lance replied. He had no interest in food; sure the suggestion was a test of dedication.

"Okay gentlemen, you know the routine. Let's roll. Cy, do you have any interest in staying with the captain? We probably won't require legal help unless we get into a jurisdictional dispute with the SF people."

"If so, call," Cy smiled. "I'll go cavort with the media hyenas."

"They're jackals," Sarge corrected.

"Make us look good," Larry called over his shoulder as he headed for the hanger.

"I always do," Cy replied, his teeth glistening in the artificial light. "Can I tell them I'm the field commander?"

"I wouldn't go that far," Bo protested. "But you can tell them you're a colleague of mine, and on occasion are allowed to hang out with me." He flashed his own smile. "Then dazzle them with your vocabulary."

"That and a little flimflam should do the trick." Cy gave a wink as he backtracked to the conference room. The three remaining Alphas headed to the hanger. The EV sat cold and lifeless until Sarge climbed into the pilot's seat.

"Is everybody ready to go? This mission is about to proceed," Sarge announced. Everyone strapped in as the EV came to life.

"It's needle in the haystack time," Jim interjected. "How'd we get talked into this?"

"We were in the conference, remember?" Sarge taxied out to the ramp, located eighty feet above the ground on the lower roof of Federal Law Enforcement HQ. "Come to think of it, you're right. How did we get talked into this?"

"Let's check out what Lance has found," Bo directed. "Three-to-one it's an empty snuff container buried in an ancient construction site."

Sarge waited for clearance from the tower. "We're probably headed straight into the twilight zone." The EV lifted off and proceeded north-northwest up the coast. Sarge considered a nice, leisurely pace so they could sightsee on the way, then thought better of it. Most rookies are too inexperienced for their own good. It'd be best to get there pronto. He accelerated to maximum cruise.

Lance continued his search, zeroing in on a bustling shopping area below. There was a quaint little sewing shop, a sprawling home center and lumberyard known as Barney's Barn Sales, plus a mighty suspicious looking restaurant. A lot of people were frequenting the eatery. That'd be the place they'd sell illegal drugs, Lance reflected as he looked down on the area. Still, the readings were faint and spread out. All three commercial establishments shared a large parking lot. Lance continued his search, knowing he'd look silly if he didn't find something concrete before the others arrived. It would be his first bust if he hit pay dirt. If not, he'd be playing the fool. He contacted the others, who were 140 miles south of his location and closing fast. Lance used a secure channel, as regs require during communication between two vehicles. "I'm still unable to pinpoint anything. The readings are just too sparse."

"Don't worry about it, son," Bo replied, though Lance was only six years younger. "Whatever it is, we'll locate it even if we have to get out the shovels and start digging."

"I'll send you some pictures while circling the shopping area," Lance volunteered. He piped his observation video via satellite to the fast-approaching EV.

"Looks normal to me, Junior." Jim checked the sensor readings on his monitor. "There's not enough for a warrant, and it certainly doesn't justify using the surveillance capabilities of the turbocraft. We can get a better look when we arrive. In the meantime, turn your sensors up to ninety percent and concentrate on each building individually."

Lance adjusted the sensitivity to the maximum allowed by law under normal conditions. All three buildings showed minute traces of tobacco residue, but hardly enough to cause concern. A thousand times what he was scanning would not construct a fully functional, ready-to-smoke, 100-millimeter nicotine delivery device.

Bo's voice sounded reassuring. "Why don't you set down in the parking lot below and check out that restaurant. Order up some lunch, but keep an eye peeled for anything suspicious. Our ETA is twenty minutes and we'll join you there. If the cloak-and-dagger work turns up nothing, we'll try the same tact in the sewing shop and lumberyard."

"I can handle that." Lance suddenly appeared more confident. "I didn't know we did undercover spy stuff in the DES. It sounds like fun."

Sarge, Larry, Jim, and Bo all laughed at Lance's reply. The commander of Alpha was on a roll. He continued, "And one more thing, Junior. Keep an eye out for anything those three buildings have in common. There must be similarities somewhere."

"I'm on it, sir." Lance sounded downright enthusiastic.

Bo broke off communications. "This might turn out to be an interesting puzzle. We'll see what Lance discovers, then discuss the matter over lunch."

"Good idea," Larry interjected. "But you forgot to ask him what kind of restaurant it is. Fast-food joints can do a number on your insides."

"You've got that right. What concerns me," the lieutenant admitted, "are the sensor readings. We might have to do some real detective work to figure this out."

"True," Jim agreed. "It's unusual to have three buildings with tobacco signatures and no clue as to what's causing the readings."

But Sarge knew what was going on. "It's the criminal element in society trying to increase our workload and overwhelm us with lack of sleep. We should be home in bed right now, or at least relaxing by the pool. Instead we're out here chasing a phantom."

FUTUREBUST3.4

Cy rejoined the conference. Senator Mackelroy was giving a detailed speech outlining all the vitally important goings-on in DC: money spent, consultants hired, experts queried; and explaining what they planned to do with the exhibit of unopened antique beer cans. The media absorbed it like a sponge, grabbing at facts and figures they secretly hoped to sensationalize. A few somber-looking reporters already realized the story had legs enough for only two days on the national level, and then (barring the unexpected, like discovering that the suspect's dad is President of the United States) it was sure to die out. Still, a reporter had to take whatever came along. This would not be a career story, but might help pay the overhead.

Captain Jackson waited in his seat as the senator, in speech-making mode, outlined his important ideas and loftiest accomplishments while in office. It is just part of the job, letting the politicians bluster on behalf of their careers. Cy sat down. "They're looking for a needle in the haystack," he quietly informed the senior officer. "It'll be used as a training mission for Lance."

"You don't think there's anything out there?" the captain whispered. "We used to acquire all kinds of funny readings when I was working the beat. But most of that cigarette litter has been picked up in the last two decades. I wouldn't think there'd be much left anymore."

"There's no telling what he's locked onto," Cy quietly replied. "But whatever it is, it's not a law enforcement problem."

The federal government's most enthusiastic anti-drug advocate had changed gears and was preaching something about how politicians should be held to the highest standards of ethical conduct and morality. Positions of power are a public trust, a sacred honor and duty. Politicians are role models to be emulated and admired for their sacrifice and service to the country. Cy leaned over and whispered out of the side of his mouth. "It'd be nice if we could pull them out of the gutter and up to par with the rest of us before we worry about higher standards. And service to the country? That's debatable. I've always wondered who's serving who."

"Quiet," Captain Jackson chuckled in a whisper, then nodded. "He's almost done, and at least verbally pointing himself in the right direction."

Mackelroy finally finished his speech and turned the podium back to his host. But before doing so, he stood proudly by Bubba's refrigerator and let the media take all the holographic images they wanted. His position, as Captain Jackson's had been earlier, blocked the mayor from the pictures. Senator Mackelroy returned to his seat after exuberantly shaking the mayor's, the captain's, and then Cy's hand in a choreographed sequence. There'd be lots of free publicity heading his way in the next couple of days, and he planned to grab him a mess and squirrel it away for later public consumption, preferably in an election year. "Like cash in the bank," he winked at the mayor.

Captain Jackson introduced Cy Bergstrom as the next speaker, then opened things up for questions. The immaculately attired attorney took control of the conference.

"Are you in command of Alpha Squad?" one reporter asked.

He'd have loved to answer with a lie, but...well, maybe...no, better not.

Cy replied hesitantly. "Lieutenant Bo MacKinsey is the field commander. That's spelled capital *M*, small *A-C*, capital *K*, small *I-N-S-E-Y*. He was wearing the leather jacket, and left to take care of law enforcement responsibilities."

"How many busts of this magnitude do you guys do in a week?" another asked.

"There's no set number," Cy replied, "but we rarely make more than ten busts a year. Drug abuse is almost nonexistent today."

Senator Mackelroy abruptly rose from his seat, stepped (lunged) to the podium and spoke. Cy had to move out of the way to give the attention-grabbing politician another shot at the glory spotlight. "And it's declining year by year thanks to our effective prevention programs and tough enforcement."

"Thank you, Senator," Cy reiterated, as the experienced old political pro, again (with more than adequate enthusiasm) shook Cy's hand before returning to his seat. One could almost hear the cash register ringing. The senator had made another deposit.

Minutes passed quickly. Cy seemed to have the media eating out of his hand. They were orderly and polite, each waiting his or her turn to ask a question.

"Was this mission any more dangerous than usual?" a lady from an Internet radio station asked. "Isn't it true the suspect was heavily armed and intoxicated?"

"This particular arrest was not risky," Cy assured. "The dangerous ones involve organized traffickers or someone who is a couple cards short of a full deck, mentally unstable; el loco." Cy spun his finger around his ear. "But those are few and far between."

"There are rumors the suspect put up a fight," another reporter commented.

"Unfounded," Cy insisted. "The suspect was taken into custody without incident. He isn't being charged with resisting arrest."

"Are you going to seize his property," a Web reporter questioned, "and if so, how much do you think you'll get?"

"I have no way of knowing the value of the property, which will be confiscated by the Feds and sold at auction after the suspect has been tried, convicted and sentenced, preferably in that order." Cy revealed his perfect smile, assuring the media that he'd just manufactured a joke.

"What will you do with the money?" a satellite TV reporter followed up.

"Probably wine, women and song," Cy replied with a shrug and another bright smile, indicating that it was not his decision.

"Better make that grape juice, women and song," a TV reporter yelled back. "And watch out for eye-catching cross-dressers. You'll get yourself in a lot less trouble that way." The whole room broke into laughter.

When things calmed down, the questioning continued. "What kind of jail time do you think the suspect is looking at?" The inquiry came from the back of the room.

"That's the judge's responsibility," Cy replied. "But minimum sentencing guidelines require at least five years for crimes of this magnitude. The suspect has no priors so it's a first-strike offense. A third strike puts you out of commission for twenty-five to life just for breathing secondhand smoke." It was another joke, though some of the reporters looked stunned. Cy continued, making a mental note to be more cautious with the humor. "Either way, it's a long time to be stamping license plates. And there's little hope of early parole. Drug abuse is not tolerated in our society." Cy glanced over his shoulder, just in case Senator Mackelroy stormed the podium to make another deposit.

"Are the *street-value* numbers Captain Jackson gave us earlier pre-inflated or should we adjust them upward ourselves?"

Cy again checked behind. Captain Jackson winked and nodded. "You won't have to tweak the stats," the attorney assured. "They've been amended according to authorized standards."

"Where do you buy your suits, young man?" an elderly reporter broke the rhythm of the questions being asked. "You're such a snappy dresser!"

"Thank you ma'am," Cy exclaimed. "But that's classified information and I'm not at liberty to say. I just thank God everything I buy is tax-deductible or I'd be in the poorhouse. They don't pay us cops enough to support and maintain a wardrobe of this caliber."

The mood lightened. Additional questions were asked until all had gotten their fill. Only one reporter complained of having nothing to sensationalize. Finally, Captain Jackson took the opportunity to wind things down. He stepped to the podium and addressed the crowd of reporters, technicians, and camera operators.

"That's all the time we have, folks. Senator Mackelroy and the mayor must get back to their respective offices, and law enforcement responsibilities dictate our presence is required elsewhere. I want to thank you for coming, and ask you to please be careful on your way out. We have a fact sheet printed up and there's stock video footage you can download to help in assembling your stories." The captain nodded a polite farewell.

Equipment was packed into carrying cases; cords wound and stored away. The politicians mingled, shaking hands with everyone they could corner. There might still be time for an interview and another deposit. Captain Jackson patted Cy on the shoulder as the two left the room. In the corridor beyond, he paused and shook his head. "How do you do it?" His tone was accusatory. "How do you keep them under your thumb like that? Only one reporter spoke out of turn while you answered questions."

"It's all in the hand gestures," Cy informed the superior officer with mock sincerity. "They can't get enough. And make eye contact. Add some voice projection. They love it."

"I'll keep that in mind," the captain replied skeptically. "But I think if you knew, you'd tell me." Cy smiled and said nothing because he didn't have a clue what the answer was. If he had, he'd bottle it and put it on the market at a hefty markup, just like some companies do with common, ordinary, everyday, run-of-the-mill water. With a product like that, one can amass a fortune. "You did make one potentially catastrophic mistake," Captain Jackson suggested ominously.

"What would that be?" Cy asked, knowing the captain was pulling his leg. He adjusted his tie using the reflection in a glass panel door.

"At one point during the questioning, you positioned yourself between a seasoned old political pro like Senator Mackelroy, and the podium."

Cy nodded. "That could have been disastrous, but I did leave an escape route."

"Like bailing out into the media entourage?" the captain smiled. "You still have the reflexes of youth." He winked. "I think we better check up on your friends. Whatever they find, it will surely be interesting."

FUTUREBUST3.6

The EV slowed over the small business district where Lance had been scanning. His Cat-four turbocraft was parked unassumingly below, slightly distant from a group of automobiles near the restaurant. Sarge circled the area to get some perspective, then descended and parked next to the other DES vehicle. The three businesses formed a triangle, with the spacious parking lot in the middle. Four Alphas climbed out, looked around, and headed toward the eatery.

"It's Chinese," Sarge exclaimed, rubbing his tummy. "I can go for that."

"Anybody see anything suspicious?" Bo questioned.

"You mean other than two DES vehicles in the parking lot?" Larry chided.

"Anything other than that," Bo conceded. "What do a Chinese restaurant, a sewing shop, and a lumberyard have in common?"

"Let's see what our young Sherlock Holmes has discovered," Jim insisted. All were curious as to what had excited Lance's sensors. They entered the restaurant, buoyed by the aroma. Lance waved them over. They pulled up chairs and sat down.

"Nothing unusual to report." Lance was apologetic as he sipped his drink, then perked up. "Try one of these Chinese Milk Shakes. They're great!"

Bo smiled, not sure if Lance was serious. Sarge continued the questioning, lowering his voice ominously. "We're trying to ascertain what these businesses have in common. What's your best guess? You can give it to us straight. Remember, we're your friends."

"There's nothing I can see." Lance laughed at Sarge's most intimidating suspect-interrogation voice. "I'm going to get another shake. Try one. They're really good!"

"Yeah, I suppose." Sarge's voice deflated to its normal level of alpha-male dominance. "Do you think they have a broccoli-flavored shake?"

"I'm game," Larry conceded. "Let's get a shake and check the other shops. We'll look more inconspicuous that way."

"You mean less conspicuous," Jim corrected dryly. "Yup, we'll blend right in, kind of like tourists. You can never tell a tourist when you see one."

The others looked at Jim suspiciously. Sometimes his deadpan demeanor made it difficult to discern if he was joking. "The lumberyard first," Bo suggested. "If nothing turns up, we can move on." He suspected there'd soon be some back-and-forth banter between the men, known as jocularity in religious circles. No telling when it might start. Alpha was on a wild-goose-chase. Might as well make the best of it.

The five officers acquired their drinks and headed towards the home center, about fifty meters across the parking lot. They surveyed the surroundings for five minutes, though nothing looked out of place. Sensors indicated nicotine in the area, but an inspection revealed little. They split up and strolled through the lumberyard, then met outside.

"Anybody see anything?" Bo quizzed the group.

"Lumber," Jim replied dryly.

"That's it in a nutshell," Larry agreed.

"Pretty much sums it up," Sarge added.

"What they said," Lance shrugged.

"Okay, it's off to the sewing shop." Bo was disappointed. "Let's see what we can find that might interest us. Try not to look intimidating."

"We'll really fit in," Sarge observed as he finished his shake. "Five cops in a sewing shop. Talk about suspicious behavior." The officers walked side by side towards the establishment. A casual observer would have thought they looked like five gunslingers in an old western movie, heading for the showdown. Appearing inconspicuous wasn't in the cards, and thus they entered the quaint little shop.

"Can I help you gentlemen," a nice little old lady inquired with a puzzled look on her face. As LOLs go, she was par for the course, wearing a dress covered in brightly colored flowers. She seemed pleasant enough—not the kind of person who'd sell addictive, health-destroying products like tobacco. Her expression hinted some confusion at the presence of five men in her shop, especially the big one standing a foot-and-a-half above her. She voiced her feelings promptly. "You men don't meet the usual customer profile. You're not here to rob me, are you? There is very little money in the till."

"No, of course not ma'am," Bo replied with a consoling smile. His good looks calmed her fears. "We're law enforcement officers."

"Cops," Sarge added gently.

"Drug police," Larry couldn't resist the temptation.

"Flatfoots," Jim added.

"The fuzz," Lance interjected. "We're the fuzz."

"We'd like to know if you've seen or heard anything unusual lately?" Bo continued. "Anything at all pertaining to drugs?"

She hesitated, looking confused. "Oh, my goodness no, officers. This is a quiet little business district. We've never had any problems like that before. Are you searching for pushers? We certainly don't want riffraff loitering in the area. It scares customers and drives down profits!"

"I understand," Bo assured. "Our sensors picked up minute traces of nicotine in the vicinity. You can't think of anything helpful?"

"Not offhand. However I'll certainly let you know if I see anything suspicious." She hesitated for a moment, thinking deeply. "I do have cloth made of hemp for sale. You didn't pick up on that with your sensors, did you?"

"No," Bo replied. "The computers filter out such irregularities, even if you had a warehouse piled with it. Your stock is certified, correct?"

"The cloth is made from one hundred percent certified fiber," she responded proudly.

Jim had wandered off to look around the store and then rejoined the others. "It's a nice shop, ma'am. How long have you owned it?"

"Why thank you," she exclaimed. "We just bought this building a few months ago. My husband and I did the remodeling, then opened the store to supplement our income. It hasn't been easy for seniors since Social Security went bust twenty years ago. Retirement is a lot harder than it used to be. We pretty much have to work to survive these days."

"That's true, ma'am," Bo agreed sympathetically. "Only the rich can put their feet up and relax after the age of seventy."

"You guys didn't help by getting rid of the tobacco junkies either," she continued, somewhat accusatory. "In olden times when people smoked, they died sooner. Social Security collapsed once life expectancy increased. The financial strain finally did it in."

Bo smiled at the accusation. "The system was in big trouble decades before we came along. It was a pay-as-you-go plan, bound to fail even with massive benefit cuts and the increased retirement age. Fifteen percent of GDP went to entitlements. The economic depression finally did it in. They dismantled Medicare and Medicaid once healthcare costs exploded."

"That's true, I guess," she acquiesced with a reluctant smile. "They raided the trust fund to pay for all kinds of wasteful spending. So maybe you guys are doing okay. We no longer have the regressive self-employment tax."

"The cloud's silver lining," Bo nodded. "But it's more than offset by the national debt surcharge. Anyway, you have a nice day." They silently filed out—five cops, no answers.

"You too," she held the door and waved. "I'm not really mad at you. Come back and visit when you're in the area with your wives. Oh, and officer?"

"Yes ma'am," Bo turned and acknowledged the shopkeeper.

She spoke sheepishly and pointed towards his pants. "If you wore trousers made of hemp, you wouldn't get rips in the knees like that. It's a very tough fabric."

"I'll keep it in mind," he smiled pleasantly. "Thanks for the fashion tip." The five officers turned and walked across the parking area towards the restaurant where the DES vehicles sat. Bo spoke first. "Did anything appear suspicious?"

"No," Sarge replied. "There is nothing illegal going on in that shop."

"Ditto," Jim agreed. "The place was as clean as a whistle."

"Just like the first places we visited," Larry insisted.

"Maybe she's selling tobacco to make up for the loss of Social Security," Lance volunteered. "She seemed a little too helpful to me."

Sarge punched Lance lightly on the arm. "There's no telling what evil lurks behind that sweet old face. She might even be an alien from the far reaches of the galaxy."

"Not likely," Jim deadpanned. "Space-aliens were not eligible for Social Security, even after all the work they did in Egypt building the pyramids."

In total surprise, Bo grasp Jim by the shoulders. "Are you trying to tell me that space-aliens built the pyramids?"

"That's right." Jim's expression exuded undeniable confidence. "I saw it on TV so it must be true. Space-aliens also built Windsor Castle and the Leaning Tower of Pisa, though they didn't have an adequate grasp of Earth's gravity when they finished the latter."

Lance laughed at their wisecracks, but spoke with disappointment. "You guys are taking this investigation seriously. That means my first bust is going to be a disaster, right?" No one responded. The five reentered the restaurant and sat down.

"So what's the answer?" Larry asked out loud, his tone serious. "We've got a restaurant next to a lumberyard, a lumberyard next to a sewing shop, and a sewing shop next to a restaurant. What do they have in common?"

All sat at the table in silence until a cute little waitress arrived. "Would you gentlemen like to order?" she asked politely, looking at each expectantly.

"A question first," Bo replied. "Do you know of any similarities between this restaurant and the sewing shop across the parking lot?"

"We both started out in business about the same time," she answered. "They opened a month after we did. There hasn't been time for us to get to know each other."

"Interesting," Bo rubbed his chin with his finger. "We'll try some appetizers, please."

"Which would you like?" she asked pleasantly. "We have quite a few to choose from, including a delicious vegetarian egg roll."

"Surprise us," he smiled. The waitress disappeared into the kitchen.

"Okay, here's what we've got," Larry announced. "Three retail establishments in the area, two starting up about the same time. A third has been here a while."

The waitress returned with a plate of meatless egg rolls. Bo leaned back in his chair and questioned her again. "Can you think of anything your two businesses had in common when they first opened?"

"I haven't considered it before. We've been too busy here. Would you like anything with those egg rolls?"

"Horseradish mustard," Sarge requested.

"Be right back." She disappeared; then returned in a flash with the condiment. "There is one thing that might interest you." She spoke while placing several tiny bowls of extra-hot mustard on the table. "When we remodeled our restaurant, we purchased most of the building products from the lumberyard next door. I think the old couple in the sewing shop did the same. I saw a load of supplies being dropped off one day. They hauled everything across the parking lot on a forklift. Anything else you need?"

"That should do it," the lieutenant replied. "Thanks much." She disappeared as quickly as she had arrived.

"Now we've got three businesses with something in common," Larry observed. "Two of them remodeled at about the same time."

"Using building materials," Jim continued the thought, "from the third." He dipped an egg roll into the horseradish. Despite his hair hanging down past his shoulders, it nearly stood on end. The stuff was hot!

Bo noticed the tears welling up in Jim's eyes. "Whatever it is has something to do with the building products. After we finish here, why don't we have a talk with the manager of Barney's Barn Sales. Maybe he can shed light on the subject." The five Alphas ate their egg rolls, each having the same reaction as Jim. Cold water quelled the heat. A napkin dried the tears.

"What kind of mustard is this?" Sarge asked as the waitress passed.

"Hot stuff, huh? They claim it's Turbo-fired." Jim laughed. Turbocharged mustard. All agreed it was very hot. The waitress refilled their glasses. After finishing off the egg rolls, the five officers rose from their chairs and tossed a pile of bills on the table, leaving a healthy tip. The perky waitress had been a big help.

The men strolled towards the home center. Jim broke ranks and headed for Lance's Cat-four turbocraft. He motioned the rookie to follow. They opened the canopy and the more experienced pilot climbed in. Lance leaned on the cowling of the sleek, single-passenger vehicle, just behind the forward, starboard thruster, while Jim energized the sensor array. "I'm going to show you something you can't discuss outside your unit."

Lance lit up like a firefly. "You're gonna tweak it, aren't you? I heard about this in pilot school but could never find out how."

"Okay, here we go," Jim announced as he grabbed a pocketknife from his pants, then pulled a couple of wires from the fuse coupler under the console. "You see these two wires—the red one and the striped blue one—we strip some insulation off like this and connect them via the infusion capacitor." Lance watched intently. "Next, we'll cut the Sat. (Satellite) Uplink to Kansas City," he pulled the fuse, "to keep Big Brother in the dark." Jim smiled mischievously. His normally calm voice hinted at excitement. "Now watch this. We'll align the sensors with the home center..."

"Unbelievable!" Lance gushed. "You're at least two hundred percent over the legal sensitivity limit. We could get into a whole lot of trouble!"

"You're right about that, Junior. I don't think I'd tell the authorities."

"Aren't we the authorities?" Lance chided.

Jim diligently continued his project. He scanned the lumberyard for illicit subatomic patterns. The Alert Buzzer sounded. "There's definitely something in there! Let's try the sewing shop."

"This won't harm anyone, will it?" Lance asked his mentor. "In pilot school they told us that super-sensitivity with NOSTRILS could..."

"Probably not," Jim cut him off in mid-sentence. "It might make them a little horny over the next couple of days. Men become ultra-potent."

"That's something I probably don't need to know about then," Lance concluded.

The alarm sounded as the sensors focused on the sewing shop. Jim winked at his trainee. "We can't do this for long or it'll fry the system. The capacitors pulse too much juice through the circuits." The sensors focused on the restaurant. The alarm went off for the third time. "Okay," Jim continued, his excitement now out in the open. "Lets try the furniture warehouse across the road. If we don't get a reading..." The alarm fell silent. Jim switched off the array. The vehicle became lifeless. He carefully sealed the wires with fast-drying silicone from the toolbox behind the seat, tucked them under the console, and reinstalled the fuse for the Sat. Uplink to Kansas City. "There's your first lesson in super-sensitivity. Don't tell where you learned it or I'll have to kill you. Now let's find the others." They closed the canopy and walked into the expansive lumberyard.

"What did you boy's discover?" Bo asked as everyone met up.

"There's something here," Jim assured. "And by the way, it'll be best if you avoid contact with the opposite sex for a few days."

"You radiated us!" Sarge laughed. "You sonovagun! But I'm too old to start having kids again. The only thing that gets stiff on a man my age is his neck." Sarge rubbed his neck, then became defensive. "I'm kidding of course; you know that, right? I'm only fifty-seven."

"I'd still be careful," Jim cautioned, looking at Sarge sympathetically.

Larry joined the others with the manager in tow. What a surprise. His name turned out to be Barney. His appearance was disheveled, but not out-of-the-ordinary for a lumberyard manager. He wore his hair in a frazzled, sticking-up-in-all-directions kind of way. His blue coveralls were dirty, though nothing like a garage mechanic's. He was scrawny and bearded with a large nose, suspenders, ratty steel toe boots, and dirty fingernails. He spoke in an unusual hillbilly dialect. They explained the situation in full.

"Toebackee signatures," the man exclaimed. "Now I've went and did it! I'll tell you bowas honest-to-goodness, I don't know nuthun 'bout such. Ain't never been investy-gatored a'fore. But I'm willing to price you out some mighty fine lumber-boards. Any-thin you want, I got here somewheres. Shore don't want you to buy from my competitors!"

"Would you mind," Bo asked with an understanding smile, "if we bring in a portable sensor, and check out your inventory? Please realize that you don't have to consent. We're just wondering why our equipment has locked on to this"—Bo almost said *this-here* but caught himself in time—"retail area."

"Well shoot, no," the manager replied enthusiastically. "I shore as heck don't got nuthun to hide. You go right 'head and chex all youze want. Let me know what'cha dis-cova. Toebackee signatures? If that don't bust the stitches out of Mama's finest wedding dress. Y'all can look around for some al-key-hal too." The manager chuckled for a moment. "Now, if y'all will a'scuze ma-self,

I godda help some of ma utha costumers. Toebackee signatures," he spoke to himself as he walked away. "Some of us is jus' gifted."

Larry headed to the EV to get the PortaSniff, and prepared the vacuum cleaner-sized unit for action. Set on molecular scan, something that'd be illegal without permission or a warrant, he waved the probe around the general area, and over some old boards nearby, causing a mild reaction. He shook his head and turned the machine off. "It's this old weathered lumber. Did they have some in the other stores?"

"On the walls near the back of the sewing shop," Jim replied. "It makes beautiful paneling. There was a rustic wooden display in the restaurant."

The manager returned to see what was going on. "What did you bowas dis-cova?" he asked in hillbilly vernacular. The guy had a way with language. He'd substitute vowels for consonants, verbs for nouns, scrambled syntax, dangled some participles, split infinitives, and emphasized the wrong syllables of words. Dang-nabit if he didn't coin new ones never heard before, yet it was decipherable if one listened closely. On TV, they'd have to translate his lexis in the crawl across the bottom of the screen.

"Where did this old weathered wood come from?" Bo questioned.

"Most'a it's 'posed to'a been salvaged from buildens."

"Where were those old buildings located?" The officers listened intently, recognizing him as a language-challenged individual.

"Well shoot," the manager scratched his head, indicating some confusion. "Proba'ly from all over the creation."

"Do you think any of it came from the southeastern United States," Bo continued, "possibly from agricultural buildings?"

"A'course," the manager replied. "This-here weathered lumber comes from everywheres old barns is being tore up and salvaged. It's been yanked off'a rundown and de-lap-i-dated structures."

"You think any of those old barns were in tobacco country?"

"Well shore." The manager looked puzzled. "People pay a premium for them old boards. Are you telling me that your ve-hickles out there homed in on lumber that was once part of a barn somewheres in the Carolinas or Tennessee? Them buggers must be more smell-sensitive than a bloodhound on a coon hunt. Can you train them gizmos to scent-out rabbits and possums?"

"It wouldn't be cost-effective." Sarge patted the manager on the shoulder. "But you could walk down the street with tobacco stains on your dentures and our sensors would latch on to you. So we're gonna arrest your entire inventory."

"I hope you bowas are fun'en with me. Y'all are pulling my leg, right?" the manager queried, as he discouraged a no-see-um that had taken a fancy to his countenance.

"Just kidding," Sarge assured. "There's nothing here we're interested in. You go right ahead and sell all the tobacco residue you want. You might advise your customers not to let their children chew on the boards, though."

"Fair enough," the manager wiped his brow. "I sure would hate to hafta dee-stroy all that-there fine product. Ta think this-here lumber could have been spoilt 'cause it was used to build a barn in toebackee country. Maybe I better sell it off cheap and get rid of the whole mess, lesson I get ma-self into a heaping mow-newer pile o'trouble."

"I wouldn't worry about it," Jim counseled. "We'll adjust the filters on our sensor platforms and it won't be a problem from here on in."

"I unnerstand," the manager replied, looking like a man who'd just dodged a bullet, probably fired from a black powder rifle. "Now you bowas have a good ole day. And keep up the mighty fine work you's doin'. That toebackee stuff use'ta be an awful plague on society. Do you know that at one time, over fourteen hun'ert people a day was dying from the stuff? Cancer and all like that. And it were legal. That kind'a thing shouldn't happen in this-here day and age, as sow-fis-tee-catered as we all are."

"It's difficult to comprehend," Jim shook his head. "I think the number was 1250 people a day in the United States. But who's counting?" The manager looked confused. Seeing the man's expression, Jim rephrased his statement. "I don't understand the logic of it either. Tobacco is the only consumer product that eventually killed one third of the people who used it. And it maimed or debilitated millions more every year."

"Oh, I knew what you was meaning," the manager nodded, his voice hushed. He seemed unnerved by the idea of a product so deadly, yet legal.

"Well," Bo informed, "I think we've solved the mystery of the toebackee-soused building products. From what I can determine, we're finished here. Gather up that PortaSniff and let's cruise." The officers thanked the manager, who still had that no-see-um buzzing around his face. They headed for the parking area. Not wanting her to worry, Sarge walked back to the sewing shop to inform the LOL that things were under control. Bo turned to the rookie. "You busted a lumber pile. What have you got to say for yourself?"

"You're not going to tell Lieutenant Griffin, are you, sir?"

"Not a chance. Let us know what to write on the report so we can corroborate your story. You might want to label it a training exercise. She'll go for that."

"Sounds about right." Lance breathed a sigh of relief. "I guess it's time you get back to HQ. I'll see you guys in a few hours. Thanks."

"We'll catch you later, Junior." Sarge had just returned from his errand. He climbed into the pilot's seat. "Don't look for us tomorrow. We'll be at home in slumber-land." The hatch closed on the EV and the motors surged to life. Lance stepped back and watched them go. Sarge lifted off, then set the four-passenger squad cruiser on autopilot. "We can take the scenic route after all," he informed as they accelerated to Mach .35. "We'll reach HQ in about an hour."

FUTUREBUST3.9

Everyone seemed in good spirits, yet Jim remained mentally distant from the group. The others were expectantly silent, wondering what would come from his high-powered thought processes. He claimed to have a photographic memory, and no one doubted it. He could recall anything. Jim turned and looked back. "Listen to this, guys. Remember what the lumberyard manager said about all those people dying from nicotine addiction?"

"You've been crunching numbers, haven't you?" Bo surmised. "We could almost see the gears turning."

Jim smiled. He'd been so focused, he hadn't noticed how hushed the others were. "You don't need a photographic memory to handle these figures. Think of it this way: 1250 people dying each day, divided by twenty-four hours. Take the first 1200 and divide, you get fifty per hour. Take the remaining fifty not included and you get about two per hour. That's fifty-two every sixty minutes, or roughly one person dying every seventy seconds, give or take. So you've got a multibillion-dollar industry," Jim winced, "employing tens of thousands of workers involved in the growing, processing, manufacture and transport of products that are killing one person every seventy seconds, in addition to injuring and debilitating countless thousands more, day in and day out! Worldwide, millions a year died from tobacco if you count all the ancillary health difficulties smokers faced. Health costs per pack were estimated at seven to ten dollars. It was an incredible waste."

"Sounds barbaric," Sarge volunteered. "But that's how it was in olden times."

"Yeah," Larry added. "We think of ourselves as an advanced, progressive, and enlightened civilization, but that kind of puts a dent in the theory."

"We've come a long way," Jim continued, "since the days of butchery in Rome, yet we allowed a deadly product like tobacco to become an integral part of our economy. A hundred thousand people died in Hiroshima at the end of World War II. Worldwide, that was just a week's work for big tobacco."

"Twenty-five percent of all fatal house fires were started by careless use of cigarettes," Sarge added. "Of course, all use of tobacco was careless."

There was silence within the group as the EV sped homeward, skimming the stunningly beautiful Pacific coastline. Each man gazed out the window, lost in varied thoughts and reflections. It seemed difficult for any sane individual to comprehend. Working in the now-defunct tobacco industry with all those people dying…well, maybe one just had to be there. But the odds of any such person going to heaven after death are slim. It's doubtful the Creator of the universe has much sympathy for those profiting by destroying other's health.

Bo finally broke the hush. "You might as well cheer up fellas. Tobacco is virtually dead and gone now. We have a lot to be thankful for. The dismantled ruins of the industry, those old boards, got us out of that news conference."

"Not a bad day's work, y'all," Larry added. "We found old beer cans and located some used lumber. With accomplishments like that, I think we deserve a paid vacation." To everyone on board the EV, it sounded like the right ide'er.

FUTUREBUST4.0

Sarge collapsed heavily into his chair after failing the routine, prescribed drug screening. His rendezvous with a controlled substance one week previous was too severe to avoid detection. The big man leaned back and closed his eyes. He was mentally fatigued; tired of the hassles, fed up with the rigamarole. It's the bureaucrats—the ones having nothing better to do than create grief for others. The same goes for lawyers—most lawyers anyway—scumsucking slimeballs billing by the minute and charging for postage.

He added politicians to the list. All they care about is the advantage of incumbency and their campaign war chests. Sarge wanted to shut his mind down but there were the doctors—practitioners of Bottom Line Triage. Hard-earned tax dollars pay for most of their education, and the result? Bill padding, unnecessary surgery, and that five-minute office visit (delayed for two hours because of overbooking) costs a week's pay. If a surgeon removes the healthy kidney or amputates the wrong leg—relax! You get a ten percent discount on hospital overcharges. Stub your toe and they'll fix you up, but it'll cost an arm and a leg. Don't talk about compassion when there's money to be made. If any healing takes place in the process, well that's just dandy. Doctors need to realize that there's a human being appended to that wallet. People so hell-bent on making money should become plumbers instead, where *all* the cash goes down the drain.

Well guess what, the bureaucrats want to talk. It used to take a week from a failed drug screening before getting the weasels off your back. Now they jump down your throat immediately. Still, this problem had been expected. Sarge typed and forwarded a detailed report as Bo requested, describing the difficulties encountered during the arrest of Robert Franklin. With so much alcoholic beer spilled, personal contamination was unavoidable.

"Come on. Time to face the music. Your friendly, neighborhood Enforcement Review Board is calling, and they want to talk to," Bo paused and pointed, "YOU!"

Sarge terminated his defeatist thinking and nodded. "How bad did I fail?"

"Egregiously!" Bo responded with a mischievous look. "They're going to suspect you're a closet alcoholic. I told you to take more showers."

"TurboSoap ain't what it used to be." Sarge relaxed, his attitude improving with Bo's humor. "What the heck, let's go see what the pencilheads have to say. It's not like I haven't been through this before." He grabbed his report and headed for the elevator to face the bureaucratic inevitable.

"That's the right attitude. There is one unexpected problem, a newcomer on the board and they say she's tough as nails."

"Great!" Sarge replied as the doors closed, his mood reverting to its previous status. "That's all I need. Some inexperienced college graduate out to impress everyone with her toughness and dedication, and at my expense."

"Some guys have all the luck. But we'll get you through this and things will return to normal by lunch. At least," Bo laughed, "that's how it usually works."

They stepped off the elevator and headed down the hall to Room 1404. The Enforcement Review Board is akin to the dreaded Internal Affairs Office most are familiar with from watching cop shows. It's like a root canal followed by a tax audit.

With uncharacteristic reticence, Sarge entered. Bo followed. They seated themselves in a nondescript waiting area on old wooden chairs coated with pealing, yellow varnish. Time passed. The receptionist looked like a librarian with her squinty glasses and loose-fitting, pink sweater. She consciously ignored them. They fidgeted. Sarge made a comment about hopefully not having to spend much time in the ERB office, but was interrupted and corrected by the receptionist, whose auditory attentiveness unexpectedly came to light. "This is not an ERB office," she became persnickety. "It's the *Enforcement Review Board Office*," enunciating the words as if talking to a child so the two men could fully comprehend the gravity of the issue. Apparently, substituting *ERB* for Enforcement Review Board had hit a raw nerve. Sarge apologized, though wasn't sure what all the fuss was about. Everyone working in the building referred to this office as the ERB, even the janitors, except they called it the *erb* office, as if the three letters spelled out a silly word. Sarge shrugged, looked at Bo, and mentally withdrew. The receptionist went back to her work, which she took very seriously, after carefully straightening her pink sweater and adjusting the glasses on her nose.

Twenty-five minutes passed. Both men took a deep breath and exhaled. "This is like sitting in a dentist's office," Sarge observed, slightly annoyed as he glanced around the room, "except there are no magazines to read."

"I'd liken it to waiting in a doctor's office for a vasectomy." Bo one-upped his subordinate and covertly chuckled so the receptionist wouldn't hear.

"That's not funny," Sarge whispered nervously, closing his legs together. He did not appreciate the lieutenant's candor.

Both men remained quiet until called, then rose from their seats and followed another drably attired assistant into the meeting area. It resembled an interrogation room, decorated with utilitarian plastic furniture. The lighting was distracted, creating shadows. Bo and Sarge sat down facing the five Review Board Members. The four male faces were familiar; this being the third drug screening Sarge had failed. But the fifth member of the board—she was an unknown quantity. All remained silent. Sarge studied the newcomer. Not a hardnosed college graduate out to prove her toughness; this woman was short, stocky, and rugged in appearance with an uncompromising glare in her dark brown eyes. He'd never encountered a more masculine looking female. Her nostrils flared as she inhaled. She had thick, bushy brows that almost met in the middle of a broad forehead. Her eyes were deep-set, spaced too far apart, and slightly askew. The jaw was square, much like a man's. Her hair was pulled back tightly in a bun. With no room left for a smile, her countenance would surely scare a little child. Sarge guessed her voice to be low and raspy—her temperament, fierce and obstinate. Demanding and uncompromising, she'd be a formidable presence during the review. Sarge now wished her more like that hardnosed college graduate he'd envisioned earlier.

The meeting was yet to get underway so Bo, clad in his fading leather jacket and torn blue jeans, leaned over and nudged gently. "I'll bet she weighs three hundred-plus." Sarge froze. The fearsome woman looked up and glared at them. Bo stopped chuckling and composed himself. No one on the review board had spoken. Ultra-woman studied the report in front of her. But now she had a frown on her face that bode ill for the hapless officers of Alpha Squad, and foretold of things loathsome and iniquitous still to come. He nudged again. "She looks like a *Bertha* to me," Bo whispered his best guess.

Sarge tensed even more. Bertha put down her report and stared, her dark eyes burning through the two officers. She knew something was going on between them. Had she heard the lieutenant's disparaging remarks? Sarge didn't know. He was surprised by an emotion he hadn't felt in a very long time. He wanted his mama!

The gentleman in the middle looked up at the officers and acknowledged their presence with a nod, but said nothing. Bertha's stare was intractable. Her eyes squinted. One side of her face seemed out of proportion with the other. The tip of her tongue slid across a pale, protruding lower lip. Bo fiercely returned her stare, then quietly nudged Sarge for a third time. "I'll bet she has man-issues," he whispered slyly. "That face could strike fear into the heart of the bravest warrior!"

Sarge pretended not to hear. He even considered grinning at Big Bertha, but knew she wouldn't buy his guilty smile. The chairman spoke.

"Good morning, gentlemen." He initiated the proceedings politely, though was not smiling. His voice sounded perfunctory and condescending. A drab looking man with a poorly fitting, dull grey suit, his facial expression revealed boredom, as if his occupation lacked excitement or satisfaction—a condition typical of desk jobs. "The lab has informed us of your circumstances. Sergeant Klassen, you have failed the screening for," he consulted his papers, "the third time, it says here. The Enforcement Review Board feels that any such default warrants an investigation. Now we're not accusing you of anything. We'd like to hear in your own words, the reasons for the infraction before filing a report with our superiors in Washington. I must inform you," the chairman continued, "that your testimony is being recorded and will be substantiated before this investigation concludes."

Sarge felt a bead of sweat running down his neck. The entire building had central air, yet this room had been neglected. The big man loosened his collar and cleared his throat. He knew of a simple solution to the predicament—an easier way to resolve current difficulties with the ERB. He could go around to the other side of the conference table and punch out each and every one of those pencilnecked geeks. Well, maybe not Bertha. She presented a threat. He'd just pound the others, return to his desk, and get to work. Problem solved. Case closed! But Sarge knew it wasn't going to happen that way.

"Lieutenant MacKinsey, do you have anything to say before we start?"

"No, Mr. Chairman. Except you haven't introduced us," he nodded towards Bertha, "to this lovely new member of the Enforcement Review Board." Sarge suppressed full-blown laughter, but a little snort managed to escape through his nose. The ERB members looked at him questioningly, somewhat shocked as he quietly regained composure.

"Thank you for pointing out our oversight, Lieutenant MacKinsey." The chairman sounded annoyed. "Where are our manners today? This is Brunhilde Burkhalter. She recently joined our staff after emigrating from Germany."

"Pleased to make your acquaintance." Bo spoke a little too sweetly.

"Likewise," Sarge nodded. Brunhilde stared as if not buying their superficial civility.

The chairman continued. "Sergeant, we'll start with your version of the facts."

With my version of the facts, Sarge contemplated, as if he'd make something up. He also noticed the ERB males barely met nominal hair length requirements for law enforcement professionals. Shoulder length would have been better but these guys had it cut just below the ears. One has to be careful with shorthairs, who are never completely trustworthy. And no one had addressed him as Sergeant in years. What a formal pain-in-the-butt. "Thank you, Mr. Chairman." Sarge held his annoyance in check. "As earlier reported, I had a run-in with alcohol during the raid conducted on Saturday, March 23rd. The suspect spilled the controlled substance when we surprised him in the commission of the crime. His shirt and pants were drenched with at least a pint of alcoholic beer. I subdued him on the floor to cuff him. Impurities transferred unknowingly. The turbocraft pilot promptly informed that sensors indicated the presence of beer on my shirtsleeve and arm. There was nothing I could do except shower and wash my clothes."

Brunhilde stared with deep suspicion, then wrote furiously in a notebook. Her thick, muscular fingers lacked requisite dexterity to properly grasp the pen.

"You didn't try to conceal the alcoholic contamination," the chairman questioned, "by taking a large number of showers?"

"Of course not. I knew the drug test was far too sensitive to have any chance of passing within a week of the incident."

"You helped in the arrest of the suspect," a third member of the panel quizzed Bo. "Why didn't you get any contaminant on your person?" Sarge was dumbfounded at the thinly veiled accusations.

"The sergeant wrestled him to the floor. I simply cuffed the perp."

"You were close to the suspect, isn't that true?"

"Of course," Bo replied emphatically. "But I only applied the restraints."

After a pause to glance at reports, questioning by another member commenced. He seemed a somewhat shy, timid man with a white pocket protector filled with pens and a black plastic comb. The guy couldn't have been forty years old, yet looked as if he'd led a very unexciting life. "You say you subdued the suspect on the floor, Sergeant. Was this necessary? Couldn't you cuff him without using so much force?"

"The man was armed!" Bo answered the query himself. "We acted quickly to insure no one got hurt. In a situation such as that..."

"Didn't you warn your squad," he interrupted, talking down to the lieutenant, "that there was beer on the premises? Didn't you inform them that they were not to get any contaminant on their person?"

Sarge wanted to laugh at the way they used the word *person*.

Bo carefully controlled his temper. "Under such circumstances it isn't always possible to avoid contact with a tainted substance. I was more concerned with making sure no one was contaminated by a bullet!" He hoped his emphasis would drive home the point that drug busts in general and beerheads in particular shouldn't be taken lightly.

The panel considered the answers. Brunhilde finally took her eyes off the pair and read her papers. One had to wonder if synaptic responses might be misfiring underneath that thick skull. She was an imposing sight at three hundred-plus pounds. Not fat, but muscular, she reminded Sarge of a picture he'd seen as a child of a female weightlifter from behind the Iron Curtain. This woman looked like she could bench-press a horse. Heredity had not been kind to her. Femininity—not her forte. *Steroids*, Sarge recalled as he stared at the hulk of a woman across the table. He hadn't seen the drugs in decades. Brunhilde surely overindulged in the prohibited chemicals during her lifetime.

"Have you ever had an alcohol problem, Sergeant?" The last member of the panel was a man who'd disappear in plain sight.

"Of course not!" Sarge replied tersely.

"Not even back when alcohol was legal?" came the follow-up.

"No, not even when alcohol was legal!"

"And you haven't had a drink, even a little one," the man held up his right hand with index finger and thumb together, "at any time since it was banned?"

"No!" Sarge replied gruffly. "I can't stand the taste of alcoholic beverages and it would violate my Marshal Arts training."

"You didn't have a drink just before initiating the mission on March twenty-third?"

"Of course not!" Sarge replied angrily. "What are you implying, that I'm drinking a controlled substance while on duty? This is ridiculous!"

The man seemed defensive in his confrontation with Sarge, who could easily pulverize him with a single punch. He explained in a way that made everything a lot clearer. "I'm simply trying to establish some facts."

"Facts?" Bo angrily inquired, irritation covering his normally pleasant countenance.

"Well," the man replied, timidly pushing bifocals up his nose, "Sergeant Klassen has a record of drug test failures involving alcohol. We are, quite frankly, wondering if he's attempting to hide a drinking problem," this time the man held up his fingers on both hands, making air quotes, "by *accidentally* getting beer on his person when he knew a drug screening was imminent. That way he could claim the presence of alcohol detected by the test was something he encountered during a job related incident."

"Would you run that by me again?" Sarge couldn't believe what he was hearing! Testosterone almost got the best of him but he maintained control. It wouldn't be prudent to climb over the table and turn the four male ERB members into tomato paste.

The chairman spoke to show solidarity within the group. "We're simply trying to establish whether you have been carefully covering an alcohol problem while at DES."

"That's preposterous!" Sarge protested, not meaning to raise his voice so much. The men flinched, though Brunhilde remained stalwart. Give her credit. She possessed more manhood than the four weenie bureaucrats put together. As a unit, they couldn't have thrashed their way out of a wet paper bag, and/or whipped a wet noodle.

Bo quickly calmed him down. "You people are way out of line!"

"We're well within the bounds of this investigation," the chairman replied smugly, as if enjoying his authority. No doubt, the four weenies were glad Brunhilde was there to protect them if things got rough. She wrote furiously on a departmental form.

Sarge regained his composure. The idea crossed his mind that maybe they were testing him to see what he was made of, an unusual but not unheard-of tactic in police investigations. They were pushing his buttons in an effort to stress him. Well he'd show them. Mrs. Klassen didn't raise her son to be no fool! He straightened his person and sat upright in the uncomfortable chair. The depressing atmosphere of the meeting had bowed his attitude and posture.

Bo nudged and whispered. "How often do you think she has to remove that facial hair? She's a fearsome sight! Look at the muscular physique. I'll bet she could beat you at arm wrestling. Get a load of those bulging biceps!"

Sarge couldn't believe what he was hearing. It was uncharacteristic of Bo to be judgmental or sarcastic, and totally unlike him to take the seriousness of this hearing with such levity. He maintained standards at a high level. Sarge didn't respond. Maybe Brunhilde wasn't fluent in English, having no idea what was being said. He stared. Despite looking at them upside-down, her notes were in English, not German!

The weenies continued their whispering conference. Sarge glanced at Brunhilde as she listened to the others—her body turned sideways. There was no disputing the facts; she did have big biceps. Eighteen inches big! He started to sweat, taking deep breaths and exhaling slowly. Blasted bureaucrats! What a waste of...womanpower, Sarge corrected. That she-male was a chunkster, a powerhouse, a force to be reckoned with; an example of female physical prowess the likes of which he'd never before seen and couldn't imagine even existed. He tried to relax. It had to be a test!

Bo studied Brunhilde and whispered. "How many men do you think she's beaten up? She must have incredible upper body strength!"

Sarge winced. Everything was surreal like in a movie. But the lieutenant's question stuck in his mind. How many men? Brunhilde certainly possessed a temperament for fighting, making her a formidable opponent for all but the strongest male. No doubt about the upper body strength either. He was glad she'd been seated when they entered the room. No telling what lower body strength she possessed. It was hard to believe she'd bother to wear a dress. She'd probably look better in blue jeans and chaps, attired like a rough-and-tumble cowboy. In a rodeo setting, Sarge could almost visualize the bull riding her. He carefully concealed a smile brought on by the absurd mental image.

The five ERBs broke up their little conference and the chairman resumed questioning. "Okay Sergeant, let's go over this one more time. Tell us in your own words what happened in the early morning hours of twenty-three

March, 2041." The Review Board looked agitated, as if being subjected to an unnecessary amount of delay—like Sarge was being evasive—an uncooperative witness. He decided to comply, not complain.

"As stated previously, I encountered the contaminate while wrestling the suspect to the floor. He spilled a substantial amount of alcoholic beer on his *person*," (Sarge figured they might like that word.) "after we surprised him in the commission of a crime, and I was tainted in the scuffle."

"Yes," a board member replied, not looking Sarge in the eye, "we know that. What we're asking is: Have you negated any relevant information from your *original* explanation?" The word was spoken sarcastically.

"There is nothing I can think of," he replied conscientiously, hoping it'd all be over soon. "Why not look at the e-doc (electronic documentation) taken the morning of the bust? It will corroborate my testimony."

"That's impossible," a board member insisted defensively.

"Why?" Bo asked, perplexed.

"It's just not possible!" the chairman repeated, appearing peeved at the query. The man would not make eye contact. What could you expect? He was a pain-in-the-butt shorthair weenie bureaucrat. The ERBs fell silent. Brunhilde scratched her chin, looking skeptically at the two officers, then made notations on departmental forms.

"She wants to fight us," Bo leaned over and whispered, "both at the same time. The testosterone coursing through her veins compels her to aggression."

Brunhilde glared fiercely at Sarge as if she'd heard the last comment, her eyes closed slightly in a squint. Definitely, Sarge thought. How could she not, sitting only six feet across the table? Maybe she'd heard them all! What then? Sarge felt a *Curtain of Doom* dropping over him. Brunhilde did want to fight. Bo was right. That look on her face was undeniable. She nodded ever so slightly as if to imply, *you and me, mano-a-mano*.

"Ever had any financial problems?" a board member asked condescendingly.

The big man regained his train of thought. "No, other than the usual everyone faced during the Great Depression."

"No financial difficulties during your career?" the question was repeated as if the questioner wasn't satisfied.

Sarge wanted to make it very clear. "No. None. Never. Zip. Zero. Zilch!" What are they implying, that I'm taking bribes? What does this have to do with a drug test? The possibility of punching them out resurfaced. It was *so* tempting.

"Any marital problems?" a board member asked matter-of-factly, as if it was his responsibility to keep track of such things in other people's lives.

Sarge replied tersely. "No, I've got a wife, three kids, and two beautiful grandkids."

Another whispering conference ensued. Brunhilde listened while watching Sarge's every move. They were clearly discussing weighty issues—something of great importance. "Is there some reason you have to draw these," the man pointed, "these doodles on your report? I really don't think that's necessary."

"It's just a habit I have," Sarge answered confidently.

"Some of them are very artistic," Bo added. Brunhilde leaned towards the chairman and glanced at his copy. Her response was noncommittal.

"Well don't do it anymore!" the chairman demanded, being as forceful as a pencilnecked weenie could. Neither officer was intimidated. If the bureaucrats did not appreciate an artistic touch...Sarge wondered if he was allowed to moon them. If it had been all men, he might have gone for it.

They went back into a whispering conference. Observing Brunhilde closely, Bo leaned over and spoke. "Just look at that profile! She might be wearing shoulder pads."

Sarge swallowed with a gulp. How could she not be hearing the comments, though she'd probably have said something by now.

"Have you ever needed psychiatric help?" the chairman asked after the whispering conference subsided.

"None whatsoever," Sarge replied conscientiously.

"No counseling of any kind, personal or otherwise?" the man asked.

"No." Personal or otherwise? What the hell did that mean?

"Do you have anything you wish to add?" The chairman finally implied he'd wrap things up. Sarge remained silent, glaring at the four. Their lack of eye contact hinted they got the message. "And you, Lieutenant?"

"No, I have nothing to add," Bo replied dryly as he leaned back in his plastic chair, with only the rear legs supporting him. His leather jacket was open at the front—arms folded across his chest.

"Very well," came the unapologetic reply.

Once again the ERBs went into a whispering conference. Sarge was relieved Brunhilde hadn't asked any questions. It appeared she'd only been an observer. God knows what she'd have queried. Apparently she had not heard Bo's comments. What a relief! They could decide whatever they wished, do what they wanted, and Sarge could get back to work. It'd be finished! He hoped to sneak past the receptionist in the pink sweater on the way out. She was adamant. *Enforcement Review Board!*

Bo nudged and whispered, making an educated guess. "They probably found her on the pro wrestling circuit. That woman could kick serious butt. I wouldn't want to get into a battle with her. You're a lucky guy. She likes you." Sarge took a deep breath. He hadn't commented previously and wasn't going to start. The whispering conference broke up. He wanted to smile at Brunhilde, to reassure her he wasn't a bad guy, but resisted the temptation. It might raise suspicions, making things worse.

The chairman rose from his seat and made a self-serving pronouncement, as if the officers were too beneath him to justify his energy or attention. "I'm afraid," he insisted with holier-than-thou self-righteousness, "that we have to direct this matter through proper channels. There are just too many unanswered questions needing further investigation. In the meantime, Sergeant Klassen is suspended from duty without pay until further notice. If you have no questions, this meeting is adjourned." And that was it. The *If you have no questions* part was perfunctory.

Brunhilde looked piercingly at Sarge as she stood up and gathered her papers. She had a satisfied look on her face, having gotten what she wanted—all three hundred muscular pounds of her. Sarge was stunned. His jaw dropped and hung open in midair. It had to be a test, he thought, some kind of elaborate test to see how he reacted. Brunhilde and the four weenies walked away, but the ground shook under her size-fourteen army boots. The men didn't turn around—the cowards! But she took one more uncompromising look at the two and then disappeared into her office.

"Did you see the hunkers on that woman?" Bo's eyes were wide with amazement. "Talk about lower body strength!" Sarge didn't know what to say. He had a perfect record, no blemishes in decades of police work. Then out of nowhere...Bo consoled. "I told you I'd get you through this." Sarge didn't realize he'd been spoken to. "Hey, did you hear me?"

The big man was completely demoralized. "What's going on?"

"Just a little misunderstanding," the lieutenant answered nonchalantly. "You've got to remember, these people do nothing all day but push paper. An occasional investigation is a form of job security. Without it, their employment would be terminated."

Sarge was flustered. "Yeah, but they're getting the top brass in DC involved. What on earth are they looking for?"

"This isn't the same office you've dealt with before. Times have changed. New management concepts are being tried." Sarge had no idea why Bo was so confident and reassuring. Both men waited. The lieutenant stood up and walked to the window. He brushed jet-black hair from his forehead and leaned against the wall.

FUTUREBUST

FUTUREBUST4.6

"Oh Sergeant. Yoo-hoo." Sarge stood up. It was Brunhilde. Though definitely not a soprano, she actually sounded like a woman—or maybe a man impersonating a woman. "Sergeant, I have to take your badge and firearm."

"I'm not carrying a firearm," he replied caustically. "And I'm not giving you my badge!"

She became defensive, hands on her broad, powerful hips. "Don't make me take it from you by force. I need your badge! It's SOP," she insisted, holding out her hand.

"Can't we work something out?" the lieutenant queried. His manner baffled Sarge. Bo's face radiated hope, as if to transmit a nonverbal cue.

"Such as?" Her voice revealed more curiosity than Sarge wanted to contemplate.

"The usual." Bo's ambiguity didn't alleviate the confusion.

Brunhilde seemed noncommittal and spoke as if throwing a challenge Sarge's way. "I'm not sure he's got what it takes." Sarge was still confused. Things hadn't made sense from the beginning. Brunhilde looked him over—sized him up. She reflected while eyeing him cautiously. "Maybe." Her grin was unwelcome. "I guess we can work something out. Come back into my office and I'll get set up. We'll see if we can't figure a solution to our little problem." She smiled ominously. "But it's going to cost you, BIG TIME!" Her hulking mass swayed as she retreated—broad hips one way, powerful shoulders the other.

Sarge grabbed the lieutenant by the arm and stopped him from following. An unpleasant realization had just occurred. "What are you getting me into?"

"Relax. Once she gets everything set up, this whole mess will be over in short order. She's making sure no one finds out what we're up to. Then we can return downstairs and get back to work like nothing ever happened."

"I can't believe what I'm hearing!" Sarge protested. "This is all so crazy! That's more woman than I can handle!"

"You're stressed out. Brunhilde will take care of everything. All you have to do is allow her to feel like she's in control, nothing more. Go on, be a man. Face the music."

Brunhilde stuck her head out and peered around the corner, her voice ringing with enthusiasm. "Okay, I'm ready. You can come in now." It was unwelcome enthusiasm as far as Sarge was concerned. He was dumbstruck, his feet frozen to the floor.

"Come on," the lieutenant directed, showing annoyance. "Let's get this over with and return to work. It's not a big deal." Sarge refused to move. "We get this matter squared away and we're home free until the next investigation."

"This could happen again?" Sarge's expression was uncharacteristically anxious for one considered fearless.

"Of course!" the lieutenant exclaimed. "We'll be dealing with similar situations frequently. It's best to face them like a man, as a necessary part of doing your job."

"I'm retiring," Sarge stated unequivocally. "No job is worth this!"

"You can't. With an investigation underway, they will suspect you're hiding something and deny your pension."

"I'm not going through with it!" Sarge shook his head. "No way!"

"So you expect me to take care of this alone? What's the problem? We're going to be compensated. It's department policy."

Brunhilde wondered what was keeping them. "Yoo-hoo," she called out in a manly voice. "I'm waiting. What's taking you guys so long?"

"We'll be right in," Bo yelled back. He grabbed Sarge by the arm. "Listen! We've been friends since I joined the force—you being a mentor to me from day one. Don't make me order you to do this! I told you from the beginning I'd get you through it, remember?"

Sarge threw up his hands in desperation. "Okay, I give up. Let's get this over with! But Mrs. Klassen better not find out. She'll divorce me and end up with the boat and the house. I don't want to lose my boat!"

Both men entered Brunhilde's office. Shaking with his eyes closed, the older man had to be led like a sightless person. She was seated at her desk: pens and pencils neatly arranged in a row; inbox to the left, outbox to the right. Her office was nondescript except for a picture on the windowsill. She spoke with calm determination. "Will this be cash or charge?" Sarge opened his eyes. "There's a five percent discount for cash if you've got it."

"How much are we talking about?" Bo questioned matter-of-factly.

"The usual," she replied expectantly. "Fifteen hundred."

"Fifteen hundred?" he nodded. "That's reasonable, but more cash than the department can spare. It will have to be charge."

"Okay, no problemo," she cheerfully announced. "Got your card?"

"Give her the card," the lieutenant encouraged with a hand gesture. "You've got the department credit card don't you?"

"Yeah. What's going on here?" Sarge queried as he opened his wallet and found the credit card. Relief appeared on his face.

"Interdepartmental shakedown," Brunhilde informed authoritatively. "If you want us to look the other way on your drug screening problems, you Alpha boys have to cough up some moola. That's just the way it works nowadays."

"I'm bribing you?" Sarge was flabbergasted. "You've got to be kidding."

"Business is business, unless you've got something else in mind that will make it all better." Brunhilde smiled and fluttered her eyelashes at the big man.

"N, No," he stammered. "I haven't got any better ideas, but..."

"We've had budget cutbacks up here while you guys downstairs are rolling in the dough. The word is you're getting a new turbocraft soon, a Cat-five. At the same time they won't even buy us paper clips. So you gotta pay! Think of it as protection money. It'll help make up for our budget shortfall."

"It's true." Bo was sympathetic to Brunhilde's plight. "They're really putting the screws to the ERB folks." He said ERB and Brunhilde didn't object. "But about that Cat-five; it's not due for three years."

"That's not what I hear," Brunhilde spoke confidently as she ran the card over the processor. "Hope you've got good credit." She pointed. "You sign right here."

Sarge grabbed a pen and signed, not believing what he was doing. "I'm bribing a police official. It's a felony to bribe a police official!" Brunhilde shrugged, remaining silent and unconcerned. She got up out of her chair and escorted the two officers to the door.

"Come on, let's go partner," Bo spoke consolingly, yet his voice sounded far away. "We've got law enforcement business to take care of." Brunhilde patted the troubled sergeant on the back as he exited the room. She didn't seem like such a bad person, certainly not as intimidating as earlier. Both men headed towards the elevator. "Are you ready to go?" Bo's voice still sounded distant, like they were at opposite sides of a room.

Sarge barely heard the question. He was mentally preoccupied. "It's a felony to bribe a police official!" he blurted. "A felony!"

FUTUREBUST4.7

"What are you talking about?" Bo shook the older man who was halfway between sleep and consciousness. "Wake up, you're having a bad dream. You've been snoozing for twenty minutes. I walked by a while ago as you mumbled something about politicians, lawyers, and doctors. I would have stuck around to hear your thoughts on diet book writers but I was in a hurry then and I'm in a hurry now. We've got to resolve the drug-test problem pronto. Come-on. Snap out of it!"

Sarge opened his eyes and looked around. He was slouched in his office chair. "I fell asleep? Is that all?" Much relieved, he checked the time and stretched. "I had the most incredible dream. There was a huge woman named Brunhilde Burkhalter..."

"That's all fascinating, but we've got to get going." The lieutenant wasn't interested in Sarge's somnolent imaginings. "We're due upstairs in five. They have a surprise for you."

"Oh God!" Sarge took a deep breath and stood up. "This I don't need."

"What's wrong? You look like you've been through the mill. Snap to it. ERB big shots don't like to be kept waiting."

The two headed for the elevator. Sarge rubbed the sleep from his eyes and tucked in his shirt. "You wouldn't believe the dream I had. There was this huge woman. She looked like an East German power-lifter, a real workhorse with rock-hard muscles like boulders!" Sarge was excited as he described his dream, complete with hand-gestures showing how big Brunhilde's biceps were.

"An East German what?" the lieutenant looked confused. The doors closed on the elevator. "There is no East Germany. You're not having problems at home are you? 'Cause you can take a long vacation if you want. We're not likely to have another bust for two or three weeks minimum."

"No, no, I'm fine." Sarge's voice calmed. "I dreamed we went before the ERB and this big woman"...the elevator opened. They walked to Room 1404 and entered.

"Hi, Bo honey," a fairly large woman greeted them with a smile. "Welcome to the ERB. I hope you boys from DES are behaving yourselves or I'll have to kick your butts around the room."

Sarge grabbed the lieutenant by the arm, then let go, smiling nervously. Bo laughed. "That's not Brunhilde. That's Doris. She's the new head of the ERB, in charge of everything that goes on. You haven't been here for a while."

"Come in boys," Doris invited. "Have a seat. Coffee? How about a sticky bun? Would you like to wrestle before we get started?" Sarge closed his eyes and banged the side of his head with his palm. Doris looked surprised at the response to her question. "Would you like to rest before the meeting?" she repeated. "Goodness, Sergeant, you look tense. Why don't you relax?"

"You do need a vacation." Bo spoke with concern. "We'll talk after the conference. Maybe you should see the police counselor."

"Not a chance," Sarge resisted nervously. "There's the possibility of another interdepartmental shakedown."

"A what?" Bo considered *el loco enorme*. Following Doris, the two walked into a plushly appointed meeting room. The floor was covered with dark red carpet. Doris sat down at a huge walnut conference table exhibiting rich brown wood grain. She again motioned towards the rolls and coffee. "No thanks, nothing for me," Bo replied as he placed his behind firmly on the sofa. "I've never trusted those sticky buns. Something about them doesn't seem kosher. Can't put my finger on it though."

Sarge eased back in a brown leather recliner. The beauty of the room overwhelmed him. An old Chinese vase sat prominently on a stand in the corner. The drapes were made of a fabric he'd never seen before. A 3D DynaView TV hung on the wall. There were handcrafted walnut cabinets containing lighted glass shelves filled with books, curios, and collectables. Wainscoting surrounded the room. To the left of the conference table was a floor-to-ceiling aquarium, with large, multihued tropical fish.

"Sure you don't want some coffee?" Doris again offered as she flicked a remote that illuminated the fish tank.

"No ma'am," Sarge replied, trying to collect his wits. "When did you remodel? It wasn't like this five years ago."

"Just last year," she continued. "It's nice, isn't it? There was so much cash floating around, we decided to put it to good use. We had stacks of money holding up our other money being crushed by the weight of additional unspent cash. And the bureaucrats kept sending more. It seemed cheaper to spend than pallet and ship back. Besides, there's no way to get a forklift up here." She paused and smiled. "Of course in the end, we did send the vast majority back to the budget people, to help pay off the national debt. You ought to see the supercomputer in the room behind the fish tank. It practically runs the place. My job is to walk around all day and pretend I'm important. That machine does everything but wipe our noses and scratch our backs. It even feeds the fish and cleans the tank. The water is duel purpose. It gives the fish a place to live and cools the computer."

"Anybody working in this office named Brunhilde?" Bo smiled at Sarge.

"No," she replied, nodding her head. "But that might not be a bad handle for the computer back there. We've talked about giving it a name, and *Brunhilde* has a certain ethos. We're tired of calling it *the supercomputer*. Brunhilde grows on you." Sarge's eyes opened wide. He took a deep breath and exhaled. "Mr. Shedmeister should be here momentarily. He'll fill you in with all the latest."

The man finally arrived with a folder tucked under his arm. He was tall, thin, and partially bald. He probably wouldn't have looked good in long hair so he wore it medium length. His clothes didn't quite fit right—a problem most skinny, suit-and-tie guys deal with. He placed his folder on the table and sat in a convenient chair, getting down to business.

"Hello Doris, hello gentlemen. I hope everyone is having a pleasant day. We reviewed the drug test, Sergeant, and reversed the results. After watching the e-doc, we concluded that through no fault of your own and with no reasonable alternative, you contaminated yourself with alcoholic beer. So that matter is closed. Now the other." Sarge was relieved, but still uneasy. Mr. Shedmeister continued. "We're going to have a vacancy in the DES command structure in about six months. You are now formally and officially a lieutenant, complete with pay increase in your next check. It should help a little. Maybe you could buy a new boat and give the one you have to Bo." Mr. Shedmeister winked. Sarge's boat is an eighty-footer, not replaceable for under a million-five.

"I don't know what to say," Sarge replied. "I thought you were going to cream me for contaminating myself. It's the third time I've done it."

"Unavoidable." Mr. Shedmeister spoke in a blunt, authoritative manner. "Couldn't be helped. Anyway, I'm late for another ERB investigation. An FBI dude has some explaining to do. We think he bribed an LAPD official. That's a felony!" Mr. Shedmeister stood up and grabbed his file. "See you all later. Take care, and congratulations Lieutenant."

"He means you, Sarge," Bo assured.

With that, he was gone. Doris broke the silence. "What are we going to call you?"

"Lieutenant Sarge," Bo offered. "You made lieutenant without going to Command School. Oh, and by the way, what he said about your boat is a good idea." All smiled.

"Plus we got a name for the supercomputer. Brunhilde sounds butt-kicking. You boys know how much I enjoy boot'en keister."

"Brunhilde works for me," Bo agreed. "It was Sarge's idea."

"Well thanks for the name, fella," she smiled. "And congrats on your promotion. We should have a party. The ERB has a bulging, well-funded entertainment account."

"Give it a few weeks," Bo suggested. "I think he needs a rest. There's been too much boredom stressing us out lately."

Both lieutenants prepared to exit the plush, comfortable confines of the ERB office. Bo spoke after eyeing Sarge for a moment. "What *are* we going to call you?"

"Let's keep it simple," Lieutenant Sarge replied, a confused look on his face.

"Sarge it is, then." The two men took leave, heading for the elevator and a return trip to their spartan seventh-floor office. They descended quietly—neither speaking. The big man figured he was in for some teasing after revealing his dream. Bo was too sharp to let it go without comment. The elevator doors opened. Bo reached up and put his hand on Sarge's shoulder. "About this Brunhilde you were describing from your dream earlier. Do you think she has a sister? Maybe we could double date next time."

He laughed while Sarge stood motionless near the elevator. Well, that wasn't so bad. If it's the best Bo can muster, Sarge wouldn't say anything—just let if ride. Of course, being a lieutenant, he could argue if he wanted to. Bo turned left into the Command Center, then stuck his head back through the opening.

"You know what I think?" He pointed his finger at Sarge.

"No." Sarge still hadn't moved. Suspicion was evident. "What do you think?"

Bo, ripped pants and all, stepped out into the hall and confronted Sarge, even though the big lieutenant was much larger than the normal-sized lieutenant. "I think this Brunhilde with the big biceps you dreamed about is symbolic of your hidden feminine side—the one psychologists claim men have." Bo noticed the puzzled expression. "You know, the deeply repressed feminine nature guys possess inside. They say us males expend a lot of energy making sure it, or she never shows herself. Well, maybe yours is trying to break away from that tough-guy facade you've been projecting."

"That's not a facade," Sarge argued with mock sternness as he stepped towards his desk. "There's a real tough-guy down inside of me."

Bo returned to the Command Center. Sarge contemplated. He could hear chuckling so he confronted the other lieutenant, who already had his feet on the desk while checking the sensor and telemetry readings from Lance's dayshift grid search, more properly termed a Population Survey. Big Brother is a firm believer in the efficacy of euphemisms.

"If I hit you real hard," Sarge assured, "you'd probably stop laughing."

"You'd never hit me." Bo smiled confidently with hands clasped behind his head. His leather jacket hung open. "There's no way. I'm too pretty to be punched out."

Dolly returned from an errand and stepped into the Command Center. She looked at the two men cautiously, as if sensing something was up. "Are you guys okay?" Her countenance revealed mild concern.

"We're just leaving," Bo smiled and yawned. "Time to go home and get some rest." The two men exited the room, leaving Dolly to her affairs. She looked at them suspiciously, shook her head, and went back to work.

FUTUREBUST5.0

Robert Franklin was escorted to the courtroom in shackles, straddled on either side by an abundantly large, uniformed officer from the United States Department of Corrections, South California District. He shuffled in, barely lifting his feet as he approached his seat—head down, hands clasped together in front due to the cuffs. The television cameras were glued to his every move. He appeared larger-than-life on the DynaView behind the judge's bench. A remote camera located over the jury box zoomed in closely on his face, revealing a somber, yet tenuously defiant mood. Bubba's yellow jumpsuit was the latest in prison attire, making suspects look silly—even clown-like. All the prisoners wore one whether they liked it or not, and it's doubtful any were ever consulted on the matter. Robert Franklin, helped to his seat by the well-muscled escorting officers, was joined by his court appointed lawyer, a man with questionable trial experience, clearly unschooled in the fine art of power dressing. His choice of suit was precipitously close to what could loosely be termed *early century used car salesman*.

"All rise." Bubba took his sweet time. "Twelfth Judicial District, Federal Court is now in session, the Honorable J. J. Horton presiding." Judge Horton, ensconced in an imposing black robe and distinguished gray hair, entered the courtroom from his chambers. He surveyed his hallowed domain, then brusquely planted his behind in the black leather chair.

"Be seated!" the bailiff bellowed. Everyone complied. Remaining absolutely quiet and somber, Judge Horton carefully mounted a pair of old-fashioned, wire-rim spectacles about his face and scrutinized a document placed on the bench before him. He gazed over his glasses at the array of spectators: including the inquisitive, the curious, and the intrusive; along with the nosy, the prying, and the snoopy. Judge Horton was an imposing sight in the shimmering black robe, sporting gold chevrons down the sleeves. He scanned the courtroom to make eye contact with everyone present, radiating a nonverbal cue down on the captive multitudes that bluntly stated: This is my domain. I'm in charge here. Challenge my authority, my preeminence at your own peril. The altitude of his bench, a full six feet above the main floor, instilled even more mastery and dominance in his position of authority, jurisdiction, and command.

Turning his attention to the defendant, he contemplated the shackled prisoner with a baffled judicial countenance. "Would the defendant please rise."

The judge, though polite, was not questioning but ordering. Bubba again took his time. "Son, I'm willing to have you released from the shackles if you give me your word you will respect this court and remain on best behavior while in our presence. We are being televised because you've garnered some notoriety since arrested. I want you to understand that this trial will be fair and judicious, but it will not be turned into a circus. One outburst, one impolite gesture, and I'll have you bound and gagged! Is that clear?"

The defendant acquiesced with a grimace. Judge Horton nodded and the officers in charge of his captivity removed the shackles. The accompanying jingle-jangle of shiny chrome-steel chains and restraints was sure to be a ratings booster in most markets where court TV is popular.

"Bailiff, would you read the charges." Judge Horton removed his reading glasses and placed them carefully on the bench, which officially started the proceedings. He positioned the gavel by his right hand and waited, unconsciously fingering the handle.

The bailiff stepped to the fore, situating himself in front of the bench where he knew the camera over the jury box could get a favoring shot of his good side. He spoke with deep conviction, calling on years of practice, and tax-deductible voice lessons.

"Robert Franklin, the defendant who stands before this court on the thirteenth day of May in the year 2041, is charged with the illegalities listed herein: that he manufactured and unlawfully handled a controlled substance; that he willfully with full knowledge of the consequences, consumed a controlled substance; that he possessed and operated an apparatus applied in the illicit manufacture of a controlled substance; that he stored the aforementioned controlled substance in a residence located within one-half mile of a school; that he possessed, with potential bodily harm to others, illegal firearms and explosives; that he held in his possession and on his person, drug paraphernalia; and that he maliciously assaulted a jail employee while incarcerated. These are the charges before the court as recorded this day, the thirteenth of May, 2041." With the pronouncement concluded, the bailiff relinquished center stage and returned to his assigned position beside the empty jury box.

Judge Horton questioned the attorney representing the United States of America. "Does the prosecution concur with said charges?"

"We concur, your honor," a young, curvy, smartly dressed female prosecutor responded confidently. She used the word *we*, not because there was more than one prosecutor, but because she represented the people of America.

The judge continued along procedural lines. "Do you have anything to add in addendum before we proceed?"

"No, your honor. All said charges are in accordance with specified requisitional parameters." Most lawyers like to talk in cool sounding legalese, and do so every chance they get. They figure it impresses others. However, an astute observer would question whether there is such a word as *requisitional*.

Judge Horton turned to the defendant and continued his procedural inquiries. "Robert Franklin, as defendant on trial, did you hear and understand all charges brought against you in court, this day?"

"We did, your honor," Robert Franklin's not quite so sharply attired, court appointed, (charity) attorney responded to the inquiry from the bench.

"And you fully understand that you have the right to plead guilty, with the possibility of a substantially reduced sentence to said charges in accordance with the plea bargain offered by the prosecution?"

"We do, your honor, and respectfully decline the offer," counsel for the defense replied, shrugging. "My client maintains his innocence and wishes to proceed with the trial, understanding that the full weight of the law may be brought to bear on him as the legal consequence of his actions."

"Very well," the judge shook his head, baffled by the response. "It is my understanding the defendant prefers the name Bubba over Robert. Addressing him as such will be acceptable. I also wish to propose in the strongest manner," he glanced suggestively at the two sides, "that we dispense with opening statements, which, though customary, are unnecessary and time-consuming. There is no jury here to be swayed by mighty pronouncements of guilt or innocence, fancy words, or pretty language. I'm interested only in the evidence and nothing superfluous either the prosecution or defense may say will influence my decision in this matter! Are we agreed?"

Both lawyers shook their heads in the affirmative, then looked at each other and grimaced, showing moderate disappointment. Giving up center stage on court TV was no small favor to ask. The judge seemed pleased. The attorneys suspected he wanted more camera-time for himself. With respect to their own situations, they came to the same conclusion: You win some and lose others.

"Then we'll recess for lunch. Court will reconvene at 1:30." With that, he slammed the gavel and quickly vanished into his chambers. Most in the courtroom stood to leave. There was the usual muffled sound of dispersing and quiet whispers. Bubba was shackled for his return trip to the holding cell, escorted in the same manner as he had entered. The cameras closely followed: one zooming in on his shuffling feet; another showing wide-angle, full courtroom; and of course the up-close-and-personal view of his countenance. All were used to produce a stunning split-screen image. There was even a handheld in the hall, following the defendant being escorted to the elevator.

The perp walk, a century-old tradition, gave viewers a good look at the accused, wearing his jailhouse suit accessorized with the chains and handcuffs the guards labeled *silverware*. The suspect couldn't help but look suspicious under such circumstances—precisely the idea. Face downcast, his heavy chrome ornamentation jingled as he shuffled along. The metallic ringing resoundingly tolled his guilt.

Court TV announcers on three different channels graphically described, minutely dissected, thoroughly examined, and deeply analyzed everything that happened during the first, brief moments of the unfolding courtroom drama—a feat in itself, considering nothing at all took place. But the talking heads did their jobs. It's a tribute to the skill and veracity of these mouthpieces that they effectively filled the void between commercials with anything other than trivial insignificance. With proceedings scheduled to restart in two hours, there'd be plenty of airtime for additional commercials, along with discussion-group speculation as to what will take place when court resumes. A biography of Bubba's life, as if he was an Olympic athlete, played on one channel. Another showed a decades-old documentary on the results of mixing alcohol with automobiles, even though Bubba was not driving when arrested. The third court TV channel replayed a previously run alcohol case, interspersed with critical analysis and detailed speculation as to its relevance to the current case. Interactive programs allowed viewers to enter convictions, feelings, sentiments, and/or opinions of the proceedings; speculate on legal strategies; or bet on the outcome.

Bubba returned to his holding cell two floors below ground and was forced to listen to the jeers of the other prisoners, many of them violent, hardened criminals who'd done serious time in the Big House and were now charged with additional crimes. Closed circuit jail TV, with a small screen in each cell, carried the ninth-floor proceedings. Bubba's offenses were serious enough to gain him a small amount of respect from the other prisoners, and the notoriety he'd acquired since his incarceration meant he was the current star on in-house television.

He settled heavily into his bunk and waited for lunch, brought by one of the escorting officers and shoved under the door. Bubba preferred better service but it was not to be. Today's entrée: *mystery meat*, same as the day he'd attacked a worker in the Los Angeles Combined Municipal Lockup cafeteria. He wasn't used to such fare and the jailers refused to give him a beer to wash it down. They didn't appreciate his lush sense of humor. He ate slowly with no complaint this time—his face expressionless and mind almost blank, yet focused. The only thought swirling through his flustered brain was what he'd say to that judge and the whole world via satellite when the opportunity presented itself. He'd pick the moment carefully—his one and only chance to speak candid and colorfully as possible. Bubba was smart enough to realize an outburst of such epic proportions could get him cited for contempt. But it'd be the highlight of his incarceration, something to brag about when he settled into his new home at the FedPen—gaining him much-needed respect.

FUTUREBUST

With lunch finished, Bubba reclined on his bunk until it was time for a return trip to the courtroom, eleven stories above. He went quietly, despite the jeers of the other prisoners.

"Tell the judge where to go, Bubba!"

"Hey Bubba. You do the crime, you'll do the time." There was derisive laughter following that remark—an oft-repeated quote from an old, TV cop show.

"Tell the judge to shove it."

"Yeah," another inmate added, "where the sun don't shine!"

"Bring us a case of beer after the show. We're getting thirsty down here."

"Cheer up, beer man! Two decades of busting boulders will get rid of that gut! You'll make a fortune with a rock pile workout video!"

The jeers died away as the elevator doors closed. No one spoke—just welcome silence. Bubba enjoyed the quiet while they lifted to the ninth floor. Then pandemonium burst upon his ears in an explosion of yelling, pushing, and shoving. He ignored the handheld cameras—lenses rammed perilously close to his face—and shuffled into the courtroom, once again being unshackled and allowed to sit quietly. All rose as Judge Horton made an entrance. "Be seated!" the bailiff bellowed.

FUTUREBUST5.1

"Are you ready to proceed?" Judge Horton addressed the prosecution brusquely, as if he was behind schedule and hadn't just finished an unnecessary two-hour lunch break.

"Yes, your honor," she assured, noticing his impatience. He nodded his approval. "The People wish to enter as evidence, Exhibit 1A, the recording taken by the police on the morning the defendant, Bubba Franklin was arrested. We will play it in its entirety."

With a motion of her hand, a picture appeared on the DynaView behind the judge, as well as several smaller monitors around the room, while being simultaneously broadcast to interested court watchers worldwide. No doubt, inquiring minds want to know.

A hush overtook the courtroom as the split-screen presentation of Bubba's drug bust proceeded. It included several views of the ground below the police turbocraft; all the sensor information taken from the vehicle; the date and time digitally superimposed in the lower left; and the audio comm. between the officers. There was a blank rectangle on the lower right quarter of the screen, which showed nothing except the letters NC. The display was in HiDef, but not 3D, technology still too cumbersome to carry on a turbocraft.

Everyone, including Bubba, watched in silence as four members of the special drug unit known as Alpha Squad neutralized the booby traps and executed the bust. The blank area on the screen labeled NC lit up with a green-gray picture penetrating the roof. The suspect was subdued, the premises secured, and a search for additional evidence initiated.

Courtroom decorum was broken twice, when the pilot informed an officer of beer residue on his skin, and when the suspect claimed they'd planted the intoxicant on him. Judge Horton ended the minor disturbances with his gavel. The eleven-minute presentation contained nothing unusual.

With the recording finished, the prosecutor continued her case, explaining that the evidence is incontrovertible. "The scenes you have just witnessed were recorded on a certified memory dot. It can be imprinted only once and is impossible to corrupt without destroying the entire recording!" Judge Horton shook his head in the affirmative. "The recording clearly shows what took place on March twenty-third, 2041. We would also like to exhibit as evidence: a TurboBrewery confiscated from the defendant's house; a sample of the alcoholic beverage; the weapons and explosives confiscated; plus a sweatshirt the defendant was wearing, subsequent to, and at the time of his arrest."

The items were brought into the courtroom on two stainless steel carts, for all to see. The prosecutor displayed the booty like a collection of prizes in a game show. Judge Horton opened the hermetically sealed sample to check the smell. A pinkie finger inserted into the package, then into his mouth, satisfied his judicial curiosity. Printed on the label was the alcohol content as tested by an independent laboratory: 22.4%. The turbocharged brew was definitely not *O'DOUL'S*.

The prosecutor continued. "The police crime lab also found the substance on Bubba's sweatshirt to be alcoholic beer; and the explosives to be of a variety used by the military. All evidence has been tracked and monitored throughout the evidentiary process by ICROG, the Independent Civil Rights Oversight Group, and is certified uncontaminated."

Judge Horton queried the defense. "Does counsel challenge the evidence or any process in which it was handled?"

"Oh...no, your honor," replied the startled, court appointed attorney, suddenly aware of being spoken to. He stopped cleaning his fingernails with a clipper and sat up straight. Judge Horton looked at him disapprovingly.

"You may continue," the judge nodded to the prosecutor.

"As for the charge of assault," she proclaimed, "the prosecution wishes to bring before this court, Mr. Clancy Thomas, the prison employee who was accosted in the Combined Municipal Lockup cafeteria."

"Proceed," Judge Horton replied. "Bailiff, call the witness."

"The Court calls Mr. Clancy Thomas to the stand!" The bailiff again made a brief but poignant attempt at stardom. It's rare indeed for the average individual to be seen on court TV in a capacity not injurious to his or her persona. Bubba was not so lucky.

Mr. Thomas entered from the rear, walked to the stand and raised his right hand, thus being sworn in and motioned to his seat, which was below and to Judge Horton's left.

"State your full name and age," the prosecutor ordered firmly.

"Clancy D'Angelo Thomas. I'm forty-two years old, born in 1999."

"And your occupation?"

"Foodservice worker at the Combined Municipal Lockup."

"Do you recognize this man here?" She motioned towards Bubba with a carefully manicured index finger.

"Yes, he's the prisoner that attacked me in the jail cafeteria." Mr. Thomas exhibited restrained anger.

"Would you describe the incident?" she continued, placing herself favorably in front of the jury box camera.

"Well, I was minding my own business, doing my job at lunchtime..."

"And your job involves?" she interrupted. "Be specific."

"My job is cooking and serving the food," Mr. Thomas answered. "I was serving lunch when that man climbed over the counter and attacked me. He grabbed a handful of the main course and forced it into my face! I was taken completely by surprise otherwise he'd never have gotten the best of me!" Bubba glared at the witness, nonverbally challenging that comment.

"Would you describe the food?"

"It was the meat being served that afternoon."

"What kind of meat...?" The prosecutor could not stop in time.

"It was mystery meat, Ma'am," he replied. "It's a canned meat served to prisoners at the jail."

"Was anything wrong with the meat that would make him react that way?" she inquired with assumed surprise. Damage control was necessary.

"No ma'am," Mr. Thomas shook his head. "Mystery meat is one of the most popular processed meats ever created, second only to hot-dogs. We have twenty-five ways to prepare it. We can even fashion an artificial turkey or ham, which we do for special occasions like Thanksgiving and Christmas. I've never heard of a complaint before that day."

"Thank you." She showed a slight loss of confidence as Judge Horton winced. Time to cut and run. "We have no further questions, your honor." Again, she used the word *we*, while not accompanied by anyone. It was spoken to express the idea that the entire population was behind her, and thus her prosecuting authority came from *The People*.

"Do you wish to cross-examine the witness?" Judge Horton queried.

"We do, your honor." Bubba's attorney came to life and sat up smartly. His use of the word *we* did not have much authority behind it, but sounded just as good. It was a part of defending his client. He buttoned his suit, adjusted his tie, and positioned himself proudly before the cameras.

"Proceed."

"Your honor, I would like the court to consider the defendant's state of mind when the admitted attack took place. My client was a productive member of society before the police broke into his house..."

"Objection, your honor!" the prosecutor interrupted. "The police didn't break into the defendant's house. They had a warrant to enter and search the premises! Must I explain how the Online Judge works?"

"No!" Judge Horton rolled his eyes. "Standards for the Online Judge are higher than...well...the legal profession itself." His self-effacing humor brought little response from observers. "Objection sustained. Rephrase your statement and refrain from making derogatory references to law officers."

"Yes, your honor." Counsel was clearly annoyed by the intrusion. "As stated, my client was a productive member of his community until his life was turned upside down by a bunch of do-gooders who..."

"Objection!" she looked angrily at counsel. "The defense is trying to portray a negative image of the men and women in law enforcement who are protecting society from the criminal element he's defending..."

"Objection!" counsel broke in yelling. Both attorneys were fuming. "I object to her portrayal of my client as the criminal element!"

"Order! Order in the court!" the judge slammed his gavel repeatedly. "I will not have this trial turned into a circus. Each of you will refrain from making derogatory statements and stick to the facts! Understood?" Still suspicious of each other, both chastened attorneys agreed in unison. That incident—a ratings booster for sure, helped draw market share from other court channels running drab, no-luster cases like celebrity parking tickets, celebrity zoning ordinance violations, celebrity shoplifting cases, or celebrity tax evasion trials. "Continue counselor!" the judge ordered sternly as he folded his arms across his chest and leaned back in his chair.

"What I was trying to say," counsel reiterated, "is that my client's state of mind was such that he didn't know what he was doing at the time of the attack. We wish to plead temporary insanity due to stress and throw ourselves on the mercy of the court."

"I'll certainly take that into consideration," the judge assured sarcastically. "Continue, but don't be accusatory of others."

"Yes, your honor. I have a few questions." The defense turned to the witness and made a feeble attempt to look intimidating, even show some manliness. He approached the stand. "You stated you had no knowledge of any complaints, is that true and correct?"

"Yes," the witness responded cautiously, eyeing counsel closely.

"Are you not aware," the defense continued, attempting to look as imposing as possible, "that an incident such as the one you described happening to yourself, occurred once before in the cafeteria just before you were hired?"

"Well, I didn't mean to suggest that..."

"Isn't it true," Bubba's lawyer interrupted, his voice revealing excitement, "that a foodservice employee involved in that incident was fired for his actions?"

"Objection, your honor," the prosecutor interrupted. "This is irrelevant."

"Objection overruled." The judge reacted quickly to prevent arguing. "There might be some merit. You may continue this line of questioning, but keep it civil and get to the point."

"Thank you, your honor," the defense sounded a bit patronizing and sanctimonious as he glanced at the prosecutor. He returned to his questioning. "Isn't it true that a fight broke out in the cafeteria between a prisoner and foodservice worker, the very employee whom you replaced after he was fired? And isn't it true the altercation was over food served to the inmates?"

"Well," the witness answered hesitantly, "that's not what I heard..."

"So now you're admitting," Bubba's attorney interrupted, "that you knew about the incident which took place just before you were hired. A minute ago you claimed you'd never heard of a complaint!"

"I never heard a complaint! Those were different circumstances..." the flustered witness replied, before he was again interrupted.

"...Of a complaint!" counsel, feeling pretty good about himself, corrected. "You said you never heard *of* a complaint. Must the record be read back to the court?"

Judge Horton nodded. He could remember what had been said. His mind worked in a legal manner and he was always cognizant of such hairsplitting interpretations. Mr. Thomas stated he'd never heard *of a complaint*, even if meaning he (personally) had never heard a complaint. They are totally different statements. To hear a complaint, he must be present at the time it's spoken. To hear *of* a complaint, he need not be, but might have heard someone else tell of it later. It was hairsplitting, even twisting the truth all out of shape, but legally correct.

"I submit to you, your honor," counsel spoke all puffed up with pride and self-importance, "that the food served in the jail cafeteria is responsible for my client's actions. He didn't go to lunch that day hoping to pick a fight with the jail staff. He wanted to be left alone. When Bubba realized he'd be unable to partake of a decent meal as he was accustomed, he lost it! He snapped!"

"Is that your argument?" Judge Horton looked puzzled and carefully scratched his distinguished gray hair.

"Yes, your honor," counsel asserted confidently. "If you knew what it's like to dine in the confines of the Combined Municipal Lockup..."

"I'll take your word for it," the judge raised his hand, palm out in protest. "Anything else you'd like to add concerning this matter?"

"Mystery meat at Thanksgiving?" the defense winced with a dismissive wave. "No further questions."

"Rebuttal?" Judge Horton turned to the prosecutor.

"Counsel need not twist and contort Mr. Thomas' words," she replied in a hostile, defensive tone. "We know what he meant. I have nothing further, your honor."

"Very well," the judge sighed. "I'll take this matter under advisement and hand down a ruling in due course. The witness may step down." Clancy Thomas looked bewildered and confused. Bubba glared as the cook was escorted from the courtroom. Judge Horton nodded. "Do you have anything else to add?"

"The prosecution rests."

Judge Horton exhaled and rubbed his forehead. "Why don't we take some time to assimilate what we've heard and reconvene tomorrow at 9 A.M. At that hour, the defense will proceed with its case." Judge Horton slammed his gavel and disappeared into his chambers. The attorneys looked at each other and shrugged.

"He doesn't seem to be in much of a hurry to get anything done."

Prosecution replied politely. "He must have something going on in his chambers that interests him more than this case. Whatever it is, it won't affect the outcome of the trial."

Counsel agreed, his expression mildly sarcastic. "It's no skin off my back. I get paid either way." The prosecutor laughed, closed her briefcase, and left the room.

Bubba shuffled towards the courtroom exit with his guards. Not that it mattered. He was going to spend some serious time in the FedPen. His mind focused on what he'd say to the judge when he got his big chance. He stepped into the elevator with his escorts and watched the doors close, temporarily isolating the men from the rest of the world. Bubba figured a verbally fortified outburst would get him sixty days tacked on for contempt, but it'd be worth it, especially on international television! He'd take full advantage when the time came. The elevator doors opened revealing his temporary abode. Surprisingly, the other prisoners were quiet—no jeering or grabbing through the bars as he shuffled by. The jail door slammed behind him and he was released from his shackles. A couple of steps and he settled into his bunk.

"See ya later," one of the guards chided. "You'll probably be off to the

Big House by Wednesday afternoon. Judge Horton makes his mind up fast on these cases. Enjoy your last nights in civilization."

"Hey listen," the other guard spoke as if having some concern for the defendant, "you're still a young guy. If you behave, you could be out in five years so don't do anything crazy. I have a feeling you'll be found not guilty on the assault charge. Judge Horton is a connoisseur of fine food. He loves classy restaurants and is surely sympathetic, in view of the mystery meat. It's only the drug and weapons charges you have to worry about." The guard grabbed the jail door and jerked it to make sure it had latched. "Sleep tight."

The guards left Bubba to his thoughts. His future hung in the balance on a dangling double-knit thread. Bubba's pro bono defense was his only hope and the guy is just collecting his paycheck and grabbing some free publicity.

FUTUREBUST5.2

Lieutenant Bo MacKinsey reclined with his feet on the desk in the Command Center at DES headquarters. Minutes passed slowly until a chime sounded to announce the midnight hour. It'd been a while since anything exciting had happened, maybe seven weeks. He scanned the sensor feeds beamed from Jim's turbocraft, looking for signs of life. The readings were disappointingly limp.

Seven weeks was a long time to wait, but not unusual. Drug abuse had dropped to almost nothing since NOSTRILS was perfected years earlier. *Neutral Operations Strategic Tactical Reconnaissance Intelligence Logistical Sensors*, an electronic bloodhound. Where would we be without NOSTRILS? Bo inquired mentally. His mind reverted to the previous bust as he hit the intercom. "Cy, what's become of Bubba Franklin?"

The DES attorney pondered. "I'll have to check."

Bo sat up in his chair. "Sarge, you guys have any donuts?"

"Our performance rating in that regard is sub par with prescribed cop standards."

"Why don't you go get some. I'm paying."

"I'll get right on it!" Sarge jumped from his chair and ran the half-dozen steps to the Command Center. "Anything in particular?"

"No sticky buns," the younger lieutenant ordered with an ominous headshake. "There's something about them…"

Larry joined them. The DES prankster smiled. "You know what bakers call the sugary glazing they put on those buns?"

Sarge didn't take the bait. Then he changed his mind. He'd known Larry for decades and figured his partner had some trivial, yet relevant information on the subject of sticky buns. "Enlighten us." Bo wondered if it was wise to encourage.

"*Sticky Bun Smear,*" Larry replied, laughing. "It's true. They call it Sticky Bun Smear. I saw it on a five-gallon container in a bakery once."

"How did I survive this long without knowing that?" Sarge smirked.

Bo put his feet on the desk and leaned back thoughtfully, suspicion evident in his voice. "Sounds kinky to me. I'm a strait-laced guy. Maybe that's why I don't like them."

"Interesting concept." Sarge scratched his head. The gears in the big man's head were turning as he contemplated the possibilities, but he knew the Mrs. wouldn't go for it.

"Take it easy, Sarge!" Bo taunted, pulling some cash out of his shirt pocket. "You're far too old for that sort of thing. I've got Cy checking on Bubba from a couple months back. If there's a court file we can access on his trial, it'll be an educating night of jurisprudence." Sarge grabbed the cash and headed to the elevator. "I'll check with Jim," Bo added. "He might want to get in on this." Feet back on the floor, he radioed his pilot, somewhere over Bakersfield, searching with disappointing results for lawbreakers to arrest. The comm. squarely framed Jim's face. "Hey, we've got something going on. Cy is locating Bubba Franklin's digital court file. Interested in watching it with us?"

"Haven't you guys got anything better to do?" Jim's voice hinted at mock severity. "I'm busting ass trying to locate the criminality in society and you guys want to watch court files. I'll bet you've got buttered popcorn." Jim nodded. "There's little going on out here. Bakersfield appears to be free of drug abuse tonight. It sucks."

"We'll pipe it out to you," Larry assured. "How much you want to bet Bubba's gotten himself into more trouble since we busted him?"

"It wouldn't surprise me in the least," Jim conceded, a concerned look on his face. "But you're the expert on mischief and troublemaking. My forte is speed and acceleration."

Minutes later Cy returned with confirmation. He typed the docket number into the computer, then transferred the signal to the DynaView. "I'll pause it until Sarge gets back. He'll want to see it all."

"Let's pipe it through to Jim," Bo insisted. "He's the one who found the guy in the first place." Larry obliged. Jim's comm. lit up:

The United States vs. Robert Franklin
Docket Number 25225-41 DES LA
S. California District
Judge J. J. Horton

FUTUREBUST

"This should be interesting," Cy observed. "There's enough evidence to convict a dozen lawbreakers, yet he didn't plead guilty."

Sarge returned from the donut shop and presented the pastry on a wooden tray lined with a paper towel. "I confirmed your story," he spoke to Larry. "They do call it Sticky Bun Smear, but assured me it has no legitimate uses other than on bakery products."

"Too bad," Bo chided. "You figured you were on to something."

They pulled up chairs in front of the DynaView, which had 3D capability, but digitized court records were rarely processed that way, short of a celebrity being the defendant. It took too much memory. Cy started things rolling. On screen, Judge Horton had just dignified the courtroom with his august, robed presence. Alpha Squad watched with interest. "Oh, good morning sir." Bo looked surprised as Captain Jackson strolled in for an unexpected, late night check of his troops.

Larry rose and moved another folding chair in front of the screen. The captain sat down, grabbing a donut in the process. "You guys look busier than usual. Normally I find you bored and wearied from lack of work. What are we watching?"

"Remember Robert Franklin from weeks past? His trial started today."

"Beer Can Bubba," Captain Jackson acknowledged. "Sure, the bust in late March. The courts must be jammed up. His day before the judge should have been completed within four weeks of arrest or he could get off on a technicality."

All gazed at the DynaView in wonder. "Would you look at that!" Bo pointed. "Bubba's in shackles. You guys were right."

"Let's see what they charge him with." Captain Jackson leaned forward. Bubba's shackles were removed and the indictment read. The last charge, that he maliciously assaulted a jail employee elicited a typical, anti-drug pronouncement from the captain: "See, you guys hauled that fellow in on drug charges and he gets into more trouble while locked up. That shows what alcohol does to people. I can't believe we didn't ban that stuff earlier!"

"Alcohol has an incrassative effect on the mind," Cy observed flatly. Just messing with them for the fun of it, he waited for the inevitable reaction. Sarge obliged.

"There's a word to think about. I haven't got a clue what you just said."

"We could look it up," Larry suggested loudly. "Or maybe Mr. Bergstrom will save us the trouble and enlighten everyone."

"In a pedantic sense, it means to thicken, but often refers to a liquid becoming more viscous. It's not ordinarily used when referring to the mind, but in this case I thought it was an apt description of what happens to people addicted to alcohol. They're thickheaded, though by no means have a monopoly on that condition. But it is harder for them to change, especially their thinking."

"Jeeze, you start uttering words like that and people will think you're very much more smarter than you really are." Bo laughed. "Then you play games with the meaning."

"Just for fun, I like torquing the import of words," Cy confessed. "In first-year law school we were taught to skew, contort, twist, garble, and dismember the facts. It gets to the heart of what lawyers do and takes constant practice to remain sharp. Even the word *truth* is different in law than normal usage. Out here in the real world, it's a pretty concrete thing. But an attorney is taught to use the best available version of the truth. It gets forged into something he can exploit in the courtroom and he's on his way to a successful completion of the case and a bonus in his paycheck."

"Maybe you should have used the word *incrassating*." Captain Jackson threw a monkey wrench into the works. Everyone's attention returned to the DynaView. They watched until court recessed for lunch. Bubba's perp walk to the elevator was included.

"Judge Horton would go easier on him if he'd pled guilty," Larry observed.

"Cy's the expert on courtroom outbursts," Jim informed over the comm.

"That's the reason!" Cy announced. "He's planning to make a scene in court. That guy's got an ax to grind. Look how many channels are covering this trial."

"I think I'll visit the courtroom for the remainder of the hearing," Bo affirmed. "Any of you guys want to join me, you're welcome to."

"Sounds like a plan," Sarge replied. "It's been a while since I've visited a courthouse. They rarely need us for testimony, with all the evidence certified against taint or defect."

Everyone except the captain agreed to Bo's fieldtrip proposal. A day in court might bring some relief to an otherwise dull shift. The digital records continued with the afternoon session. The recording taken from the turbocraft was played in its entirety.

"You see that?" Jim spoke in an upbeat voice. "That's my work. I've made you TV stars, and what thanks do I get? No money or gifts. No affectionate pat on the back or heartfelt congratulations…"

"We do love you," the captain interrupted Jim's lamentation. "We're getting you a Cat-five turbocraft. Wait 'til you see what that thing can do!"

Total silence. The announcement was unexpected. Jim broke the quietude gently. "Maybe you do love me. I hope it goes faster than the Cat-four."

"And a whole lot more," Captain Jackson replied. "I'll fill you in when we take delivery next week."

"Next week!" Bo was caught off guard and out of character. "They aren't supposed to be available for years!" Sarge scratched his head and shrugged.

"That's what I've got to talk to you guys about." Captain Jackson spoke with some reservation. He clearly wanted to change the subject. "Now let's calm down and watch the court record. They're about to call a witness."

Clancy Thomas was sworn in as Cy increased the volume. No one spoke while he described the confrontation with Bubba at the jail cafeteria. All sat in stunned silence, not knowing if they should be shocked or laugh out loud. Larry seemed troubled. "He attacked the cook with mystery meat."

"Assault with a deadly weapon." Jim spoke with his patented, deadpan voice. "I just spilled coffee all over the cockpit. The maintenance guys are going to be upset. It'll need a complete system's check."

"I think we missed something." the captain insisted. "Run it back."

Bo leaned over to pick up the donut he dropped. "I better get a vacuum."

"No, leave it for now," the captain ordered. "Let's watch the court file."

Cy backed up to the correct spot, then replayed the classic duel of wits between opposing attorneys. The DES legal eagle leaned forward and studied the scene closely. "Look at those two go at it. My guess is they are either having an affair, or are about to start one." The judge slammed his gavel to regain order.

"Talk about affairs…" Captain Jackson cleared his throat and motioned towards the DynaView, which held Judge Horton's impressive judicial embodiment.

Everyone remained silent. The defense was tearing down Thomas' story. Then the courtroom drama concluded. Judge Horton abruptly adjourned the proceedings and retired to his chamber. The men stood up, dusted themselves off, and regrouped. Captain Jackson broke the silence. "I'm going to miss this place when I retire. Law enforcement has its moments. I haven't seen mystery meat used as a weapon since junior high." He smiled at Bo. "You'll be gunning for my job, won't you? Well, I've got to be on my way. Thanks for the fine hour of judicial review. I'll see you guys in the morning. Behave out there, Jim." The pilot nodded. Captain Jackson strolled from the Command Center and headed to the hanger where his SkyLimo waited. The Alphas returned to their desks and tasks unfinished after cleaning up the mess on the floor. They couldn't forget what they'd seen. Was Bubba's predicament funny, or semi-tragic?

FUTUREBUST5.3

Two o'clock in the morning and Bubba paced in his cell, contemplating his upcoming courtroom outburst. He needed ideas—something to ring the judge's bell. Bluntly suggesting where to go wasn't enough. The idea revolved in Bubba's head like a hamster in a squirrel cage. He knew where he stood. One chance is all I'll get, he calculated. It will be best to wait for the end of the trial when they least expect it. Then the whole world gets it!

Four hours later, the sun rose in the east. Two stories below ground, Bubba couldn't see it, but he was still thinking.

Breakfast was served at 7:30. Bubba wasn't hungry, however he ate anyway. He was also given a new prison suit. They wanted him looking nice for the cameras. The guards with him from the start of the trial, arrived to take him upstairs. He was not shackled, just handcuffed due to good behavior. They walked to the elevator. His two well-muscled companions took hold of his arms and waited as they rose to the ninth floor. The doors opened and the three men walked out into the hall crowded with curious onlookers and those ever-present television cameras. Bubba entered the courtroom. In the back he saw familiar faces, the men of Alpha Squad who'd entered his house weeks earlier. The gears turned ominously in his head.

"All rise. Court is now in session. The Honorable Judge J. J. Horton presiding."

Honorable is right, Bubba reflected. I'll honor him soon enough!

"Please be seated," Judge Horton nodded. He scanned the courtroom, surveying his domain from the bench. His elevated perch gave a decided high-ground advantage in projecting power, authority, dominance, control, and jurisdiction. "I want to remind you that this is a court of law and this trial is being televised on several court channels. I'll tolerate no outbursts or improper behavior. We are here to try the defendant and I expect everyone to behave with dignity." He looked at the defense. "Are you ready to proceed?"

"We are, your honor." The judge nodded. Bubba's attorney ambled out from behind his table as if to take center stage. He paced back and forth in front of the court. A double-knit suit clung to his pudgy frame, revealing a body out of balance with normality. The jacket had two buttons strenuously engaged near the middle, while others at the top and bottom were free to allow for flab and tummy sag. It gave the lawyer a shape reminiscent of what bodybuilders call a *girley man*. His cheeseburger physique strongly suggested he'd been hitting the transfats a little too assiduously. He cleared his throat and proceeded in grandiose fashion.

"Your honor and members of the court," counsel held his head high. "We are here today to determine the fate of the man seated before us in the defendant's chair," the attorney pointed at Bubba, "in a fair and equitable manner. Society deems it necessary to impose statutes; edicts by which we live together; ordinances we believe will help us become a more caring civilization; precepts, nay laws which…"

"Excuse me counselor." Judge Horton addressed the defense. "Let's not overdo the speechmaking. I know you rarely get a chance for grand and noble oratory in Bankruptcy Court. Your wish to inspire us with admiration for our legal system is commendable, and I'm sure millions watching around the world are full of gratitude. However, I'm not interested in your rhetorical skills. Please, just get to the point."

"Yes, your honor," counsel recoiled. He regained composure and cleared his throat. "But there are times when the rules we as a people have imposed on ourselves for our own benefit, and in our own best interest, become offensive, oppressive, an abomination of justice, a detriment to growth and happiness of the individual…"

"Counselor?" Judge Horton patiently interrupted. "Are we going to have a trial or religious revival? I'm willing to give you leeway, but don't take advantage of my generosity and patience. I know we're on television, but this isn't the Supreme Court."

"Uh, yes your honor," counsel replied, perturbed by the interruption.

"Remember," his honor pointed out, shaking a judicial index finger at the lawyer, "defend your client to the best of your ability but don't bore me with speeches."

Counsel had to regain composure, regroup, and organize his ideas into something usable. He returned to his table and gathered up some papers.

"You're bombing," the prosecuting attorney whispered.

"I know," he whispered back. "This case is hopeless. The guy's guilty and we both know it." Bubba pretended not to hear.

"Try some constitutional arguments," she suggested in a hushed voice.

"Your honor," counsel turned and faced the judge, "I want to submit here today that the arrest of Bubba Franklin was unconstitutional; that he was harassed by the police and should be set free at once!"

"Okay," Judge Horton replied, "humor me."

"Your honor," the defense now spoke with confidence, "the raid on Bubba's domicile took place without a proper warrant, signed by a living, breathing judge. How can it possibly be legal to…?"

"Excuse me again," the judge interrupted. "The police acted in good faith with a *No Knock* warrant from the Online Judge, served in the early morning hours because of mitigating circumstances."

"The Online Judge is nothing but a computer programmed to take data from the police surveillance vehicle known as a Cat-four turbocraft and analyze it. If the data is deemed adequate by an electronic brain, it spits out a document which allows law enforcement to break down a suspect's door…!"

"Objection, your honor," the prosecutor interrupted, looking thoroughly perturbed. "The Category-four turbocraft used by the police is not a surveillance vehicle, but a law enforcement tool. And they didn't break down anybody's door. They safely blew the entrance using PuffCharges, people-friendly explosives..."

"I get your point," Judge Horton raised his hand to stop the impending advertisement for Cuddly-Soft Dynamite, a popular name-brand. "Sustained. Continue your argument, counselor, but don't defame the police."

"Yes, your honor," the defense recoiled. "What I'm saying is that a warrant, not directly sworn out by a living, breathing judge, is an inadequate instrument of the law to justify entering the residence of a citizen of this great and just land of ours. We are a nation of laws, not men and machines, and we..."

The judge preempted counsel's impending speech. "Your argument is duly noted, however Congress and the PATRIOT III Act disagree. The Online Judge is under constant, around-the-clock supervision by court appointed magistrates in the Kansas City, Missouri nerve center, who oversee all actions taken by the electronic legal system and can instantly override any decision deemed incorrect. In addition, any online warrant can be overturned by a living, breathing judge, as you so eloquently refer to us, and few ever are. Over a quarter million have been served since its inception in law enforcement and acceptance by the Supreme Court fifteen years ago, with only a handful thrown out. The software for the Online Judge is refined and clarified each time a warrant is deemed incorrect, and it's to the point now that very few are considered for reversal. The record of the Online Judge far surpasses in fairness and equity the judgment of flawed human beings in our legal system."

"But your honor..."

"And as you already know, I didn't see anything in the database to warrant a review. If I had, it'd have been dealt with immediately. Not only that, but the drug sniffing sensors known as NOSTRILS are remote-calibrated twice a week by sworn officers of the court in Kansas City. And Congressionally appointed technical officers oversee their actions. We'd be very fortunate if everything in our society were as fair and impartial. So the ruling stands. The warrant is legal. End of discussion!"

A brief silence ensued as counsel came to terms with the court's decision. There was just too much precedent behind the Online Judge for this appeal to work. The defense tried another tact on the technological front. "Your honor, I would like to submit to the court that techniques incorporated in the arrest of Robert Franklin violate the doctrine of Separation of Church and State." Judge Horton gestured reluctantly to proceed. "Your honor, the Neutrino Camera mounted on the Cat-four turbocraft can see through walls. It is the defense's contention that only the divinity known as God be allowed to peer through solid structure and that the police have no right to spy on the people this way."

The prosecution was about to object, but Judge Horton waved her off. "Is that really your argument? I don't think it's going to wash, counselor. No surveillance, audio or visual, took place until after the turbocraft's sensors detected illegal drugs on the premises; until after a warrant was issued; and until after the police discovered illegal firearms within the domicile. Neutrino Cameras have saved countless law enforcement lives in the last ten years, and they're here to stay. Now do you care to try again?" Judge Horton quickly realized he shouldn't ask such a question of a grandstanding defense attorney, so he preempted. "And don't tell me that the police violated the defendant's rights when they used blast retardant to safely diffuse his booby traps. There are no civil rights abuses there, unless you consider those against the officers." There was a very brief pause.

"And furthermore," the judge continued his preemptive strike, "don't try to convince me that the sensor array known as NOSTRILS is unconstitutional. That has long ago been determined by the Supreme Court not to be the case. Those electronic sensors probe at the subatomic level, well below the point of ownership of matter. The Supreme Court has clearly noted that an individual has complete ownership of his molecules, such as his DNA, but not the atoms contained therein. Those scanners search for subatomic patterns and in no way infringe on the privacy rights of individuals, who do not have legal ownership or control of such particles. It is not considered an unreasonable search under the Fourth Amendment. NOSTRILS was approved for use under an addendum to the PATRIOT III Law when it was reaffirmed and updated in 2018. Now, do you have any *legitimate* arguments to present?"

"It may not be unreasonable, but it is also not a reasonable search."

"The Supreme Court has already said that," Judge Horton replied. "The Constitution protects us from unreasonable searches, nothing more. It does not guarantee searches will be reasonable. There is a grey area in-between with some legitimate arguments claiming a search may be neither reasonable nor unreasonable. You already know how words and meanings are twisted within the law. You did it yesterday to the prosecution's witness. Now, any other ideas you want to try?"

"How about police brutality?" the defense asked sheepishly.

"Not likely," his honor replied.

"Freedom of Assembly?"

"Explain." Judge Horton tolerated this, knowing the defense was almost finished.

"My client has the right to assemble whatever he wants, according to the United States Constitution. The TurboBrewery should not be considered illegal because…"

"Nope," Judge Horton raised his hand in a *Halt!* motion. "You're stretching it to the limit and beyond. I could be out playing golf so don't try my patience! Besides, that Mark V, 261B TurboBrewery with Froth Enhancer is German-engineered so it's not protected by the American Constitution."

The defense retreated to his notes. Bubba fidgeted, looking bored and annoyed. "Why don't you try a bleeding-heart argument?" the lady prosecutor whispered. "No one can ask for more than that."

"He's not going to buy it," defense whispered back.

"It's all you've got," she replied. "And besides, we're paid by the hour."

That statement rang a bell. He nodded and turned smartly to face the judge. "Your honor, I'd like you to consider my client's past. He was born into a family of boozers. His mother was an alcoholic working in her father's bar. When pregnant with child, she became intoxicated. This man who sits before you, ingested alcohol before he was born. He spent nine months of embryonic life swimming in a sea of alcohol. After birth, he nursed at his mother's beer-contaminated breast. He was born an alcoholic, raised an alcoholic, and unable to break his addiction as an adult. He has been unfairly targeted, picked on by a society which doesn't understand or care about the consequences of..."

"Are you trying to break my heart?" the judge interrupted sarcastically. "I appreciate your sympathy and concern for your client but I can't allow you to continue with this argument. I too, was raised by an alcoholic parent, way back in the olden days when it was legal to drink Devil Liquor."

The courtroom broke into amused laughter. Judge Horton smiled, gratified his comment had drawn a positive response from the onlookers. He held up his hand to quiet things down. Bubba's attorney contemplated an appeal, meaning more hours away from boring bankruptcy cases. Unbeknownst to him, the judge's comment wasn't enough to get a case overturned. The term *Devil Liquor*, an old standby for preachers, is not considered prejudiced or judgmental. Alcohol put more people through hell and damnation than Satan in his wildest dreams could hope for. Judge Horton continued.

"The argument doesn't wash. With the help of treatment and anti-addiction drugs, I gave up the sauce when it became illegal. And look at me today. I'll admit it was hard, but I succeeded and so did most everyone else. I'm afraid I'm going to rule you out of order. Now do you have anything more you'd like to add which will aid in the defense?"

"Could we take a one hour recess?" counsel asked disappointedly. "I'd like to consult with my client."

"Done!" Judge Horton slammed the gavel without hesitation. His vehemence almost cost a pair of wire-rim glasses parked a little too close to the point of impact. "This court recesses for one hour, at which time we will probably reconvene long enough to consider another recess for lunch." Judge J. J. Horton disappeared into his chambers.

The Alpha boys stood up and stretched. Bubba was escorted to a locked conference room where he and his attorney could consult. Everyone else queued from the courtroom and headed for the coffee bar. "Bubba's attorney will attempt to convince him to throw in the towel," Cy informed. "This could be over before lunch."

"It sure gets exciting," Sarge yawned. "Now I know why I didn't become a lawyer."

"It's not too late to lower your standards a half-dozen notches and head off to law school." Cy laughed and shook his head. "Our next shift starts in thirteen hours. We might as well get some rest. The judge knows of Bubba's propensity for outbursts so that shouldn't be a problem. Besides, he has the mute button. The slightest sign of things getting out of control and he'll cut the signal to the outside world. Only the people in the courtroom will know what's going on."

"I'll bet Bubba doesn't realize he has that button," Bo replied. "He thinks he's going to be a TV star. Either way, we can watch it on the DynaView tonight at work. Whose turn is it to bring donuts?"

Everyone looked at the attorney. "Okay, I get the message," Cy acquiesced. "But it's not going to be donuts. I'll bring something healthy."

"Tofu," Sarge warned, "and you'll be stuck in a locker."

"Got it," Cy replied. "But it'd take all four of you to get me in there. I get claustrophobic." All smiled as they headed for the door. Cy questioned rhetorically. "I wonder what's available in the FBI lounge?"

FUTUREBUST5.4

Lieutenant Bo MacKinsey exited the courthouse, deep in thought. He sensed things were out of kilter, skewed as if the cosmic equilibrium of universal mind-stuff had shifted along elemental vibrational wavelengths; the space-time continuum was out of whack with generally accepted parameters; psychic balances weren't jiving with planetary inertia. In short, something didn't seem kosher. Bo laughed at the flakey thoughts running through his head. It sounded like the first pages of a *Psychic Romance* novel. He'd consult with Jim on the matter. The pilot had spoken of hearing mystery novels playing in his head.

Bo left the Civic Center after the ten o'clock recess with Cy, Larry, Jim, and Sarge, but decided to head home instead of grabbing a bite to eat with the others. He enjoyed fresh air and exercise: walking or cycling when something was on his mind. He strolled up Broadway and stopped on the freeway overpass, gazing down at the automobiles. Things looked quiet for the most part. Rush hour traffic had receded, thus the MFIP, Motorist Frustration Incendiary Potential was down to acceptable levels. Those following such things can tune to Road Rage Radio, billed as *high-octane coverage of lively highway exchanges*. It's part of a disturbing trend. Anything confrontational, belligerent, or in-your-face, some media mogul is sure to exploit.

He paused to take in the moment. The stately hybrid Elms planted along the roadway two decades previous to replace the dying palm trees, were awe-inspiring, fully leafed-out. Bo leaned on the overpass railing and stared at the midmorning traffic, his mind focused inward. Realizing the bright summer sun was affecting his eyes, he donned a pair of sunglasses, then turned his attention northeast towards the Golden State Freeway, a couple miles away. Something was going on over there. He could see Cat-three media turbocraft swarming like bees, heading northward. They looked so small in the distance, yet Bo knew he was witnessing a televised chase. The police turbocraft, painted in the colors blue and white, (thus were referred to as *Blue & Whites*) could easily follow for hours. Bo could not actually see the chase, just the turbocraft above.

He watched in troubled silence. The suspects often tried to run, reeking havoc with traffic patterns, needlessly endangering life and property. It's a forgone conclusion they'd be caught. An automobile can't outrun a turbocraft—never had and never will. The media followed, hoping to get a ratings booster—great live pictures of the chase and maybe a spectacular crash. There were at least two-dozen media Cat-threes overhead.

As they disappeared into the distance, Bo ran the list through his mind: The Police Chase Channel, Mobile Surveillance TV, the High-Speed Pursuit Channel, On-the-Run Network, Speed-and-Crash, and a shameless media company known as CRUNCH, which implied lots of accidents. One called itself FirstChase, claiming to be first on the scene of any high-speed pursuit. Another: The Pursue Review, a daily encapsulation of police pursuits in the country. All are media corporations that specialize in chases, covering the entire nation with satellite feeds. If little is happening live, there are plenty of decades-old reruns, complete with slow-motion, in-depth, play-by-play analysis. High ratings and profits drive the networks. In a way it's sad and troubling, but people love it. Truly, society is flawed.

Bo turned his back to the railing and looked west, the sun now behind him. His mind focused on the Franklin case. Bubba's arrest had troubled him from the beginning, including the FBI dudes who arrived with Dolly. Though both had hair covering their ears and foreheads, only one retained locks down past his shoulders (the guy with the pony tail). The other looked like a mop-top cop needing the services of a good barber. Strange! Who ever heard of shorthair

FBI dudes, except maybe on old TV reruns. Things were imperceptibly moving towards a new and possibly unwelcome paradigm.

FBI is the largest tenant (IRS was second) at HQ, with floors 1—6, 8—12, and 15—36, including all but six of the allotted parking spaces in the underground garage for the first thirty-six floors. The fourteenth floor had two of those spaces, leaving DES with four.

DES and FBI got along fine, except after a major drug bust when all the glory focused on drug enforcement. At such times, FBI jealously guarded its sovereignty and could even be vindictive. Those four spaces would inexplicably be reduced to three. In business more than a century, the feds had enough Congressional backing to throw weight around, and weren't afraid to do so.

In a fit of anger, Sarge once referred to the FBI as the Federal Bureau of Ineptitude when they screwed up a case both agencies worked on together. It was budget time and the Feds knew a big seizure would bolster their crime-fighting image in Congress. Money was scarce during the depression. Spectacular arrests meant publicity. The Feds jumped the gun, trying to make the collar of a drug kingpin before being fully prepared, and without DES knowledge or cooperation. In an attempt to steal the glory, they blew the case—turned it into an embarrassing failure. The drug kingpin got away and later taunted the FBI by giving a live phone interview on talk radio. Never apprehended, he expanded into terrorism and contract killings of government officials—not a bad sideline for a former tobacco executive. Sarge swore on the brass bell of his new boat that he'd someday catch the guy.

His loudly worded derogatory comments didn't go unnoticed by the Feds. Still, there was no one at the bureau large enough, strong enough, or fast enough to intimidate the big man. But the next day, down in the parking garage, three of those ubiquitous, dull, clunky-looking black Fords with plain-jane hubcaps were parked in precious DES spaces and they didn't move for weeks. The gesture was meant to intimidate.

During less severe parking space droughts, Dolly, Sarge, and Larry had seniority; though Sarge and Larry arrived at work together, and Dolly worked days. Fortunately, FBI didn't know that. Captain Jackson always rode his favorite perk, the SkyLimo, so three spaces was no sweat if it became necessary. Walking or bicycling to work was the only fashionable pastime Bo involved himself with. Cy likewise, along with Jim—they live in or near downtown. The mechanics, Big Al and Zeke, rode the city bus. That often left one space for the lowest guy on the totem pole, Lance. His 2038 GTX Ford looked great sitting there anyway, the only hydrogen fueled muscle car ever mass-produced, and it made FBI dudes green with envy.

Bo recalled how the whole building had gathered around when Lance first started work. The rookie nervously called security to keep the Feds from rubbing their hands over the custom yellow paint job, which included a tricolor holographic, three-part offset racing stripe running the length of the vehicle. He also asked them to stop kicking the titanium wheels. Lance understood why they liked the car, even appreciated their compliments. He just didn't want them leaving finger marks and smudges all over the Synthwax shine.

Bo took a lung-expanding breath as his mind returned to the FBI investigators at Bubba's house. Could shorthair cops make a comeback? Fat chance! It'd be like steam engines replacing Maglevs, or double-knit suits becoming popular again. He looked down at his faded jeans. The left knee sported a small, one-inch hole—just barely started. The right knee—considerably larger. Still, it's way too early to think about a new pair. Bo smiled as he leaned on the railing. There's a company on TV marketing pre-ripped jeans. That means his *rip-shred* style is coming into fashion. He'll consider donning unblemished clothes if that happens.

Bubba's lawyer might have a field day. Fashion-wise the guy is a real pro, and from Bankruptcy Court. No doubt, plenty of criminal trial experience to be gained over there. The legal profession sure is generous when it comes to defending the poor, less privileged, destitute, disenfranchised, or underfinanced. Oh well, Bo sighed to himself, they're lawyers. They thrive at the bottom of the social-consciousness ladder, a couple notches below doctors. Anything you get from such people is a pleasant surprise. Keeping attorneys from scraping absolute bottom are corporate CEOs, drug dealers, and weapons smugglers. God help us if any of them decide to reform. There'd be nowhere lower for lawyers to aspire to. Well, maybe diet books. But Bubba's counsel wore double-knits, much like a TV weatherman...heck, you'd have to go back seven decades to the 1970s to experience such an abomination, except maybe for used car salesmen! Double-knits won't come back into fashion. Hopefully never. God help us!

Bo shook his head. How would one describe Bubba's lawyer? Sarge, with no malice intended, would call him a *twerp*, defined as a person who wore double-knits in court. Larry would see it differently. The guy's a *dork*, defined as a foolish lawyer attired in double-knits. Cy would refer to him as a *klutz*, a lawyer lacking fashion sense. And Jim wouldn't say anything—just shake his head and mimic the guy's mannerisms. But Jim's photographic memory might settle on the word *dolt*. Dolly would wince and refer to him as a *spaz*, using that label with anyone who made her nervous. So that left *dwebe*. That's what Bo would call him. He wondered what the word signified. When he got the chance, he'd check a dictionary.

Dork, Dolt, Twerp, Klutz, Spaz, and Dwebe—all once used by adolescents to taunt classmates. But over time, the meanings changed. Each is now apropos only to attorneys. Bubba's lawyer should think seriously about a complete image-makeover home-study correspondence course, initiated by getting rid of the double-knits.

Then there's Lance. He often used the word *doofus*—probably the way to go. A doofus attorney! But Bo had no idea what a doofus was either. He'd ask Lance later.

Bo crossed the overpass and resumed walking towards his parent's quake-resistant luxury apartment, sporting a large and adamant doorman one tipped handsomely to get past. Bo lived in a less well-to-do apartment a few blocks further on—a building standing on the sight of old Dodger Stadium—part of a huge mega-mall, apartment complex. Bo resides twenty-three stories above left field. He gazed at the highrise structures north of his current location, which concentrated so many people in a small area.

The Los Angeles Online Herald and Gazette recently reported that the city picked up four additional seats in Congress due to the increased population from the 2040 census. The last ten years made a difference. South California now had eight percent, or thirty-seven of the 465 seats. Much less densely populated, except for the San Francisco-Sacramento megalopolis, North California had nineteen seats, or four percent. But together, the two Californias had fifty-six seats, or twelve percent, plus four Senators.

Of course, the East Coast whiners were not happy. The Boston-New York-Philadelphia-Baltimore-Washington megalopolis lost a dozen seats a decade previous after warmer temperatures and catastrophically elevated sea levels chased scores of coastal lowland residents westward to higher ground. Though prohibitively expensive and difficult to maintain, they managed to dike Manhattan, but it was too little too late. Gale-reinforced waves easily roll over twelve-foot dikes—typical for a *government* project. At additional cost, the water must be mopped up before mosquitoes breed in warm puddles and ponds, causing an outbreak of antibiotic-resistant yellow fever or malaria.

Then there's the Fresh Kills landfill disaster on Staten Island, NY. Millions of tons of garbage were in danger of washing away during Freak Tides, (very high water) and storm surges. It became the costliest superfund site of all time, taking decades to clean up. All this occurred after a catastrophic collapse of the West Antarctic Ice Sheet in 2027. Sea level rose nine feet with no end in sight. Those twelve-foot dikes had to be augmented and reinforced at huge additional expense to the taxpayer! Another result of higher sea level in the New York area is that Long Island is no longer as long as it used to be. Most of the eastern forty miles disappeared under high tides and a menagerie of perfect storms. Too bad! It was a top-drawer neighborhood. The fastest way for any real estate bubble to burst is for the area to become a mosquito-infested swamp. Rising sea levels made it a snap. It's now protected by federal law as a sanctuary for migratory waterfowl using the Atlantic flyway to reach breeding grounds in Canada.

Washington DC had a different problem related to global warming. Congress was forced to think ahead because it was too late to try any other option. Previously, the lowest point in town was above sea level. But no more, and lawmakers are squeamish. Afraid of getting their feet wet, they decided to move the city to higher ground before things get too damp, and a study was commissioned to determine the feasibility. Despite cutthroat competition, a site, christened New Washington, was picked in West Virginia. It'd be a 120-year project moving every historic building and monument, and cost unknown hundreds of billions. But the new city might look much as the old had, minus one small detail known as the Potomac. A senator from West Virginia controlled the Appropriations Committee so prospects look good. Sea level is rising and can't be stopped.

True, there's little to be gained by letting the rest of the town rot. They'd tried that before and it didn't work. So if the government clears out, DC will convert to a theme park with an emphasis on water, including oceanfront condos built on stilts.

South of DC, there are other large population centers, with Atlanta leading the way. It's one big town now, stretching north into the Blue Ridge Mountains; south to Macon; and east and west to the state lines. Further south: the once thriving Miami-Ft. Lauderdale megalopolis is now under water. However proactive Orlando survived thanks to a $70 billion reclamation project. Storm surges swamped Daytona Beach, but the 500-mile race is still an all-American tradition in February. The high banked curves at the raceway double as dikes. Little else has changed. Speeds are frightening with plenty of crashes. To see the race live, anchor your boat in the lot and wade to the grandstands. Get there early before the good seats are gone.

Fort Myers and St. Petersburg-Tampa were destroyed in Gulf Coast hurricanes. Pensacola also went under the waves. The United States Navy now trains carrier-based fighter pilots in Buffalo, New York where the climate is more seasonable.

Sure, looking at things positively, Atlanta is still high and dry, as long as it doesn't rain too hard. But southern Florida, and Louisiana Cajun country are gone. Alabama's coastline suffered terribly when the beautiful and historic city of Mobile was destroyed. It went under the waves despite a massive attempt to save it. Yankees from as far north as Minnesota and Wisconsin came south to pitch in with everything they had, but to no avail. The Gulf had the final word and swept everything away in a single, powerful hurricane.

That's the real tragedy. The Mississippi Delta and Bayou country are submerged, along with other Gulf Coast marshlands. The Everglades disappeared. Hurricane Nigel eventually destroyed Miami. Though the storm had a sissy name, its winds were devastating at over 180 miles per hour. New Orleans was destroyed by higher sea levels. New & Improved Orleans is built a few miles north on higher, more stable ground. If wanting to take a nice seaside drive through Louisiana, Interstate 10 is where you'd head. With the Florida Keys washed away, the southern-most point in the contiguous United States is now in Texas, and the locals are proud of it.

Except for a stilt city (a hundred thousand refusniks who wouldn't leave their homes) which sprang up in the shallow water that was once south Florida, people fled by the millions, taking with them their coveted seats in the House of Representatives. Many ended up in Atlanta, which infuriated the natives who didn't want to see their city overrun by *Southerners*. But Floridians were desperately searching for a patch of dry ground, to set down roots that wouldn't get washed away by the first high tide. The state of Georgia is one of the most populous in the country, behind South California, Ohio, Alaska, Michigan, Wisconsin, Minnesota, and Idaho. There's hardly room for a peach tree to grow. You can live anywhere as long as it's not near the coast, which moved inward by miles in some places. The Outer Banks are now protected reefs, the perfect habitat for pearl oysters. Interstate 95 between Savannah and Jacksonville was washed away by high tides and storm swells. It didn't matter. Both cities are a fond memory.

Global warming is not a popular subject. People figured things out fast once it was too late to save the coastline. Care to purchase an option on beachfront property in Arizona? Scientists speculate that if all the ice on Antarctica and Greenland melts, sea level will rise hundreds of feet. Lake Ontario is only 236 feet higher so it might become part of the ocean. Even Niagara Falls could be threatened. Skyscrapers in coastal cities will have to deal with serious moisture problems on lower levels.

Despite Global Warming being ignored in the early part of the century, it turned out to be a very big issue. In a sense, the US was one all-consuming nation placing itself above God. There were solutions too, plenty of them if instituted in time. There was too much concern for the economy over the environment. The halfwits in government forgot that the country's economic foundation is dependent on the environment. They figured things out only after it started to disappear under saltwater and they found themselves carried by a riptide towards impending doom.

In contrast, forward thinking Californians prepared years before with progressive planning and zoning, and High Water Dissipation Structures. They admirably accomplished the engineering goals of saving the Pacific shoreline and preserving sensitive coastal ecological sites. So federal spending-wise, the heartland, along with the West Coast feasted, while the East Coast famined.

Proactive thinking does pay off handsomely; however getting people to plan ahead is difficult, especially if it involves spending money to achieve a far-off result. Maybe it's nothing more than the fact that the two Californias seem to have good karma. But if sea level continues to rise, that shoreline will be gone also. An additional seven feet has been predicted by 2080.

Still, everything about global warming isn't negative. Southwestern states, along with northern Mexico, went from dry and arid to lush and tropical with additional rain. And you can now purchase oceanfront property in northern Canada up near the Arctic Circle with no money down. And what comes to mind when the word *Greenland* is spoken? Green land, of course. Lots of it, a whole unspoiled continent. After ocean currents changed directions, some of the nicest beachfront condos in the world were built on the southern slopes of Greenland. The large chunk of land finally, after centuries of trying, lived up to its name and did so spectacularly. If anyone is interested in a timeshare lease contract, contact Lars Eriksson or Sven Johansson in North Copenhagen. They thought of it before anybody else. And Greenland's freshwater, aged thousands of years while locked up in glaciers, is bottled and shipped all over the world, sold under the labels: Greenland, Age-Old, and Glacier Melt. It was thawing anyway, so why not bottle it?

A little-known island emerged from the icepack just above the Arctic Circle as the polar caps receded. Spitsbergen—most people had never heard of it, located north of Norway, but the reindeer know where it is. Previously, no one cared if the place existed. It's now considered a summer retreat for the rich and famous—a land of the midnight sun.

Bo smiled as he continued past his parents' apartment, deciding not to stop in for lunch. He contemplated how hard it must have been to work as a drug cop before NOSTRILS was invented. They'd fly over residential subdivisions in rickety helicopters equipped with Infrared cameras (probably unconstitutional) that detect heat radiating from structures, indicating excessive use of electricity for grow lights or drug labs. But most drug busts back in the old days involved painstaking undercover work along with paid informants. Tedious, time-consuming, and dangerous, investigations often netted only the small fish, leaving the sharks swimming in a pool of money. That's just the way it worked out. Bo mentally tipped his hat to the old drug fighters. There was substance abuse, broken marriages, and suicides among officers because of the emotional strain of such work.

Later, things got a little touchier, Supreme Court-wise. Big Brother's rise to prominence was initiated. NOSTRILS came first, an electronic version of what police dogs had been doing for decades—sniffing for drugs, only on a much larger scale. Big Brother was searching! Big Brother was intruding! That, of course is all true. Big Brother had always been a big snoop. But the

Fourth Amendment contained the word *unreasonable,* the focal point of legal arguments. High-priced Constitutional lawyers made a fortune splitting hairs until unreasonable was defined more in step with dangerous times. Fighting terrorism was the justification, though NOSTRILS worked equally well in all law enforcement situations. No doubt there was some semantic hocus-pocus at the high court, but it wasn't the first time that happened. NOSTRILS made it through the controversy with closely defined working parameters and plenty of judicial oversight. The technology, if used in moderate amounts, is non-invasive, non-drowsy, non-habit-forming, and most important, nonaddicting. It works at the subatomic level, well below the molecular protections guaranteed by the Fourth Amendment. However, drug use proponents labeled the Supreme Court's decision *an odious deprivation of liberty*—fancy language from the malcontents.

It was the Neutrino Camera, or NC for short, which finally became the real *Big Brother* issue. A camera that could see through walls! Early versions developed in the last century were so rudimentary, no one gave them a second thought until the cloudy, distorted, and indecipherable picture began to clear up with technological advancement. Again, the Orwellian cry of Big Brother was heard throughout the land. Of course it didn't wash. With a warrant, and even without a warrant if part of the NSA, one could listen to conversations and/or videotape activities. The Neutrino Camera just made it a lot easier, and the Online Judge, a whole lot quicker.

The inexorable march of technological progress in law enforcement was unstoppable, and early-century terrorism was the catalyst. As the decades passed, the complaining slowed to a trickle. The results were spectacular. Bad people were easily located and stuffed in jail using a molecular scan with a sample of DNA. Of course, a warrant was required. Good people were left alone unless a rogue Attorney General gained control of the Justice Department. But that happened only four or five times in the last century. The one *given* is that society must implicitly trust the people who wield technological power. The DES earned this trust over the decades. Even the NSA reined itself in and learned to live within the confines of the Constitution. And wonder of wonders, people trusted the IRS. They had to. IRS is the only regulative body of government making sure everyone not covered by loopholes pays their tax liability. Say it isn't so? There's no argument from the wealthy. Most now realize that paying their fair share is the patriotic thing to do, like serving one's country in the military. The rich routinely choose the former. It's easier to shell out cash than put one's life on the line.

Still, Bo didn't like the Neutrino Camera. It's so intrusive with private residences—a fine moral line to walk. Even with the okay from the Online Judge, he considered it an invasion of privacy and infringement of rights—not to mention that if used, judicial oversight is intensive; paperwork oppressive. Besides, most cops get into the business, at least partially for excitement. The NC creates so much of an advantage, there's hardly even a chance to get shot at. The perp's actions are an open book. Old time cops handled drug busts with courage and bravery, facing lethal firepower from violent perps. Bo felt modern cops could do the same. Deep in his heart, he hoped his hesitance would not get an officer under his command killed in the line of duty. The NC is most advantageous to society if kept within the terrorism arena. No one cares much for the civil rights of such people.

Finally, The *BEAM* was invented. Yes, The *BEAM*. It stands for "Blocking Energized Anti-Magnetism". Bo laughed. The word must be spoken with exaggerated emphasis, foreboding, and fear evident in the voice and eyes. For decades, the military sought ways to disrupt the electromagnetic field around an object like a tank or truck, or even a radar site, rendering it temporarily useless, but not destroyed. Previously, they learned how to mess up the electromagnetic field around a large site like a whole city. They could even do a battlefield. But excessive damage was the problem: lots of fried circuits on otherwise salvageable machinery.

On the civilian side of things, the *BEAM* had the potential to stop a vehicle in its tracks: electronically kill the engine, yet it's not as easy as it sounds. Focusing on a fast-moving object like a car is touch-and-go. The *BEAM* has to be aimed carefully or it might disturb the bioplasma surrounding the driver's body, thus endangering other motorists with the possibility of a crash. The *BEAM* dramatically slows metabolism and lowers the body temperature of living creatures. It also reduces oxygen uptake by the lungs, thereby inducing sleep. It has the potential to be a very big crime-fighting tool, but the Supreme Court limited it to nonhuman living creatures. Law enforcement calls it Freeze-drying.

More technological advancement is needed before the instrument can be fully utilized. But the writing's on the wall. When perfected, it'll be feasible for a police turbocraft to stop fleeing vehicles, thereby eliminating high-speed free-for-alls on the highway. Disrupt the electromagnetic field around the motor and the car or truck will not run. The chase is over—the danger avoided. Every police force in the country drools at the possibility of ending its worst nightmare—pursuit scenarios, forever and for all time. Good riddance. Too many lives, both civilian and law enforcement, have been sacrificed in the past.

The ramifications aren't lost on the various television channels that specialize in such matters. Police chases are considered prime viewing by such entities, and the pursuant advertising revenue is substantial. Competition between networks is fierce: who can get the most spectacular chases and thereby the greatest viewership. These channels constantly advertise that they are first on the scene with the latest breaking chases, the best camera equipment, highest speeds, and most dangerous situations.

In a big city like Los Angeles, as many as forty media turbocraft might be involved in a chase, counting local and national news channels. They'll swarm the action like hornets, creating havoc in the skies. The government proposed banning such coverage due to the skyward danger, but there's that pesky First Amendment to deal with. And besides, once The *BEAM* can be aimed safely, the problem will be solved. No more police chases!

For the networks making their bread and butter thus, the milk and cookies will soon be gone. The advertising moola will dry up—their cash cow slaughtered and ground into pet food. Bo had long ago decided the sooner the better. In the meantime, the multifarious chase channels are grabbing for every crumb; fighting fiercely for market share. It's all nonsense but what to do. If the soap operas get a little tiring, switch to a current live highway chase going on somewhere in the world. Viewing never has to be dull or boring. It's reality TV run amuck, and says something about the nation we'd become. Bo knew it wasn't a positive reflection on the people of America.

From a technological standpoint, NOSTRILS was the best thing to come down the pike since two-way radio. Older technology won't even pick up on tobacco and alcohol violations—of course no one was concerned with such things in those days—and it always involved someone looking through the device, snooping into the affairs of others. NOSTRILS found Bubba without straining an electronic nose hair. It'd sense anything from bubble gum (if it happened to become illegal) to explosives—homing in on distinct, easily identified subatomic patterns. At a million dollars per copy, it can be made small and light enough to fit into a turbocraft, which is not much bigger than a large bathtub (though considerably more maneuverable). NOSTRILS and the NC are the most successful law enforcement and antiterrorist devices ever invented. Congress made them legal when they upgraded the PATRIOT III Act, which stands for: *Provide Appropriate Tools Required to Intercept and Obstruct Terrorism.* It did just that. If a bad guy needs locating, load a sample of DNA into NOSTRILS and head to his last known whereabouts. It put a big dent in the ongoing terrorism menace. But nonconformists have another idea of what PATRIOT stands for: *Pervert America's Treasured Rights by Idiotic, Oligarchic Tyranny.* So who listens to fanatics?

As for Bubba, he'd soon be heading to the FedPen, like all users of dangerous drugs have been doing for the last century or so...well, not all users. We're back to that alcohol-tobacco sticking point again. In the old days, only selected drug abusers went to prison: the counterculture, low income, barrio-ghetto-slum-inner-city addicts ended up in jail; their possessions confiscated and families devastated. With alcohol, even a (fatal accident) drunk driver could get off with a suspended sentence if he had the money for a good lawyer. And tobacco—who cared about the millions of casualties every year around the world. In the US as elsewhere, too much money was being made! But that's all past. A new marshal is in town and he has NOSTRILS—Supreme Court endorsed—in his holster. To paraphrase Bobby Fuller: You can fight the law, but the law's going to win.

Bo continued walking. He thought about Judge Horton and his chevrons. Judges wear such robes only on special occasions, usually when cameras are present. Bo contemplated His Honor's distinguished gray hair. Heck, old guys always look distinguished, even shorthairs—even when they turn out to be communists. But that's what bugged him: image-consciousness. It's shallow—incorrect—hollow and empty. How he disliked image. It's a cover for lack of substance, character, emotional depth, or core moral values and human decency.

He entered his highrise and took the twenty-three flights of stairs on foot for a little extra exercise and added time to think. The D. A. will confiscate Bubba's house, courtesy of the Controlled Substance Confiscation Act. The money pays expenses incurred by society to put drug abusers in jail. Those laws are tough on addicts, making down-on-their-luck individuals even *downer*-on-their-luck when they get out. But that's what the people want—GTLs, Get Tough Laws. The politicians have said it for decades. The law is the law! Can't coddle criminals!

Bo locked his door, lay down on the couch, and turned on the Big Screen—channel 141—Mega Court, Mega Cases, Mega Controversy, and Mega Sentences. Six minutes of advertisements followed—thank goodness for the mute button. He hoped the individual who'd invented it ended up a millionaire. Incessant pitch men sold everything from shaving cream guaranteed to make your girl go crazy, to Super Toasted Oatsters, (along with Sugar Fortified Toasted Oatsters) the cereal that's *Smart for your Heart*. When Bubba's case recaptured the screen, Bo had long since rested his head against a pillow, closed his eyes and dozed off to sleep.

FUTUREBUST5.65

Bubba stared blankly downward, sulking at a table in the tiny conference room. He said nothing and had no interest in listening to his attorney. Bubba wanted to think about what he was going to say to that judge—an outburst of epic proportions shaking the very foundations of the world! He'd come up with a plethora of insults over the last twenty-four hours, drawing on his experience in the military and the manly language used when the boys got together. But a few more ideas wouldn't hurt. He wanted to tell the whole world where to go and he had the forum to do just that. Nothing could be more ideal, short of a spot on talk radio. But as offensive and spirited as it sometimes is, producers would never let him say what he wanted, the way he wanted. Bubba did not intend to waste a golden, court-appointed opportunity. He couldn't believe they were all so stupid.

His attorney was yakking something about a belated plea bargain, but he didn't hear a word spoken. Bubba sat silently and contemplated—lost in his own world. His best bet for an outburst would be just after lunch when full tummies cause most to let down their guard. That's when it would take place. So far, he'd been a good boy—on best behavior—causing no trouble in the courtroom. They wouldn't suspect a thing. He'd let everyone on the planet know how he felt about their laws, and precisely what they could do with them!

"Do you have any feeling on this matter?" his court appointed lover-boy asked, as if the guy really cared. Bubba knew he was more interested in impressing that good-looking lady prosecutor with charity legal work. Women eat that stuff up. It proves he's sensitive. What else she saw in him, God only knew. But like most lawyers, the guy was an opportunist, exploiting a gravy train of free publicity in front of the TV cameras to make a name for himself, something to cash in on later. Well, if that's the case, Bubba would show him how it's done.

"No," Bubba replied gruffly, not looking up as he spoke.

"It's your life," counsel responded tersely, shaking his head. He knocked on the door. Two guards escorted them back to the courtroom.

Bubba sulked. He was contemplating five years on the rock pile and his attorney wears fashions from the 1970s. No one the defendant knew could even remember those days. Bubba slouched in his chair. He wanted to look demoralized, like a beaten man—like he had no fight left in him. Then they'd find out how wrong they were!

An hour passed. It was 11:00. Everyone expectantly waited for the judge to reenter. The recess had been for only an hour. The bailiff stood ready to announce the arrival of His Honor with a timely *All rise*, but the judge hadn't signaled his return. They waited. Another hour passed slowly—it was now just after noon. Bubba was getting antsy, but kept still. He didn't want to jeopardize his chance at bad-boy celebrity stardom. 12:15—the judge still had not returned. He was an hour and a quarter late. The guards were concerned, yet dared not do anything. 12:30—no judge. The minutes ticked by slowly. 12:31. Bubba started to fidget and squirm. One of the guards approached the defense and put his hand gently but firmly on Bubba's shoulder, then squeezed as if to say: *Keep cool, dude. Nobody's going anywhere.* Then finally, at 12:34…

"All rise. Twelfth Judicial District, Honorable Judge J. J. Horton presiding."

"Please be seated." His honor sat brusquely at the bench, looking harried and upset, though he was clearly trying to conceal his emotional discomfort. "I'm sorry for the delay but it was unavoidable." He shuffled papers and tried to focus. "Does the defense wish to add to what was said earlier?"

"No, your honor," Mr. Double-knit replied with a shrug. "Other than to ask that the charges be dropped." Bubba looked miffed. He'd hoped there would be further vindication involved in his defense. He didn't think it'd be over that quickly. There had to be more. His lawyer hadn't said anything of consequence. Bubba looked at the judge in confusion.

Horton continued: "In that case, I'll hand down my ruling immediately."

There was an audible gasp within the courtroom. Such decisions usually take twenty-four to forty-eight hours, involving thoughtful deliberation and the weighing of facts. Bubba was caught off guard—his carefully planned outburst about to be preempted. It could not be executed if…he had to do it right then, at that very moment or the opportunity would be lost forever. He was just about to EXPLODE!!!

Judge Horton was surprisingly swift with his pronouncement. "On the charge of assault: guilty! Thirty days, sentence suspended. On the charge of illegal weapons and explosives: guilty! One year plus timed served. On the charge of possessing drug paraphernalia: guilty! Sixty days. All other charges are dropped!" *SLAM.* His Honor walloped the gavel with awesome authority. "This court is hereby adjourned!"

Everyone sat stunned as the judge rose from his chair and disappeared into his chambers. The courtroom remained momentarily silent. Muffled cheers could be heard coming from deep in the building through the ventilation system. A slight murmur began to mount, first slowly, then with pronounced momentum. People looked at each other in confusion as if to say: What's this all about? What does it mean? Finally it began to sink in.

Bubba had essentially been acquitted! He was looking at no more than fourteen months in the klink. He might even keep his house if willing to try some do-it-yourself handyman legal work while incarcerated. Bubba's attorney was ecstatic. He grabbed his client by the shoulders and shook him. The double-knit lover-boy knew he had just hit the jackpot. He'd essentially won a court victory in front of millions of viewers. There'd be interviews, party invitations, maybe an appearance on a late night talk show. He'd need an agent and a manager to look after his affairs while he lapped up the gravy in celebrityland. He was definitely going to need a new wardrobe!

FUTUREBUST

Bubba didn't understand the implications. Guilty! Guilty! What was all the commotion about? Why was his attorney so happy to see him go to jail? Then slowly, it hit him too. He'd be a free man in a little over a year. A free man! Not ten years nor five. He'd be out of the slammer by next summer. He'd rub elbows with the corrupt CEOs and politicians in the minimum-security wing—a piece of cake! He grabbed the double-knit clad girley-man and almost hugged him. Drug offenses are serious business. Three convictions often mean life in prison, and thousands had been so sentenced since the 1990s. But he'd be free in fourteen months. A done deal! Damn, if he'd just had a beer to celebrate. It was an unforgivable lost opportunity to get drunk.

The prosecutor was shocked, shrugging her shoulders in disbelief. "Nice job," she congratulated. "Any idea what just happened here?"

"Not a clue," counsel replied, standing straight and tall, attempting to button his jacket. Two days in court with the same outfit; he felt proud. "You owe me dinner at your place. Let me know when it's convenient."

"I'll do that," she said, still shaking her head. Looking inconspicuous as possible, she picked up her briefcase and ducked out the door with everybody else. The two guards with Bubba from the beginning, put the cuffs on their smiling prisoner and escorted him to his holding cell. Four hundred twenty-five days at *Camp WalkAway*, and he'd be a free man.

FUTUREBUST5.7

Bo awoke at 11 PM, rubbed his eyes and checked the clock—already late for work, sleeping in his clothes on the couch. The Big Screen was still on, but Bubba's trial ended hours earlier. Bo mercifully slept through the broadcast, thanks to the mute button (an invention having world-shaking ramifications right up there with the wheel, fire, electricity, and Pro Wrestling's Battle Royal Rumble—a high ratings, unlimited, no-holds-barred, ten-man, everyone-against-everyone free-for-all that the promoters swore was not rigged in advance. They even put up a million dollar bond payable to anyone who could prove otherwise.).

Bo sat up and gazed at the television, hardly enthused by the MegaCourt's latest offering; an ancient rerun of some old Hollywood celebrity-type movie star actor's much publicized trial for slapping a cop during a routine traffic stop. He rubbed his eyes and read the headlines scrolled across the bottom of the screen to see what he'd missed, expecting news of Bubba's conviction, plenty of mandatory jail time and a hefty fine for good measure. Five years would be the minimum for the crimes Bubba had perpetrated on society.

Bo's eyes opened wide and muscles tensed as he gazed at the screen.

Fourteen months plus time served? It didn't make sense! He grabbed a clean shirt, keys, wallet, then commandeered the express elevator to the ground floor, hailed a taxi and paid the driver double if he'd step on it! Minutes later he arrived at Federal Law Enforcement Headquarters in downtown Los Angeles, bolted through the entrance without even waving to the foxy, late night FBI receptionist, jumped the security scanner, then took the stairs to the seventh floor and turned towards Cy's office while still buttoning his shirt. The DES attorney looked up from his desk, startled at the harried intrusion.

"Blind date?" the drug-busting legal eagle spoke with a muted smile. "You're running pretty fast."

"Did any of you guys see what happened at Bubba's trial after we left?"

"No one said anything." Cy grew concerned. "Was there an outburst? I thought the judge had a mute button."

"No outburst." Bo caught his breath. "I saw on the late-night headlines that Bubba's sentence was only fourteen months plus time served. He should have gotten sixty months and a fine." Bo shook his head and shrugged, arms outward in an *I don't know what's going on here* pose. Unusual. Bo always knew what was going on.

The DES attorney looked mindfully stunned and perplexed, putting a finger on his chin. "In three minutes I can have every bit of public information on Bubba ready for analysis. Other than that, it's a question mark to me."

"Do it! And check on Judge Horton at the same time."

"Horton? Are you thinking bribe?" Cy's eyebrows rose simultaneously. "Consider it done. But remember what I've told you in the past."

Bo shook his head and smiled for the first time since he'd arrived, then calmed Cy's fears. "I'm not asking for any illegal searches. She won't have to visit you in prison."

Cy spoke vehemently. "It's a promise I intend to keep. More lawyers are incarcerated for shenanigans, misdeeds, crime and/or evil than any other profession. Mama made me promise to avoid trouble after I passed the bar. She always was overprotective."

Bo nodded as he exited the legal office, then stopped, putting his head back through the door. "Route the requests via IA, just to be safe."

"You want I should make queries through LAPD's Internal Affairs computer? Sure thing, Boss." Cy's speech mimicked a backwoods bumpkin sheriff's deputy. "You'd think they'd have figured it out by now." Bo nodded and left the room. He was feeling both demoralized and excited. Normally, work involved lots of watching and waiting until Jim's sensors unearthed a perp. Things would get exciting for a few hours, then another month or two of tedium. But DES had not lost a case since…Heck, he couldn't remember losing one. Bo knew he'd find out what went wrong if it meant turning the judicial system inside out. That alone would alleviate the boredom.

He headed to the Command Center, sat down and contacted Jim, who was fifty miles out from HQ, searching for drugs in the Lake Forest, Mission Viejo area. The pilot looked at his comm. and noticed Bo's expression. "What's up?" Jim had not heard the news.

"How fast can you get to Judge Horton's?" There was no explanation.

Jim didn't question the inquiry, though his eyes narrowed. He typed Judge J. J. Horton's name into the computer. Instantly GPS showed His Honor's residence and Jim's current location. The pilot interpolated. "About twelve minutes."

"Make it eight! Confirm everything is normal in his neighborhood!"

Jim wrested control of the turbocraft from the in-flight computer and banked hard towards Glendale, throttling up full as he made the turn, a maneuver the FAA frowned on over residential areas because Jim didn't have a G-suit. He sucked in his gut, grimaced, and accelerated to over 325 miles per hour in seconds, then hit AFA (Auxiliary Fuel Augmentation), juicing the mix with a nominal bit of Pryotec (fuel accelerant). The thrusters kicked in hard to 445 mph, jamming him into the seat. M-CAS, the Midair Collision Avoidance System, showed clear sailing below two thousand feet. The sky was empty all the way to Glendale.

Back in the main office, the InstaPrint kicked into gear. Cy's web search was reaping results. Sarge left his chair to check it out and Bo joined him after ending the conversation with Jim. "See what you can find on Robert Franklin and Judge Horton. In case you haven't heard, Bubba received an extremely light sentence for his crimes. I want to know why." Sarge appeared stunned, but complied without saying a word. Bo continued as they walked to Sarge's desk. "Look for clout: political, financial, or any other noxious form thereof that might have swayed the judge. If His Honor has been threatened, I want to know who, where, and why. If he was bribed…" Bo didn't finish. He walked back to Cy's office. "It was an open-and-shut case. Can you think of anything?"

"We can watch the court record for ourselves."

Bo returned to the Command Center and scanned the monitors. Jim was halfway to Glendale, covering seven miles a minute at three hundred meters. The first two thousand feet of airspace is reserved for turbocraft. Higher than that he'd get mixed up with general aviation.

The comm. showed Jim's face was intense, concentrated on the task-at-hand. He'd been a turbocraft test pilot two decades earlier during initial certification, and had many stories to tell about those days—he could fill a book with them. At times like this, the man has no fear. He'd have less than a second to react to a major malfunction or be augured in. Jim was flying above Interstate 5. If he crashed, it'd be into concrete, not houses. The freeway was essentially empty at this time of night.

Mesmerized by the monitors, Bo watched city lights gliding quickly behind. The vehicle had four external cameras showing any direction he wanted. He switched from one to another. Jim's speed made it difficult to focus—hard on the eyes. Bo leaned back in his chair to think. If Judge Horton had been threatened or was in some kind of trouble, it might already be too late, making for a very difficult night. However if bribed, something not uncommon just two decades previous in the twenties...

Bo closed his eyes and pondered the situation, both personal and professional. Like the others in the office, he had a good stable job, a successful career. He had his whole life ahead of him. And now out of the blue—if this incident involved a bribe—he was about to investigate a federal judge. He even had Jim tearing across town in hopes of uncovering anything relevant. The possibility was slim, but...He glanced at the monitors as Jim decelerated over Glendale. Bo reviewed the Franklin bust six weeks previous. His mind probed the ether, searching for clues, answers; a reason for the unexpected outcome. The mental exercise turned up nothing. He was stumped, something not supposed to happen to a man of his character. The phone interrupted. It was the captain. Bo could see the senior officer was not pleased.

FUTUREBUST5.8

An astonishing judge of character, Captain Jackson knew what was going on like he had eyes in the back of his head. In fact, Bo often wondered if that's why the senior officer wore short hair. The captain was also adept at interpersonal analysis. Both men gazed at the other's expression on their respective phones.

"We're checking out the judge's neighborhood." Bo glanced at the turbocraft monitors as Jim hovered directly over the target house at four hundred meters. Nothing seemed out of place. He started westward towards what looked like a small park, though it was hard to make out in the dark. Bo's attention returned to the phone.

"I wouldn't worry about the judge," Captain Jackson spoke cautiously. "He's probably okay. I'll bet you're tearing up cyberspace right now." Bo didn't answer, waiting for him to continue. "You're search might not yield much, but give it a try." The captain rubbed his chin and thought carefully about what he was going to say. "That Cat-five we talked about last night is sitting on the factory floor in Las Vegas right now." Bo's eyes widened with surprise—caught off guard again. "That's right," Captain Jackson noticed the expression, "it's ready to go. Send Jim to Vegas on the Maglev. He can grab it and be back by 10 AM." The senior officer's eyes lit up. "Wait 'til you see what it can do!"

Bo exhaled as if doing a yoga exercise. "I didn't know it'd even been field-tested and approved for service yet. How'd they get it through certification so fast? Yesterday you tell us its development is years ahead of schedule and now I find out it's already flight-certified." He looked at the captain with a stunned stare. "This is completely out of character for me. No one's ever supposed to pull the wool over my eyes!"

"The Cat-five's existence is a secret," Captain Jackson explained with a nod. "Those not in the inner circle know only that the vehicle is in R&D, the earliest stages of planning and design. As far as answering your question on airworthiness certification"—Bo had not asked a question, but he remained silent—"we've been chosen to finish the testing."

Another stunned expression. "By who?"

"SecDef (Sec. of Defense) and the Pentagon," the captain replied matter-of-factly, as if he wasn't dropping a bombshell. "He doesn't know it yet, but Jim has volunteered to field-test the new technology. Most of the best, old-timer turbocraft test pilots in the country have retired, and those that remain don't have the military background the Pentagon is so fond of. So Jim got the job!"

"What difference does a military background make for a civilian vehicle?" Bo immediately wished he hadn't asked. Captain Jackson smiled sympathetically. Bo sat quietly, unsure of how to react. With an elbow resting on the desk, he knocked his fist against the side of his head.

"Still with me?" Captain Jackson watched the reaction on his phone. "I wanted to tell you guys earlier but it wasn't possible. The Pentagon boys are finicky about stuff like this!"

"What were you thinking when you agreed to this? We could be in over our heads."

"I'm not yet certain what's going on under the surface. And you're right. We may be in over our heads but we'll probably survive." Bo wasn't sure the word *probably* was a good or bad thing. The captain continued. "The objective is to get our new equipment up and running ASAP. Don't forget, the Pentagon was involved in drug interdiction before!"

"Yeah," Bo reminded, "a halfhearted effort often used as justification for wasteful spending. The results speak for themselves. WoD failed." A moment of silence followed.

"I'll tell you what, lieutenant." The captain rarely addressed him by his rank. Bo waited for the inevitable ultimatum. "You and the boys can bail if you want. Talk it over. It's your decision. Let me know tomorrow."

Lieutenant Bo MacKinsey was already outgunned. Darn child

psychology—it's mighty effective. Using the word *bail* implied he was chicken. "You're *Tom Sawyering* me. If that thing's so good, we'll give it a try. But the Pentagon?"

"Need-to-know," the captain answered without telling him anything. "I'll fill you in when it's necessary. In the meantime, go get the Cat-five and let's give her a rip. It'll take your mind off that court case." Bo looked at the screen but didn't like the expression on the captain's face. The senior officer obliged. "And there's one other thing I *forgot* to tell you." The word was used facetiously. "The CIA may be involved. But of course, that's rumor, innuendo, conjecture, speculation, half-truths, and some disinformation mixed in! Then sprinkle paranoia on top. And you didn't hear it from me." He smiled. "In fact, you and I have never met. You don't know me."

Bo laughed at the captain's humor, then changed the subject. "I hope it isn't as bad as all that. By the way, I'm arming everyone in the office. Things are getting unpredictable." He decided to inject his own humor. "Nonviolence is a good thing, but has its limitations."

"The pro wrestler's credo," Captain Jackson smiled, his voice sounding tired. "I'll see you in the morning, if not sooner."

Bo ended the transmission and closed his eyes. Some unproductive paperwork fell to the floor as he leaned away, landing in various hard-to-reach locations around his chair. He looked with detached annoyance, deciding to leave it and concentrate on more important matters. He wanted to make sense of the whole mess, collate and distill what he knew, or at least suspected. Need-to-know? That's just great. Disinformation? Even better.

He dissected the situation. There was Judge Horton handing down an irrational and professionally embarrassing sentence to an abuser of dangerous drugs. Plus a secret, uncertified Cat-five turbocraft ready years in advance of schedule, a hint of disinformation in itself. Also, the possibility of unwelcome and meddlesome Pentagon involvement in drug interdiction, probably illegal in the civilian arena. And the CIA—the Firm watching who-knows-who doing God-knows-what. On the home front, he had Cy involved in a cyber-search of a federal judge, and Jim snooping around His Honor's neighborhood in hopes of stumbling over a clue that might unravel the mess. Bo rubbed his forehead and decided to call his pilot.

Jim's face could not be seen on the screen. He was in covert mode—lights out in the turbocraft. "Look," the pilot spoke quietly, "I've scanned the area thoroughly. There are no firearms or explosives, and no finely honed atomic structure moving around."

"No knives."

Jim spoke figuratively. "There is a carbon based protein-covered life form roaming the neighborhood. It has the atomic structure of a collie."

"Lassie's on the prowl."

"Laddie," Jim corrected. "Is it a civil rights violation to call the pound?"

"We'll let this infraction ride."

"Great. But I don't want to push. It's a bigger crime to violate someone's rights than to kill them!" Jim was being marginally facetious.

"You might as well come back to HQ. Captain's got an errand involving mortal danger with a side order of paranoia."

Jim's eyes lit up like a cat. "Risk and danger I'm okay with," the pilot hesitated. "But paranoia?" He ended the transmission and quietly maneuvered his turbocraft out of the bushes where he'd been concealed for the last five minutes. The natural landscape provided cover for his small, agile vehicle while surveying the neighborhood. No one could have seen him except by sheer coincidence. He was just too good at that sort of thing.

Jim throttled up minimally, elevating toward the open, uncluttered sky. The Cat-four, not much larger than a bathtub, (with four TurboThrust motors attached) made a sound equivalent to a ventilation fan. Not loud under minimum power—more a whirrr—it blended into the hushed sounds of the late-night environment. Jim illuminated his *NightSun*, a powerful spotlight recessed in the bottom of the turbocraft. The residential hillside was artistically landscaped and professionally groomed by lawn care and gardening specialists. It's a fine, out-of-the-way place to live, if blessed with enough green to pay the bills. Jim knew Glendale was not within range of a cop salary, not even a captain's. Still, he liked to visit.

He turned his vehicle south and disappeared into the night, wondering about the undescribed errand, and why the word *paranoia* came attached as standard equipment. Jim had dealt with such mental anomalies in his brief but tumultuous past-life as a pilot for the Firm, which is another way of saying the Company, the CIA, or Central Intelligence Agency. He still had enemies there—people who held positions of power and would not forget. *Paranoia*. Jim didn't like the sound of the word. It messed with his mind. Those people flat-out did not agree with what he'd done. They had questionable principles. What happened is not important at this time. It occurred two decades previous when he was hungry for excessive excitement. He had no interest in refamiliarization! Just plain, ordinary, vanilla-wrapper excitement would suffice in most instances.

Arriving at HQ minutes later, he parked his vehicle in its allotted space and headed to the Command Center. Bo MacKinsey was slouched in his chair, head back, eyes closed, legs stretched out, an arm dangling limply. He looked like the victim of a heinous crime in a mystery thriller. Papers were scattered here and there on the floor, indicating a ruckus had taken place in the commission of the crime. The Command Center was eerily quiet. Jim looked at the victim, stepped confidently forward and kicked him in the leg. Bo opened one eye in annoyance and shrugged. He didn't want to be disturbed. Jim kicked again.

"Your assignment," Bo sat up straight. "The Cat-five we talked about last night—it's ready. You're off to Vegas. Then we begin the testing!"

"Whoa pardner," Jim spoke cowboy English. His face revealed suspicion. "What's this you say? It's true that I once was but am no more a turbocraft test pilot. Please explain in detail, and be thorough. Leave nothing to chance."

"I'll fill you in on what I know at the moment." Bo spoke with little assurance. He considered remaining silent as an indication he knew nothing. "The Cat-five is uncertified, at least there've been no field tests. You're doing flight and systems checks." He looked at Jim apologetically. "This situation involves the Pentagon, along with your former employer." Bo finished the briefing calmly, though he figured Jim's reaction would not have the same placid characteristics.

"You're joking!" Jim held his vehemence in check, in deference to the lieutenant who was clearly in the dark. "Are you saying I've volunteered? I hate to be the bearer of bad tidings but I'm not liking this scenario so far." Jim's voice was edgy, but not overly emotional. He rarely became emotional.

"Neither am I," the lieutenant replied. "But Captain Jackson *Tom Sawyered* me into it just minutes ago. You're involved in some sort of covert procurement, testing, and deployment of the new sensor platform. Apparently its capabilities are right out of a harebrained sci-fi novel!"

"So we're the first to get one?" Jim inquired, his demeanor changing. He seemed more receptive—less hostile—warming to the idea that a little normal excitement might be heading in his direction. It hadn't been all that many years since the Cat-four was unveiled. "I hope it goes real fast! By the way, test pilots make a lot more money."

"I'll check on that." Bo looked suspicious. "You're forty-four, right?"

Jim kicked Bo in the leg again. "Smart aleck! You think I'm in a midlife crisis and need a brand new top-secret, untested turbocraft, along with the danger it entails to shake things up and make me feel like a youngster again? Well I'll have you know that you're probably right. You just wait until you're my age!"

"You know where to go," Bo smiled. "There are Maglevs leaving for Vegas every hour. You can be back by 10 o'clock if you steer clear of the showgirls. And no gambling!" (Bo sounded adamant about both suggestions.) Jim grabbed a bear claw from the—as advertised in the bakery across the street—*Cop tested and certified* pastries. Between DES, FBI and IRS, plus the occasional LAPD order, the claim was justified—true as stated. "Sarge has the department credit card," Bo volunteered. He perked up. "Get some rest on the way. It's going to be a long day tomorrow. And one other thing." Jim started to leave the Command Center but waited for further instructions. "Take a BugSwatter from FBI surplus! *You never know...*"

Bo left the sentence unfinished, his voice trailing off in an air of mystery and intrigue. Jim nodded. It was sound advice, especially with paranoia in the pipeline. The pilot procured the required credit card from Sarge, who diligently read through the Internet-search material. Jim headed for the elevator and Union Station, only a short walk from HQ. He'd shuttled the two Cat-fours from the factory in 2036. What the heck, it made for nice relaxing work—almost like a paid vacation, giving him time to contemplate *paranoia*. Jim could almost hear the word bouncing around in his skull, with an echo and a maniacal laugh to add suspense.

FUTUREBUST5.9

Cy entered the Command Center with a paper that he dropped in front of Bo, then waited for a reaction. "Turns out Bubba has clout after all. Take a look. Larry found it in the information we gleaned off the Web."

Bo read the paper and nodded, showing little surprise. He'd suspected something was up. His suspicions were justified. "We're talking heavy-duty clout." He dropped it on his desk nonchalantly. "Jeeze, who'd have guessed Bubba's related to a Commander-in-chief of the United States of America, the fourth President of the US of A!"

"It's amazing what you can dig up on the Internet. Our whole lives are in there. However, due to the inordinate age of the former president, it's highly unlikely he had anything to do with Bubba's success."

"You're probably right," Bo acquiesced. "James Madison's long dead. If you told me he was related to one of the founding fathers, I'd have guessed Ben Franklin."

"That's interesting," Cy pondered. "For a guy who hated history class, you knew James Madison was the country's fourth chief executive. Care to explain?"

"Eighth grade," Bo shrugged. "We had to memorize the Preamble to the Constitution, the Bill of Rights, the first paragraph of the Declaration of Independence..."

"When in the Course of human events..." Cy spoke reverently.

"That's the one. And the Gettysburg Address—thank God Lincoln had the good sense to be brief, plus the presidents up to the forty-seventh."

"And how many do you still remember?" Cy queried.

"That's easy. Washington, Adams, Jefferson, Madison, Monroe, then Adams Jr. I think. Don't ask me any more than that. If Bubba had been related to the twenty-third, I wouldn't have a clue without looking it up."

"Me neither," Cy insisted. "But Jim remembers all that stuff after reading it once."

"So that's it on Bubba? How about Horton? Any skeletons hiding in his closet?"

"His Honor has a longstanding reputation as a hard-line judge. In the early years they called him 'Hang'em High Horton'. He was a fearsome advocate of stiff sentences, including no mercy for drugs. He was beloved by the politicians and the people. Horton is said to be the originator of the phrases: 'Drug abuse, never turn'em loose,' and 'Three strikes, you're out. That's what it's all about'. But he's as clean as a whistle. However, the illicit affairs alluded to last night... Horton may be getting a little more than his fair share!"

"You're digging into the judge's past?" Captain Jackson entered the Command Center, looking tired and forlorn. He grabbed a chair and sat down. "I don't think you'll uncover anything that easy. Whatever happened in Beer Can Bubba's trial involves more than just the two of them. In fact, they may be pawns." He put his hand on his scalp and rubbed, looking down at the floor. Actually he appeared exhausted. "I couldn't sleep and decided to get some work done. This whole thing's got me tied in a knot!"

Sarge and Larry entered the Command Center. "We're going to look at the court record," Cy volunteered, "and see what happened after we left this morning."

"It might turn up something," Captain Jackson shrugged, but it was clear he wasn't placing a bet. "Anyway, judging from what we saw last night, it's got to be better viewing than what's on TV these days. Have any of you guys seen the Conspiracy Channel lately?"

"We don't watch that sort of garbage." Sarge spoke with so much assumed gravity and self-righteous bravado, everyone laughed. "We watch the Debate Channel exclusively. Us highly educated enforcement officers would never abase ourselves with conspiratorial trash. We prefer to strengthen and improve our minds with righteous intellectual stimulation!"

"So you've been watching the Conspiracy Channel also?" the captain turned in his seated position and looked back at Sarge. "I do understand what you are saying about the Debate Channel. It's the highest rated on TV, but it wasn't always that way."

"What do you mean by that," Cy queried. "Debate has been number one for as long as I can remember."

"Well," the senior officer continued, putting his hands on his thighs, elbows out, in a pose of exaggerated wisdom older men often project, "it was before your time. But back in the olden days around the turn of the century, nobody paid attention to such offerings. In fact, a Sunday of football games received more in-depth discussion and analysis than any presidential election ever did!" Captain Jackson got everyone's attention with that statement, proven true after a prestigious university in Massachusetts completed exhaustive studies. "One of the reasons we had so many unsolved problems was because no one openly and fairly discussed anything. Oh sure, there were a bunch of hotheaded radio talk show hosts hawking their own brand of Political Problem-solving Perfection, but they were mostly pretentious, self-indulgent mega-mouths backed up by pea-brains who liked to hear themselves yak. Those goofballs had the intelligence of sawn cordwood and were nothing but a decrepit monument to *Unthinking America*—people who believed if they repeated ignorance and lies enough times, it would miraculously transform into Truth!" Captain Jackson seemed annoyed, then regained his train of thought. "Actually they had the aptitude of a bucket of rocks, but that's neither here nor there. Anyway, debate was not an integral part of the American political landscape."

"*Firing Line,*" Cy protested. "Wasn't it honest-to-goodness debate?"

"That show was decades ahead of its time," the captain admitted with a smile. He seemed reinvigorated. "As you guys know from watching reruns in syndication," he turned and looked at Sarge, "the show was hosted by a man named *William F. Buckley Jr.* He was a fine, upstanding American in the best tradition. Buckley worked for decades as the only advocate for televised debate. But in the end it all went for naught. He fled the airwaves at the turn of the century, leaving a giant void in American political and intellectual thought."

"And no one tried to fill his shoes?" Concern showed on Bo's boyish face.

"No one could have," the captain answered authoritatively. "The thing that stood out about Buckley was his vocabulary!"

"It's the stuff legends are made of," Cy added respectfully.

"That's right. It was the biggest vocabulary in the known universe." Captain Jackson spoke with reverence. "Buckley used words in ordinary conversation that I'd never heard before. He was a brilliant man. In fact, when Webster's announced the release of their new, 21st Century Unabridged Deluxe Color Edition Dictionary, the big fat one that weighs ten pounds or more…"

Cy pointed to a copy of that very edition on the reference table in a place of honor, along with: *The Columbia Encyclopedia*; *Bartlett's Quotations*; *The Medical Desk Reference*; *The Oxford English Dictionary*; and a full color, holographic, double-deluxe special edition of The Autographed Encyclopedia and Almanac of All-time Greatest Pro Wrestlers, including an appendix listing midget wrestlers of the past century, plus a glossary of the most used pro wrestler terms and phrases. Everybody's favorite was *shut-up juice*. Where else could one look up such an expression and actually discover an answer?

"Anyway," Captain Jackson refocused attention back to the matters at hand, "when they printed up that big, fat dictionary, Webster's advertising campaign loftily announced that it almost certainly contained just about every word Bill Buckley knew. They had to print them by the thousands, though no one actually believed the exaggerated claim." He hesitated, clearing his throat. "More likely, that dictionary is nothing but a compendium of Buckley's vocabulary. He even supported decriminalization of dangerous drugs, an attitude that raised a few eyebrows. I suspect he was concerned with the hypocrisy of WoD and how it affected people's perception of fairness within the legal system. It's funny but I don't recall how that old guy died."

"My uncle had quite the vocabulary," Bo announced with a smirk and a nod. "He'd employ one cumbersome utterance after another, even while conversing on the most mundane topic. Tragically, he succumbed after choking on a big word."

"Kudos on the testimonial." Sarge turned back to the captain. "What gave a boost to televised debate?"

"Buckley's show was a forerunner of the number one television pastime today. But the real reason for debate's success goes back to the Great Depression. You guys probably don't know this, but in the 1930s, they had economic problems too."

"Today it's known as the Great Recession," Bo informed.

"That's right," the captain looked surprised. "But in the olden days, they thought what happened in the 1930s qualified as a depression. It turned out the real thing didn't occur until 2013, and is only now receding. The problems that caused the economic collapse of our lifetime were easily solvable: avoiding tax cuts and loopholes targeted to the rich; too much government debt, etc. We had an unsustainable lifestyle based on huge amounts of cheap, imported energy that diminished noticeably when oil-producing nations became politically unstable. Combined with inflation from the medical profession and executive salaries, job exports and a weakened dollar initiated a recession. There was no way out at that point and the economy collapsed when the stock market panicked. Global warming was the last straw fifteen years later and made things a dozen times worse. When the heartland turned into a dust bowl, well, you guys know about the starvation back in the late twenties. Two billion people died, worldwide! Then coastal cities started dropping off into the sea—terrible for those affected."

The captain paused. He shook his head in disbelief, thinking of the suffering they could have avoided. "If we'd tried some sensible debate and discussed the problems, instead of arguing or rug sweeping, none of it would have happened. People learned their lesson after that. Things have changed. We're now interested in our political and economic systems. It's all over TV.

Debate is number one. Mr. Buckley would be proud. We have shows like: Within Reason; Point-Counterpoint; Devil's Advocate; For Your Consideration; Diametrically Apposed; Debate—Yesterday and Today; and Heated Exchange; though that one is a little too controversial for an old fart like me."

"You missed a bunch," Cy insisted enthusiastically. Still he was impressed. It was obvious the old guy's memory cells were active. "I like: Debate or Debacle; For the Sake of Argument; and my favorite is: Say *What?*"

"A good selection," Captain Jackson nodded approvingly. "How about you, Lieutenant? What are your favorite shows?"

The captain was testing. "Gee, I don't know," Bo smiled. He put his fingers to his chin and rubbed intelligently, feeling the stubble of his beard. "How about: That's a Loaded Question; and Formal Debate—Past and Present. You guys know how much I love history. And of course Firing Line reruns." Bo passed the hot potato to Larry.

"Contention and Controversy; Subject to Change; That's Debatable; and Practical Debate—Analysis and Instruction, are my favorites," the DES prankster smiled. The others weren't sure whether to believe him or not.

"And you, Sarge?" Captain Jackson turned and glanced from his seated position. "You started this whole thing."

Sarge nodded pleasantly. "You think you've got me, don't you? I'll tell you what my favorites are: This is Debate; Get to the Point; and the Saturday night ratings leader, Debate-a-rama. Last weekend they had six Elvis Impersonators from the IBEI dressed in full regalia, debating the King's best number one hits. You can't beat that! The only thing I dislike about the Debate Channel is that it's a premium add-on—$12 a month, real money nowadays."

"Lets watch Bubba's trial," Cy interrupted. "We might discover some answers in our own little mystery." He downloaded the file and initiated the recording at the morning session when the defense presented its case. Bo and Captain Jackson were already seated. Sarge and Larry grabbed chairs while Cy leaned against the Command desk.

On screen, Bubba's double-knit defense took center stage, trying every diversionary tactic known to man—in the sense he clearly wasn't prepared to defend his client and didn't want to reveal his incompetence on international TV. He tried various methods of flimflam: the flamboyant-orator method, the pseudo-Constitutional method, and the bleeding-heart method. All are effective in some circumstances, but none made an impression on Judge Horton. Recess was called. There was a brief pause, then the record restarted as court reconvened. The five DES officers watched as His Honor, looking stressed, entered the courtroom and without hesitation gave Bubba the bargain of a lifetime. Disturbed, everyone remained silent until Cy spoke. The attorney sounded confident.

"I'm going to roll it back," he suggested. "See if you can tell me what went wrong." The last minutes of the courtroom drama were played again. A visibly distracted judge entered the courtroom, asked a question, and swiftly handed down his verdict. "What do you think?" Cy quizzed. Everyone remained silent, so the DES legal-eagle answered his own question. "Decisions affecting a defendant's life usually take twenty-four to forty-eight hours!"

"He changed his mind suddenly," Bo swiveled in his chair. "Before the break, he wasn't buying a thing the defense said."

"Recess for one hour was called at 10:02 AM," Cy pointed out. "The time is imprinted on the screen in the lower right. We left the courtroom." Cy rolled the record backward. "Look when they reconvene, 12:34 PM. That's two and a half hours, plus!"

"Someone got to him," Captain Jackson shook his head in disappointment.

Larry tapped the senior officer on the shoulder. "DCS. Digitized Courthouse Surveillance. If somebody entered his office, it's on file."

"Can you access those surveillance logs?" Bo leaned forward. Things were moving along quickly.

"You want I should route the request through LAPD's Computer?" Cy smiled slyly, again using that mediocre imitation of a backwoods southern bumpkin sheriff's deputy.

"You guy's aren't still doing that?" Captain Jackson shook his head and sighed heavily, then changed his mind, "Well, what the heck."

Cy went to work using the Command Center computer. His request to Internal Affairs for secure courthouse surveillance information was accepted after the proper LAPD codes were entered. Cy smiled mischievously. "Which camera do you want?"

"Access the building layout," Bo suggested while leaning forward in anticipation. They might solve this mystery without even leaving the office.

Cy did as he was told. The building layout came up on the screen, clearly showing each camera location. WideView #941 was in the ninth-floor hallway, thirty-five feet from the judge's chambers. Cy accessed the picture, then put it in fast forward search, starting at 8 AM. Looking rested and refreshed, Judge Horton entered his office four minutes late. People scurried up and down the hallway as if having super fast-twitch muscles energized by a powerful stimulant. The entire area was visible. No one would be able to enter the office unobserved.

"This should be easy," Sarge announced. "Whoever got to him is going to be right on camera. The surveillance log rolled along until 9:45, then went blank. Everyone looked at Sarge disparagingly. "Okay, I spoke too soon," the big man admitted with a disappointed shrug. "So it's not going to be that easy. The log has been erased."

Cy objected. "That's impossible. The signal was disabled. Whoever got to Judge Horton knew the courthouse security system and shut that camera down electronically because they are cross-referenced to cover all areas with at least three views. It'd be difficult to physically disable a camera without another catching it."

"No one can get in without a security pass," Captain Jackson insisted. "The system tracks everyone, including visitors, just like Big Brother."

"Jurors have special passes, so do the media and witnesses, officials and employees." Cy was thinking out loud. "Scanners follow everyone by their DNA imprint. An alarm will sound if anyone is where he or she should not be. Let's try the visitor's entrance, camera #11 on the west side of the building. This person is very talented at cloak-and-dagger." Cy accessed the record, starting at 7:45 when the doors were unlocked. He again ran it in fast forward search, 12X normal speed.

Everyone watched for eight minutes until Captain Jackson stopped the log. "Run it back a few minutes, then forward at normal speed." The five officers scrutinized in silence as visitors filed in, one by one through the detectors. Nothing appeared out of the ordinary until 9:21.

"Freeze the picture!" Captain Jackson ordered, raising his hand in a *Halt* motion. Five people were on camera near the entrance to the building; two were guards. Everyone stared at the still image, then at the captain. "Look at that guy on the screen," he pointed. "Cy, can you enlarge and enhance?"

An elderly gentleman dressed in a finely tailored, white three-piece suit, white tie, and a white derby hat stepped through the detector, casually putting a hand over his face as if to rub his forehead at the exact moment he strolled by the security camera. Cy enlarged the image.

"Print that out, please." The captain pointed. "Look at the way he covers his face as he passes. There is no way to know the camera location unless he'd studied the same floor plan we have. Those cameras are virtually invisible to the naked eye. His attempt to conceal identity could be considered suspicious behavior!"

"It might also be purely innocent." Sarge played devil's advocate in the discussion. Cy went out in the hall and grabbed the picture off the InstaPrint.

The captain took the photo and studied it, then handed it off to Sarge, who stared, then handed it back to Bo. The young field commander shook his head. "He certainly has distinguished gray hair." Bo handed the full color, digitally enhanced printout to Larry.

"That fellow in the picture," the captain assured, "isn't a casual observer of any court proceeding. In fact, he's not as old as he appears!"

"Wait a minute!" Larry seemed mesmerized as he gazed at the photo. He shook his head in disbelief like he knew the guy, or at least had seen him before. Still something didn't add up. "That's Uncle Roy. But it's impossible!"

FUTUREBUST6.0

Larry tried to grasp the situation. He looked carefully at the picture, then gazed at the image on the DynaView. Uncle Roy had been an old man twenty-four years previous. He was surely deceased—dead and gone by now. After watching the court record of Bubba's trial, everyone congregated in the Command Center. Only Jim was missing. He'd headed off to Vegas to pick up the new turbocraft.

"He's not as old as you think," Captain Jackson informed. "Do you fellows know who LeRoy is?"

"Only from what Larry told us," Sarge shrugged. "I never saw the guy."

"Well that's him in the picture. In fact, I'd guess he's about sixty. The man is deceptive. I've never seen him without a masquerade, but have come to recognize his cover. Some people think the idea of a disguise is passé, being that we can scan a person's DNA and ID them. But LeRoy is very skilled. He could dress up as a beautiful woman and win a beauty contest. His DNA imprint is somehow forged. He plays the part of the super-spy, but I don't know if he actually believes that or is using it as a ruse."

"Uncle Roy is in his sixties?" Larry was suspicious. "If you know that, it means you must be his mole."

"That's correct, at least partially," the captain informed. "I was approached by LeRoy shortly after you refused an offer to spy on DES for the Firm, and agreed to his proposal, figuring someone would do it sooner or later. That way I could keep tabs on everything, and promptly inform my superiors of the situation. In actuality, we fed so much disinformation to the CIA, it's hard to believe they kept me on for so long."

"So you were a double agent?" Larry was stunned.

"DES bamboozled the Company for years. We began to think they were flimflamming us by letting us hoodwink them. It's called dis-disinformation. In order to counter such an animal, you need anti-dis-disinformation." The captain rubbed his head slowly, then continued. "I had to keep you from getting a promotion in order to prove my loyalty to the Firm. Of course, that was easy to do. It's one of the reasons I ended up in L.A. after you guys settled here. The CIA pulled on some fat strings to make that happen. It had nothing to do with procuring NOSTRILS as everyone thought. So I worked as an agent with the full knowledge of senior staff in DC. We milked the situation for all it was worth."

"What does Uncle Roy have to do with Judge Horton and Bubba?" Cy inquired, not sure he was grasping the picture.

"Years ago we suspected the CIA was setting up a secret organization to distribute alcohol and tobacco products. They needed cash to make up for budget cuts."

"Wait a minute," Cy interrupted. "Do you mean to tell me that Congress and the Administration knew about this?"

"Not until DES discovered the plan and informed them."

"Then why did they need more money after the organization had been downsized?"

"The CIA is an entity unto itself," the captain continued. "It exists for national security purposes, but is also a self-perpetuating organization with a secret life of its own. If Congress reduces funding, they get it somewhere else to continue doing whatever is necessary for survival. The institution, first and foremost, protects itself and its interests."

"That's par for the course within the Military-Industrial Complex," Larry grimaced. "Interests of the country are secondary. They always protect numero-uno."

"True," Captain Jackson replied. "But the CIA is probably no longer part of the MIC. There is too much infighting between the various military and intelligence organizations at budget time. And all the work they do domestically is difficult to categorize, unfunded by Congress. Money to spy on other government agencies must come from covert sources. The Firm refuses to share resources with or trust other agencies like the FBI or NSA, who are probably doing the same thing. They are constantly quarreling. And Black Ops? Covert dollars must be untraceable, especially when it involves America's anti-democratic activities in foreign countries, like destabilizing democratically elected governments that are not meeting the US's double-standards for *Free Enterprise Purity!*"

"And Judge Horton?" Cy reminded the captain.

"Judge Horton and Bubba may be pawns in this whole mess. When we discovered what the CIA was up to, a half-dozen DES moles in various regional offices fed highly coordinated amounts of negative-anti-dis-disinformation to the Firm, trying to undercut their plans. It worked for a while, but when the CIA realized we'd been hustling them, they confused the heck out of us."

Bo had it all figured out. "They were leading you on, right?"

"Pretty much. But the key is determining when they figured it out.

Without that, it's impossible to know if they forwarded reverse-negative-anti-dis-disinformation.

"You could have countered all that with inverted reverse-negative-anti-dis-disinformation," Bo informed coyly.

"You're making things more complicated than they have to be," Captain Jackson replied. "They'd have used counter-inverted reverse-negative-anti-dis-disinformation. Anyway, I'd guess Uncle Roy and the other mole-handlers paid a price career-wise. For revenge, he may be doing everything possible to undermine DES and make us look incompetent. Bubba's success in court accomplished that at an international level. The Company is still PO'd at us. I'm betting they have black market drug operations going to supplement cash reserves."

"So now we're up against the CIA," Bo observed sarcastically, "or at least some spooks holding a grudge against us. It makes a wonderful plot."

"I wish it was that simple. There is also the Pentagon," Captain Jackson winced.

"And their interest in this?" Cy queried. He was still baffled.

"That's Need-to-know." Captain Jackson spoke as if apologizing for his lack of openness. "I'll fill you in when I can." There was grumbling, but everyone acquiesced. They had no choice in the matter, short of beating the truth out of him. It all sounded like a story one might watch on the Conspiracy Channel.

"I still don't understand why we are testing the Cat-five ourselves." Bo shook his head in confusion, not used to having the wool pulled over his eyes.

Captain Jackson gave the most thorough and comprehensive explanation he could without revealing anything relevant or important. "When it arrives in a few hours, it will have only Navaids. The sensors will be installed later."

"And the reason for this?"

"The main components were shipped from Hong Kong and are now in L.A. There is no point in sending them to Las Vegas for installation. We can do that here. Thus Jim is showing up four days early. There are people out there who do not want us to have that vehicle. So I'm jumping the gun by getting it here in advance of the schedule. Hopefully, the bad boys will be caught off guard. A Cat-five turbocraft, along with a complete sensor package is too much of a temptation."

Cy appeared troubled. "And who are the bad guys in this scenario?"

Captain Jackson mirrored his concern, then answered the question in an honest and forthright manner. "My guess is, one way or another, we're about to smoke them out."

Bo sat up in his chair and confronted the captain. "Jim could be in a lot of trouble!"

"He could be. You gave him my message?"

Bo nodded. "I told him to expect paranoia back in his life at any moment."

FUTUREBUST6.1

Jim awoke as the Maglev decelerated on approach, twenty miles outside of downtown Las Vegas. He covered his eyes, surprised at how bright it was, even though the sun was an hour from rising. Any sane person had to wonder what the electric bill for the desert metropolis came to. "These trains are way too fast," he mumbled while tossing a pillow onto the empty seat next to his. The magnetically levitated ride is like traveling on a cloud—over 330 miles per hour and almost no feeling of movement except for the scenery whizzing by. At night it's spooky.

Maglevs saved the transportation system during the depression, drastically reducing the use of automobiles and airplanes. Both were overworked infrastructures. Construction created jobs for engineers to sandblasters and increased demand for concrete to copper wire, backhoes to bulldozers. The cost per passenger-mile is two cents, far below an automobile or aircraft. A Maglev is the only place Jim violates the three by one hundred rule.

Electricity to power the Maglev system is generated pollution-free by huge windmills located in the plains states, from the Dakotas south to Texas. America got a late start in windpower. Politicians in DC were too busy protecting the fossil fuel conglomerates to concern themselves with the long-term sustainability of the economy. Sizable campaign contributions saw to that. But during the Great Depression, there was a desperate need for clean, cheap electricity to power the economic recovery. By 2040, windmills alone generated more than the total US output at the turn of the century. And the price dropped drastically because the damn stuff is virtually free.

Jim rubbed his eyes. Flashing lights were visible and there was nothing subtle about the purpose. After rounding a curve, he could see the eye of the luminous hurricane, the Neon Jungle—hotels, casinos, shopping malls, at least thirty square miles of sin and decadence. He loved it.

As the Maglev entered the station, he stood and rubbed his hands together while gazing out the large window at a thirty-foot holographic billboard. A beautiful model enticed travelers to have fun, see the sights, and part with hard-earned dollars at one of the many gambling establishments. Jim wasn't going to fall for that pitch. It'd be the casino losing if he entered. His *gift* would see to that. Gambling was in his blood!

Some people thought it a myth, the idea of a photographic memory, but

Jim knew different. He could briefly look at the page of a book, close his eyes and read it back verbatim. No limit—one page or a hundred. He'd tell you the twenty-third president was Benjamin Harrison, but anyone would know that.

He looked down the rows of seats as people detrained. Maglevs are exceedingly fast, the swiftest ground transportation ever invented. Jetlag is possible on these magnificent trains. Future technology promised speeds of 475 miles per hour. "Mach .6 is far too fast while traveling so close to the ground!" He wiped the sleep from his eyes and made a mental note to stop mumbling, a habit that could get out of hand. Bo would mention *el loco enorme* and offer vacation time to sort things out. Jim enjoyed his job. If drug abusers lurk in the vast expanse of Los Angeles, he wants to catch them pronto. Keeping his town of twenty-four million residents drug free is a matter of pride. Sunning himself on a deserted beach accomplishes little in that regard.

The train was headed for Denver. End-of-season ski enthusiasts wanted to trek into the mountains one last time before the late spring blizzards turn to liquid and head for reservoirs that supply the west with water. That makes the snow duel-purpose.

At 5 A.M., Las Vegas was bustling. Across the boulevard from the station, Jim spied a newer casino and nightclub. He had plenty of time and was in a money-hungry, victimizing mood.

Inside it was a zoo—lights flashing; people yelling; gambling (something that should have been banned along with other dangerous drugs) was in full swing. People carried on as if there was no tomorrow. Even 24/7 couldn't satisfy. The PA played the song *Eight Days a Week*—one of an ancient rock group's many number one hits. Jim inferred a subliminal message in the lyrics. Live for today. If gambling seven days a week does not satisfy...

Gaming is clearly a drug. Many wanted to ban it in previous years because it often ruined finances and destroyed families just like alcohol. But others considered it a *pursuit of happiness*. Debatable? Did gambling give happiness? One lawyer spoke up on the subject. "We could write plenty of Constitutional laws to make sure you never find any, but there is no point in overdoing it." His statement actually made sense. Gambling remained legal. It might have been a tough law to enforce. NOSTRILS couldn't pick up the subatomic patterns of blackjack, craps, or roulette. When the techies figure out how to do that, society might embrace a ban. So despite the suggestion that he steer clear, Jim acquired some chips and seated himself at the blackjack table, hoping Bo wouldn't mind the cash advance pilfered from the DES credit bureau.

The dealer seemed reticent, as if not wanting to toss any cards across the table. After a delay, a large man in a finely tailored suit stepped near, hands clasped behind his back. His attempt at being nonchalant made him stick out like a sore thumb. Jim motioned the dealer to commence. However, luck being what it is...Well, after winning $1100 in nine minutes, two gentlemen joined the first and escorted him rigorously and with some embarrassment (to the casino as well) out the door. Photo ID Recon Surveillance (PIDRS) was cross-referenced with other casinos, thus they were sharing databases. Jim had been kicked out of every casino in the city, a pretty good record considering he didn't live there.

"You guys have no sense of humor," he complained, wondering if he could get them any madder than they were. The FullView glass door was courteously held open as he flew by. He dusted himself off and headed for the mall. They'd graciously cash his chips for a four-percent fee, and allow him to shop without hassles.

Sarge's grandkids liked toys. Jim picked out a laser-guided soccer ball and a remote-controlled dinosaur that ate smaller, meeker—not included, sold separately—forms of life. The same goes for the rechargeable fuel cells.

He strolled down Flamingo Road as the dawn approached, counting his money, aware Bo would require a large ROI, Return On Investment to straighten out the problem with DES credit. That left him with about fifty bucks.

He decided to take in a concert and there were plenty to choose from in the immediate vicinity. Most bands on the popularity down-slope will agree to do shows anytime of the day or night. After foolishly spending their fortunes on fur coats and private jets, they'll work the early morning hours, at least until bankrolls swell to an acceptable level of bloating. Often there are legendary groups from the turn-of-the-century on the nostalgia rebound. As previously stated, many had spent themselves into oblivion during initial years of success, and need a financial booster. It costs a lot of money to maintain a private zoo, or pay for the upkeep of a six hundred-room mansion. One rock star even has a portfolio of fine, antique cars valued at $240 million. He is in his nineties and works to pay for insurance and preservation. Las Vegas is a mecca for such talent.

Jim stood in one location on the street and could see nine marquees open for business at that early hour. The choice seemed unlimited, as long as one liked *pissed-off-at-everything* bands. There was a group known as The Drool—their music definitely oozed out in liquid form. They needed to get more acoustic, less electronic to solve that problem. Two theaters down, a rapper named UpChuck was doing four shows a day. The guy is good—Jim had seen him in L.A. He also noticed DiddlySquat and Maggot were in town. And who could forget The Barf, a group that broke up then got back together then broke up then got back together ad nauseam. Jim figured it was their way of garnering free publicity. Twenty years previous, Maggot was sued by another band called Maggot Breath. Lots of free publicity there. Both released new albums at the time, reaching an understanding on the legal issues. Then there was the time UpChuck and The Barf performed at the same outdoor festival. The ramifications are obvious. Further down the street other bands are playing, including Hairball, an Ironic Rock band that shaves their heads. (A study by a prestigious university in Massachusetts found over twenty garage bands had named themselves Hairball in the last forty years. But only one made it to the big-time.) UpYours is another pissed-off-at-everything band. The AntiBodys are known for lack of clothing during a show. Jim wasn't in the mood for any distended male eye candy. Slug's hit, Rambo's Lullaby was number one for six weeks. They were playing later.

Jim finally chose a band he'd never seen. A bunch of scrawny, sixty-year-old crotch-grabbers dressed in skintight black leather, Blabber Mouth wasn't as good as their name would imply. Jim liked their hair. Purple mohawks went well with the mauve (open toe) high heel shoes. He made a mental note to see another legendary band from the turn of the century when time allowed: Kiss Off. *Pissed off at everything* is definitely in vogue.

FUTUREBUST6.2

By 8 A.M., Jim was at the turbocraft factory office, a small brick building in the midst of a sprawling, sixty-acre manufacturing facility. "This is a surprise," the man at the desk informed. "With DES, huh? I'll have to check."

Jim sat in a chair and waited. Phone calls were made. The office help furtively glanced at him with confused looks, as if they'd seen his face on a "Wanted" poster. Over twenty minutes passed—then finally a clear, positive response from an office manager who'd personally taken charge of the situation. "Your vehicle isn't here. It's in the Secure Area. That thing must be something special. The rest of us can't get anywhere near the site without the risk of being shot. Other than a phone number, we're not sure the place exists. None of us has ever seen it. We've been informed that if we get caught out there, we'll be dealt with!" The guy shrugged. "And if there is a turbocraft waiting, more power to you."

Jim nodded. "How do I get there?"

"We'll give you a lift," the man replied. "You should take some water. And I'll have to see your Class-A Pilot's license along with C-PID" (Certified Personal IDentification).

Jim showed the required documents, signed necessary papers, and put the pen back into a glass filled with writing utensils. A young secretary kept looking at him funny—like she was psychic—like she knew he was about to die or something. He wondered if she had information he'd appreciate knowing.

She said nothing, just stared and chewed on her pencil. Jim fired up his high-powered mind and analyzed the situation. Best to be on guard.

A uniformed security officer brought an old, obsolete, broken-down vehicle known as a HumVee by the front door and they were off to the Secure Area. It turned out to be twenty miles from the factory office, in the middle of nowhere—only desert sand in windblown piles. The nearest building: a newer hotel-casino complex about ten miles away. "Here you go," the officer informed. "Pretty desolate, but GPS says this is the spot and that sign confirms it." The guy pointed to a steel post. "You're on your own. Someone will come by to get you, I guess."

He soon disappeared, leaving only tire tracks behind. A warm day was in store. Jim was keenly aware of the sun. It was hot and very bright—normal for the desert in springtime. He waited with his hands in his pockets, his bag of toys by his feet, wishing he'd heeded the advice and brought a bottle of water. A scorpion scurried across the desert floor, leaving a trail of tiny footprints that disappeared over a dune. It was getting hotter, though Jim was not seeing mirages yet. He dug his boot into the sand and spread it around some. "Anything one can do to make the desert more presentable..." He noticed the sign was so sandblasted to be almost unreadable. The rusty steel post leaned. But it was just as the guy in the office said:

> Top Secret Secure Area
> No admittance.
> Violators will be shot!

Jim wondered who the brainiac was that put that sign there. Without it, no one would have been the wiser. Sand graced the landscape. There was nothing of interest for miles. He could barely see the outskirts of Vegas through the heat-distorted void. Eighteen minutes passed, then he heard a noise some distance away. A short, pudgy man in a business suit with a pug-like bulldog face exited a hidden access. From a distance, the guy reminded him of a Marine drill sergeant he'd once known. Jim watched cautiously as the two converged. "General Hortomer," the fellow stuck out his right hand in anticipation. "Air Force, retired."

Jim shook it perfunctorily, but said nothing. Because Air Force people are generally strait-laced and likable, something about the guy didn't sit right. He looked more like a Marine. That's not to insult the Marines. Most Corps officers are okay, but still a little cranky since budget cutters in Congress transferred them out of the Navy and into the Army. It was a common sense move. The Navy did not need its own army. It already had an air force, so the Navy and Air Force were combined to cut costs and streamline. Four armed services under two commands. It helped the Pentagon live within budget constraints on a lot less money. But traditions die hard, especially in the Marines. Give them credit. They threw one big temper tantrum trying to regain sovereignty.

"This is a surprise. So you're the DES pilot who's going to put our little toy to good use," the general winked. "We were expecting to deliver to L.A. ourselves." He hesitated. "But I guess this will work out. I had to call my superiors to get the go-ahead or I'd have been here sooner. Come on downstairs and I'll show it to you. You thirsty?"

"I'm fine, thanks." Jim cradled his shopping bag and followed. The guy had used the word *toy* to describe the Cat-five. Maybe he was being facetious. The two men stepped into the dimly lit tunnel as the trapdoor closed behind them. They walked at least a quarter-mile through the corridor. Light was provided by a string of bulbs hanging Christmas tree-fashion from the ceiling. Despite several tunnels leading off in different directions, they continued in a relatively straight manner. Jim counted his steps. They were descending downward. He almost laughed—his thoughts being superfluous. It wasn't possible to descend upward—not unless one lived in China.

"DES, Los Angeles was handpicked by SecDef," the general informed. "I sure hope this vehicle does the trick." Jim had no idea what the guy was talking about. All he'd been told was to expect the reemergence of paranoia. "If we succeed at this mission, it'll be a great day for the MIC."

Jim pondered as they continued down the corridor. Those are three letters he did not like to see used together, capitalized, and in that order. "I certainly hope so," he tried to sound upbeat and positive. He knew he wasn't a fan of the MIC, a tightly knit organization of PACs and special interest groups; military contractors and weapon manufactures, consultants, pork barrel spenders in Congress, extreme rightwing political think-tanks, and a few fanatical, high-ranking members of the Armed Forces—people who often profiteered handsomely from the honor and glory of soldiers, sailors, Marines, and airmen who'd made the ultimate sacrifice for their country. The group is also known as the Iron Triangle, the crème de la crème of money-wasters in government. The initials MIC derive from a term coined by the thirty-fourth president of the United States in his farewell address to the nation back in the middle of the last century. That document became known as the Eisenhower Prophesy. The guy had been an old-fashioned Republican, one of a rare breed that died out soon after. He believed in fiscal responsibility. Twenty years later, the party had done a complete about-face and over the next thirty years, spent the country into oblivion. More than half of Jim's paycheck is relieved from his possession because of the need to pay off the national debt left to future generations by those spendthrift Republicans who believed deficits didn't matter.

Military-Industrial Complex! The label had an evil connotation to any taxpayer who didn't relish funneling a big percentage of his paycheck down a rathole into government waste, fraud, and abuse. There were news stories from the early part of the century that resurfaced now and then, of $2.3 trillion (give or take) of MIC money that could not be properly accounted for. Of course that didn't mean it was lost, stolen, or mismanaged. They just couldn't account for it! But as the decades passed, horror stories of Iron Triangle waste and graft were unearthed, despite vigorous efforts to keep the information secret. The news usually made exclusive debuts on The Pentagon Waste Channel, which was 100% dedicated to the discovery of past abuse by the Military-Industrial Complex. The tiny network had won countless awards over the years, and did a great public service in revealing the truth about waste in government; that the lion's share (90%) was in the form of excessive Iron Triangle spending.

Such waste was the primary reason for burgeoning deficits that initiated the Great Depression. A century later, people will still subsist at a lower standard of living, shelling out higher taxes to pay down that debt. Shunning personal responsibility, previous generations could not have been more fiscally negligent. Apparently they lived without a care in the world, dumping all the difficult, unpopular sacrifices into the *devil-may-care* file. Babies born in the late-21st century will still be repaying the debt when they retire.

The two men came to a doorway. The general put his face close to a small camera for Retina ID (RID). The door opened into a large underground complex with pipes running in all directions across the ceiling, and late model computerized machine tools on the floor. They stood on an elevated steel landing. The Cat-five was displayed on a revolving work platform. Jim was flabbergasted. There were at least twenty guards in the vicinity. One wore the Green Beret.

He bit his lip...a little too hard he decided. Must be repressed anger. The whole scene seemed a touch off the wall, like those old *James Bond* movies the public is still fond of, though today they're taken in the abstract. Jim walked to the railing and looked down at the prototype vehicle—a Category-five turbocraft. For an instant, his mind flashed back to the first time he'd seen the Cat-one in 2019. A thrill had gone down his spine. What a beautiful sight. That vehicle led him into all kinds of excitement, first as a test pilot, then flying it for the Firm. The turbocraft had been a paradigm shift in technology. It was so safe and efficient, small helicopters were phased out. Now, decades later, he got the same feeling but didn't know why. Jim noticed no exit to the facility large enough for the vehicle. An anomaly—it seemed troubling. Maybe they planned to build, but not fly it. "How are you going to get that thing out of here?" he asked, mystified. "We must be a hundred feet underground."

"Just about," the general smiled. "Let's go have a look." The guy didn't answer him. Was he hiding something? A twinge of paranoia fired through Jim's mind.

The two men descended a flight of galvanized, expanded-steel steps until at the same level as the turbocraft, slowly turning on a skid-resistant platform as if being unveiled at a car show. All they needed was a model in a bathing suit sitting on the cowling. Knowing as much about the MIC as he did, Jim figured they probably just forgot. A guard asked to inspect his shopping bag. The toys were cleared by security. The guard liked the soccer ball. "'Bend it like Beckham'." Apparently, he had gotten one for his kids.

"So that's it." Jim tried to sound intelligently enthused as they walked to the platform. "It was rumored to look like the Cat-four."

The general winked and smiled. "Superficially, they're almost identical. It's your standard single-passenger, four-thruster configuration. But this is not your father's turbocraft. There is more here than meets the eye!"

"We've been looking forward to the first flight." Jim placed his bag of toys on the floor and continued the *I know what's going on* charade. He stepped onto the slowly revolving platform. "Of course, the secrecy of the project kept us from learning anything about it. But we'll be able to kick serious butt with that baby!"

The general patted the turbocraft affectionately. "You're going to be amazed. In law enforcement, this thing should be illegal." The twinge of paranoia changed to a pang. A wave of his hand and the revolving platform stopped. Hortomer grabbed a cloth and removed a smudge from the canopy. His next statement brought on a twitch of paranoia "But the law isn't relevant in this instance."

"Probably not," Jim quickly fabricated a lie. "At least not under these circumstances." He felt he better qualify the statement, not wanting to sound totally unconstitutional. Jim changed the subject to something he understood, sending a prayer skyward, hoping *The Lord Would Provide*. "Now what's this I hear about more speed?"

"Whoa baby! Come here and look at these turbines!" They circled to the other side. "You ever hear of Pulsating Thrust?" The general was obviously a very proud parent. His expression radiated deleterious glee.

"Only in theory," Jim lied again—out of necessity, not compulsion. He didn't have a clue what the guy was talking about.

A smile crossed the officer's face. "My boy, theory just became cold, hard fact. Technically, the Cat-five is not even a turbocraft. It's too advanced! This platform's been redesigned, top to bottom, inside and out." Jim gazed at the front, portside motor—the cowling removed for inspection. It didn't have the same rotor displacement as the TurboThrust motors now in service. Many parts appeared more compact. The turbine blades—the meat and potatoes of the thruster—were not gently curved, but wiggled back and forth in a most unusual pattern. "This is a quantum leap in technology!" the general bragged, interrupting Jim's inspection. "This baby has 175% more power, yet consumes less fuel!" If true, Jim's aforementioned midlife crisis is toast. Hortomer laughed. "And that's not the real story. You could slip in and out of church during services without being noticed." Jim smiled at the example of quietude, but looked skeptical. "There is negligible exhaust disruption," Hortomer explained. "The thrust backwash is dissipated between pulses so less air is forced out behind. Thus minimal disturbance accompanies an active motor. And 175% more power!"

Jim wasn't going to believe without proof, but withheld his skepticism. "You're telling me that I could land this thing next to a litter barrel and not disturb the garbage inside, not even the loose paper and cups?"

"Just about," Hortomer qualified. "There is almost no air forced out the backside. It's dissipated between pulses, kind of like inhaling and exhaling at the same time. We've neutralized the vortices inside the motor!"

"Unbelievable!" Jim was not acting for the benefit of the general. But experience told him..."So what's the downside?"

Hortomer quickly returned to earth. "There are some erratic flight characteristics, but you'll be able to keep things under control," his voice lacked some of its former confidence, "as long as there are no FCM malfunctions." (Flight Control Modules)

Jim grimaced, but remained closemouthed on the matter. He didn't want them to think he was a weenie pilot, afraid of a little HSID, High-Speed Instant Deceleration, or UC/T, Uncontrolled Collision with Terrain. Pilots who fret over negative possibilities are labeled complainers and whiners. Wasting mental energy accomplished little. Jim hoped to glean more information. "This technology is classified?"

"The CIA doesn't know of its development," Hortomer became overconfident. "They probably think R&D is developing a new tractor."

Jim doubted his former employer was in the dark. In fact, it wouldn't surprise him if the Firm already had plans in place to procure such a vehicle—maybe this very one! And they probably didn't care how they got their hands on it, just as long as they did! If the general claimed they didn't know, it meant they weren't supposed to know but almost certainly did. The Firm knew before the President was informed, which precedes SecDef. And a retired Air Force general working in the development of a farm tractor guarded by elite commandos? It all pointed to paranoia, just as Bo predicted.

The general opened the canopy and stepped in as workers gathered around. Jim leaned over and rested his palm on the cowling of the low-slung vehicle, but a guard motioned him back. He couldn't help noticing that it felt different from the Cat-four. Another thing. Why use commandos to guard technology? Soldiers that can speak three or four languages fluently and shoot the apple off your head at a hundred yards with a hastily drawn sidearm should be out in the world chasing bad guys and evildoers.

Hortomer gloated. He flicked a switch that powered the console. "Computerized preflight and pilot ID!" The general was like a kid in a candy store. He touched a finger-actuated switch on the armrest. The turbocraft's cowling changed from dull grey to flat black, matching the display platform's hue with incredible accuracy. Jim jumped back in surprise. Even the Green Beret cracked a smile. Hortomer was amused. "Far out, isn't it? From a distance of a hundred yards, it'll diminish into its surroundings. We call it Chameleon Skin."

"Variable camouflage!" Jim was stupefied. "I'd heard rumors it was in R&D, but didn't think it possible except in sci-fi books written by hallucinogenic dreamers with overly vivid imaginations."

Hortomer laughed at the spirited description of fiction writers. "On a clear day, people looking up will not even know you're there. The bottom of the vehicle turns azure blue, a holographic effect. No matter what angle it's viewed from, it matches surroundings perfectly. But power consumption is critical. There's a supercomputer as big as a golf ball located under the seat that sucks so much juice, you may feel the heat on your behind. If it gets too hot, turn on the AC." Hortomer shut down the display.

"And with virtually no sound coming from those Pulse Thrusters, the vehicle will disappear into thin air. You're sure the CIA doesn't know about this?"

Hortomer elaborated. "If news leaked, they'd be real upset. The CIA boys are sensitive that way." He paused—to clarify—but didn't. This brought on a jolt of paranoia. "It's one of the reasons you were handpicked. Your top-secret disagreement with the Firm is well-documented." Jim frowned. A well-documented secret? But it had made the national news. That's why the Firm was so PO'd. He went public with one of their dirty little unconstitutional secrets. Hortomer continued. "There is no radar, ground-based or satellite, capable of registering an echo. Nothing can discern its electromagnetic emissions or track it in flight."

The general's tone mystified Jim. He let it ride. "When can I have it?"

"You get her back to DES, Los Angeles by 10:30 A.M. and the options will be special-delivered upon *confirmation of arrival*." There's that inflection again. This brought on a sizable shock of paranoia. The general continued. "We've already put your DNA imprint into the C-PID module so she's ready to go. I'd like to hear it's operational next week. At that time, you'll have FMA."

"Sounds good!" Jim feigned excitement, realizing something was out of whack. "I'll never get it back by 10:30. It's after nine now."

The general laughed. "How fast does your Cat-four travel at full throttle?"

"Four-fifty MPH, if I use AFA," (Auxiliary Fuel Augmentation).

Hortomer winked. "Add 175% more power to Mach .6 and you'll be back by 10:30."

Jim agreed, a positive look crossing his face. Again, he didn't want to sound like a weenie pilot. But he was starting to suspect..."What about tech support? Parts?"

"It's all taken care of, 110%," the general assured as if it wasn't.

Paranoia punched Jim in the gut. The last time he'd heard someone say that, it nearly got him killed. He remained nonchalant, showing a total lack of concern. He was into something unsavory, and besides, he hated clichés. Anybody using *110%* is covering something. Jim took a moment to admire the turbocraft. What he really wanted was time to think. The general mentioned FMA, Full Mission Authority—CIA-speak, giving carte blanche to do anything necessary to successfully conclude an operation. The military never used such terms, being concerned with rules of engagement and accepted conventions of combat. No one in the Armed Forces is ever given FMA because it means going beyond the limits of international law. Jim was already in the CIA's crosshairs. They'd grab the Cat-five somewhere between Vegas and L.A. His status as a living being was in question. "Great, no problem. I'll fly her back to L.A. and we'll get the ball rolling."

"Good enough," the general nodded. "Return the way you came. By the time you get outside, this vehicle will be waiting to take you on the flight of a lifetime."

"But how are you going to get it out there?" Jim was puzzled. "There's no exit."

"You just leave that to us," he assured with a grin. "GodSpeed." The guy would've made a great politician. He didn't mean what he said, and didn't say what he meant.

Jim grabbed his bag of toys and climbed the stairs as a technician reached into the cockpit and fired the thrusters. He stopped on the landing and looked back. The Cat-five idled with virtually no sound. It seemed surreal. They waited for him to leave. He gave them a confident *thumbs-up*, opened the door, and stepped back out into the corridor.

FUTUREBUST

FUTUREBUST6.7

"I'll be back in Los Angeles by 10:30," Jim mumbled sarcastically. "I'll be lucky to see that city again." And the comments about the *flight of a lifetime* and *confirmation of arrival*—the general was taunting. Jim knew the guy was CIA, and Hortomer knew Jim knew. The general implied he is already toast—might as well not fight it. And G*odSpeed?* Jim shook his head in disgust and walked towards daylight.

"A *great day for the Military-Industrial Complex.* Thieving Profiteers!" He hadn't mumbled this much since his days at the Firm. A bad habit was regaining a foothold in his consciousness despite best efforts to refrain. The entrance opened. He climbed from the tunnel into the bright and cheery sunshine. The idling turbocraft was 550 meters from where he stood. The Secure Area appeared secure. There was no trace of where it had come from, not even footprints. Remote control, no big deal, he thought, making sure he didn't mumble. Walking to work a few days previous, he'd passed an individual who was not only mumbling, but accentuated his one-sided conversation with hand gestures. It's sad how some people end up.

Jim approached the Cat-five and circled slowly. Careful preflight confirmed it to be the same vehicle he'd seen inside the facility. He knew they weren't going to let him drive it home without a GPS tag. Jim removed the credit card-sized BugSwatter Bo had suggested he carry, and activated it, running the security device over the vehicle to scan every inch. He located a tiny electronic dot the size of a pinhead, hidden right on the canopy where he'd have put it himself. Best satellite reception is topside on a synthetic surface. They gave me a decoy, Jim figured. Too easy. He found another after a minute's search, stuck securely to the nosecone. The rest of the vehicle was clear.

Stowing the toys in a large storage compartment behind the seat, he jumped in, shut the canopy, strapped himself, grabbed the controls, and throttled up. The turbocraft lifted almost silently, with minimal sand swirling around as he hovered ten feet above the desert. Jim marveled, turning the vehicle around in one place like the needle of a compass. Then Excessive Acceleration Syndrome (EAS) got the best of him. He gunned it.

That was definitely a capital mistake. The idea of 175% more power had slipped his photographic memory. His noggin snapped backwards into the headrest. The Cat-five accelerated like nothing he'd experienced before. Jim held on for dear life, thoroughly enraptured by the speed. He gained altitude to avoid slamming into a dune (UC/T), instantly rising to six hundred feet, then leveled off for two minutes. An uncomfortable shimmy rudely manifested at 340 mph. He eased the throttle, bringing the turbocraft back under control and into a hover after flying past the fifty-first floor of the brand new, recently completed *U-Bet* casino and hotel complex. Jim smiled and waved at the startled couple looking down at him from their fifty-second-floor window. Life's good. Another casino to try out. He turned the vehicle north and headed for the hardware store in the mall, using recently acquired caution, along with considerably less throttle. Jim parked near the Maglev station and walked to the store.

A pair of work gloves was a buck, and a two-liter bottle of water: one-twenty. A small can of denatured alcohol costs a buck forty-nine, and a roll of paper towels: forty-nine cents. The sales tax used to pay off the national debt brought the bill to just under five dollars. Only eighty cents tax. But the water wasn't included because it's a necessity—the tax charged on three dollars of purchase. Combined with state and city, it's over twenty-five percent.

Jim also bought a postcard with some spare change, wrote a note, and mailed it, just in case he didn't make it back to L.A. in one piece. Then he went to work on the tenacious little GPS tags. After a minute of soaking, rubbing alcohol loosened the stubborn, self-sticking bugs. They were a big improvement over the GPS tags of yore—the ones needing super-glue to attach. These little buggers have microscopic electron(ic) tentacles which latch onto any surface, and hold so tight dynamite can't dislodge them. But a dab of alcohol makes the tentacles retract, as long as the liquid is applied within four hours. If not, the tags become a permanent part of their environment, held together at the level of atomic structure—a true self-sticking technology.

Jim headed into the train station and pressed the tiny homing devices on a window near the back of the Los Angeles bound Maglev, being careful to place them the same distance apart as they had been on the turbocraft. As the denatured alcohol evaporated, the tags reattached themselves with a super-tight electron(ic) grip. A station employee looked suspiciously at the pilot—Jim showed his badge and the matter was resolved.

With that task completed, he headed back to the parking lot and jumped into his ship. It wouldn't start. He flipped up the cowling and noticed the battery was disconnected. The magneto had provided electricity. Paranoia was now the norm. He reconnected and prepared to leave. Jim reached into the electrical compartment and dislodged a fuse for the transponder. He didn't want ATC, Air Traffic Control following his every move. He also pulled the plug on GPS navigation and the radar altimeter. No matter. He was fine as long as he remained under VFR (Visual Flight Rules) and used M-CAS (Midair Collision Avoidance System) sparingly. There's simply no way to know what method they'd use to track him. He fired the thrusters and took off in the wrong direction, heading southeast towards Flagstaff.

Lake Mead was stunningly beautiful in the sunshine, though he didn't have time to sightsee. The stripped down Cat-five is the vehicle of choice if in a hurry, a rocket at over 620 mph. It did have one nasty flight characteristic: a violent shimmy between 340 and 400 miles per hour. Jim throttled-up through the turbulence—the first thing they taught in flight school. More power negates handling problems. He inhaled gratefully.

The thrusters were quiet enough to make a sound system worth considering. Jim hung on for dear life only twenty-five feet off the ground, flying *nap of the earth* for the first forty miles, then increased altitude for safety. In less than twenty minutes, the outskirts of Flagstaff vanished behind. He slowed to 410 miles per hour to save fuel, then made a paranoid-induced right turn towards Yuma.

That Maglev left the station a quarter hour ago, Jim thought. It'll be halfway to L.A. before they figure out what happened. He leaned back in the seat and relaxed. The turbocraft fit like a glove. It made him feel as if he was wrapped in a protective envelope of speed. "Okay, let's think about this." Jim spoke out loud. He didn't care. No one would hear. "They planned to force me down in Death Valley or the Mojave Desert where I'd have been left to die. Once they realize I'm missing, the search will commence between Vegas and L.A. Approaching downtown Los Angeles from the southwest may make it possible to get to HQ in one piece. The only variable—the Firm's lack of civility. If they can't steal the Cat-five, they'll destroy it," yet Jim had no idea why.

He eyed the comm. It was full military. With certain access codes and a whole lot of know-how, one can listen in on any frequency desired, including secure CIA, State Department, NSA, and even intercept LFL communications. Those codes are impossible to break, unless…he went right to work. With only two-dozen, twelve-digit sequences to unravel, how difficult could it be?

Skyscrapers at Prescott were visible in the distance as he sped through the morning heat. He marveled at the greenery below. Parts of Arizona had once been arid; mostly sand, sagebrush, and cactus. But that was the old climate. Changes in ocean currents sent plenty of wet weather across the southwest. It's a whole new environment down near the Mexican border—farms and forests. People who claimed global warming was negative turned out to be partially wrong. Of course, the fact that a dozen coastal cities were destroyed by hurricanes made it a hit-and-miss proposition.

Thirty-five more minutes and Yuma, Arizona passed before he was able to break into Secure Access. Jim put the comm. on scan and turned west towards Tijuana. Being busy with flying and code breaking, he'd forgotten to try out the Variable Camo, or Chameleon Skin to sci-fi fans. A touch of the finger-actuated sensor brought the system to life. The turbocraft shuddered and slowed, then automatically kicked in more power as the vehicle regained velocity. The cowling of the Cat-five turned green. The rainforests of Baja Norte were below.

He throttled up. His head jammed into the headrest as a warning buzzer interrupted the high-speed reverie. Jim had an extensive knowledge of acceleration, but he'd never felt anything like that. AFA was untested, an invitation for further research. He punched—but no response. No Pyrotec in the can. Surprise! They didn't want him running away.

Luxuriant Tijuana disappeared behind in a blurry flash! He was quickly out over the ocean. The top of his vehicle turned deepwater blue as he slowed to 380 miles per hour. The turbocraft shook violently and kicked like a bucking bronco, so he throttled back up to four-fifty. HQ was only twenty minutes away. That's when the comm. came to life. "I'll be bumfuddled," Jim shook his head. "They *are* looking for me."

..."located just east of Tijuana!" a static-filled voice blurted, "now heading up the coast at 3-3-0. We're closing!"

"Splash that turbocraft," came an order from some unknown command. "And no collateral damage this time!"

Jim slammed on the brakes, throwing the thrusters into vectored reverse. Except for stout, industrially woven safety harnesses, he'd have gone right through the canopy. "I hope the flight control modules hold out!" Jim grimaced painfully as negative G's dug into his chest. He was not wearing flight leathers, a specially padded suit that helped in such situations. The rapidly decelerating turbocraft slid into a sideways, airborne skid, followed by a violent shimmy. Years of flying experience brought things back under control after he'd tipped over edgeways for a few seconds.

Jim lowered the vehicle until it was just off the ocean surface. The thrusters created barely a ripple. The Cat-four would have produced all kinds of spray. He held perfectly still and looked up. Twelve seconds later, two F-42s streaked overhead. They were painted black with no ID.

..."Where the hell is he?" the comm. blurted.

..."We must have flown past him!"

..."Damn! This system doesn't track close enough."

Jim rammed the throttle forward while staying at sea level. The 42s held formation, then banked out over the water, slowing to Mach .4. Jim's only hope was to stay behind and pray to the *Everywhere Spirit*. He looked at the cowling. The color matched the surface of the water so closely, it was hard to tell where one ended and the other began. The sun was very bright, yet no reflections bounced off the Chameleon Skin or the canopy. Jim again thanked Great Spirit for his thoughtfulness.

..."He doubled back," one of the pilots bellowed. "Split up and find that sucker or our heads will roll!"

"Hopefully," Jim smiled. Turbulence from the 42s buffeted the turbocraft. He was violating the three by one hundred rule and adjusted upward to twenty feet above sea level.

…"My screen is blank!"

…"Continue a sweep to the south. I'll head up the coast."

One of the F-42s went into an 8-G turn, coming around so quickly it almost took Jim's breath away. He could not match the fighter without slowing, and just managed to keep himself behind and below. Without a high-performance G-suit or flight leathers, six G's is the most he'd realistically endure.

"I'll follow you north then," Jim muttered, regaining concentration and focus after he nearly blanked, something that wouldn't have happened in his younger days.

The unmarked F-42 accelerated to Mach .85, roughly 645 miles per hour. Jim followed, well below and eighteen hundred meters behind as they screamed up the coast. He hung on to the guy's tail until arriving at Long Beach, just minutes from HQ, then broke formation and headed towards shore, gaining enough altitude to jump over a senior highrise. There'd be safety and plenty of hiding places in the city.

…"He was right on your tail the whole time!" the comm. blurted.

…"I don't see him! Where the hell did he go?"

By that time it was too late. Jim flew into the middle of an industrial park and stomped on the brakes, hiding inside an open warehouse. A black, unmarked F-42 screamed overhead, going in the wrong direction.

It took forty-five minutes of shucking and jiving for the Cat-five to weave it's way through town. Jim took a very roundabout path, spending lots of time between buildings, under bridges, and behind big elm trees in an effort to remain hidden. The F-42s were relentless. They could not locate him, but knew his general vicinity. One pilot had mentioned being unable to track close enough. Jim was baffled. He slipped into the hanger at HQ a few minutes before noon with twenty pounds of fuel still in the tank. Everyone came out to meet him, including Captain Jackson.

Jim throttled back to an idle, then switched off the motors. He raised the canopy and stepped from the vehicle, noticing that he was sweating profusely. The supercomputer under the seat was hot.

FUTUREBUST6.9

There's something about Jim's personality that appreciates humor during a stressful moment. "You're late. I said no showgirls." Bo smiled.

Jim explained his situation. Security protocols were instituted, though the immediate threat had dissipated. Automated Air Traffic Control informed them that two F-42s were heading east towards the Mojave Desert at a low altitude and high rate of speed. Building security was tightened. Under DefCon Delta, C-PID would be required for the elevator. The main doors to the hanger had to be closed and secured, something everybody hated to do because it eliminated sunshine.

"I got caught counting cards again," Jim admitted. "Those casinos are sharing databases because I've never entered that particular building before."

"The casinos must be taking that sort of thing seriously if they sent two fighters after you. How much is missing from the till? Can you pay it back with interest?"

Jim laughed at the jokes. He knew Bo wanted all his money, not just the interest. If he complied, there'd be no questions asked. Jim tossed his wallet. He also reached back into the turbocraft for the shopping bag, carried from Vegas in a roundabout way at very high speed. It'd have been a shame to get shot down and the toys end up in the drink.

"Let me see that," Sarge grabbed the bag. "Not bad. A laser guided soccer ball. Can't miss with one of those. 'Bend it like Beckham'." Jim had heard that expression used twice, but still drew a blank.

Troubled by what had happened, Captain Jackson directed the conversation back to the current problem. "How did you escape F-42s? Their record is sixty-nine kills to no losses. I put you in some peril out there."

"They seemed to know my general vicinity but were unable to track closely," Jim guessed. "All in all, that is an incredible vehicle. The technology is many steps up from what we're used to." He jumped back into the Cat-five and retrieved his water. Dolly joined them and handed him a towel. He took a long drink and wiped his brow, then leaned back and closed his eyes to decompress. Time to show off the Cat-five. "Check this out. It's got duel climate control. You need that in a one-passenger vehicle. And cup holders. I can fill at least four cups of coffee. They thought of everything I don't need. I hope they didn't neglect the things I do need. I haven't found the chute pull or the fire suppressor yet."

Captain Jackson removed a paper from his pocket. "I've got to call the shipper. We're getting 3D-capable cameras small enough to fit on a turbocraft, a three-mile detection range on the NOSTRILS upgrade, plus subsurface penetration capability down to twenty-five feet depending on the soil type and density. On top of that, the upgraded Neutrino Camera will no longer give off that greenish tint. It will be in computer-simulated, living color." Captain Jackson smiled and put the paper back in his pocket. "This is the first in the country. Eventually, there'll be six searching for illegal drugs."

A couple of FBI dudes stopped in to look over the new machinery. They informed of an intelligence report from the NSA, just in, indicating there might be an attempt made to kill Jim. "An NSA retrieving station in Roswell, New Mexico picked up repeated mentions of the words Black Ops from various secure phone calls," the FBI dude explained. "That wouldn't be unusual, except the statements made were not in reference to any particular operation." He pulled out his notes and read. "The assortment of callers expressed the same somewhat confusing idea. NSA picked up four different calls with someone ordering," and he quoted from his notebook, "'Terminate Black Ops'. Now that could mean anything, as in an order to abort a covert mission. But the NSA computer spit out your former CIA code name and put two and two together. They think you are probably in some sort of danger."

Jim nodded. At least they were sharing data. "Tell them thanks. I'll be real careful." There was nothing like a little well-intentioned information from the National Security Agency to raise Jim's spirits. But they had done the best they could under the circumstances.

Everyone except the mechanics (Zeke, and Big Al) and Jim left the hanger and headed into the office to get some work done. The seventh floor was locked down tight. The FBI dudes decided it might be best if the whole building was put under a security ban—no unsupervised visitors until the bigwigs in DC lifted the order.

Jim laughed again. A security ban. That's oxymoronic.

Big Al eyed the Cat-five. Advanced technology is always exciting. He'd soon be overly protective of his machinery. "Pulse Thrusters," Jim pointed at the motors. Big Al scratched the top of his head with a greasy hand. "There's a manual in the storage compartment. Everything else you need is in the computer. And a full military comm."

"Sounds good," Big Al nodded his approval. "I'll have her figured out by this afternoon. But that comm. is coming out pronto."

Jim seemed uneasy, troubled by what had happened. He left the hanger and walked into the Command Center where Dolly and Sarge were watching the monitors. "Would you call my apartment?" he asked.

"Sure," Dolly replied. "Who are we to talk to? You live alone."

"Just call." He said no more, looking worried. Dolly rang up his number. It was busy. Jim looked down at the floor.

"Who's at your apartment?" she asked.

"No one," Jim answered. "I just wanted to see if anyone's been there yet." Jim looked at his co-officers who seemed confused, so he elaborated. "The bad guys. They have already torn the place up. That's why the phone is busy. They probably pulled the monitor right out of the wall."

"I'm going home with you," Sarge demanded. Jim didn't argue. He knew Sarge would not acquiesce.

"I just hope the photograph of my Great Great Grandfather is okay."

"They wouldn't steal it," Dolly comforted. "They couldn't know its value."

"You're probably right," Jim agreed, though he was clearly worried. He informed Bo of the postcard, just in case he'd crashed in the desert. It would arrive the next day.

Captain Jackson understated the obvious. "Looks like we smoked them out!"

FUTUREBUST 7.0

Sarge accompanied Jim to his apartment. Paranoia had gripped the pilot earlier that morning and it wasn't about to let go. He holstered his firearm, locked the door, and reset the home surveillance. Professionals knew how to disarm a burglar alarm and break in without drawing attention to themselves.

The place was a mess. "Those guys were real pros," Jim grimaced. "They've trashed everything." Sarge picked up a leather recliner with the seat neatly slit, so as to require reupholstering. Jim shrugged as if he had seen it all before. "They were making a statement that they can get to me. I've got to wonder what they were looking for."

"They can get to anybody. If the bad guys are determined, it'd be impossible to stop them." Sarge looked like he was about to punch someone out. Jim gave him the BugSwatter from his pocket. He swept the room, but found no surveillance devices.

"I'll be all right. You can go. There is little harm done."

"I can help you clean up," Sarge volunteered.

"Thanks for the offer but I'll do it later. Everything's under control." Jim pointed to the picture on the wall, which was unmolested, the most valuable item in the apartment. Despite hanging at a slight tilt from the ruckus, it remained undamaged.

"You don't think they'll be back then?"

"It's just a warning," he replied.

Sarge knew Jim wouldn't underrate the situation. He left fifteen minutes later after they righted the sofa and refrigerator. The latter was still working, so they restacked the salvageable food and wiped the floor. Jim noticed a bag of cheese puffs was missing from the cupboard. The vandals helped themselves, and were probably sitting around watching TV, munching on his puffs. If L.A. wasn't such a big town with ten thousand people eating them right now, he'd grab his Cat-four, fire up NOSTRILS and find those suckers with an atomic scan. All he needed was a sample. He looked around in hopes they'd opened the bag and dropped one on the floor while stuffing their pie holes, but no such luck. The guys were professionals. They wouldn't leave that cheesy a clue.

The Big Screen on the wall was also untouched. At least the vandals showed some class. They were messing with his mind—a subliminal voice echoing through his head. *Next time we'll do a more thorough job.*

Near the front entrance hung a five-inch-square picture of Jim's distant Great Grandfather. Lost in thought, he gazed at the photo for several minutes. While standing amidst scattered belongings, Jim contemplated his ancestor, sitting proudly on horseback. The face possessed so much character. Jim knew all the stories by heart, legends told and retold, generation-to-generation. Still he felt an unbridgeable gulf between the present and his ancestry. That man had lived in another place and time. It might as well have been another world.

Did the chief have an inkling of what the future held for his people? Jim contemplated the unlikely. A kind stranger from California gave the 170-year-old photo to his family, back when they lived on the Rez in South Dakota. It's said to be priceless, at least in some circles. An Indian on horseback—there's nothing unusual about it, and the quality is not the best. But it is the only known picture of his ancestor, despite claims that two others exist. One expert decided Jim's family was unrelated, asserting the great chief had no relatives who survived. Jim knew it was possible to get an expert to say anything. This involved an intangible, the element of faith in the validity of stories handed down across the years. The warrior in the picture was his ancestor but he couldn't prove it. They didn't have DNA samples back in the 1860s. His mother kept the photo until she died, then it became his. That happened thirty-nine years ago.

The picture transcended the barrier of time. Jim's distant Great Grandfather had lived free out on the plains before the Dakotas became states. He had to fight for all he held dear and was killed at a young age for no reason other than he would not give in.

Jim retreated to the bathroom for a hot shower, then retired to his sleeping quarters and reclined on a blanket. He pondered how hard his ancestors' lives must have been, wondering if he could ever live up to what he felt would be their expectations of him. Before the white man, things had not been so bad. After the white man came, their way of life was ruthlessly destroyed and the tribe nearly exterminated. It was not pleasant. A troubled, restless sleep darkened his consciousness. When he awoke, he realized he'd been dreaming of something important, but could not remember what.

Judge Horton accosted his thoughts. Jim wondered if the magistrate hadn't already disappeared. Conspiracies crowded in, making the DES pilot's head spin. He contemplated his experience in the Cat-five. The country's most seasoned turbocraft pilot wouldn't allow such an episode to pass without critical analysis. If any lessons could be gleaned from the encounter, Jim would distill and file them in his extraordinary memory.

Once the Cat-five passes final certification, five additional vehicles will be put into service in major cities. Airworthiness documentation is a relatively minor project—the new vehicle being nearly identical to the previous technology, at least on the surface. But the thrusters will require a thorough evaluation, with performance characteristics documented, and the vibration problem resolved. Big Brother was on a roll. That issue had long since been resolved in most people's minds. Hopefully, the new technology wouldn't upset the applecart and send everything toward a slippery slope of mistrust and suspicion. One had to wonder.

He grabbed a small box from a dresser and headed to HQ, walking the distance in fifteen minutes. Alpha colleagues wouldn't arrive until later. Work was the best way to clear his mind. No point in worrying about what he had no control over. Security was tight as he entered the Federal Law Enforcement Building. Those FBI dudes were not kidding. They wouldn't let him in without cross-referencing his C-PID (Certified Personal ID) with a molecular scan. That's kind of funny. He couldn't prove he was related to his ancestors, but he proved he was himself. They let him through with a nod. One FBI dude shook his hand.

FUTUREBUST7.1

"How's it going with that thing?" Jim, arriving upstairs, interrogated the head mechanic.

"Not bad." Big Al wiggled and looked up, his face showing dried grease smeared across like war paint. He was upside down in the cockpit trying to connect a sensitive electronic module deep under the console. "There's not much to it," he grunted. "Just pull the component out of the box, slide it in, beat on it with a hammer to make sure it's set, then calibrate. If that doesn't do the trick, hit harder with a bigger hammer until it understands who's boss. Sophisticated devices aren't stupid. They learn quickly." The *Big* in Al's name did not refer to his physical stature. He was smaller than average. He also had an unusual sense of humor.

"Everything fits then?" Jim smiled and sat down on the cowling. It was nice to be at work where things appeared normal, discounting the unusual security. He rubbed his hand over the Chameleon Skin.

"Like a glove," Big Al replied, changing position. "This thing's built from scratch, one piece at a time. It's got to be a prototype." He pushed himself back out of the vehicle. "Usually they put wearing parts that need the most service where you can't get at them without removing something else first.

This is better designed." He paused. "But it still points to a sizeable pay raise, crammed with perks, bonuses, benefits and freebees."

"A fatter check? Why's that? I'm the test pilot."

"It don't operate unless put together proper," Big Al smiled slyly while making fun of his own intelligence. "And remember, it has to be assembled correct—real careful-like or something might not work. There's no telling what could happen. I'd hate to hear you had some awful midair technical problems." Big Al changed his vernacular from grease monkey to Ph.D. economics professor. His life before joining DES had been in the ivory towers of academia, followed by a tour of duty as chief economist in a multinational corporation. Then he went into investment banking as a corporate raider. His goal at that time was to make money. It didn't matter who, what, why, or where. Only how much. Later he changed his mind, deciding money wasn't that important. For a Ph.D. in economics, that's heresy. He moved to another, more fulfilling line of work. Still, one has to fight for every penny to make it in the world. He explained. "The inflation rate will top a half percent this year. With skyrocketing prices and kids to feed, how can I be expected to worry about whether the new machinery is assembled to specs?"

"Sounds to me like you're threatening my health and wellbeing." Jim laughed. "If I can weasel more money out of the department, I should be able to get some for you, is that it?" He paused, handing Big Al the small box he'd brought from home. "You install this for me and I'll see what I can do."

"See," Big Al shook his head, taking the cardboard container, "you guys aren't so bad at economics after all. Come over here and I'll show you something." Big Al placed the tiny sound system on the pilot's seat and stepped back to the starboard-rear motor. He peeled away the Chameleon Skin, exposing the technically advanced innards, then pointed a greasy finger. "Those are high-speed turbines, but it's the damnedest blade configuration I've ever seen. They revolve faster than the turbines in the Cat-four. When you hit Mach .45 or a little over 342 miles per hour airspeed at sea level, the outside edges of the blades are revolving at the speed of sound. That's what causes the vibration. As you continue to accelerate, the turbines go supersonic until the entire length of the blade transverses the sound barrier at precisely 401.3 miles per hour, if figured mathematically, again at sea level. Then the problem dissipates, you're safely through."

"So there is a little sonic boom right within the motors," Jim nodded. "Are you sure this vehicle is designed to go fast?"

"Actually, it's designed to go faster or slower. However, it has a little problem between 342 and 401 MPH."

"Anything I should be worrying about?"

"Not really," the mechanic concluded with a shrug. "It just makes for a bumpy ride." He paused ominously. "As long as the Flight Control Modules don't fail."

"Crash and burn?"

"There'd be nothing left. She'd disintegrate," Big Al explained. "Normally you could control the situation and land without the FCMs, or just deploy the ballistic parachute. But if you're between Mach .45 and .52 during a failure…"

"I haven't even found the chute pull yet. So what's the solution?"

"For now, just ram through the danger zone. Don't spend any time there. When we get a fix, we'll install it. Or you can stay below .45, and no problem."

"I don't think that's going to happen." Jim folded his arms across his chest. "You know how much I enjoy speed. I've got to have an ample supply of acceleration under my butt or I'm miserable to get along with."

Big Al smiled and nodded, as if there was some truth in what Jim said. "One more thing I want to show you." He stepped back to his toolbox, grabbed a shiny electronic device the size of an old cigarette lighter, and handed it to the pilot.

"Haven't got a clue," Jim shook his head in the negative, tossing the gizmo up and down. "Explain, and it better not have anything to do with economics."

"It's a sophisticated homing device," Al informed. "Zeke found it buried deep in the bowels of the machine. He's got a sharp eye."

Jim was stupefied. "But I used a BugSwatter on the entire vehicle! There is no way I could have missed it. Besides, look at how big it is!"

"It was easy to overlook," Big Al consoled. "A BugSwatter would never locate this little booger. It doesn't send out a signal."

Jim shook his head. "Then how could it be used for tracking?"

The mechanic shrugged. "Zeke claimed he read it in a spy novel. He thinks it absorbs outbound signals sent from a space-based transmitter, creating a hole in the signature pattern. It works like an electronic vacuum. Whoever is tracking you looks for a lack of signal or reflection. That little device soaks up all the broadcast transmission in its vicinity, creating a void in the spectrum—the opposite of current technology. It tells them where you aren't, which is almost the same as locating you, only not as accurate. They interpolate, then figure horizontally. There is no way to know you're being watched. It's the perfect method of tracking someone who doesn't want to be scrutinized."

"So it can't pinpoint location, just the general vicinity." Jim's voice held a note of concern. "Big Brother is getting real sneaky. How did Zeke find it?"

"It was secured behind one of the airframe struts." Al raised his eyebrows slightly. "With normal maintenance, we wouldn't have found it for six months. You're lucky to be alive! Zeke figured when you slipped away from the GPS tags, they flooded the entire southwestern US with an imperceptible homing signal, via satellite. A barely detectable void appeared over Arizona and you'd been located to within 2500 square miles, give or take. At that point, they scrambled the F-42s, which could focus in and narrow your whereabouts down to maybe a hundred square miles. After that they probably went visual. It's slow and cumbersome, but effective."

"How does Zeke know about this device? I've never heard of it."

"He's got an awful lot of useful information locked up inside his head," Big Al conceded. "The guy's an avid reader of spy, and sci-fi novels." Jim tossed the gizmo into the air, catching it as it fell. "Zeke figured the device probably cost over one million dollars. And the entire system, including R&D, a billion dollar project!" The tossing abruptly stopped.

"That's not an expense born by anyone but the big boys. It looks like I've made some unwelcome friends in high places."

"No doubt," Al agreed. "Zeke wants to dissect the device but I figure we better not. Maybe we can send it back to DC as a practical joke."

"Let's keep it for now," Jim suggested. "You've removed the power?"

"Just after we found it," Al assured. "We considered taking it over to the Maglev station and putting it on the train to Alaska. They'd have chased it all the way up the coast!"

"That's a bit dangerous for the passengers. The nutcases flying those 42s would fire at anything. Remember, your typical fighter pilot is not an inhibited personality." Jim shook his head, realizing he had done much the same thing with the GPS tags. He was also ticked off, having underestimated his adversary. Big Al's demeanor implied there was another problem to resolve. "Shoot," Jim encouraged, wondering what else could go haywire this early in the game. He prepared for the worst.

"We're missing one module," the mechanic shrugged. "It was on the bill of lading when the courier delivered, but not in the shipment from Hong Kong."

Jim looked puzzled, then annoyed. "Let me guess. DSP for NOSTRILS?"

"Why did you guess Deep Subsurface Penetration?"

"Because everything else is just a better version of what we already have. The new subsurface modules are state of the art, a capability the military wanted years ago but technical difficulties made it a tough nut to crack. Current technology allows me to scan up to five feet underground. DSP penetrates twenty feet or more, depending on soil type and conditions. It'd have easily gone through a ten-foot thick concrete bunker, a capability the cartels don't want us to have! Drug dealers literally go underground to avoid the law."

Al looked apologetic. "I hate to be the bearer of inauspicious tidings, but you're right on the money!" He never used the word *money* frivolously.

Jim was clearly disappointed, but left with few options. "We'll have to look into this, but my guess is that we're out of luck. It's a blow to drug enforcement in Los Angeles."

A long minute passed. Both men were immersed in thought. Jim couldn't help but notice the mechanic's expression, a look warning those nearby that something was cooking in the grey-matter located between his earrings. Al seemed cautious with his words. "I was thinking about the bad boys wanting to get this vehicle. If things get hairy, could you land on Sarge's boat without scratching the varnish?"

"Easily," Jim assured. "Piece-of-cake."

Al's eyes grew wide with wonder as he observed the senior DES pilot. Then the mechanic shrugged nonchalantly. "It'd be a great place to hide the Cat-five, making the *Big Boozer* an aircraft carrier!" Jim laughed. Big Al pointed at the new equipment. "You think this is legal?"

"Need-to-know." Jim shrugged. "But we'll do our best to make sure."

FUTUREBUST7.2

Evening rolled around, then late night. Al had finished and gone home hours earlier. Things were quiet in the hanger. The Cat-five was nominally complete—all electronic components installed with one glaring exception. Jim ran through a computerized check. The electronic brain informed him that the DSP, the Deep Subsurface Penetration Module was improperly integrated, definitely a *duuuhh* moment. Leave it to computers to figure out the hard stuff. Consolation? His new vehicle included a high fidelity sound system, however the left-hand, law enforcement side of his brain much preferred DSP.

The modules were considerably smaller than on the Cat-four, making for a nicer design inside. Removing the storage box behind the seat might create enough space to haul a passenger. It'd be cramped, but doable with a shoehorn. Jim read from the onboard computer. There was nothing new—it just worked better and from farther away. The missing component troubled him. Whoever took it knew what he was doing.

An FBI dude in camo fatigues and body armor stopped in to make sure everything was okay on the seventh floor. The guy carried an old rifle. He also had an unusual backup gun, and a vicious looking knife strapped down near his ankle.

"Nice gun," Jim motioned at the antique. "Is there enough firepower there?"

"It's a Winchester carbine, circa 1876. It'll handle just about any contingency. But I also carry a German-made MP-5 machine pistol in case things get ugly."

"An eclectic assortment of weapons. You're lucky to be part of a well-regulated militia," Jim affirmed. He pointed at the knife. "That's out of reach."

"Not if you are struggling close-quarters on the ground. My name is Buford. I'll be patrolling floors six through ten." They shook hands. "This is great. I haven't had a chance to dress up in camo for months. You've provided the first excitement in awhile. Everybody's volunteering for overtime. We'll have agents on the roof, just in case they repel onto the building. It's CIA guys we're after, right?"

"Right," Jim laughed. "At least I think so. We're not sure. You're going to be disappointed though. They won't be coming back. They've already made their point."

"How so?" Buford didn't like what he was hearing. He was after thrills. It isn't often one gets to shoot at CIA guys. For decades, FBI has lived with the fact that CIA is its superior in intelligence gathering. The Feds are treated like an incompetent little brother, to be tolerated, endured, and occasionally slapped upside the head. It is annoying. The two agencies don't talk.

"They tore up my apartment," Jim informed and pointed to the instrument panel, "plus they got our most important upgrade. This vehicle has ostensibly been neutered!"

"What'd they take?" Buford asked as he squatted.

"Deep Subsurface Penetration, the last piece of electronics I'd want to give up."

"Too bad," Buford agreed as he stood up. "That would have shaken things up. The bad guys always hide underground like rodents. It suits them."

"How do I get in touch with you if we need help?" Jim asked spryly.

"Just call 911," Buford countered. "Talk to you later." He continued his patrol, hoping for a chance to capture a CIA agent. The two agencies had been feuding for decades.

FUTUREBUST7.3

The other Alphas wandered in at 11 o'clock, grumbling about tight security. Jim informed them of the missing module.

"We'll order another," Bo announced, attaching some unappreciated humor. "A bureaucratic investigation should add excitement to our lives."

Jim scrutinized those standing around, including Sarge and Larry. "What's our plan of action then?"

"You're going to check up on Horton. Maybe he'll lead us to that Uncle Roy fellow. I'm concerned. Bribed judges were once dime-a-dozen, but recent studies at Harvard have shown only thirty percent are vulnerable to cash advances today. I hope we don't end up going back to the bad old days."

"We could fire a GPS tag onto Horton's butt with a TurboShot," Larry laughed, "as a deterrent to him skipping town."

"Wow!" Sarge rubbed his behind. "The hospital would be his first stop. He'd think he'd been stung by a bee."

"Yeah," Bo agreed. "A forty-pounder!"

Cy was the last to arrive, wearing a baggy pinstriped double-breasted suit reminiscent of gangster fashions from a century before. "Security is tight!" he admonished. "They did a scan of my new outfit. I hope those sensors don't ruin the creases."

"All you need is a violin case," Jim commented enthusiastically, looking up from his four-engine throttle rocket. "Is that tax-deductible?"

"If the Firm is spying on us," he smiled and adjusted his tie, "I want them to wonder about our sanity. That would surely make it tax-deductible, being used in a job-intensive way. If they think we're crazy or disturbed..." Cy shrugged in explanation. "It's much harder to intimidate one whose sanity is in question."

"We'll keep an eye out for that," Bo smiled. "Anyway, if the Firm is after us, we can use the long-range capabilities of the Fiver to our advantage."

"I still like the GPS tag scenario," Larry added. "If we fired at vastly reduced pressure, he'd end up with a big red welt on his butt a quarter inch thick and as big as a silver dollar." Larry shrugged at the other's skepticism. "Okay, the welt would be bigger, but who's going to measure it?"

"As far as shooting the judge in the keister," Bo shook his head, "can you imagine the lawsuit and medical costs to remove the tag? The way they latch on to foreign surfaces with their electron(ic) tentacles, denatured alcohol would have to be used immediately."

"You could always try dynamite," Sarge suggested dryly. "A couple of well-placed sticks might be enough to detach the most tenacious GPS tags."

"Explosives aren't an option." Bo's smile was stern but understanding. "Blowing up a judge's ass is frowned on in legal circles, right Cy?"

"If he took a bribe, we'd have probable cause. Our ultimate goal is to flush out Uncle Roy," Cy insisted. "But what do we do if we catch him?"

"Make him an offer he can't refuse," Bo replied as he looked at Cy's suit.

"I'd sure like to meet him again." Larry spoke absentmindedly. His countenance troubled the very observant lieutenant. Larry's face held an expression indicative of possible chaos, mayhem, and all-around inconvenience for civilization as a whole. The DES prankster continued, noticing the others were waiting for his up-close-and-personal assessment of the CIA miscreant. "The guy has an unusual charisma behind all that sarcasm. He likes to talk. If we bend him to our ends, the information we acquire would be priceless."

"It's risky," Cy advised. "The bad boys are going to be after the Cat-five. Possibly we won't have to find them. They'll find us."

"That's just peachy," Jim assured. "They do know where we are." He paused, looking inward at the mental vastness, then came back to the plane of consciousness others inhabit. "I think I'm about ready to try this bugger out. I'll head to His Honor's house and feed a scan back to you. It'll be our first test of the new sensor platform." He pulled the canopy down and fired the burners. The four motors throbbed briefly as the vehicle came to life. The hanger doors were opened. Two heavily armed SWAT guys stood by and watched. Jim taxied out while Sarge, Larry, Cy, and Bo walked behind. If it had been a Cat-four, the thrust would have messed up their hair. But the Fiver—there was virtually no exhaust. It seemed surreal, almost like flying saucer magic.

Jim waited for clearance from AATC, then throttled up and lifted away from the building, hovering out over the street some hundred feet below. The most experienced turbocraft pilot in the country waved to his compatriots, gave them the peace sign, pointed the Fiver towards Horton's domicile, and poured on the coal. The SWAT dudes observed the scene with amusement. Bo watched the Fiver disappear full-tilt into the night, wondering how many times he'd warned his pilot not to smoke the tires. It never did much good. Consolation? Jim hadn't done a simulated wheelie.

The men enjoyed the cool night air, spending a few fleeting moments gazing at the Milky Way. Bo returned to the office. The phone was ringing. He ran to the Command Center but it was too late. Caller ID said it was the LAPD. He returned the call and found himself talking to a precinct captain. "We have a report that Judge Horton turned up missing. Thought you might be interested."

Bo frowned at the oxymoron but let it pass without comment. "I sent a turbocraft to his neighborhood, just to be safe."

"Photo ID Recon picked his image out of the crowd at LAX. He's definitely gone, maybe on the run. But we have no proof he's done anything illegal. Our hands are tied until something concrete turns up. You guys have more authority in these matters." The captain smiled. "One other thing. The Chief wants me to suggest you stop using our Internal Affairs computer for searches. We use FBI's secure access."

"I'll make sure it doesn't happen again," Bo promised. "Maybe we'll switch to the NSA's computers upstairs. They'll never figure it out."

The captain winked in agreement and hung up. Things were getting weird. Judge JJ on the run? There's little chance of it being a scheduled vacation—his docket filled with cases. Bo reclined in his seat, wondering about all the security surrounding the building. He had talked to the SWAT dudes out on the roof. They were in no hurry to return to normal either—overtime and all. The other Alphas entered the Command Center, grabbed chairs, and huddled around the turbocraft monitors.

Jim's voice and image came over the comm. "These are the first 3D pictures ever sent from a turbocraft. I can't believe they've reduced the cameras to portable status!"

"We'll patch your feed to the DynaView to get the 3D effect." Cy made the needed connection with a few taps on the keyboard. The big screen lit up with a breathtaking view of Hollywood, seven miles from HQ.

"It's spectacular!" Sarge couldn't control his enthusiasm.

"Like mountain-fresh air," the DES attorney waxed poetic.

"Yeah," Bo seemed troubled. "What they said."

"You ought to see this view." Larry was mesmerized. "I think it's better than what you've got out there in the real world."

"I doubt it," Jim admonished with a smirk. "Don't try to con me. I'm not trading jobs with any of you. I'll be within range of residential Glendale in two minutes unless you're in a big hurry. There is always more speed." Bo kept quiet. He didn't want to spoil the moment.

"Take your time, partner," Sarge's eyes were bulging at the picture. The big man brushed his hair back. Everyone watched as mile after mile passed silently beneath the turbocraft. Bo switched views from his Command Console—front to back, side to side—using the remote joystick and camera selection switch Zeke installed earlier that afternoon. All worked flawlessly.

"Try zooming in," Cy suggested. The lieutenant reached back over the desk and remote operated the camera looking towards Glendale.

"What are you doing with my equipment," Jim protested. "Leave'em be!"

"We're just playing," Bo laughed, his mood more upbeat. "How far are you from Horton's house? Do I have time to fool around with the split screen?"

"No you don't," Jim replied, checking the GPS. "Three miles, the outside range of the array. I'll zoom in if you'll kindly return control to me." Bo released the remote. Jim placed the turbocraft on hover and focused toward an upper-middle class neighborhood where the judge resided. "I'll find it in a minute." He added night-vision enhancement, zooming in until the house encompassed the entire DynaView. "There it is, a three-story Tudor. What do you think?"

"It's a little ostentatious," Sarge conceded, "but the Mrs. might go for it if it came with a cleaning lady."

"The camera," Jim laughed. "What do you think of the image?"

"Just like looking out of a window," Larry replied, still mesmerized by what he saw. "Those 3D views make me want to reach out and grab, and from three miles away. That would certainly make us the long arm of the law."

Cy frowned at the use of trivial, law enforcement humor. The four Alphas gazed at the DynaView with wide-eyed fascination. Bo spoke. "Sit tight, Jim."

The phone rang again. It was the Federal Bureau of Investigation, Central Command, Los Angeles, a dozen floors above DES Headquarters. Bo listened to the sector chief. "We've got some information for you DES guys," he informed. "Judge Horton left town. Photo ID Recon picked him up at LAX hours ago. Then it spotted him in Dallas, followed by Miami. We don't know what happened to him after that. Maybe Havana."

"You guys were following him?" Bo was puzzled.

"After that decision he made in the Franklin case, every law enforcement computer in the area had his name top and center. We've got a BD program incorporated in our CrimeStopper software package." Bo looked confused. "Bribery Detection," the sector chief informed, "developed back in the twenties when graft and corruption was rampant. It's slow, but still works pretty good."

"Thanks for the information," Bo was double-troubled as he hung up.

Jim switched on NOSTRILS to scan the neighborhood. He fell silent, detecting an anomaly in the instruments before it was obvious to the others. The turbocraft pilot possessed a tracker's instinct ingrained in his genes. Bo routinely checked the comm. "Your thoughts?"

Cy, Sarge, and Larry shifted their attention to the comm. Jim remained focused, checking three different displays. He rubbed his chin and looked at the lieutenant. "I'm picking up a neutrino disturbance, dissipating slowly. Someone operated a powerful camera near the judge's residence earlier."

"You have probable cause," Cy informed. "But for what?"

"The judge apparently skipped town," Bo informed the others. He noticed Jim's baffled expression. "Scan the neighborhood at the subatomic level. Turn off the telemetry. Then you might as well come back in."

Jim looked disappointed as all Command Center screens went blank except the comm. in the center of the main display. Bo turned toward the phone. It was Captain Jackson calling from his living room. The senior officer liked to check up on his graveyard shift from time to time. "How does the new equipment work? I've been wondering and decided to call."

Bo, mindful of what the captain had done to him last night, opted to have some fun. "I can't really say without first consulting my attorney."

Captain Jackson grimaced. "Okay, I deserved that. Now answer the question."

"Everything's spiffy, if we discount the missing DSP."

"I'm glad it's going so well," Captain Jackson capitulated. "But I've decided to keep my distance from the new machinery, as close as I am to retirement. Wouldn't want to jeopardize those much-anticipated golden years. Sometimes technological advancement boggles the mind. We'll get an expert opinion as to whether it's legal."

Bo agreed. "You know Judge Horton flew the coop?"

Captain Jackson nodded. The senior officer appeared agitated. "There's one tidbit I wanted to share with you guys. Uncle Roy phoned. Normally he'd show up unannounced. He wants to talk. I think the Firm is concerned about the new technology. He's extremely anxious to meet Jim. Apparently, no one on his side of the fence figured the Cat-five would make it to Los Angeles—assuming it would be in their hands before we got a chance to look it over! They underestimated, which is precisely why I sent Jim. It was to be delivered by a factory pilot. Had that been the case, it, and one dead pilot would never have gotten to L.A."

"I'm sure Jim is anxious to meet him. When is LeRoy going to show?"

"Soon, at HQ," Captain Jackson assured. "Keep an eye on him when he arrives. He can't be trusted. Make sure he plants no bugs in our midst. Watch him like a hawk! He's probably behind Horton's disappearance." Bo was about to make a suggestion, but was preempted by the captain. "And don't bother arresting him. No matter what the charge, he will be set free within the hour. I already tried it twice in the last decade."

"Got it. See you soon." Bo ended the transmission, shaking his head in wonder. He was troubled, yet relieved. "So we've already achieved our objectives for this evening."

"It looks like it." Cy tried to lift everyone's spirits. "I'll go downstairs to the lobby and wait. We should order a pizza. You think spies like Italiano?"

"We'll find out." Bo was instantly receptive. "Take care of the arrangements, Larry. Put it on the card. The bean counters complain we don't use expense accounts adequately. They hate the extra work when we return money."

Larry and Cy departed. Sarge sat down and stared at the blank monitors as the phone rang for the fourth time that evening. The call originated from Roswell, New Mexico. "I'm Commander Bosley, NSA," the man informed courteously. "I just got a note here on my desk that says you are planning to use our computers for classified requests." The guy sounded serious, though he clearly had a sense of humor. "I wanted to inform you that it probably isn't a good idea."

"I was joking, sir," Bo smiled. "I guess our phones aren't secure either."

"*ECHELON ULTRA* can penetrate any secure access. By the way," Bosley smiled, "that information is classified. Anyway, try busting into IRS, or Homeland Security computers. Then call back and tell me how you did."

Bo nodded, noticing caller ID listed the number as *Classified*. Still, it was a golden opportunity to get info from the specialists. "Do you have any idea who might be using a Neutrino Camera here in Los Angeles to spy on a sitting federal judge?"

"Probably the CIA."

"But who would want him out of the way?"

"Probably the CIA."

"Any idea who'd scramble two, black, unmarked F-42s and try to shoot down a civilian turbocraft?"

"Are you sure it was civilian?"

Bo acquiesced. "An experimental vehicle with military applications."

"Probably the CIA," Bosley repeated.

"But why do they want my pilot dead?"

"You better talk to the CIA. If there is anything you guys need, feel free to give us a call." The phone went blank.

Bo leaned back in his chair and contemplated. Strange things were happening with few clues to piece the puzzle together. And someone out there wanted it that way. Jim returned at a very high rate of speed and parked in the hanger. He entered the Command Center. "That thing's uncertified," Bo reminded. "You could wait. The paperwork I'd be wading through if you'd crashed and burned. Have you no feelings for your fellow man?"

"I had to test the airbrakes," Jim insisted before continuing. Bo seemed distracted. "You ought to see on top the building. They have six SWAT guys tethered to the roof, pointing their guns at everything that moves."

"So what happens next?" Sarge shrugged. Jim shook his head.

"I think I can help you out," an elderly gentleman replied. His bodyguard accompanied him, a big man named Dirk with a nametag on his lapel. Cy escorted them into the Command Center. Uncle Roy removed his jacket and handed it to Dirk, who hung it in the main office. Then the bodyguard stood by the door with his chin up, feet slightly apart, hands clasped in front while looking big and tough. It seemed LeRoy needed protection while in the domain of law enforcement. The guy spoke sarcastically. It was obvious from where all the bad vibes originated. "Judge Horton left town. We kept an eye on him to verify he didn't change his mind, turn chicken, and rat, thereby reneging on our deal. The Firm is sending him to TobagoBago where he'll be gently encouraged to live happily-ever-after. We bought him a full half-acre plot. He's not important so don't lose sleep over it, and please don't interfere." Uncle Roy said *please*, but was not being polite. "Horton was a hard-line judge. We needed someone on the bench who'd be more accommodating, someone with—how shall I put it—a more forgiving heart. Forget your silly law enforcement prejudices. There are important issues to discuss!"

"This is simple," Cy nodded. "Arrest him and be done with it." Uncle Roy laughed. So did Dirk as he stood with his back against the wall just outside the Command Center. Cy handed Bo a device taken from LeRoy. He placed it in plain view on a nearby counter.

"You don't want us recording you. Fair enough." The device, an electronic scrambler, would make it impossible to record a conversation unless one happened to have a counter-scrambler, which could, of course, be subverted by an anti-counter-scrambler. No matter, DES offices are not bugged. No point in encouraging Big Brother.

FUTUREBUST7.6

The Alphas were amazed at Uncle Roy's candor. Bo, sharp as usual, made a speculative observation, though his comment was terse. "So the Firm removed an unsympathetic judge, in case you're caught selling contraband."

"I wouldn't use the word *removed*," Uncle Roy insisted. It was clear the two had a deep, intrinsic personality conflict, as if they'd been enemies in a previous life. "We could call it a vigorously intimated early retirement." He seemed pleased with his choice of words and stared piercingly at Bo, as if dealing with a greenhorn too far beneath him to be worth the trouble. His tone softened minimally. "Judge Horton submitted his personal termination notice after the Firm forced his decision regarding Robert Franklin. We figured it would embarrass and intimidate DES if Bubba was given a lenient sentence. The Company likes to go into any negotiation with a dozen aces up our sleeve. We saw Horton as an impediment to progress. So a hint of blackmail, a thinly veiled threat of extensive bodily discomfort, and presto-chango, the judge is nowhere to be found. Horton was a patsy, having had far too many illicit affairs for his own good. It seems he was getting more than his fair share. What a shame if his wife found out. Divorce court isn't his forte. She'd have taken him to the cleaners."

Standing outside the entrance to the Command Center with hands clasped in front of him, Dirk laughed quietly. He had everything under control.

No one in the room interrupted the spy. Larry mentioned that the guy had a tendency to talk. They'd let him ramble—see if he'd tell them anything useful. Uncle Roy glanced at Cy's gangster pinstripes. "Consider adding a violin case to that outfit. It's very intimidating." Without waiting for a reply, he turned to the only Lakota native in the room. "Jim BlackOps. I read your

CIA file recently. I'll bet someone could write a *Clancyesque* book about your experiences." LeRoy's facial expression was baffling, making it difficult to gauge whether he was really interested. Jim quietly nodded, arms folded across his chest as he leaned against the wall. His own expression revealed intense scrutiny. He said nothing. It was clear that CIA types didn't always trust each other. "They're still upset with you," LeRoy continued, his voice softer, as if looking for a button to push. "Just this morning you survived the last day of your forty-four-year life." Uncle Roy spoke with cynical admiration. "You've gained moderate respect from those wanting to erase you from the face of God's green earth. Escaping an F-42 is impossible and you got away from two at once! That demotes their combat scorecard with one tie. You've ruined the aircraft's perfect record!" Uncle Roy shook his head and smiled, yet his voice hardly exuded sympathy. "About the minor in-flight difficulties—no hard feelings, I hope." He sat down on a nearby chair. "I'd like to know how you accomplished such a feat?" Jim remained silent. He reached into his pocket and pulled out the MED (Mysterious Electronic Device) Zeke found deep inside the turbocraft and handed it to LeRoy. The CIA miscreant nodded. "They must be very, very angry at you."

"Would you tell us why you're here?" Bo spoke with all the politeness he could muster. "You mentioned having a dozen aces up your sleeve." Bo felt he had a more appropriate location for all those playing cards, but decided to keep things civil. No point in provoking the man.

He was ignored. LeRoy gazed at Jim and offered a plausible explanation. "It was the perfect opportunity to exact revenge—you all alone in the middle of nowhere. There are people at the Firm who'd like nothing better than to see you splattered across the desert in your new turbocraft. It'd make a wonderful alibi. An experienced pilot killed while flying an untested, uncertified prototype." The sarcasm got very deep. Uncle Roy spoke as if seeing it through their eyes. "Too bad, it's such a shame. We're going to miss him, but he was a test pilot— he knew the risks." Dirk, standing tough with his back to the entrance, turned and looked into the Command Center. He said nothing. Everything was under control.

"Which did they want more? Me, or the new turbocraft?"

"Your new turbocraft is no threat," LeRoy laughed. "They wanted you. But old grudges are hard to assuage and those people can be vindictive. There are top officers in the Firm who had their careers sidetracked because of you."

Jim understood the warning. "Do you think they will try again?"

"If you give them cover, possibly another accident scenario. I'm guessing you have a little time. If anything happens in the near term, they'd be the first ones questioned." A good explanation, Jim knew he was telling the truth but he did not know why.

"And the reason you are here?" Bo asked again.

Uncle Roy got right to the point. "I'm here to make a deal with DES in Los Angeles. We'd like to come to an understanding. I'm sure there is common ground to work from if we put our heads together." The guy seemed to enjoy concocting ambiguous sentences.

"So you precede your peace offer with embarrassment and intimidation," Cy observed flatly. "That's an interesting tactic when up against overwhelming odds." LeRoy looked annoyed, as if realizing that DES was in fact holding all the cards.

Sarge wondered how much trouble it'd be to throw the CIA bad boy from the office and be done with it. He'd have to beat up Dirk first, despite the bodyguard being almost as big and twenty years younger. Maybe LeRoy could be turned over to the FBI dudes for target practice. Sarge's gaze was direct. "You will also take the opportunity to find out all you can about our new sensor platform."

His sadistic smile returned. "We don't want your toy." Uncle Roy grimaced in disgust, as if only an amateur would ask such a thing. "But about that missing module. It's a painful loss I'm sure. DSP for NOSTRILS would have been a welcome enhancement."

"I don't suppose you'd give it back?" Jim asked quietly.

Uncle Roy just smiled. "You see, it's these misunderstandings that cause so much friction between us. We're not after the Cat-five, yet this morning... the consequences could have been *such* a tragedy." Sarcasm? The guy possessed no other philosophy, except maybe cynicism. "It's highly unlikely you'll acquire a new DSP module anytime soon. The manufacturing facility is a smoking ruin. Terrible thing, fire, when it gets out of hand. It will take months to rebuild, barring additional unforeseen difficulties." Uncle Roy seemed proud of himself. Dirk, standing tough outside the door, smiled in self-congratulatory satisfaction.

FUTUREBUST 7.7

Captain Jackson arrived with Larry and motioned everyone out to the main office. The Command Center was too cramped. Larry placed his stack of pizzas on the counter near the refrigerator. Uncle Roy sat down on a chair while Dirk stood near the InstaPrint in that same pose: feet squarely apart, chin up, and hands clasped in front of him. The guy said nothing—just looked forward. His noncommittal expression implied he was so intimidating, he didn't even need to look the part. The senior officer spoke as if to assume command. "Can the CIA give up money acquired through the sale of illegal drugs? From what I understand, it's already figured into the domestic surveillance budget."

"It's good to see you, Jacko." Uncle Roy spoke with never-ending sarcasm. "I'm not here to negotiate an end to the sale of controlled substances. In fact, we're in dire need of even more untraceable cash. And as always," Uncle Roy leaned back, clasping his hands behind his head, "we don't have to be accountable to anyone. That's just the way the spy business works." The sarcasm waned, providing much needed relief. "There are problems facing both our organizations. The Firm needs your sympathy and cooperation."

"Your mother must be real disappointed in you," Sarge commented dryly. Dirk glanced at him but said nothing.

Bo laughed at how the tough guys reacted to each other. He'd put his money on Sarge, who'd just break Dirk's leg and be done with it. No point in making a fuss, throwing punches, or smashing up the office. And *Jacko*—Captain Jackson's code name—pretty funny also.

Uncle Roy turned to Larry and grinned. "Don't I know you? Yes. You're the young man who raided the Capitol Building a quarter century ago with no backup. I told you there'd be a ruckus if you exposed the truth."

"We did okay," Larry observed. "Lawmakers were introduced to the democratic process after that. There was no longer any need for term limits."

Uncle Roy nodded. "But the system isn't in as good shape as you think. It's still controlled by money and special interests, just as it was then. No matter what ethics laws are passed by the do-gooders in Congress, the dark side finds ways to undermine them. They don't even hide the fact they're doing it."

Larry didn't argue the point. "I've got a question for you." Uncle Roy looked reflective and waited. "Where did you relocate your operations after Congress was busted? We checked everywhere, dragging the new drug sniffer around town for two years, but dangerous drugs like tobacco and alcohol were still in the area."

Uncle Roy nodded. "We stayed a few steps ahead, yet occasionally you were within hours of catching us. We relocated to a top-secret vault deep under the reflecting pool next to the Lincoln Memorial; an abandoned command bunker the President could go to in case of attack. It worked like a charm until our hideout sprang a leak. Remember when the water mysteriously disappeared from the pool eighteen years ago? We got flooded. I had Ulrick," Uncle Roy hesitated and smiled, *"terminated* for his incompetence." Dirk made a smirk and shifted his weight as Uncle Roy continued. "He was supposed to maintain the facility. Lots of Cubans were destroyed. Congress had to do without for a month. After that—well it was getting hard to make a buck selling alcohol and tobacco. Our leaders became less addicted. Smoke-filled rooms—a thing of the past."

"So we won," Larry prodded the spy.

"It looks that way," LeRoy replied perfunctorily. "Today we supply reactionary groups hiding throughout the country. Plus there are always the business execs with their tax-deductible entertainment accounts. Those people love exchanging shareholder money for drinking and smoking pleasure."

Captain Jackson changed the subject. "How is it you managed to get back into the good graces of the Firm?"

"Oh, that little misunderstanding," the spy pooh-poohed. "Yes Jacko, you managed to embarrass me some. But I wasn't the only one fooled by DES. Some big shots were also bamboozled and they felt the only reasonable course of action was to excuse the mistakes. That's what's so heartwarming about the Firm. It can be an especially forgiving organization."

"So you were pardoned," Cy observed. "How very fortunate for all of us."

Uncle Roy chuckled at Cy's counter-sarcasm, gazing at the attorney's attire. "Some were cleared of malfeasance, others were not. Risk assessment is critical. In this business, you survive by the skin of your teeth." LeRoy looked thoughtfully sentimental. "'There is a destiny that shapes our ends; rough-hew them as we may.'"

Jim dropped his hands to his side in disgust. "So now we're quoting Shakespeare. I'll give you another you might want to work on." LeRoy looked at the turbocraft pilot slyly. "'I don't know, I thought it just sounded distinguished-like.'" Jim spoke in his best imitation British accent, something Native Americans probably shouldn't try. "Stir that one around in your martini for a while."

"Touché," LeRoy replied. "I recognize that quote, but can't put my finger on it."

Dirk exhaled loudly and shifted his weight, tired of the disrespect aimed at his boss.

"You've been reading Bartlett's," Captain Jackson commented.

"You guys are really getting in your licks. That's to be expected. It's not often one gets the chance to beat up on a spymaster."

FUTUREBUST7.8

"Why don't we terminate the hostilities and enjoy a bite to eat." Larry dutifully prepared the pizza purchased minutes earlier. He handed a paper plate to the *spymaster*.

"Italian Pie," Uncle Roy appeared pleased at the suggestion. "Are you sure it's safe to consume? Goodness-gracious, I didn't know cops dined on such sumptuous fare. My recollection is that the average law enforcement officer's highest culinary aspirations reached their pinnacle with donuts." Again, he seemed pleased with his choice of words. "You boys are full of unexpected sophistication!" Dirk smirked.

"You had to get in the last swipe," Bo observed as he helped himself. "That's a sign of insecurity, don't you think?"

Dirk was offered pizza but declined with an expression of disapproval. Larry returned the paper plate to the counter. "This is pretty good." He attempted to end the verbal tussle between the two sides, directing his question at Uncle Roy. "What is it you're offering us? Why should we make peace with the CIA?"

"To make life easier for everyone," LeRoy replied, his demeanor now serious. "The Firm could be a powerful ally against conservative special interest groups and PACs making up the Iron Triangle, in their attempt to legalize harmful substances like alcohol and tobacco. You'd be amazed how many congressmen and senators they've bought off. There are more legislators under the influence (of $$$) now than at any time since the National Rifle Association went bust. It's not hard to visualize a day when controlled substances are legal. You'll need powerful help on that front."

"Why don't you start by giving us a list of legislators," Jacko encouraged with a pizza-filled hand gesture, "leaning towards legalization. Then we'll discuss your idea."

Uncle Roy quietly contemplated the counteroffer. "*Leaning* is not the word I'd use—more like stumbling head over heels." He handed his plate to Larry and pointed at the Vegetarian Supreme. "I'll give you one name, then you decide if my overture is worth considering. Are any of you acquainted with the senior senator from Kentucky? Truckloads of money can change a lawmaker's mind, even a man of principle. You'd never believe such a staunch anti-drug advocate could about-face so quickly. But few outside the Firm know of the conversion of Senator Jake Mackelroy."

"How long has Mackelroy been in the Iron Triangle's pocket?"

"Twenty months," the spy conceded after licking his fingers. He went right at his new slice, then continued. "The Firm attempted counter-bribes to win back his anti-drug support, but to no avail. The Iron Triangle had too much money invested. We don't even know where the loot is so we can't blackmail him back to our side. That makes it a tug of war between the MIC and CIA to buy as much Congressional support as possible. The winner will have a big say in the future of DES as a law enforcement organization. Our immediate concern is the lack of ready cash to influence powerful people in our direction. That's why we need you guys to look the other way. A moratorium on certain turbocraft flights would be helpful. With a quick infusion of hard currency, the Firm can rebuild its covert resource base and regain a footing against the MIC's drug legalization juggernaut. But if we don't have the cash to make counter-bribes, our only option is blackmail. We prefer to avoid using negativity and concentrate on positive methods of purchasing clout."

Cy shook his head in disbelief. "You say the MIC is buying influence in Congress. They've done that for years. What's the big deal?"

"The big deal, my dear boy," Uncle Roy exuded condescension, "is the rate at which they are doing it. Years ago, Congress allocated excessive sums of money for the military, and DOD turned and waved the dollars in legislator's faces. If a lawmaker maintained a solid record of voting for Pentagon pork, the brass could direct a disproportionate chunk to that district. That created jobs and votes for the politician, who then became dependent on the Military-Industrial Complex for monetary support to maintain his seat in government. To reciprocate, Congress voted for even more Pentagon pork. It was a vicious circle. Of course all the legislators claimed they were impartial and open when it came to excessive military spending. But their denial fooled no one. This carrot and stick persuasion worked wonders for bloated military spending. It's impossible to identify who controlled the federal purse. Why, do you know that most of the legislators on their respective Armed Services Committees were from states where DOD spent the vast majority of its money?" Uncle Roy became more sarcastic than usual. "Of course, that's *purely* coincidental! But it was a cash-and-carry government. The Pentagon even had an office where members of Congress were graded according to support. They kept a dossier on each member with a numeric scorecard. That's how they decided where military spending would be funneled."

"You're pretty ticked off about this, aren't you?" Sarge inquired. Dirk fidgeted.

"To be perfectly honest," the spy mellowed, "we at the Firm were quite jealous and would have used similar tactics. But it just didn't work out that way. Our methods tended to create bad vibes and hurt feelings. Such negativity never yielded the results the DOD achieved. The Firm is the black sheep of government agencies because of what we do. Intelligence gathering is not glitzy or glamorous. We get down-and-dirty, which makes us less attractive to legislators, thus it's harder at budget time. The gravy goes to the Pentagon glory boys. But money is better spent in the gathering of intelligence than used for military purposes. We were the ounce of prevention; they were the pound of cure." Uncle Roy got back to his main topic. "But there are limits to everything. Pork no longer acts as an infinite catalyst, with fewer dollars to squander now. The Great Depression saw to that. So you take one small step further and the MIC is now into outright bribery!"

"There's a detail to be ironed out." Cy interrupted. "Remember what Mark Twain said about influence in Congress? It takes lots of money to buy a crooked politician, but loads more to keep the honest ones quiet. Where is DOD getting the cash? They've been complaining of budgetary shortfalls for decades, claiming they are the most appropriationally challenged department in the government."

"They get by with few problems. Their supply of *green influence* is almost infinite."

"You mean to tell me," Jim was incredulous, actually showing some emotion, "they finally decided to eliminate the waste, fraud, corruption, and abuse; then use the money saved for defense purposes?" He spoke symbolically, being that Pentagon waste was much greater in the early part of the century when they believed that money grew on trees and was there for the picking. Current Pentagon budgets are much reduced from pre-depression levels.

"That's very astute." LeRoy seemed impressed with the pilot. "But sadly, no. That is not how they accomplished their objectives."

"They didn't decide to save money by cutting back on medals?" Cy asked.

"Wrong again," LeRoy shook his head. "But a good guess also." Uncle Roy paused, as if to keep his audience in suspense. He also requested another slice of pizza. Larry heaped three on his plate.

"Well," Sarge encouraged gruffly, "are you going to enlighten us or do we beat it out of you?" Though he'd not moved for some time, Dirk shifted his weight after Sarge's remark. He seemed agitated, as if the statement challenged his preeminence in the room.

"Bribes are paid by military contractors within the Iron Triangle. The money is first laundered, then spit back out as entertainment funding so it can be deducted. It's a two-fisted bargain for them." LeRoy looked at Jacko. "We need to get together on this, if only temporarily. Legalization would be a bonanza, via the sin taxes. We'd be one of only seven countries condoning dangerous drugs!"

"An interesting proposal," Jacko agreed. "You won't mind if I think about your offer, then get back in touch?"

"Fair enough," the agent conceded. "But I'll get back to you. There is no way you're going to know where I am. Remember, we're secretive." The spy stood up and handed his plate to Larry. "Wrap it up, I'm taking that with me."

Cy walked over to the coat rack and grabbed LeRoy's jacket. Dirk reacted too late to prevent the act. He did not appreciate the courtesy. In fact Dirk was pissed. He got really hot, but remained under control, looking at LeRoy for instructions. The CIA miscreant smiled. It didn't bother him. "You're looking for my hair on the jacket. You thought you'd grab a DNA sample and enter it into your sensors."

"It would be a great way to follow you," Cy shrugged.

"It was foolish." LeRoy spoke as if Cy was another rank amateur. He pulled a little plastic packet containing human hair out of his pocket. "I always carry decoy samples to spread around. I get them at the barber shop, a place you guys obviously do not often visit." Dirk cooled off. He laughed at Cy's inexperience. "I thank you for the pizza. It was quite good. Maybe a bunch of cops can teach an old spy some new tricks." Uncle Roy stopped and became very serious, looking at Cy. "You wouldn't mind telling me where you hid the GPS tag on my jacket when you grabbed it? That was another amateur move."

Dirk wanted to punch Cy out, but restrained himself out of minimal civility, and maybe some grudging respect for the young attorney's taste in suits. A fight is not the best way to maintain fine clothes. Cy smiled mischievously. "It's stuck just inside the collar. But I'm sure a BugSwatter would find it."

"True," the spy agreed. "You don't have any denatured alcohol, do you? There's no other way I know to remove a GPS tag. Can you imagine getting one stuck on your skin? Without immediate attention, surgery is the only option."

"You forgot dynamite," Sarge suggested. "It's known to work in a pinch."

Dirk glared at Sarge, telepathically implying that he'd just done them a big favor by not punching someone out—his way of maintaining nonverbal control in a situation where he had none. He was outnumbered (by Sarge alone). By glaring contempt at the most imposing member of the L.A. DES, Dirk was staking out his turf, implying he wasn't afraid of any of them—a tough act to ignore.

"Well," the spy smiled at Sarge's idea, "I'm not suicidal, at least not yet. I'll have to drop this jacket off at the Salvation Army later. You'll soon be tracking some old vagrant as he walks the city looking for spare change."

"I'm afraid that's your only option," Sarge concluded, ignoring Dirk. "We can make sure you get a letter of apology from the Enforcement Review Board and a check for reimbursement if you think it will help. I know Doris likes to write checks."

"I don't think that's necessary." LeRoy pocketed his scrambler. "You guys watch your step and I'll see you in a couple days." He left, followed by tough-guy Dirk. Larry escorted them downstairs. Sarge and Cy dutifully cleaned up the mess from the pizza. Larry returned after a few minutes.

FUTUREBUST 7.9

"Security's tight. They were suspicious of LeRoy. Dirk didn't like the scrutiny but went through okay. LeRoy scanned as an anomaly. The machine claimed something was different. I told them he is the same person as when he came in." Larry laughed. "It's crazy. How long do you think this will last?"

The others shrugged. Bo looked thoroughly disgusted. "The way LeRoy talks, they didn't want our new sensor platform, just the guy in it."

Jim smiled and nodded. It made him proud to think they wanted him dead. He had really messed them up—such that they were still looking to get even. But they'd have to wait for another chance to plant him in the ground at high-speed. On the positive side, if he had to go, that's how he preferred.

"Do you think we should be making deals with the Firm?" Cy inquired.

"I can't answer your question," Larry informed, "but we'll be able to track Uncle Roy." The others looked at him quizzically. "I sprinkled some GPS mini micro-tags on the pizza, kind of like added seasoning. We'll be able to follow him wherever he goes. That's what the scanner picked up on. He's carrying them in his stomach! And once those things latch on to his insides…"

"How did you manage to get tags on his pizza without him noticing?" Bo asked. "He watched like a hawk while you served."

"Well," Larry looked sheepishly at the others, "I didn't exactly put the tags on his slice alone. I sprinkled all the pizzas before leaving the restaurant."

Captain Jackson put his hand on his head and took a deep breath. His facial expression registered identical to the morning Larry had trashed the patrol car in the Pentagon parking lot. The captain's tone was serious. "Are you saying we have GPS tags in our digestive tracts?" Cy picked at his teeth with trepidation.

"At this stage of the game," Larry conceded awkwardly, "we each probably have more than one bug up our ass. All we have to do is figure out which are up LeRoy's. There were fifty in the package. How long can it take?"

"An entire package!" Captain Jackson was mortified. "Those things cost $250 apiece. The bean counters will order an internal investigation!"

Bo winced at the senior officer's unintended humor. "If GPS tags attach to our insides—and they will very soon—there are only two ways to dislodge them!"

"So it's either alcohol or dynamite," Sarge agreed, trying to boost morale. He couldn't help but see the humor in the situation. "That doesn't leave much choice. Does anyone know where to get high explosives? I don't think Puff Charges have enough punch."

No one thought that was funny. Alpha was now in dire straits. "The dynamite option is out," Bo protested. "We'll have to get falling-down drunk or those things will be stuck to our insides for a long time. It'd be just like Big Brother!"

Captain Jackson shook his head and sighed. "Don't anybody do anything rash until I explain our situation to Doris. Then we can rid ourselves of these tags under laboratory conditions. But this whole unit is going to fail the mandatory drug screening."

Bo's apprehension was still evident. "Let's hope she is as forgiving as the CIA. In the meantime, Larry, you have a job to do. Catalog every GPS microtag on that pizza. Legal or otherwise, we'll track him and see what he's up to."

The captain was concerned, but brought other matters to the fore. "LeRoy implied the CIA has a few judges in their pocket. No doubt they've replaced hardnosed magistrates like Horton in as many courthouses as needed, likely putting the most effort into areas where illicit drug operations are active."

"So we have to check out every new judge in the U S of A, to locate CIA replacements," Bo agreed. "Also, hardliners suddenly turning soft will be suspect. If we do this correctly, it'll lead us to the CIA's hotspots around the country. Signs of judicial softness will indicate where they are working the illegal drug trade." Bo seemed upbeat despite the difficulties at hand. "With luck, we could crush their entire enterprise."

"LeRoy?" Sarge insisted. "Why don't we just arrest him?"

Captain Jackson summarized. "He'll be released fifteen minutes after we lock him up. The guy carries a get-out-of-jail-free card in his pocket."

Sarge capitulated. "But what about this Pentagon thing?"

"He's probably twisting the truth to fit his own ends," Captain Jackson insisted. "Listen, last winter when I was in DC at the National Law Enforcement Convention, I overheard a big shot say, and I quote, 'Drug wars cost money. Sin taxes make money.' You put two and two together and we've got trouble. Some members of Congress may be considering legalization of dangerous drugs to tax them for additional revenue, which will be directed towards the Iron Triangle."

Bo leaned back in his chair. "Congress will never go for sin taxes, even if it means cash for their districts. It would be tantamount to the government involving itself in an immoral business partnership with cartels engaged in the drug trade."

"Read your history," Larry interjected gently, patting Bo on the shoulder. "Years ago, government routinely used sin taxes to finance spending. It was a mind-boggling immoral transfer of wealth from the addicted, to the merely greedy." Bo, being too young to remember, looked surprised, then downward in disgust. He did not argue the point.

"Lets go out on a limb for a moment," Captain Jackson continued. "The Iron Triangle may want drugs legalized. They're extremely conservative—market oriented, so why not let the consumer decide. Get people addicted and inflict heavy sin taxes, using the windfall..." He hesitated, then came at the problem from another direction. "Look, since the Great Depression started in 2013, the Pentagon budget had to be slashed. At the depths of economic uncertainty, the military spent less than $55 billion a year. That's all that was available. And those were the most uncertain times this country has ever faced. The national debt notwithstanding, with the severe difficulties now subsiding, they have much less money. This year's budget is $85 billion, a fraction of before. People found out during the teens and twenties that we could cut spending drastically, yet still defend the country adequately with a reasonable amount of money. They never forgot the lesson. Iron Triangle waste was a major cause of deficits and the economic collapse that followed. Once you multiply untold hundreds of billions in waste with decades of interest, you've added trillions to the national debt."

"You're speculating about all this, right?" Cy queried.

Captain Jackson shook his head. "In the past, there was often a dichotomy between the best interests of the country, and that of the Military-Industrial Complex. When they conflicted, the MIC always won out, walking away with huge appropriations and profits for participating industries, but little good for the country. You guys should read the history of the B1 bomber. It cost tens of billions to build the fleet. But if you add five percent interest on the national debt over forty-five years, plus expenses to maintain the whole fiasco, you've got over $200 billion wasted before the damn thing was mothballed. And that's just one useless weapons platform! It's highly doubtful that the B1 ever made any difference to our interests. But no one did a cost-effectiveness study. The B1 was a strategic bomber converted to a tactical platform because there was nothing else to do with it. That wasted more money. It was built to create jobs in the aerospace industry and had nothing to do with national security. They compounded the error and built the B2, followed by the B3. People got really upset when they found out that of the $3.1 billion spent on each B3, $1.8 billion was gross profit for the manufacturer. It cost $1.3 billion to build the plane. Then came the B4. All the unnecessary spending, with interest compounded on the national debt adds up to a trillion dollars wasted."

They were shocked at the numbers Captain Jackson was throwing around.

"And the past may be coming back for a visit if the big spenders in Congress have their way. The Iron Triangle is behind it all. I'm sure of it! Their attitude is that market forces should be allowed to dictate public policy instead of using common sense, or God forbid, some wisdom. A casualty of such thinking might be the long-term survival of our civilization. But the MIC never looks that far ahead. They're only interested in the money they can stuff into their pockets now, with no regard for who pays the bill or puts their life on the line!" Captain Jackson rubbed his forehead in frustration. "This is the kind of issue that could split the country apart. Even within the Pentagon, there will be widespread opposition to using sin taxes to finance unnecessary spending.

They are not immoral people. That's what's so interesting. During the Great Depression, those huge budget cuts had a hidden upside for the Armed Forces. With the money gone, Congress was less able to force useless or dangerous pork barrel weapons onto the military. The Pentagon regained some control over its destiny, thereby directing resources to programs that made sense militarily. The generals were no longer hamstrung by a Congress looking to funnel money to individual districts. But the MIC does not like the idea of the Pentagon brass influencing the purse strings. The generals tend to go with the best interests of the Armed Forces, but military contractors want that money spent profitably for them, and Congress wants the money helping reelection chances. They were headed in different directions, which eventually broke up the power of the Iron Triangle during the Great Depression. Now it sounds like several factions have reorganized and buried their differences. These people are downright evil! If they combine powerbases, they'll again control the purse strings. And their actions will never be in the best interest of the country!"

Everyone looked at Captain Jackson. He understood their doubts and misgivings, but continued unabated. "Unfortunately in a turf battle this complex and lucrative, the MIC will be holding all the aces. The Constitution gives the power of the purse to Congress, and those guys were considered the hypotenuse of the Iron Triangle. Any other questions you guys want answered?"

There was silence until Larry spoke. "LeRoy mentioned staying one step ahead of us back in DC, getting wind of our plans and clearing out in the nick of time."

"That's Need-to-know," Jacko replied, his voice much subdued.

FUTUREBUST 8.0

Lieutenant Bo MacKinsey pretended nothing was amiss as he walked into the DES office. His shoulder-length locks were brushed to create the look of a Hollywood celebrity, big-hairstyle pompadour. He was dressed in a fine black leather jacket radiating a lustrous shine as one might see on a new, investment sports car in a prestigious auto showroom. Bo's slacks were state-of-the-art with a designer logo stitched near a belt loop just above the right cheek of his twenty-eight-year-old keister. Black leather shoes exuded a newly polished glow creating feedback with the luster emanating from the jacket. He removed the outer garment and hung it on the rack in the main office, then adjusted his cuff links.

"No tie?" Sarge gave the younger officer a nudge. "You know we're not going to church. There was no reason to dress up."

"I thought I'd come to work attired better than usual. Don't worry. This will not become precedent. I just received my first lesson in a correspondence course from the Acme School of Image Makeover. It says to try new clothes, guaranteeing you'll be judged by appearance and not your character." Bo shook his head in disappointment. "I hate image consciousness but I guess it's nothing a good drunk won't cure."

"You sure look fine," Cy joined the conversation. "Normally you dress like we just hired you from the *will-work-for-food* line at the Mission."

Bo acknowledged the truth. Normally he did look rough around the edges, like the proverbial undercover cop. But that's his prerogative. He was definitely not an image guy. Besides, it's cheaper to pick up nice, pre-worn clothes at the Salvation Army Store.

Everyone turned as Doris entered. The head of the ERB clutched a cardboard box, the contents jingling as she carried her cargo into the main office. She glared at each member of the elite drug-fighting team until she had encircled them with her mood. Jim, Cy, Larry, an immaculately dressed Bo, and Sarge fidgeted. Captain Jackson had the curtains drawn over the window that looked into his office. It was just after 5 A.M.

Doris was determined to make a point. If rumors reached the higher-ups, Alpha would come under a full-scale investigation, making their lives miserable for weeks. There'd be hearings, reports, unwanted media attention, even disciplinary action if Big Brother went by the book. And they'd have to reimburse the department for all those GPS tags, out of their own pockets. Only the Pentagon is ever allowed to waste money with impunity.

How would the public react if they found out? An entire squad of DES professionals getting drunk on the job—for medicinal purposes of course. It would create an international scandal. If the story leaked, she'd have to absorb the blow, and however she justified, the public wouldn't buy it.

How about scientific analysis? Five DES officers and their captain took part in a binge drinking experiment for scientific testing, discovery, and exploration. Yeah, right! The conspiracy theorist would have a field day. Alpha continued to fidget. Captain Jackson entered the main office to face the music. Doris looked squarely at the senior officer. "So what do you have to say for yourself? You of all people, getting into a mess like this! And all those GPS tags going to waste. They aren't cheap. The bean-counters will get suspicious if we don't find some way to cover this up!"

"I can't even reveal what's going on," the captain rationalized. "It's Need-to-know."

"I suppose the fate of the world is resting on your shoulders," she replied, indicating she'd get to the bottom of the situation if it took…Everyone looked down as she tapped her feet. She was wearing steel toes.

"Truthfully," Captain Jackson continued, distracted by the threat, "this matter is more serious than I can explain. We just may be on a Mission from God, as corny as it sounds. Under the circumstances, ingesting GPS micro-tags was the only option at our disposal. We didn't mean to swallow them ourselves, but in hindsight there was no alternative."

Larry breathed a quiet sigh of relief. The captain had backed him up.

"Do you realize that once they latch onto your insides, it'll take nothing short of high explosives to dislodge them? You were taking an awful chance with your health!"

"The risks are worth it," he assured. "We're into a plot so deep, we'd need a six-volume book to explain it all. Hopefully, you'll support us through to the final chapter."

"Don't butter me up as if I'm a character in some cheap paperback novel."

"We're not talking cheap," Captain Jackson insisted with mock sternness. "If we were characters in a book, it'd be a quality hardbound with pretentious, glossy cover and BIG NAME author, released by a large, prestigious publisher to fanfare and excitement; maybe even a jug band concert included in the festivities."

Doris cracked a smile. Larry decided to push the outside of the envelope, something he was adept at. "And once published, you've got to think about a movie deal, plus the big-dollar star that will be playing you."

"So I'm on the big screen as well." Doris laughed. "You guys are creative. But cancel the concert and have a hoedown instead." It was now clear that Doris would lighten up.

"You're forgetting action figures," Sarge added, seeing she was receptive to humor. Maybe it'd be nothing more than a glancing blow. "I almost got an action figure contract with my movie deal, all those years ago! Imagine the impact that would have on your life."

"What about me?" Cy noted confidently. "I'd be the best dressed little action figure ever. And all tax-deductible outfits and accessories are sold separately."

"Action figures sound cool." Bo put the icing on the cake. He was dressed for it. "I can see it now, a twelve-inch high Lieutenant Bo MacKinsey, complete with leather jacket, and pants with holes in the knees."

Doris smiled, shaking her head. "Okay, you guys have made your point. But the idea of getting a book printed by a publishing house is far-fetched. You have to be a celebrity for them to even look at your manuscript. They'd never give a group like us the time of day. Think more in terms of *Print-On-Demand*." After Doris shot down their dreams of a big publishing deal, she returned to the matter-at-hand. "I've always supported Alpha in the past and I'm not going to stop now. But I sometimes wonder what you're doing down here on the seventh floor. So as far as I'm concerned, this matter is closed when those GPS micro-tags are heading to the sewage treatment plant. How we explain this to the bean counters, I don't know. We'll work on that later. Just be thankful there was enough booze in the evidence locker. I brought up a half-dozen bottles of *ever-blissful intoxication*," Doris spoke with sarcasm, "to help you on your way. One apiece should get you blitzed."

She continued. "I can still remember what my uncle used to tell me when I was a little girl, small enough to sit on his lap. The guy was a raving alcoholic, hopelessly addicted to his bottle. Sobering up temporarily after one of his legendary benders, he'd apologize profusely and give us an explanation for his behavior which at the time seemed plausible." The men listened with rapt attention. Doris had grown up in an alcoholic family. Childhood experiences affected her deeply, contributing to strong feelings against Devil Liquor. "After going on his usual tirade, breaking furniture, yelling at everyone and causing havoc in the house, he'd stomp out the door and disappear. When he returned a day or two later, we always got the same excuse to smooth things over and make it all better." Doris now spoke in a low, manlike voice as she quoted her long dead uncle: "'The first two quarts of whiskey I can handle. It's the third that always does me in.'"

She looked at each member of Alpha, knowing all had strong, anti-drug attitudes of their own. On a roll, she continued her lecture. "Do you guys know why alcohol is the most dangerous drug? It's because the dependency is both physiological and psychological. People used to drink socially, as if there's security in numbers. They lost control of their lives by the millions, a human tragedy of unparalleled proportions."

"I think what happened," Captain Jackson added, "was that people were well aware of the addictive qualities of heroin or cocaine. The vast majority regarded those drugs with extreme caution, even fear. But alcohol didn't have that. They assumed they could play around and not get hurt, and some weren't hurt by it. But you can make that claim about all dangerous things. However, those that became addicted found themselves in dire straits, unable to control their problem. Alcohol's stealthy—its victims having no idea of the trouble they'd fall into."

"What you are saying," Cy nodded mischievously, "is that we better be careful while we imbibe."

Doris smiled. "You're lucky I like you guys so much. If the other squad was involved in this fiasco, I'd be getting suspicious."

Jim changed the subject to divert criticism. "In a way, alcohol and tobacco were the first WMDs, Weapons of Mass Destruction ever invented." It didn't help.

"You're also expected to see the police counselor after this episode is over—no complaints. Then this affair can stay under wraps. But if I don't get glowing reports about the whole lot of you, I may have to spill the beans to the higher-ups."

"Thanks for your support and consideration," Captain Jackson replied. "The last thing we need is an internal investigation. As soon as I can, I'll fill you in."

"Is it absolutely necessary," Sarge inquired, "that we endure the head-shrinking? I always get self-conscious when counselors ask how I feel. It makes me want to punch them out. If it got out of hand and I lost control..." Sarge smiled sweetly. Jim and Larry were in complete agreement.

"It's a prerequisite to continuing in this line of work," Doris proclaimed, uninfluenced by the casual warning. "And you are not allowed to punch out the psychologist. She is only five feet tall, 110 pounds. That will guarantee more head-shrinking." Doris looked at Jim. "The last thing I need is an alcoholic turbocraft pilot bumping into tall buildings while searching for drug abusers to arrest. This isn't *Police Squad*!"

There was grumbling, but everyone knew it was for the best. Without speaking, they checked out what she'd brought from the evidence vault—six bottles of assorted alcoholic delectation, each decades old. Sarge reluctantly grasped a bottle of Mexican Tequila. Larry, a rare, priceless quart of *Southern Comfort*. Bo studied his bottle of 100% pure *Jack Daniel's*. Cy gripped a blessed quart of *Toastmaster* Vodka. He was sure the liquid would taste dastardly awful and wasn't looking forward to drinking it. Jim shook his head in dismay as he picked up a bottle of *BeefEaters*. To him, it was nothing but firewater with a funny name. Maybe he'd become a vegetarian after this episode finalized.

Each bottle should have been in a museum, but that had been tried before. Put $500,000 worth of booze on display and some jewel thief breaks in and steals it. The curator usually decides it is not worth the security risk and additional insurance premiums.

A jug of vino remained, alone and forlorn on the table. Captain Jackson looked at the deep red liquid. Able to remember when alcohol was legal, he decided to have pity on the poor, hapless gallon of wine. He cradled the jug in his arms like a small child. "This is going to hurt me more than it hurts you." Then addressing everyone in the room, "I sure hope it gets better with age. Otherwise I'm in a whole heck of a lot of trouble." Though cruel, it'd have been wise to force the wine on his subordinates. They wouldn't know the difference anyway. But as the senior officer, he'd do what's best for his men and drink it himself, if necessary, going down with his ship.

Doris noticed their expressions. For the first time she was unable to contain her amusement. "You know, sometimes I wonder about you guys. If I didn't know better, I'd suspect you fabricated this to get your hands on controlled substances. Are you sure you're not a bunch of closet alcoholics?"

Everyone smiled at the insinuation, though Sarge was taken aback. "Who'd dream of such a thing? I can't believe you'd entertain the thought."

"I was joking," Doris reassured. "I couldn't resist. But so help me, this better not happen again. I don't want anyone else seeking a bottle of medicinal alcohol to remove GPS micro-tags from their innards. By tomorrow, most of the DES officers in this building will be suffering from the 100-proof flu. As far as I'm concerned, if you want to chunder (blow chunks), come up with something better than ingesting electronic devices."

"You know how creative we are," Bo assured.

"I've got work to do back upstairs. So get to it. You've got serious drinking ahead of you but I don't want to witness this. And under no circumstances are you to share with those FBI SWAT dudes on the roof."

Bo frowned. "Those guys are protecting us."

Doris gave him another dirty look, then turned to answer the captain.

"Are you sure you won't help me finish off this bottle of fine red wine? One way or another, I'm going to need assistance before the day is through."

"Well thanks for the invitation, sailor," she replied, "but I shouldn't involve myself deeper than I have to. I've got a nice cushy job watching over my supercomputer and don't need anything to jeopardize that relationship. Brunhilde could smell the alcohol if we hooked a Breathalyzer to her." Doris started to leave, then turned. "I've asked Dolly to watch over things while you're inebriated. If she needs my help, I'll be down in an instant. In the meantime you fellas behave as much as possible under these unfortunate circumstances." Doris disappeared, leaving the men to deal with their drinking problems.

FUTUREBUST8.3

"A woman will always abandon you if she thinks alcohol consumption is getting out of hand." Captain Jackson sat on the floor with his back against the wall. He held up his bottle so the ceiling lights shown through the deeply colored liquid. Then the nearly retired officer broke the seal on the outlawed beverage and removed the cap, hooking his little finger through the glass ring on the neck of the bottle. The others sat beside him. "It's best," he informed his partners-in-crime, "to maintain a close working relationship with the floor while consuming quantities of alcohol. Gravity does unpredictable things. It's also way too early in the day to drink, but we're all friends here. If a man can't get drunk with his best buddies before breakfast, what good are they?" The others held up their bottles in agreement. "Down the hatch." The captain closed his eyes, raised the jug to his lips, and took a healthy, eye-popping, better-than-ten-second pull on the outlawed grape juice. The five Alpha's watched in amazement. Captain Jackson lowered the bottle, shook his head, and wiped the excess on his sleeve. "You know it's a shame," he spoke after analyzing the taste, "but this stuff doesn't get any better with age!" He raised the jug and took another long swig, then placed the bottle on the floor. "*Rotgut*, that's what we called cheap wine back in the olden days. This is going to be a very difficult drunk."

"I'm sure glad I missed those years," Bo informed. "Why would anyone want to drink something called rotgut?"

Captain Jackson closed his eyes and swallowed hard, stopping the drink from returning to the environment whence it came. He spoke as if giving an order. "Come on everybody, let's tie one on!"

Cy looked confused. "Tie one on what?"

Bo didn't understand. "What are we going to tie it with?"

Sarge laughed. "It's an old expression. It means to get really drunk."

They looked at each other and shrugged. Sarge's explanation didn't help.

"I'll tell you something, son," Captain Jackson volunteered. "You're holding a fortune in your hands. An unopened bottle of *Jack Daniel's* on the black market fetches $105,000! So give it a try. There are people who'd part with their life savings to get a taste."

"It's that good, huh?" Bo was astonished. "Might as well give'er a crank."

"A little advice. Drink it slow and easy," Captain Jackson informed the rookie alcoholic with a palm-down hand gesture. "A sipping whiskey is supposed to be savored. And besides, a wholehearted gulp...!" Bo cracked the seal and opened the bottle, making sure none spilled. No point in getting thousands of dollars worth on his new shirt.

"Sounds like good advice," the lieutenant nodded. "I hope this stuff lives up to its reputation. A virgin drunk should be memorable." He raised the bottle and allowed a mouthful of amber liquid to flow into his life experience. Captain Jackson waved his hand as if to say, Stop! Too Much! But it was too late. Swallowing the beverage with a gulp, Bo waited for the taste to reach the consciousness-centers in his brain. The others watched with fascination. After a pause, Bo's jaw dropped. Grabbing his chest, he exhaled, then inhaled shallowly, as if choking. He closed his eyes and shook his head. Slowly, painfully, breathing stabilized as he pounded his breastbone with a clenched fist. Bo looked at the others with tears in his eyes.

Sarge reached over and patted him on the back in a fatherly fashion, as if to console. "So what do you think of your first snort?"

Breathing abnormally, he shook his head but finally responded in a gravelly, hoarse voice. "Wow! That stuff really packs a wallop." He took another deep breath and asked a difficult personal question. "Do I have to down the entire bottle to get drunk?"

Captain Jackson laughed. "I don't think so. Three or four gulps like the one you just took, with a half-dozen more for good measure should dislodge those GPS tags. Then you can spend the day contemplating a headache."

Larry, Sarge, and Jim looked at their bottles with disdain. Three seals were hesitantly cracked and the three anti-drug activists faced their dilemma. Cy remained unconvinced, waiting to see what transpired. "Let's do this together," Jim suggested. "On the count of three." The men eyed their bottles and looked at each other.

"Okay," Larry agreed. "Let's give it our best—on the count of three."

"On the count of three." Sarge nodded his approval.

Silence ensued. They looked suspiciously at each other. Thirty seconds passed. There was mistrust in the air. Jim squinted as he gazed at Larry. Larry looked at Sarge. The big man shook his head in disgust and spoke with Alpha Male dominance. "Aw, to heck with it. 3—2—1—go." Sarge raised the bottle to his lips and took a shot glass-sized gulp. Age and experience taught him how much to swallow, though he'd never been a drinker. After four additional snorts in rapid succession, he closed his eyes and shook his head. What followed was the customary, long-drawn-out *"Ahhhh"*. He lowered his bottle to the floor and looked at the others, eyes open wide with tears. "Well go on. Get to it.

Take little gulps, not big ones. You guys will do okay." His voice exuded the confidence of a burp.

Jim and Larry shrugged and followed suit. They raised the bottles in a toast, then down the hatch. "Wow!" Larry wiped his lips. "It's been a long time. That stuff really tastes bad. What on earth were we thinking all those years ago? Why would anyone want to drink such an atrocious, disgusting, evil, foul…"

Jim continued the descriptive narrative, "…hideous, horrible, horrid, loathsome…"

It was now Sarge's turn to show off his storehouse of adjectives, "…nasty, nauseating, obscene, and offensive…"

"…Repellent, repugnant, repulsive, and revolting…" Captain Jackson chimed in…

"…Sickening, unwholesome, and vile liquid?" Bo finished the multi-personalized statement with some disappointment evident. "What a rip-off. You guys left me with only three adjectives. Each one of you got four."

"How about we add wasteful to your list?" Cy suggested. "That'd give you the required number, equal to everyone else."

"Thanks," Bo affirmed. "I couldn't have done it without you."

"I'd add some descriptive flavor of my own," Cy assured, "like base, distasteful, unsavory, ghastly and highly uncool, but you guys ran through your list in alphabetical order and I wouldn't want to disturb the flow."

"That shows good judgment," Captain Jackson observed. He had already cleared out a quart of his ripe, red, rotgut from the top of the gallon jug. "And speaking of not disturbing the flow of things, how about getting started on that elixir you're holding? You haven't even opened the bottle."

"I'm getting my courage up," Cy assured. "I've never done anything this intimidating, not even when I was a kid growing up on the mean streets of Beverly Hills."

"No excuses!" Bo ordered. "You've got to dislodge those tags from your insides or they're going to be stuck forever. You don't want to go into surgery, do you? Face it like a man. The rest of us will back you totally. They taught us that in Command School."

"Okay," Cy agreed. "But I'm going easy on this stuff. I sure hope it doesn't taste offensive." He opened the bottle and sniffed the fumes emanating from within. There was a subtle but not offensive odor. Cy felt encouraged and decided to give it a yank.

Captain Jackson cautioned. "Slow and easy, son. That stuff is stronger than you think. Wodka packs a punch few people can handle. Only the Russians drink it straight."

"Well," Cy replied with renewed confidence, "if the Russkies can do it, I can too!" He lifted the bottle to his lips and took a full-fledged, two-shot gulp. Then, without hesitation, took another just as the effect of the clear, supposedly tasteless liquid reached his center of perception. What followed could only be described as a geyser of vodka spurting forth. He dropped the bottle, spilling a valuable (at black market prices) amount on the hardwood floor. His eyes bulged as he coughed, trying desperately to clear the airway. The DES attorney inhaled and spoke, using his well-equipped vocabulary to its fullest.

"Whoowaa!" he exclaimed, a word that would be futile to look up in the dictionary. Cy quickly regained control of his bottle. "You were right!" Pause. "That's powerful!" He continued to breathe deliberately, trying to regain a rhythm. "But I'll tell you the truth…" he coughed, "it's not bad. I can see why the boys tested their manhood on this stuff. It really slugs you!" Cy took another belt to clear his windpipe, using caution gained from experience. All things considered he handled the rest pretty well.

Captain Jackson pointed to the spill. "That's the equivalent of a sports car." Cy couldn't believe it. Sixty thousand dollars on the floor and no way to salvage and cash it in. He got up, grabbed a sponge, and wiped the spill away, trying to grasp how such a small amount of liquid could be so expensive. Even the juice squeezed from surplus diamonds, used as a perfume by fancy, rich ladies, wasn't so valuable.

Captain Jackson congratulated his crew. Their alcoholic baptism was complete. He stood up using both hands on the wall to steady himself, then headed for the Command Center. The others followed. Out the window, Sarge could see the SWAT guys milling around on the roof, making sure no CIA commandos attacked the building from the air. The big man felt better. Everything would be okay. They lined up and sat down on the floor with backs against the far wall. Captain Jackson gave another order. "Now let's clear these bottles down to the halfway point and put our GPS dilemma behind us." He sounded more self-assured than usual.

Bo took some gulps of his medicine. He lifted his bottle level with one eye closed and tried to gauge the amount left. Like good sports, they continued cautious but unhindered with medicinal drinking. Time passed quickly. By the time they were forty-five minutes from sober, things were looking rosy. "Doris sure has been accommodating," Sarge announced.

"She seemed pretty pissed—I mean *pissed* in the American sense of the word, not the British," Larry replied conscientiously with a burp.

"You're probably right," the captain capitulated. A ten second pull on his jug helped. "This stuff is tasting okay. Maybe it gets better with age. It just needed a little aeration."

The others laughed sloppily, punctuated by more alcoholic burps, and continued their inebriational journey. Most of the bottles were half empty.

Each drank slow but steady, lost in clouded thought processes. Finally, a semi-intoxicated but well dressed lieutenant put his arm on the senior officer's shoulder and made a slurred admission. "You know, I don't care what the others say about you, Cap'm. You're an alright fella."

Captain Jackson nodded in good-natured disagreement and took a long pull on his decades-old wine jug, determined to finish it off. He knew how easy it was, while drunk, to get into a fight over absolutely nothing. "That's definitely a true statement," he admitted with a mighty belch, the first manly burp of the morning.

Bo's eyes were half-closed, as if it was way past bedtime. "I've got to ask you something. Wouldn't this liquor taste better if we dumped it all together and drank it mixed up?" No one answered. Bo had asked such a silly question. Of course it would taste better if they combined resources. And sharing is always the best thing to do, just like their mothers taught them when they were little.

After a silent five minutes, Sarge broke the quietude. "Do any of you guys know what that pink elephant is doing out in the main office by the refrigerator? If we don't stop him, he's sure to steal our donuts."

"You're not really seeing a pink elephant, are you?" Jim inquired. "Cause I don't see him. And besides, there's not enough room for more elephants. The green one and the purple one are already squeezed in pretty tight." Jim's mood darkened. He grabbed at Sarge's bottle. "Let me try some of your liquor."

"Forget it!" Sarge pulled his supply out of reach. "No, I'm not really seeing pink elephants. That's just something people joked about back in the olden days. I was trying to be humorous!" The big man belched long and loud, a full five seconds. "It's better than being obnoxious, which is how most people ended up while on this stuff." He gazed at his bottle suspiciously. "By the way, do you guys know what *proof* stands for?"

"Mine is better than yours!" Jim taunted.

"The bigger the number..." the captain replied, losing his train of thought.

"I'm out of luck. Mine is only 80 proof. You guys got better liquor than me." Bo anguished. His words sounded antagonistic and blameful.

Alpha Squad was well on its way to total inebriation. Dolly entered the Command Center and stared at the six intoxicated officers sitting with backs against the wall. "You guys look like something out of an old movie. Six drunks lined up in a row. I'll bet if I pushed one, the whole bunch would tumble in unison. Anyway, I'm going to have some of the leftovers with Lance. He's assured me there is nothing better than pizza for breakfast."

Dolly left the room. The six drunks didn't respond. They were too far into goofyland. Lance appeared in the doorway, chomping on a piece of cold Italian pie with the works, amused by the scene in front of him. Only twenty-two, he'd never seen a drunk before—the legendary beverages were banned years before his birth. Now six blitzed individuals slouched against the wall, right before his eyes. He shook his head in jovial disbelief while continuing to down the pizza. Bo looked up at the hotshot rookie with a slushy smile.

"Great pizza," Lance held up a large, drooping slice for all to see. "It's loaded; got everything on it: peppers, onions, olives, double cheese, even broccoli. You guys must have had a real party last night!" He took another bite.

"Yup," Bo slurred his speech. "We had a groovy party." He seemed dazed, lost in oblivion, his grin self-congratulatory. The young lieutenant was doing great—not a care in the world. He closed his eyes and allowed his chin to droop forward against his chest, as if exhausted. The moment passed. How fortunate that he'd gotten dressed up for his virgin drunk. Everything seemed hunky-dory. Then his mood transformed! He tried to stand but couldn't. Gravity had changed directions just as Captain Jackson warned. He spoke with difficulty and a couple of false starts. "Tell...tell..." Bo burped. A bomb went off inside his skull. His eyes were as big as saucers. "Tell Dolly," he stammered, grabbing his stomach, "not to eat that pizza!" Lance hesitated, unsure what the lieutenant was getting at. "Tell her!" Lance jumped back towards the kitchen.

Bo struggled to stand, finally succeeding with the wall as a prop. Dolly suddenly appeared in front of her drunken comrade. "What's this about not eating any pizza?"

"Whoa!" Bo staggered against the wall. "Where did you come from?"

"Lance told me not to eat the pizza," she reiterated. "I wondered what it was all about." The rookie looked at his unfinished slice with disdain, placing it cautiously on the command console—as if treated roughly, it might explode.

"Did you eat any pizza?" Bo pleaded, his vision blurred and head throbbing.

"No, not yet. I was warming my slice up. What's this all about?"

The other drunkards began to realize what had happened. Bo leaned carefully against the wall. "That's the pizza that still has GPS tags sprinkled on it. We were going to salvage them so the bureaucrats don't get suspicious. Thank goodness you didn't eat any!"

Dolly didn't like what she was hearing. "Well what about Lance?" Bo looked cross-eyed and unfocused, losing track of his thoughts. "What about Lance?" she asked sternly, wanting to grab him by the arm and shake, but was afraid she'd knock him down.

Bo rubbed his scalp and refocused, looking around until he found the pilot squarely in his line of sight. He squinted and spoke with self-assurance. "As for you my young friend, we'll have to get you some medicine!"

FUTUREBUST8.7

Doris wasn't pleased, however said little. There was no point in jumping up on a soapbox to give a speech to a bunch of drunks. They wouldn't remember anyway. This time her good nature prevailed. She returned from the Last Chance Liquor Store with a gallon jug of a homemade concoction labeled XXXXX, then motioned Dolly to come away from the others. "Keep an eye on those guys. They're not in good condition. Call me if you need help." She turned to go back to her regular job, hoping the current stint as bartender was over, then stopped. "By the way, don't play country music. People get too emotional. Years ago, studies done by a prestigious university in Massachusetts suggested that men are thirty percent more likely to get in a fight if listening to country music while drunk."

Dolly was surprised, but agreed to the ban. "It doesn't look like we'll get any law enforcement done today, either."

"Make sure they don't wander out on the roof. The SWAT guys will get suspicious if one of our officers falls eighty feet to the ground and bounces back up." Doris retreated upstairs.

Captain Jackson staggered side-to-side until he made it from the Command Center out to the main office. Stabilizing his position by holding onto a chair, he eyed the unopened gallon jug on the counter. His vision was blurred but he knew what was in the container. "That's White Lightning. I remember that bust. It's been years. Why would the evidence guys keep that stuff around?"

"I have no idea." Dolly looked at the captain cautiously. She opened the bottle and poured a large glass. A splash spilled onto her wrist.

He noticed the liquid on her arm, then stammered. "You're history now. There's no way you're going to pass a drug screening in the next two weeks." He made a suggestion that seemed quite logical to his flustered brain. "Might as well get drunk with the rest of us. Doris will fix everything." Captain Jackson started to lose his balance. Dolly had to get him safely seated in a chair. Lance laughed at the sight of the drunken senior officer.

"Pass, on your offer. I have no interest in fooling around with that stuff." Dolly couldn't imagine how a perfectly rational human being could become so disoriented.

Lance picked up his glass of moonshine and eyeballed it suspiciously. "Is this stuff really going to get me drunk?"

"It shore will," Dolly assured in redneck dialect. She used the corny impression because the other guys did it all the time. "That-there is genuine shine. Have at it."

Lance carefully sipped and then slowly drank the entire glass—the only person in his high school graduating class that had ever done so. Steam would have spurted from his ears, but that only happens in old cartoons. "Not bad," he observed, handing the glass back. "Tastes like racing fuel. It's hard to believe high-test could be homemade. I sure hope this stuff does the trick. I don't want an operation."

The other drunks had staggered from the Command Center into the main office. They'd seen Lance drink the entire glass of shine without spitting any out. He seemed immune to it. They clambered towards the counter and stared pie-eyed at the best looking bartender they'd ever beheld. She grabbed more glasses and poured for anyone who wanted any. Her idea was to get rid of the stuff. Cy drank two glasses, then searched for the elephant Sarge had mentioned earlier—not a problem unless he actually found it. Bo asked why they call it white lightning when everybody can see it's clear and doesn't have any sort of electrical charge. He was learning stuff they don't teach in Command School.

"Drink up, everybody. This is your one and only chance to try some genuine foot stomping, butt-kicking, rip-roaring, shoot'em-up, kick-ass white lightning. There aren't many places left in the US of A where they can still manufacture this stuff and not get caught."

Doris returned to the party with small paper sacks. She gathered up the bottles and placed them in the bags, then handed them to their rightful owners. "Here, if you're going to play at being drunks, you might as well look the part."

Lance had already finished his third glass of shine. Though a rookie, he decided to taunt Doris. "Can I try some cigarettes with this alcoholic liquor?"

Doris gave him a dirty look. She was trying to get Captain Jackson's gallon jug into a paper bag, but with no luck. "Line up," she insisted. "I need a picture, just in case I'm short of spending cash someday."

Dolly positioned the novice alcoholics against the wall near the InstaPrint. They offered little resistance. Only Lance understood what was happening but went along with the gag. His upcoming inebriation hadn't kicked in. Still throttling up, he smiled and sipped on his fourth glass. "Blackmailing an officer of the law is serious business. You could get into a heap of trouble."

"Hush up," Doris chuckled, "or there will be no more liquor for you. Tomorrow they won't remember a thing. That's why I need this picture." She focused the holographic camera on the seven officers. Lance raised his empty glass in a toast, and the photo was taken. The flash from the camera just about knocked the photogenic group to the floor.

Jim regained his balance and tapped Lance on the shoulder. "Follow me," he suggested, trying to readjust his eagle-like vision.

Sarge, Larry, and Captain Jackson leaned back against the wall. The three appeared disheveled and exhausted. Sarge looked cross-eyed at his bottle and started to complain. "This chakita isn't very strong!" He had difficulty enunciating words. Cy stepped sideways and made a desperate attempt to grab the jug of white lightning. Lance poured a glass, drank it, then chased it with another. Jim stumbled into the elevator doors, (he'd forgotten they were there) righted himself, and continued towards the hanger.

"Here, let me get that for you," Dolly volunteered. Cy motioned that he didn't need any more alcohol in his system. Too dignified to burp, he carefully rejoined the others on the floor. Lance grabbed Cy's glass and headed well-supplied out to the hanger. Doctors with knowledge of such medicine would have considered his prescription filled, several glasses back. A mule-kick to the head was in the works. He found Jim out in the hanger.

"I gotta show you something." Jim spoke haltingly, pointing at the brand new Category-five turbocraft. "Look at that vehicle. Isn't it gorgeous?"

Lance teetered, setting his glasses on a barrel. "It's a beauty!"

Big Al glanced at the two pilots. He was fifty feet from the discussion, working on the EV's flight stabilizers. The mechanic shrugged and focused on his work.

"You know," Jim put his arm on Lance's shoulder, half to steady himself, half out of affection for the rookie, "that thing might be Mach 1 capable." His head was swimming. "I had it right to the sound barrier before I backed off, and I wasn't afraid either. I could have gone past like butter through toast." He laughed as if he'd said something funny.

"No kidding?" Lance was off balance. "I'm sure glad I joined DES." He burped and squinted, rubbing his head. It hurt, but he managed to continue his thought. "There was little chance I'd ever race big-time. I could test-drive, but some big name would suck up all the glory on race day." His expression changed from disdain to confusion. "Big Al explained why things always go like that but I didn't understand a word he was saying."

"He was learning you with economics," Jim concluded, looking pie-eyed and unstable. The pilots leaned against each other for support. "Probably had something to do about advertising. That's what makes the DES so great. A couple of dudes like us will be flying the most advanced turbocraft in the world." Jim's tongue was tangled in his mouth. "You know what else I learned me today?" Lance burped. "Two intoxicated DES officers," Jim stumbled momentarily, then laughed as if it was just a silly mistake, "can stand together drunk a lot better than apart. We're supporting each other's addiction."

The shine mule-kicked. "Maybe we better sit down. I'm feeling…"

Both men staggered to the Cat-five. Big Al again looked over at the two, wondering what on earth they were doing to his new vehicle. Something didn't seem right but he shrugged it off, fully aware that pilots had quirks and idiosyncrasies. Present company excluded, some are prima donnas.

"You know what I think?" Jim looked at the rookie. Lance blinked his eyes like he couldn't see straight. "We better take this baby for a spin and see how fast it'll go."

With great mental effort, Lance considered the proposal. "Dolly will kill us."

Jim answered enthusiastically. "That's the beauty of it. We're in no condition to fly so we'll let the Fiver do it on autopilot. What could be more fun? We could be out there now, searching for illegal drugs."

"It would be great," Lance conceded with continued mental difficulty. "But..."

"We're not that drunk anyway," Jim assured, regaining his balance. "It's a once-in-a-lifetime opportunity to take a scenic tour of Los Angeles while..."

Lance felt nauseated and clutched his stomach. He recovered after taking deep breaths, deciding it might be a good thing if he went out for some fresh air.

Dolly located her errant alcoholics. "What are you two doing out here?"

Big Al glanced at the three drug enforcement officers, wondering what in the world was going on. He picked up a rag, wiped some grease from his hands, and mumbled to himself. "Pilots, they're as temperamental as big, fancy Hollywood celebrity-type, movie star actors." He frowned. "At least they don't end up in therapy as much."

Dolly was pissed in the American sense of the word, not the British, but she spoke in a hushed whisper. "I ought to drag you back into the office by your ears like a couple of schoolboys! Did you really think you could go out for a ride in your condition? Now get in there!" She shook her head in disbelief, retrieving the two glasses.

They entered the main office together and staggered to the opposite wall where the others had passed out. The senior pilot strained under intense mental effort, as if to cognize an epiphany—profound and enlightening. He finally got the words straight in his head. "I'll tell you something, junior." Jim focused in an attempt to teach the rookie. "Women can be so insensitive. They don't understand the bond that forms between a man and his machinery. There are genuine feelings of closeness that bind a pilot to his vehicle."

"It is truly a beautiful thing," Lance agreed with all the gusto he could muster, just before he passed out on the floor.

FUTUREBUST8.9

"There are twelve unauthorized GPS micro-tags at the treatment plant, and one more lodged in a crack in the sanitary sewer about ten feet below the surface of Alameda Street," Larry announced. "We have our binge-drinking episode to thank for that. We've also recovered thirty from the uneaten pizza so we saved $7500." He smiled as they applauded their accomplishment. "I sprinkled fifty on the pizzas."

"So where are the others?" Bo gazed at the monitor. A look of confusion crossed his face. He analyzed the information on the screen, then shook his head in disbelief while Sarge, Cy, and Jim gathered around. "What would five GPS micro-tags be doing at the homeless shelter?" Bo considered the ramifications. "No! Say it isn't so."

Larry laughed. "You've got it. Uncle Roy is living incognito at the homeless shelter while in L.A. Who'd have guessed?"

"That's the last place I'd have looked for him," Sarge admitted.

"There's two still missing," Cy informed.

"You crunched down on one." Larry smiled. "Don't worry. We'll deduct $250 from your paycheck and everything will be even. There's another at the dog pound. LeRoy must have fed pizza to a stray pooch. Maybe the guy has a heart after all."

"You gotta feel for the captain," Sarge added. "That rotgut was really hard on him. He'll be back to work in a couple days. But he did leave us a note." Sarge read from the office memorandum left by the senior officer. "Next time you find any unopened antique beer cans, save a twelve-pack for emergency situations. Sorry about my little alcoholic miscue. I tried my best to hold it all down." Everyone nodded in agreement.

FUTUREBUST9.0

Larry gazed at the GPS monitor, following ever so closely the outward movements of one LeRoy, (last name unknown) AKA Uncle Roy—self-proclaimed spymaster, all-around troublemaker, and CIA miscreant. The live, living, and breathing subject of questionable scrutiny, Uncle Roy was leaving the homeless shelter where he lived incognito in all his surreptitious splendor and glory. DES would have to inform him of his stomach viruses, but short of surgery, the bugs were now a permanent part of his anatomy. Although some spies and secret agents are known for their ability to withstand extreme pain, it's unlikely as Sarge might suggest, that LeRoy try the dynamite option of removal. Larry hoped the CIA operative harbored no deep, irrational fears of surgical operations. Some people are scared to go under the knife, even when the most experienced surgeons do the slicing and dicing.

That 140-proof *shine* Doris supplied, would now be useless. The GPS tags had already woven their tenacious electron(ic) tentacles into the living fabric of his insides and tightened an unbreakable grip for all eternity, ostensibly becoming one with surroundings. In fact, it's beside the point. Dolly converted the unused liquor into fuel. The EVs were capable of burning anything from vegetable oil to nitro. Total black market value of the alcoholic fuel: $145,000. She poured the white lightning into the Cat-four AFA canisters, thereby saving on Pyrotec, which costs over $200 a gallon. The rotgut Captain Jackson failed to consume was saved. Dumping it into the fuel tanks did not seem prudent. And sending it towards the treatment plant is also a no-no. NOSTRILS might pick up on straggling alcoholic particles for months if not years, wreaking havoc on drug searches. The sewers would require turbo-flushing by city crews. She decided to pour it into the ocean, at least thirty miles from shore. Two weeks later it'd dissipate enough that NOSTRILS wouldn't react. DES was not planning any Population Surveys out among the tuna anyway.

Jim entered the room, grabbed a chair and sat next to his colleague. Both watched the screen. "What was it you said to Uncle Roy when you insulted him?" Larry questioned.

Jim smiled. "'I don't know, I thought it just sounded distinguished-like.' I was quoting the great *George Harrison* from the movie *A Hard Day's Night*."

"Of the Beatles, then," Larry recollected. "I remember that band, though they broke up long before I was born. A Diamond Commemoration for the release of *Sergeant Pepper's Lonely Hearts Club Band* is planned for next year. Ringo's still alive. I'll bet that old geezer is past the century mark." Jim agreed, but seemed unusually quiet. Larry decided to clear the air. "Are you ticked at me for getting you into a situation like that?"

Jim shrugged. "I'd hoped to get through my life without ever drinking a drop of that disgusting stuff. But the battle against drugs seems more important. However I did want to ask about the legality of this surveillance."

"Root around in the Patriot Act and you'll find the Shadowing Clause allows us to maintain surveillance on anybody we're suspicious of. It hasn't been overturned by the Supreme Court yet, so what the heck."

"That was the Unwarranted Supervision Clause," Jim corrected.

Larry seemed conflicted. "No, I think you're mistaken. It's the Shadowing Clause." Jim looked skeptical. Larry gazed at him hesitantly, then retreated. "I probably better not go up against your photographic memory, huh?" Larry seemed troubled. "Then what's in the Shadowing Clause?"

"Look it up and let me know what you find. It might also be relevant to our situation. By the way, the Unwarranted Supervision, or Hoover Clause was ruled unconstitutional decades ago." Jim winked and diverted the conversation to a more scholarly subject. "Hopefully the brilliant light I recall wasn't a UFO, because I'm not fond of them flying in my airspace."

Larry was surprised by the statement and decided to take the bait. Jim had surely been provoked and would exact revenge in his own unflappable way. "You've never actually seen a UFO, have you? That light you remember was a flash from Doris' holographic camera. She's getting a poster-size print made."

"Need-to-know on the UFOs." It's inevitable. Jocularity. In a religious sense, one joke begets another. Jim pointed to the ceiling and whispered. "Shhhhh. We shouldn't be talking about aliens. They've got listening posts. Our conversations are monitored."

"There are no aliens listening out there. You're thinking of the National Security Agency." Larry was relieved by Jim's upbeat mood, knowing the man had good reason to hate alcohol—his parents killed by a drunk driver when he was a child. Larry's full attention returned to the tracking screen, locked onto the intestinal fortitude of the infamous Uncle Roy. "He's coming this way. Look how he drives around the block before heading in our direction, running misdirection plays with his vehicle!"

"Shadowing is still an effective form of tracking someone, even after dark," Jim informed his co-officer before changing the subject again. "You didn't happen to watch Devil's Advocate on the Debate Channel a few nights ago, did you?"

"Nope," Larry admitted, while still focused on GPS. "Was it good?"

"One of the best I've ever seen." Jim sounded a little excited, which for him is a lot excited. "They discussed the possible downfall of western civilization and how the descent into the abyss was precipitated by events that took place at the 1999 Ryder Cup."

Larry turned, amazed by the statement. "What happened at the 1999 Ryder Cup that had such world-shaking ramifications?"

Jim shrugged. "I tuned in late and was hoping you'd fill me in."

"No can do." Larry had been set up. The gears were already turning. Revenge would be sweet. "The Ryder Cup was a golf tournament, wasn't it?"

"I think so." Jim didn't sound too sure. "I'd never heard of it before the other night. It's hard to believe something that momentous, even from the standpoint of subtle humor, could happen at a golf match. Anyway, it was the Debate Channel's annual showcase on refined and artful wittiness, probably the best television of the entire year."

"I'm sorry I missed it. We should download a copy from last week's listings. You know, that network makes over $50 million a year running those old *Firing Line* reruns in syndication. Debate is profitable. It brings in more revenue than Pro Wrestling."

"What about golf?" Jim queried."

"They say golf is a microcosm of life," Larry replied cautiously.

"Not true," Jim spoke as if it was all a crock. The duel of wits had started. "Actually, bull riding is the real microcosm. You start in a cage, then it's out the chute into the arena of life. You're involved with something a lot bigger than yourself, and a rough ride is in store. If you hang on long enough, you might do okay. Most can't cut the mustard and are bucked off too soon. Better luck next time, if there is one."

"You may be correct." Larry's assumed gravity was a tip off. "Truth is, golf tournaments are rigged, just like Pro Wrestling. They play the match following a script, with a plot calculated to stir the deepest feelings of righteousness within the audience. The players get together days in advance and carefully plan strategies. They figure out who will win the round and what their individual scores will be. On a hole-by-hole basis, they know who's going to end up in a bunker, in the rough, or closest to the pin. They even blow two or three foot putts, which is a dead giveaway someone else is supposed to gain a stroke. I once saw a guy miss the hole by inches, yet his ball kept going downhill and ended up in a pond. He purposefully blew two strokes with one shot. It's all rigged in advance, predetermined from the get-go. Then the supermarket tabloids run those sordid stories of love, sex, and seedy romantic betrayals among the tour's elite—all that passion, lust, desire—and presto, you've got big time TV ratings for a silly game." Jim didn't say anything, deciding he'd better think on it for a while. "And speaking of a silly game..." Larry laughed, his attention returning to GPS tracking. "LeRoy is driving the wrong way up a one-way street to discern whether he's being followed. He must be paranoid!"

"He has good reason to be spooked," Jim conceded, "if you will pardon the pun. A spy with his awareness and longevity develops a sixth sense telling him when something's out of kilter." Jim was speaking from experience. "He feels he's being watched, but has no idea from where. However, there's a ticket in his future from Satellite Traffic Surveillance if they can ID him."

"Yeah, I'm sure he's got that rusty old Cadillac registered with DMV. We should let Motor Vehicles know where they can find his antique land cruiser. I'd like to see his face when he gets the ticket while reclining on a cot in the homeless shelter and realizes his cover is blown."

Jim smiled, unconsciously fingering a string of turquoise beads hanging from his neck. "We could have a lot of fun with this but better not tip our hand."

Larry capitulated reluctantly. He liked practical jokes as long as no one got seriously hurt, permanently disabled, or ended up in traction for an unnecessary length of time.

By 3 AM, LeRoy's battered vehicle was only blocks from Federal Law Enforcement Headquarters in downtown Los Angeles. Jim scrutinized the monitor. "He's making progress. I'm out of here. I really don't want to meet with him again this soon."

"Can't say I blame you," Larry replied. "It was over two decades between visits for me. But it's funny. I grew to like the old fellow. He spared my life and I sure got a nice leather chair out of the deal. Still, the only solid conclusion I ever came to regarding LeRoy is what Sarge said—that his mother didn't love him when he was a little boy."

"It wouldn't surprise me," Jim acknowledged. "That's true of a lot of CIA types." He rose and returned his chair to its former resting place. "What really puzzles me about the guy is his profession—I mean what he did before being recruited by the Firm."

"I've had years to ponder that question. My guess is a psychiatrist."

"CIA people are a hard lot to explain. I know they hold grudges." Jim hesitated. "You want to hear something really profound? Sarge once claimed that you were named after a member of the *Three Stooges*." He remained perfectly serious and shrugged. "But for the life of me, I've never been able to figure out which one!"

Larry smiled, making no response. Topping such a remark would take some thought. Jim quickly headed towards the hanger. On the way he informed Bo of LeRoy's impending visit. Jim wanted to check on his Cat-five, which had just undergone a detailed examination required by the certification process. He had no interest in talking to Uncle Roy, knowing he'd be briefed later if the spymaster had anything constructive to say.

FUTUREBUST9.3

Big Al was laboring on the Delta Squad EV, keeping the vehicle polished and ready to go on a moment's notice for the frontline officers. Zeke was sick and he'd fallen behind. That meant long hours. Plus, there was the special-duty certification process to deal with.

An FBI SWAT dude headed back out on the roof to watch for bad guys. It had been seven days since the building was locked down, and they hadn't captured a single CIA agent. Expectations were high in the beginning, but as time slipped by, it was obvious the Firm wasn't coming back. The Cat-five had been out on a dozen test-flights and attracted no unwanted attention. As Jim said earlier, they had made their point.

Off to the left about fifty feet, the Fiver rested in its parking spot with the rear cowling open. Since Al was the only one working, the vehicle looked neglected. The mechanic wiped his hands on a rag, threw it on the floor, and stood up. "Take a look at this." The grease monkey motioned towards the turbocraft. He pointed down inside the vehicle at two little electronic modules, each no bigger than a book of matches. Both were secured to struts. "It's got a one hundred percent computer controlled fire suppression system. Plus, the ballistic parachute is electronic—no cable deployment."

The mechanic's revelation troubled Jim. He bent over and looked into the vehicle's innards. "Is that it? Is that all that stands between a pilot and incineration on impact?"

"Those little boogers are the brains." Big Al shook his head in dismay. He looked at Jim with resignation. "I'm sorry, buddy, but for the time being there is nothing I can do. They're supposed to be rubber mounted, per the onboard plans."

Jim grimaced. "There is no way you can install the old-fashioned fire suppression system in this vehicle? I've survived two violent, high-speed crashes with the previous safety equipment. Why would they change it?"

"A retrofit would be difficult. I'd have to cut through reinforcing struts, then install two new canisters of extinguisher foam and route the cables to the cockpit. It would be a mess. But I'd do it if I could. On the positive side, I've already ordered parts for the ballistic parachute out of the book for the Cat-four. They should be here in a week."

"A week?"

"They're backordered from Hong Kong. The factory has no spares. They are using *just-in-time* inventory management, as if the idea of efficiency has run amuck. So we wait. But I think we can install a manual chute pull with about eight hours of work for two guys if I use a sledgehammer. Until then, you'll have to live with what we've got."

"What are the odds those little chips could malfunction and fail to provide fire suppression or an emergency chute?"

"Preflight says they're functioning." Al scratched his nose with a greasy finger. "I assume it's been thoroughly tested and refined, but wouldn't want to bet my life on it." Jim shook his head in dismay as Al continued. "As far as I'm concerned, the old system was fine. Now you are totally at the mercy of electronic impulses and a bunch of ones and zeros in the software package! The rubber mounting is easy. I'll have that done pronto."

"If it ain't broke, why do they meddle with it?" Jim was puzzled. "I'll bet some government bureaucrats were involved in this decision."

"Possibly some payoffs," Big Al conceded.

"So you think economics played a part in this?"

"Money talks!" the mechanic replied, shaking his head in consternation. "You'd be surprised how much *monetary influence* is floating around in the big outdoors, and there are lots of low-ethics shysters ready to grab. Some company with connections came up with this system and decided to cash in. Same for the chute. The CEO called a PAC. They informed lobbyist who had buddies in Congress who put pressure on officials who oversee bureaucrats making recommendations to design engineers who stuck the gizmo into the plans. It's a government contract. Those boogers are manufactured in an influential congressman's district whose constituents are working at the factory. They contribute dollars and votes to the politicians who win reelection, and everybody's happy except you."

"It stinks! No matter where you look, money is influencing decisions that should be made on merit. And it's at its worst in politics. Sometimes I wonder what's going to happen to us as a society!" Jim dug his hands into his pockets.

"Possibly the same thing that happened to your people years ago," the mechanic replied cryptically. Both men stood in silence, then Big Al continued. "Did you still have the photograph of your Great, Great Grandfather on the wall after the bad guys trashed your apartment?"

"Thankfully," Jim replied, glad to be leaving the last subject behind. "Honoring our ancestors is a tradition. They made us what we are. Unlike the white culture which worships sex, violence, and money, ours revere the sacred ground they walked on, or what's left of it." Jim paused. "And while we're on the subject of elders, wasn't yours a Fed Chairman?"

"That's right," Big Al smiled. "In fact, it's one of the reasons I left investment banking. We used to buy up companies and tear them to pieces..."

"You mean dismember them," Jim interjected graphically.

"You've got it," Big Al admitted. "Then we sold off the parts to make a huge profit, leaving hundreds of people unemployed in the process."

Jim studied his facial expressions. "What changed your mind?"

"Two things." Big Al seemed ashamed. "One was my Grandfather, God rest his soul. I didn't feel the grandson of a Fed Chairman should be groveling in such a heartless, cutthroat business enterprise. Not that I'm so high-and-mighty, but it was beneath the standards he set for the family. You go into something like that purely for personal gain, with no concern for others. You know, there are people who actually admire such behavior. I think they need their collective heads examined!"

"So you saw the light," Jim encouraged. "And what was the second?"

"I didn't want my kids growing up under corporate raider standards. They came home from school one afternoon and asked what I do for a living. I felt so ashamed. What could I tell them? They even wanted to go to the office for a firsthand experience of my professional activities. It was a homework assignment they were required to write a report on." Big Al again hesitated. "In so many ways, what we did was counterproductive!"

"Don't they justify corporate raids by claiming it roots out inefficiency and excess?"

"Maybe. But all we wanted was easy money. Efficiency is an excuse to cover the disgusting nature of the work! Corporate raiders know what every lawyer learns the first day of law school. The fastest way to acquire wealth is to take someone else's. Then ship all the jobs to China and give yourself a pay raise!"

"Interesting," Jim concluded. "Past and future generations influenced your decision to move on. Maybe there is hope for the White Devil."

The mechanic smiled at Jim's characterization. "That remains to be seen."

"So now you're a grease monkey working in drug enforcement," Jim added spryly. "Do you feel you're accomplishing anything here?"

"More than before. A Ph.D. in economics can gain you a lot of financial security..."

"If there is such a thing," Jim interrupted.

"If there is such a thing," Big Al conceded, "you can get a whole lot of it in a hurry. But it also made me feel useless. Money isn't real anyway, yet they don't teach that in the classroom. You have to figure it out for yourself."

Jim nodded in agreement. "My people could have taught your people that centuries ago. But the whites were too busy cutting down the forest and killing the animals. Men digging for gold destroyed much of my homeland in the Dakotas. The ancient ones called it *the yellow metal that makes men crazy*. My Grandfather back at the Rez says white people have one, overriding fear—that someone else might make the last dollar." Al smiled. "By the way," Jim became serious. "You pulled that military comm. out of the Fiver, right?"

"Yesterday. You think they want it back? It's a sophisticated device."

"It's possible the Pentagon doesn't know we have it," Jim speculated. "They don't worry much about keeping track of classified laptops, secure comms, and the like. There are even times when ordnance turns up missing." Both men smiled at the oxymoron, though it was no laughing matter. "Anyway, I wanted that thing out. Get Zeke to look it over."

Big Al nodded, remaining quiet. He was wearing a look that made one wonder what was going on upstairs right under his toupee. He eyed Jim cautiously. "What were you and Lance up to a week ago? You both looked sick. Then Dolly came out and dragged you away by the ears. That's mighty suspicious behavior, even for prima donna pilots."

Jim laughed and sat down on a fifteen-gallon barrel, contemplating his answer. It was a golden opportunity to have some fun, being that Larry had bested him in the jocularity department a few minutes before. He figured he'd start slow and easy. "Need-to-know."

"Uh huh," Big Al shook his head. "Real secret agent stuff I suppose."

"Naw, nothing like that." Jim folded his arms across his chest. He paused for effect, then cranked it up a notch. "I guess I can let you in on our secret."

"That's good news," Al ribbed the pilot. "Let's have it. And it better be high-quality or I'll be looking for more reliable information from Lance."

"Okay, it's like this. We all got drunk that morning."

"Yeah, right! You must think I was born in a barn and raised by wolves. Come on, you can do better than that. Give it another try."

"No, really." Jim tried to sound sincere. "We got drunk for medicinal reasons."

Big Al remained unconvinced. He leaned against a tool cabinet. "So you expect me to believe you got drunk in preparation for a Mission from God?"

Jim shook his head and laughed. "We were drunk but I can't elaborate. It's strictly Need-to-know. Scout's Honor." Jim made the *Scout's Honor* sign, proving beyond any doubt that he was telling the truth. There was almost nothing more fun—save for flying—than messing with the grease monkey's highly educated thought processes.

"Well I'm not buying it," Big Al was obstinate. "DES officers do not spend their time drunk, Mission from God or no! That stuff's illegal, you know."

Jim enjoyed the moment. "It wasn't just Lance and me either. All the

Alphas were plastered, even Captain Jackson. Doris, up on the fourteenth floor gave us the liquor."

"Right!" Big Al replied sarcastically. "I'll tell you this though. I once knew someone who was related to a person who had a friend that was employed by a guy with an uncle who smoked marijuana back in the sixties. But that's as close as I've come to any kind of drug use or intoxication."

"Well, you're doing okay then." Jim stood up and patted the mechanic on the arm. "But we really were drunk."

Lance came through the door and out into the hanger. He walked toward the two men and joined them, noticing both were silent. Big Al seized the opportunity to question the rookie. "Were you drunk a week ago?"

"Yup," Lance replied matter-of-factly. "First and last time for me."

"You've got him trained," Big Al admonished. He slapped Jim on the shoulder. "I can't win with you guys. I'll see you tomorrow."

"Did you have any problem installing a rumble seat?" Jim asked as the mechanic walked from their presence.

"Nope," Big Al replied, heading back to the EV he was working on earlier. "Drunk...my ass!"

"What's with him?" Lance protested, shrugging. "What'd I say?"

"He doesn't believe we were drunk." Jim clued the younger pilot in. "I guess I can understand his skepticism. Alcohol is illegal, you know." Lance smiled. "Anyway, welcome to the graveyard shift. This is the time when all the world sleeps, but we at DES remain vigilant. Nighttime is when the dark, evil, foul, and disgusting things that happen in the world...uh, happen." Jim smiled. "I guess I'd never make a very good writer, would I? That was a poorly constructed sentence. Anyway, are you ready to give the Fiver a try?"

"I'm ready as I'll ever be!" Lance announced. "Let's rock and roll."

"Jump in." Jim closed and secured the rear cowling on the vehicle. He also grabbed a portable fire extinguisher just in case. "I'll squeeze in behind and we'll be on our way. Your Cat-five certification was faxed this morning from DC. As far as I'm concerned, anyone who can hold his liquor as good as you should be able to fly anything he wants."

"Keep it down," Lance whispered. "That stuff is illegal."

Both men situated themselves in the single-person vehicle—the rookie comfortably in the pilot's seat—Jim shoehorned behind, sitting sideways on Big Al's handiwork. His left shoulder was up against the back of the seat, his knees scrunched against his chest. It was an uncomfortable position, but he'd be okay for a couple hours. Then Lance, wide-eyed and bushy-tailed, fired the Pulse Thrusters, scanned his instruments for anomalies, cautiously throttled up, and taxied out to the ramp after Big Al opened the doors. The mechanic pretended to drink from a glass, shaking his head in the negative. Lance smiled as he was cleared for departure by AATC. The SWAT guys gave thumbs up. They knew that vehicle was the reason they were dressed in camo and carrying lethal firepower while collecting overtime. What more could one ask for in a job?

Neither spoke as they headed out over a subdued city. Lance decided to cruise the Strip, and with the push of a button deleted the drug search planned by the supercomputer up on the fourteenth floor. Jim nodded in approval. The rookie was learning fast. He headed west, allowing time to take in the view. Below, the traffic was light. Above—"Look at the night sky! Now I understand why you work this shift. It's beautiful out here!"

"Yup, sure is. I wouldn't give it up for anything." Jim smiled in his cramped back seat. "You won't be able to fly this shift until I'm dead and gone. That's the advantage of seniority. I get to do what I want, you don't."

Lance laughed. "Until you're dead and gone, huh? I can wait. I'm patient." He smiled. "But if it happens sooner than later, all the better for me."

Both men took in the celestial scenery for ten minutes as they overflew Sunset Boulevard. With very little activity below, Lance didn't bother to turn on NOSTRILS. No point in ruining the evening with a troublesome Population Survey. Big Brother needs a vacation. Some thought him a little too intrusive anyway. All that government meddling could try one's patience.

When they'd seen enough, he changed directions. "I wanted to ask you..." he looked over his shoulder after accelerating to Mach .33. "Man, this thing is smooth!"

"What's on your mind?" Jim inquired in teaching mode.

"The headache and nausea I had after I regained consciousness? It's called an overhang?"

"Nope," Jim replied, "but you're close. It's a hangover. Don't ask me why." The more experienced pilot decided he should enlighten the rookie. "It also looks like I have to teach you the economics of turbocraft fire suppression later." Lance turned on the stereo system and found some Rock and Roll tunes to add atmosphere to their journey. The eighty-year-old stuff was still the best. Then the Cat-five sped off into the darkness.

FUTUREBUST9.7

Larry headed down to meet Uncle Roy and escort him upstairs. He'd have to endure a complete scan both ways to ensure he's the same person. It's all rather risky. If the SWAT dudes discover a Company man, they'll scramble to get first shot.

He entered while Larry chatted with a late night FBI receptionist. "What a surprise." Larry used every ounce of acting ability he possessed. "We didn't expect to see you back here for a few more days. What can we do for you?"

"You can build some ramps nearby." LeRoy shook his head in frustration. "It isn't 4 A.M. and there's no place to park. I walked two blocks to get here!"

"Life can be brutal," Larry chided.

LeRoy seemed impatient. "Don't get clever with me, young man. Remember, I spared you, years ago. You should be grateful."

"I am," Larry conceded, amused at being called *young man* by someone apparently his own age. "Your boys didn't appreciate me. Where's Dirk?"

"Dirk's a jerk." Leroy sounded peeved. "It's hard to hire good help these days. He's more interested in chasing women than doing his job."

Larry motioned with his hand. "You better step over to that security monitor. We have to make sure you're not carrying any listening devices."

"I wouldn't dream of planting a device in your office."

"That's good to hear," Larry countered. On a roll, he'd already topped Jim and now threw one over LeRoy's head. "You're absolutely sure you weren't tracked? Your presence here could be embarrassing." They rode the elevator upstairs. Twenty seconds later, the two men entered the main office.

Bo greeted him with a skeptical handshake. Uncle Roy refused the courtesy.

"Where's Jacko?" the CIA operative questioned gruffly.

"At home in bed, but he left you a message," Bo replied sternly. "Quite frankly, no one here believes your story about bribery. It's over the top and well down the other side—ridiculous!" Larry nodded his approval. Uncle Roy was visibly angered, but said nothing as Bo read him the riot act. "We suspect you've concocted an elaborate scheme to move large amounts of contraband. We don't even believe this has anything to do with the Firm, but is a fabrication to enrich your personal finances. Word on the street is that high-priced Cuban stogies are available. So no peace pipe with drug runners!"

Uncle Roy pointed his finger in warning. His momentary silence was ominous. The spy was PO'd to the point of boil-over and let go with a vengeance. "You want to talk about stupidity, I'll teach you a little something on the subject." Larry started to chuckle but held back so as not to disrupt things. LeRoy didn't realize he had just made a joke. This seemed to be a night for jocularity. Then the spymaster commenced his sermon.

"When I was here earlier, I told you of growing corruption in the halls of power. Influence peddling has been pervasive in government for decades. Do you know what people in Congress call graft? A *Tolerable Indiscretion*! The Capitol is filled with tolerable indiscretions, along with a wink and a nod. Another example is *Excusable Ethics Lapses*. An inquiry into unethical behavior is labeled *Unwarranted Oversight*. Bribes are euphemistically referred to as *Redundant Paychecks*. Kickbacks are *Contractor Honoraria*. And closed, no-bid contracts are called *A Gimme*! Special tax loopholes for corporations are referred to as *Drano*!" LeRoy wrung his hands together, then regained control of his anger, as if calling on years of practice. "You are nothing but a choirboy, lieutenant!" He looked at the ceiling. "The innocence of babes. How naive!" Bo and Larry remained silent. No point in provoking the man. Better to let him blow off steam—referred to as *venting*.

LeRoy cut to the chase. "You need a crash course in politics to get a better idea of how wrong you are. Congress is neck deep in corruption."

Bo was thinking maybe they should escort the guy to the elevator and send him packing. He wasn't telling them anything they didn't already know.

LeRoy calmed down. "A good analogy is the aging process. It happens so slowly, you hardly realize it's taking place. But as the years pass, changes become evident. Look at a photo taken ten, or even five years earlier and you're surprised at the difference. Corrupting influences within government work the same way. They creep in like a cancer eating at the fabric of democracy. I've seen this first hand. Working for the Firm, I have a front row seat. Ethical standards are lowered such that we don't realize it's happening. Something totally out of bounds today, might within a decade be casually accepted as harmless, or welcomed as positive. Read your history about the greed of the 1980s. It's a perfect example. As I said the other day, it's only one small step from influence peddling to blatant, outright bribery. Some warped philosophies insult the Constitution, hiding behind Free Speech as if this vital principle of democracy can be purchased from political leaders. I'll tell you one thing. Free speech becomes very dangerous when only the rich can afford it!"

"It's that denial we discussed more than two decades ago," Larry summarized. "And you're right about Free Speech. It is dangerous when only the rich can afford it—distorting democracy. I can't believe a Supreme Court would debase itself to accept such a premise."

LeRoy seemed relieved. "Can either of you dispute what I have said?"

"No dispute," Bo conceded the point, caution visible on his face. "Influence traded for campaign contributions is latent corruption, both immoral and unethical. However, outright bribery, even if it is just one baby step further into the cesspool of money-politics, is illegal. Where's the proof illegalities have taken place?"

"Secret money funneled from the MIC is categorized as *Incentive Contributions*. We've become desensitized to this behavior. And you need proof?"

"So all you offer is philosophical proof," Larry observed. "It's not much to go on."

"I also have a hard time believing," Bo reiterated, "that the fine line between influence peddling and bribes has been crossed, no matter how desensitized we've all become."

"Well then," Uncle Roy was growing impatient with his precocious students, "let me give you an example straight out of the historically documented past. Are you aware that the federal government, some forty years ago, subsidized the growing of tobacco?"

"What!" Bo couldn't believe what he'd just heard. "The government subsidized the growing of a plant used to produce a toxic, poisonous product that killed thousands a week in this country? That's absurd!"

"Fraid not," Larry disagreed. "LeRoy's right. Didn't you read your history?"

"I skipped that class frequently," he admitted, now visibly shaken by the revelation. "How could something like that happen?"

LeRoy was pleased he'd made an impact. "Money buys influence. How could any ethical person accept cash from such an industry, then claim the money wasn't the issue? And in the same breath, they graciously voted for subsidization of the most deadly consumer product in the history of the world, while *overlooking* the contributions they received." An awful lot of sarcasm spewed forth in the emphasis of that word, but this time it was wholly justified. Larry realized LeRoy was the king of sarcasm, the undisputed champion of the world. He'd never again butt heads with the master. The man had made his point, and wasn't even finished. "Even bullets and bombs haven't killed as many people as tobacco!" LeRoy revealed caustically. "I don't think those legislators feared God, or they would never have allowed such a practice to continue."

The young lieutenant was stunned, like someone had just punched him in the stomach. "Get him out of here," Bo ordered. "The answer is still no!"

Larry pointed the CIA operative in the direction of the exit. LeRoy was shouting as they left the main office. He stomped his feet like a child, told to go to bed without dessert. "Do you know how they define *political influence* in DC?" he yelled as they headed for the elevator. "Not intellectual authority, not the ability to convince and sway opinion..." LeRoy bellowed as Larry gently shoved him forward..."not even celebrity star-power!" The doors on the elevator were about to close. Larry had Uncle Roy by the arm to keep him under control. "Wealth!" LeRoy screamed as the doors sealed the two men off from the rest of the world. "Capital wealth!" Both exited on the first floor. LeRoy was shown his way out after being scanned. "That kid should have read his history lessons!"

FUTUREBUST9.9

Larry didn't reply—quickly returning upstairs. Bo had turned white at hearing Uncle Roy's comment. It was impossible to believe. Tobacco: a government-subsidized product! Larry found him out in the hanger sitting on a barrel near the wide-open vehicle entrance, his head between his legs. The SWAT guys looked concerned.

"Am I really a choirboy?" he looked up as Larry approached. "I had no idea that the federal government subsidized a plant responsible for killing hundreds of millions of people worldwide." Larry put his hand on the young officer's shoulder. He said nothing. "Are we that tolerant of corrupt, unethical behavior as LeRoy has suggested? Could he be right?"

"I don't think I can answer your second question," Larry consoled. "The answer to your first is I hope not, or we as a society are in deep trouble. Your reaction to his statement is encouraging. If everyone was equally stunned about what happened, we'd be making progress."

Bo sat up as the color returned to his face. He took a deep breath and exhaled, then walked to the edge of the landing platform and looked out over the surrounding area. Larry followed. They gazed at the view of the historical monument across the 101 Freeway. A half-dozen Maglevs were parked at Union Station waiting for their departure times. They could even see the newly refurbished county jail complex known as the Combined Municipal Lockup; and the businesses of Chinatown, a few blocks away. Bo looked up at the Milky Way and breathed deliberately until his head cleared. Life was full of unwelcome surprises. Like stories in the history books of gladiators killing for barbaric sport; of people treating it as a joke. *Unbelievable*—government subsidized tobacco!

Bo finally broke the silence. "You know, LeRoy's a hypocrite."

"The guy's a *philosophical* bloodsucker," Larry opined. "As long as drugs stay illegal, he's in clover. He can have his cake and eat it to."

A wind gust kicked up over the building, blowing Bo's hair in his eyes. He brushed it away and looked at Larry, who was doing the same. "Let's get to work." He turned and retraced his steps. "You've got to keep an eye on that guy. I can tell he's up to no good!"

FUTUREBUST10.0

"He's heading up the coast." Larry stood by a GPS tracking monitor focused on Uncle Roy. The others were in the Command Center gazing at the wall-mounted DynaView linked to the Cat-five, patrolling 110 miles west-northwest of HQ. It was past noon but everyone stayed to help out. LeRoy had taken flight and they wanted to see where he was going, courtesy of the Hoover Clause in the PATRIOT III Act. (The fact that the Hoover Clause had been ruled unconstitutional was irrelevant to the current situation. Elsewhere in the document, Article 423b, Subsection 14, Paragraph 9 states that if the person under observation does not realize that the surveillance is illegal, then the law need not be precisely adhered to—i.e. what he doesn't know won't hurt him. Such incongruities are common in Patriot III, because no one in Congress took the time to read the bill before it was passed and signed into law. Also, the glossary at the back of Patriot IV defines *constitutionality* as "an inconvenient nuisance".)

Bo was pacing, still ticked off at LeRoy for what he'd said a week earlier. Most eyes however, were locked on the spectacular 3D image of the Pacific Coast Highway just west of Santa Barbara, besmirched only by the presence of a rusty Cadillac. LeRoy's hands were clearly visible on the steering wheel even with the camera five thousand meters behind and slightly to the left. He was speeding towards an unknown destination.

Lance was flying the turbocraft he and Jim had been testing nonstop for the last two weeks. Jim sat behind his student, sideways and scrunched up in the rumble seat Big Al had fashioned. Lance queried as he zoomed in on the car. "How's the picture?"

"It's splendid! We can almost smell the exhaust belching from his tailpipe, which," Larry looked closely at the screen, "appears to be held secure by a coat hanger."

"Splendid?" Sarge inquired, brushing hair from his forehead. "You could have replied it was groovy or rad or even far-out. But splendid?"

"The Brits use that word," Cy defended the fancy English vernacular. "It sounds rather like an aristocratic response to Lance's inquiry. Bloody good!"

"We're not carrying any pollution detection devices on this vehicle," Jim mused from his cramped back seat. "But if we were, I'm wagering anybody who'll bet, we'd have that bloke up on an emissions charge."

"Well stay tight on his blooming ass," Dolly ordered, as she watched with the others. "Figure out where he's headed."

"I know where he's going." Lance radiated a prophetic smile. The Cadi sped on at ninety-five MPH. Considered fast for a car, it was a little slow for the turbocraft. To keep things exciting, the occupants of the Cat-five would have preferred four hundred-plus mph. Regardless, it handled splendidly at low speed.

Bo sat at the Command desk. Concerned, he looked straight at the comm. framing Lance's face. "What do you mean you know where he's going?"

"Yeah," Jim tapped the rookie from behind. "What's up with that?"

"He's headed for Lompoc. About four weeks ago on a routine scan, I picked up minute traces of tobacco. I thought it was an anomaly and brushed it off."

"Why didn't you inform us?" Bo reclined in the chair and turned towards the 3D DynaView mounted on the wall.

"Not after what happened a few months back," Lance objected. "I didn't want to bust another lumber pile. It was too faint to worry about. There was just enough time to get a fix, somewhere in the vicinity of Lompoc."

"What's this about a lumber pile?" Dolly became mildly peeved. "You guys aren't keeping vital information from me again?"

"I'll fill you in later," Bo, somewhat embarrassed, glanced at his female counterpart. "Lance, do you remember the day?"

"I was cruising between Santa Maria and San Luis Obispo in the Cat-four, taking the scenic route back to HQ when NOSTRILS briefly registered signatures. It might have been the twenty-fifth."

"Cy," Bo sat up straight in his chair, "grab that Data Register from the turbocraft scan files. Let's see what we can discover."

"I'll have to get the security pass from Doris." Cy headed for the elevator.

"Anything else you can tell us? This could be your first big bust!"

"Nothing I can think of," the rookie replied. The onrushing Cadillac appeared to head for Lompoc, just as Lance claimed.

"You probably picked up on an underground installation," Jim patted Lance on the head like he was a schoolboy, "which was too deep to latch onto. In the few seconds someone opened and passed through an exit, the readings elevated. As the door closed, the scent was lost."

Everyone scrutinized the DynaView as the Cadi accelerated up the coast. LeRoy had a scrambler installed or STS (Satellite Traffic Surveillance) would have ticketed him. The 3D view was so spectacular, all watched transfixed. "What kind of mileage do you think he gets?" Larry asked.

"No more than twenty miles per gallon," Sarge opined. "My boat gets better than that!" (Probably not true.) The others laughed. "There aren't many people around who still use gasoline motors. He must be getting his fuel at an airport or marina."

Uncle Roy made a wheel-chattering left turn in the direction of Lompoc. "I think the kid is right," Jim informed from his cramped back seat. "He's turning off the 101 and heading up Highway 1. There is very little between us and Lompoc."

"You're getting awful close to Vandenberg Air Force Base," Dolly advised. "We better inform them of what's happening. Who's in charge up there?"

"That would be Lieutenant General William 'Billy-boy' Walthers," Jim replied, shifting his weight to ward off a backache. They had been out on patrol for ten hours with only one stop for donuts and gas. That made them eligible for hazard pay. Regs required a donut stop every four hours. They were also running low on fuel.

Dolly looked up the number of the base commander and mumbled. "I'd still like to know a little more about that lumber pile."

Jim leaned over and pointed to a spot on the armrest. The Cat-five shuddered, then regained stability and speed as Lance activated the Variable Camo. "We'll move in closer," he informed. "I'm betting he might have some contraband in his trunk."

Lance accelerated the Fiver hard. He pulled to within 2200 yards of the Cadillac, then leaned forward and activated the sensor array as they decelerated to match the speed of their quarry. Jim congratulated him for an earnest pursuit.

"You've got that boy trained." Bo's voice radiated concern. "He closed the distance by almost two miles in just over forty seconds. How does the Fiver feel through aggressive acceleration?"

"Splendid," Lance replied in a poor quality English accent. "The shaking is mostly gone from .45 to .52."

"It's quite remarkable," Jim agreed. "We can all be thankful that Big Al gave up hostile takeovers to pursue more important goals. I appreciate the smoother ride, pilot sensitive steering, and the genteel flight manners this vehicle exhibits. And it has enough cup holders to satisfy a family of four."

"Plus the duel climate control allows me to keep the temperature at a comfortable sixty-eight degrees, while Jim prefers sixty-seven back in the rumble seat." Lance adjusted the sensor array from full wide-scan and focused it on LeRoy's gas-guzzler, now only six miles from Lompoc. The alert buzzer immediately sounded.

Fifteen feet from the Command Center and the same number of seconds later, the InstaPrint came to life. A warrant had been issued. Sarge grabbed it off the machine and read the results out loud. "The Online Judge wants that character picked up, paddled, and stuffed in the FedPen!"

"The suspect is nearing his destination." Lance adjusted the camera so those at HQ could see the surroundings better, then lowered his altitude to eight hundred feet. "We'll hold back two miles to avoid detection."

A telephone lit up. It was an incoming call from Vandenberg Air Force Base. "L.A. DES," Dolly swung her chair around and answered.

"Lieutenant General William Walthers returning your call," an Air Force captain on the screen replied. "One moment." A middle-age man appeared. He was dressed in Air Force blues with three shiny stars glittering on each shoulder. (Plus room for more if he managed to get the four-decade-old Missile Defense Shield up and running.) He had brown hair with touches of grey. Mutton-chop sideburns highlighted his features, similar to what Elvis Presley once wore. There was a poster-sized photo of the legendary rock & roller in a chrome frame on the wall directly behind, where the Commander-in-Chief is usually hung. General Walthers had his priorities, preferring the King to the President. He sat at his large, well-equipped workstation. A ten-gallon hat rested on the corner of his desk in plain view, along with a small teddy bear propped against the oversize headgear. The cute and fuzzy toy had a model of an ICBM, an intercontinental ballistic missile safely tucked under its arm.

"Lieutenant General Bill Walthers here. What can I do for you folks?"

"We might have an enforcement situation up near your place," Dolly informed the base commander. She gazed at the screen, noticing how pronounced his sideburns were.

"Does it involve cigars?" the general inquired bluntly.

The others turned their attention to the phone. "We think it might. How'd you know?"

"This is strictly between us," the general directed. "Three weeks ago, I busted a colonel down to a captain. He had cigars in his possession—said he picked them up in Lompoc. We don't tolerate dangerous drugs or deviant behavior here at the base. It could jeopardize our mission standing and readiness. I had to keep it hush-hush for fear of alerting the media. You know how those people latch onto a story like it's their meal ticket and blow it out of proportion. They'd sensationalize the actions of one officer who had a serious judgment lapse, as if the entire base is wasting away on drugs. I saw it as an embarrassment to the Air Force best kept under raps."

Dolly acquiesced. "The press can be a pain in the butt. However this may be bigger than a few Cubans! You destroyed them, right?"

"They were used as ballast in an ICBM test. I doubt much was left of them after the missile was destroyed." The general looked troubled. "You don't think it could have anything to do with tobacco cartels, do you? Those people are the scum of the earth. I had relatives who died of lung cancer, and some of them didn't even smoke!" The general became concerned and angry. "If the cartels are operating in this area, I want them rooted out and crushed ASAP!"

"We'll know more soon," Dolly informed. "I'll keep you abreast of the situation."

"You don't have to tell me anything," the general commanded. "Just get them out of here! We have a launch countdown sequence due to start in thirty-six hours. You tidy up this mess for me by sundown and I'll be one of the DES' biggest fans. Let me know if you need assistance within our boundaries." The base commander was silent as a look of disgust covered his face. "We've got a few warheads on-site that I'd like to ram up their...!" His demeanor was fierce for a general officer, then tension eased and he regained composure. "Well, you know what I mean."

"It'd be a tight fit for all but the biggest asshole," Dolly affirmed.

"Do any of you at DES know how to insult a drug dealer?" General Walthers asked, as if posing a riddle.

"Don't think it's possible," Dolly replied flatly. The general nodded his approval, smiled, and the screen went blank. She shifted her gaze to the comm. Lance and Jim stared back at her. "Did you guys get that?"

"The general definitely doesn't like cigars," the rookie replied. "But I can't see what's so wrong with it. If a guy wants to suck on a stogie once in a while, why make a fuss?" Jim lightly slapped Lance across the back of the head. The pilot turned and laughed.

Dolly winced after hearing the comment. "The law is the law. Besides, those things smell awful. Have you ever been close to a cigar smoker?"

"I only saw tobacco once, in an anti-drug class back in high school," Lance admitted. "It's hard to believe a pile of dried leaves could kill so many people."

Everyone's attention returned to the DynaView. LeRoy exited the main road outside Lompoc. The car turned onto a driveway and backed into an innocent looking garage in a residential subdivision. The turbocraft was a mile back, hovering at treetop level.

Cy returned from his errand. "I've got the data you requested. I ran it through the computer for analysis. Looks like it was faint traces of cigar tobacco."

"So I was on to something after all," Lance congratulated himself.

"It's your first big bust," Jim admitted. "Now why don't we peer into that garage? It might be worth all the paperwork to observe LeRoy's operation. If my guess is right, it's nothing but an entrance to an underground facility."

"Go ahead with the surveillance," Dolly confirmed. Lance fired up his full color Neutrino Camera and watched as it penetrated the wooden structure.

LeRoy descended a flight of stairs heading to a concrete bunker. Lance adjusted the focus and depth of field. The sensors elevated, then returned to normal as the heavy door was pulled shut.

"That's why LeRoy was concerned about DSP capabilities," Jim observed. "He's dug in just deep enough that our present sensors can't locate him."

Lance focused on the facility. NOSTRILS wouldn't penetrate the bunker but the Neutrino Camera could. Everyone watched with fascination. "Wow!" Sarge put his hand on his head as an inside view appeared. "Would you look at that? LeRoy's got himself one heck of an operation. There must be a couple thousand boxes of stogies warehoused there. This has to be a regional distribution center!"

"And at $100 per smoke," Jim agreed from his back seat. "He's got everything but a CSI, a Cigar Store Indian. Prepare a bunk at the FedPen!" Jim was silent only a moment while the implications sunk in. "You've got to admit, LeRoy is pretty good if he can run a business on the side without the CIA knowing. Or maybe he's not in the Firm anymore. That guy might be a total fraud." The suggestion gave everyone something to ponder.

"This could be a real hefty bust," Dolly congratulated enthusiastically. She was suffering from an acute case of ADS, Arrest Deprivation Syndrome, having missed the last six busts during the graveyard shift. "He must have two thousand boxes stashed away!"

"Could be worth ten mil," Cy suggested. "Street value could easily be inflated to $25 million. The media is going to eat this up!"

Dolly's ADS was evident to all in the room. "Lance, scan the area around LeRoy's operation. Check for underground escape routes. Count the employees he's got and for God's sake, don't let anybody spot you. Check for weapons, booby traps—anything relevant. Then get your tail back here pronto. I want you refueling in ten minutes."

"Yes Ma'am!" He was totally enthused.

"Don't break the sound barrier on the way back," Bo cautioned. "I knew Chuck Yeager, and you're no Chuck Yeager."

"You're always taking the fun out of everything," Jim replied from his back seat. "We'll keep it under control. See you guys in ten. Too bad the Cat-five isn't certified for in-flight refueling yet. We could just sit here and wait."

FUTUREBUST10.3

Captain Jackson and Big Al entered. Dolly had kept the senior officer apprised of the situation. "Cigars, huh? With impending retirement, this could be our final bust together and it looks substantial. I'd sure hate to go out on a piddly-ass note!"

"It's a chance to grab yourself a heap of glory before leaving," Bo insisted through the laughter.

"A nice, healthy chunk of glory would feel good right now. I'm going to miss this place." He shook his head in amusement. "Well, not everything. I won't miss rubbing elbows with the mayor. She calls weekly, demanding we find a drug abuser to bust so she can sit in on the news conference. She thinks she got shortchanged on the last one."

"What will you do during retirement?" Dolly asked. "Sit in a rocking chair and keep time on your pocket watch."

"I'm going to buy a big lawn tractor and mow my lawn as often as I feel like it. That's every man's dream. I know using a lawn service would impress the neighbors more, but a man's got to do what a man's got to do." The captain then unloaded a bombshell on his subordinates. Nothing could have prepared them for what he was about to say. The fact that he'd been acting secretive; that he'd uttered *Need-to-know* when not wanting to divulge information—it all broke loose like a dam bursting. This announcement registered on the Richter Scale. He spoke words that were music to everyone's ears. "I'm also going to grow my Afro back. I'm tired of short, kinky hair." Those assembled looked at the senior commander in astonishment. They'd been arguing against his rebel hairstyle for years. Despite never being spoken out loud in law enforcement circles, the captain's short haircut made him somewhat of a freak and embarrassment to others. "Yup," he insisted, "I'm returning to the old hairstyle. Remember how I looked in the twenties?"

"Whoa!" The statement surprised Larry. "You had a righteous head of hair when we were in DC. With greater than a four-foot circumference, we couldn't even put a cap on you in those days. It was one high-class look!"

"I still like the Afro best, and that's what it's going to be," the captain insisted. "Only difference is it will be grey." He shrugged. "You guys weren't the only ones pestering me to get with the times. My wife's been on my back for ten years. She claims I look like a redneck. That's hard for a man to take."

"You've restored my faith in humanity," Bo agreed. "I was starting to suspect communist influences." Captain Jackson smiled. Bo is right. Everyone knows commies always wear short hair. It helps them blend in with other uncivilized types.

"You'll look good. Besides, that will give us two *Fros* at HQ when you visit," Big Al agreed. He motioned towards the DynaView. Lance and Jim had finished the *prebust*. "Look at all the cigars. Do you realize where most of them would have ended up?"

"Does this have anything to do with economics?" Bo asked.

"Sure does. Those stogies were headed for corporate boardrooms. Who else would drop a C-note to suck on burning tobacco?"

"Explain," Sarge encouraged, though it wasn't a prudent, well-thought-out request. The big man got a few dirty looks, but Al relished connecting economics with daily lives.

"Big execs love to spend shareholder's money. Fat cats do it all the time. They've got the private jets; the corporate yachts; memberships at country clubs and hunting lodges; opulent offices that rival a palace; corporate parties and entertainment; the top-floor executive suites in swanky hotels around the country; the chauffeur-driven stretch limos; even personal salons that pretty-up their swelled corporate heads; and the list goes on. It's deductible as a business expense so there is no tax on the money. But it still comes out of shareholder's pockets and is subsidized by taxpayers. Just like those cigars. They're hidden from view under the guise of corporate entertainment. Back in the olden days they had a name for sanctioned drug abuse: the three-martini lunch."

"I had no idea corporate welfare was so pervasive," Larry added. "I thought it was nothing more than tax shelters and loopholes to keep from paying income taxes."

"You wish," the mechanic replied. "And that's not the worst of it!" They all looked at him. He shrugged his shoulders. "I don't make this stuff up. Corporate execs can donate huge sums of money to PACs. Guess which they donate the most to?"

"Those that push for tax breaks," Sarge answered without hesitation.

"Correct!" Big Al exclaimed. "Shareholder's money is passed out to politicians who keep the laws skewed in favor of corporate welfare and excess. The big boys get dinner and a cigar paid for by the shareholders. And the TurboFilters that de-ionize the smoke so you can't detect any drug abuse—those are tax-deductible also. They come in under the entertainment equipment loophole!"

"How much does corporate welfare cost the treasury?" Bo asked, looking peeved.

"Over $200 billion annually," Big Al replied, "a lot of money to everyone except our friends in the Iron Triangle. And the voters could end it but they don't seem to care. That money would help pay off the national debt."

"Come on everybody!" Dolly sounded impatient, as if LeRoy could move his entire inventory in the next hour. "We won't solve that one today. Let's go! We've got a bust to execute. Jim and Lance are on their way back."

Sarge, Larry, Al, and Cy headed out towards the hanger. Dolly noticed the men didn't have the same aggressive edginess as normal before a bust. They also realized LeRoy would not be able to remove his inventory before they arrived to liquidate it for him, even if he knew they were coming, which he did not. Uncle Roy could not run or hide. He was within their grasp, about to be caught red-handed. His career as a purveyor of smoking pleasure would soon take its last, painful gasp.

The officers remained in the Command Center in a prebust state of mind, running through the precautions. Captain Jackson rubbed his thumb against his chin. "If we reel in LeRoy," he suggested, "as a source of information he's history."

"Could he lead us to bigger fish?" Bo asked.

"He may not even be active with the Firm," Captain Jackson replied. "I've called five times over the last couple of years and they won't talk about agents, past or present. That doesn't surprise me. However, FBI and NSA had no information on LeRoy either. It's as if he doesn't exist. The Firm may have kicked his ass out years ago, but he still has contacts and uses them extensively. All I'm saying is that if you have strong feelings on this matter, air them now so as not to get into split-second decisions in the field."

"Agreed," Bo affirmed. "The chance that he leads us to bigger fish is slim. There is no way to know, but any information he reveals could be disinformation. Or it could be genuine. What about that little tidbit on Senator Mackelroy?"

"And your instincts?" Captain Jackson asked.

Bo considered for no more than a second. He answered directly, as a commander must, even under pressure. "We take him out of circulation today!"

Captain Jackson looked at Dolly. "I follow intuition, not instincts," she insisted. "And I concur. We end LeRoy's fun and games now. Tomorrow we can ship him back to DC in manacles and let the big shots figure out what to do with him. That may be more revealing than any information we could get out of his unreliable mouth. If they let him off with a wrist slap, political interest in drug enforcement is waning." The two men nodded. Dolly's suggestion made sense. How would the higher-ups deal with their bad boy? Knowledge gleaned might reveal valuable information as to the future of their agency.

"It's a go then," Captain Jackson announced with an uncharacteristic lack of certainty. He headed for the hanger. The lieutenants stared at each other.

Dolly shook her head sympathetically, realizing what the senior officer must be going through. "It's his last bust."

"This is the final chapter of his long and distinguished career. It's got to hurt. He just handed the command over to a new generation." Bo nodded thoughtfully. "It's a change of the guard. We're the future." They sensed the responsibility that had fallen on them. The decision was theirs. In fact, Lance was her protégé—the bust under her command. "Are you okay?" Bo asked, concern showing on his face. "If it's about that lumber pile, it was nothing.

Lance homed in on some boards salvaged from tobacco barns. He asked us to substantiate his report stating we found a wrapper from a stick of nicotine gum."

"I remember," Dolly laughed and shook her head. Still she wasn't as confident as normal. "No, I'm not concerned with that lumber pile. Do you realize that during Captain Jackson's lifetime, drug abuse went from rampant and out-of-control to almost nothing? His career spanned a very successful timeframe." She hesitated. "One other thing. Everyone wears body armor! Those are *take-no-prisoners* guys."

"Done," Bo agreed. "I'll tell them. If you do, they'll complain."

"Let's do it then." Dolly motioned towards the hanger. "Oh," she stopped before they had gone far, "keep in mind. This is the first day of the rest of your life."

Bo understood the gravity of her statement. *"These are the good old days,"* he replied. They resumed their trek towards the future.

FUTUREBUST10.6

"Lance just left with enough fuel for another six hours," Captain Jackson informed the two lieutenants. Everyone grouped together. He spoke as if briefing a superior officer of the prebust progress. Preparations were complete. Everything was ready except for one detail. Bo informed them of the body armor. They complained, but also complied.

"Body armor is so uncomfortable," Sarge protested.

"So is a bullet," Dolly reminded. "We're not taking chances. Everyone stays alive."

Cy strapped on his bulletproof suit. "These getups give me a chance to dress awkwardly and they protect my clothing from blood and bullet holes."

"We all look like zombies," Jim teased as he stretched his back, having sat in one scrunched position far too long. He'd stayed behind after Lance refueled.

"Yeah," Bo ended the discussion as they continued to suit-up. "But we're alive and we're going to stay alive. Those guys are more dangerous than an ornery beerhead."

Big Al strolled over to the lockers where the front-line officers were prepping. He held a cardboard box no bigger than if containing a pair of children's shoes. Jim turned and glanced at the grease monkey. "It's for you." Suspicion. "Don't worry, it's been scanned."

Jim's pocketknife was buried deep under the body armor. Captain Jackson obliged, cutting the tape with a pair of nail clippers. Inside, surrounded by a plethora of annoying multicolored foam peanuts was a clumsy looking electronic module. A small piece of paper was taped to it. Jim glanced at the note, then put it in his mouth, chewed and swallowed.

"You want to explain your actions?" Dolly demanded. "I know you are not gastronomically inclined towards paper and ink."

"It was a twelve-digit phone number with a five-digit area code, plus a little note." Jim winked. "Top-secret spy stuff. Need-to-know."

"A five-digit area code?" Captain Jackson surmised. "That's a government number. You and your photographic memory better not forget! Are there any instructions?"

"Nope," Jim grimaced at the aftertaste as he looked at the device suspiciously. "It's too small to be a replacement DSP. I've got no idea what it does, but it's certainly for the Cat-five." Jim handed the box back to Big Al, who closed and secured the package.

The mechanic scratched his head in confusion, then confronted Jim. "I found some stripped wires under the console of Lance's Cat-four. Could he know about super-sensitivity this early in his career?"

"That's Need-to-know also," Jim smiled.

"We can deal with it later," Dolly insisted. "Let's get going!" The bust was delayed for ten minutes while everyone suited up. By the time they cleared the ramp, Sarge piloting the Alpha EV, Jim piloting Delta, Lance was hovering three hundred yards from LeRoy's tobacco warehouse, holding the high ground.

Minutes later, the raiding party closed on its destination. The two EV's flew in formation. They didn't take the scenic route up the coast. No one was interested. Lance piped a video feed of LeRoy's garage back to the rapidly approaching squad. Nothing was happening to warrant concern. He switched to the full color Neutrino Camera that effortlessly penetrated five feet of dirt separating the concrete bunker from the surface. Dolly, in the Delta Command and Control seat located behind the pilot, and Bo in the Alpha C&C, pored over the video. LeRoy was overseeing his operation. Because of the high-tech capabilities of the Neutrino Camera, L.A. DES had him right in the crosshairs. His tobacco smuggling operation was about to go up in smoke.

Everyone had been silent for ten minutes. Jim finally broke the solitude with a simple request. He was speaking to both EVs. "I've got to tell all of you something. I've been in on lot of busts with you guys. And on every one of them I was fifteen hundred feet above any possibility of getting hurt. I've watched you guys take all the risks and accept all the danger while I was hovering out of harm's way."

Dolly interrupted. "This is no time to mush out on us!"

"What I'm getting at is that I want to be on point. Sometimes while sitting up there in the turbocraft, I felt like I was not carrying a fair share of the load." She made the decision. The matter was settled. They flew towards Lompoc.

"Hold your position," Lance radioed. "LeRoy's coming out!" Both commanders were glued to their respective screens. They watched as LeRoy exited the bunker, then headed up the stairs and back into the garage where that rusty old Cadillac was parked. He opened the trunk and tossed in a large trash bag, standing there transfixed as if lost in a daze.

"What's he got in that bag?" Bo glared at his screen.

"One moment," Lance tuned the sensitivity of the Neutrino Camera and focused on the trash bag. He adjusted the depth of field and zoom. The view went through the black plastic. "Two ply," he commented. "Money! The man doesn't want his stash busting open!"

"Jeeze!" Dolly proclaimed. "Look at all that money. It must be ten pounds of hundred dollar bills!" Both Enforcement Vehicles were hovering five miles from LeRoy's illegal activity, not the best thing for a heavy EV. It consumed fuel. "Looks like he's going for a spin with a sizable wad in the trunk."

LeRoy settled into his land yacht. Lance switched from the NC to normal surveillance and concealed himself behind a large tree. The garage door opened and the Cadi pulled out onto the driveway making a rubber-squealing turn for the main road. The guy seemed to have a fetish for screeching tires.

"It's kind of funny," Larry opined as he watched LeRoy on the monitor. "He has all that money yet drives a pile of rust and torn vinyl. It's a perfect camouflage. Who'd suspect the driver of a wreck like that would have bags of money in the trunk, or bother to stop him."

"They might if he's Black, Latino, or Indian." Jim caught everyone off guard with his comment. There was a brief silence.

"Or if he's a lawyer," Cy broke the stillness. "The police have to be ever-vigilant when it comes to lawyers."

"That's true," Jim agreed.

"Let him go!" Dolly brought things back into focus. "We need the element of surprise. With his insides bugged, we'll pick him up in an hour."

"Roger," Lance acknowledged the order. "You are clear to move in and take the bunker. Those guys are equipped only with small arms."

FUTUREBUST10.7

The final miles were covered in two minutes. The EV's landed by the building LeRoy had vacated. The neighborhood was rundown—a remnant of the Great Depression—yet still middle class. The six officers wasted no time.

FUTUREBUST

Lance kept an eye on everything from his airborne perch, hovering ninety meters above the carefully hidden underground bunker. "You'll have to blow the latch on the heavy door," he informed through their person-to-person comm. Sarge grabbed a crowbar and pried the service entrance open.

"These guys thought they'd never get caught," Dolly observed. "There are no perimeter defenses."

"They gambled we'd be unable to locate their facility," Jim guessed. "Without LeRoy leading us right in, it'd have been difficult. He's definitely budget-conscious."

Weapons were drawn. Larry handed Jim a clump of explosives: Puff Charge enhanced with an additional dose of Protex. A little extra *oomph* wouldn't hurt with such a heavy door. They headed down the stairs together.

"All clear," Lance radioed. "The door swings inward. The neighborhood is quiet."

Jim placed the charge on the latch, poked in a detonator and stepped back. He sheltered himself with a portable blast shield. The others were stacked up behind. "Me first, you follow," he whispered. "Let me take the first volley!"

"Let's do it," Dolly ordered. "Take covering positions."

"Go!" Lance informed them. "The door is clear."

Jim grabbed the remote and blew the door lock. The heavy entrance swung slightly inward. Shoulder first, the bust proceeded. The standard cop greeting rarely helps. Perps tend to do the opposite. This instance was no exception. "Freeze, DES!" He knelt down, gun drawn, using real ammo, not rubber-dubbers. The bad guys were surprised, but reacted instinctively. They drew and fired!

"Damn!" Lance grimaced. "Four shots, four hits!" He swallowed hard. The rookie had never experienced such firepower used against another human being. Uninhibited gunfire usually portends an inauspicious start to the drug-busting festivities.

"They bounced off, Junior," Jim assured. He held his fire while everyone took cover behind shelves. It was now seven well-equipped officers against four lightly armed drug suppliers. He decided to talk them out of their hiding places. If successful, there'd be less paperwork for Bo and Dolly. "I want you guys to consider the situation you're in." He spoke loudly to the trapped stock boys. "There are twelve of us. We have the only exit to this bunker sealed off. We have tear gas and flash-bangs. And those bullets you just tossed our way bounced off body armor. Think about this very carefully. Do you want to see the sunrise tomorrow or are you looking for a permanent residence, six feet under?"

"One of them is circling to get a better shot," Lance informed the team. "Jim, turn thirty degrees to your left and fire waist high!"

Jim fired through the shelves stacked full of 50-count boxes of stogies. The bullet obliterated some smokes, then hit the concrete wall just inches above the head of the man crawling on all fours, trying his luck at a forced escape. He hit the deck and winced. "Don't do that again!" Jim ordered. "Slide your weapons out on the floor where we can see them!"

"Forget it!" one shouted. "We finish this thing here!"

Jim looked disgusted, but out of compassion for the drug-pushing scum, decided to try again. "You're going down in a blaze of glory for your boss, is that it?" He was thinking way ahead of the cornered men. "Didn't you boys notice that he left just before we got here? It's part of an arrangement we worked out. He walks with a bundle of cash while you guys take the fall, a good deal for everyone except you. Now let's try it one more time. Shove the weapons out on the floor and you'll have a nice, hot meal waiting for you at the brand new Combined Municipal Lockup. I'll even make sure you get chocolate pudding for dessert. It's that or a one-way trip to the morgue!"

"They're thinking," Lance radioed. "The pudding has them wondering."

Dolly whispered. "Nice bunch of lies. I hope it works. By the way, all such trips to the morgue are one-way." Jim smiled acquiescence. He'd been inadvertently superfluous.

"Weapons are coming out," Lance informed as he watched the various screens in his turbocraft. Four handguns slid on the floor.

"You boys lie real still," Jim ordered. "Arms outstretched!"

"They're doing it," Lance acknowledged as he watched his NC monitor. "They're all yours." Jim stood up, followed by Dolly and the others. The four men were cuffed less than a minute later. It was a wrap. "I'll call the paddy wagon." Lance, relieved it was over, leaned back and exhaled loud enough that the others heard it. The rookie pilot checked his GPS monitor. "Do you need me here? Uncle Roy is thirty miles back down the coast, moving at a good clip. You want I should go see what he is up to?" Lance used the voice of a backcountry sheriff, an impression he'd picked up from Cy.

"I think we can manage," Dolly replied. "Go keep an eye on LeRoy. Did you get a good recording of the bust?"

"I got a great recording!" he replied enthusiastically. "I'm beaming the e-doc to headquarters. Captain Jackson sends his congratulations. I'll follow LeRoy for a while. Maybe he'll lead us to a money laundering operation. If nothing happens by the time we get downtown, I'll have LAPD pick him up."

"Sounds good. LeRoy has no place to hide."

Lance radiated enthusiasm with the successful completion of his first bust. "Hey, did you see the SWAT guy's? When I left the hanger, they wanted to come along."

"They knew we might get some action," Jim replied. "Yeah, we noticed. It won't surprise me if a couple sign up for DES recruitment."

"Great." Lance whirled the turbocraft around and headed down the coast in search of one LeRoy (last name still unknown), AKA Uncle Roy.

Bo collected the slugs that hit Jim and put them in a plastic bag. They were Teflon-coated brass—cop-killer rounds that easily penetrate a bulletproof vest. The firearms were individually bagged and labeled. "Get those guys out of here," Dolly ordered.

"Where do you want them, ma'am?" Sarge asked, as if it had all been a walk in the park. He had one miscreant, and Jim, Larry, and Cy each had one.

"Park their butts up in the garage," Dolly ordered. Jim handed his trafficker off to Bo. The four marched their captives up the stairs in compliance with orders. Taking them alive had been a worthwhile objective. The bad boys made it to the garage under their own power—easier than carrying their wounded bodies up the stairs on stretchers. They had also saved tens of thousands of dollars in hospital bills. That chocolate pudding was looking like a bargain. Might as well sprinkle some coconut on top as a bonus.

"Look at all those smokes." Jim was astonished at the number of stogies. "Fifty in a box at one hundred dollars apiece. That should easily give us twenty-five mil exaggerated street value."

Dolly laughed. "It's a lot easier than counting each smoke. It'd take too much manpower to figure the exact value." She picked up a box, broke the seal, and dumped the contents on the floor, then crushed the valuable product into the concrete with her boot. "Five grand down the drain. Even during their heyday, the MIC never wasted that much so quick." She checked the label. "They're Cubans all right."

Jim began figuring in his high-powered mind, regarding the reference to Iron Triangle money-wasting capabilities. "Don't know if I can agree with your assessment, at least not like it was back at the turn of the century. Think of it this way. Sixty minutes times twenty-four hours." Jim pondered for a second. "That's 1440 minutes in a day, times 365." He looked at the ceiling and made the calculation. "A half million minutes in a year."

"Where did you learn to do all that figuring in your head?" Dolly asked. She had a hard time believing he could execute complex multiplication mentally.

Jim calculated. "Now, we have 525600 minutes in a year, times $5000 per minute"...he closed his eyes. "Wait, I'll get it. Five thousand dollars wasted a minute only comes to a little over two and a half billion a year. The Iron Triangle used to waste that in a week or two. And that's with time off on weekends and holidays. You're not even in their league!"

Dolly smiled and shook her head. "I didn't mean it literally."

He conceded the point. "But it gives some idea of how much money was wasted every year by the Military-Industrial Complex, which President Eisenhower warned us about eight decades ago. It had to be more than $100,000 a minute, or fifty-some billion a year before the Great Depression. Stomp as many Cubans as you want and you'll never keep pace with Pentagon waste." Jim closed his eyes to make another calculation. That's over $1600 a second, or a box of cigars every three seconds, twenty boxes a minute. You'd be doing quite a dance to keep up. And that's not even our biggest problem." Dolly looked surprised as Jim continued. "What on earth do you want to do with all this tobacco? If we don't handle this mess carefully, we're going to have elevated signatures every time we come up here. Your boots will have to be destroyed or they'll excite the sensors. We'll have to be miles from HQ before turning on NOSTRILS!"

They looked at each other for a moment. "Let's burn it all!" Dolly insisted. "We better haul this garbage to the dump and burn it in the Turbo Incinerator. I don't want to do it in a residential area. Secondhand smoke isn't good for the children."

Jim agreed. "We'll have to get this place sanitized with a TurboVac. Make sure you keep a box or two as evidence. It's hard to believe people pay a hundred dollars for these stupid things. The surgery to remove a lung increases insurance premiums. There was once seven to ten dollars of medical expenses for each pack of cigarettes sold!" They left the scene of the crime and started up the stairs together. Halfway up, he stopped and pointed to the indentations in his body armor. "That was a good idea. Those bullets would have done more than tickle without it." In the garage, the body armor was removed for comfort's sake. The transport arrived thirty minutes later. Cleanup commenced. The cigars were destined to go up in smoke, though not in the usual way.

FUTUREBUST10.9

Dolly sat in her EV. "Lieutenant?" Lance's voice held a hint of urgency.

"Go ahead, Lance. What's happening up there?" She gazed at her monitors. One held Lance's worried face, and two more showed LeRoy's vehicle in the distance. Lance had tracked it down and was following a mile behind.

"It's getting crowded around me. I think the media is aware of our M-SOC."

"Damn!" Dolly cursed. "Bo, get over here," she yelled at her counterpart, who was overseeing the investigation. He ran towards the EV and stuck his head through the hatch to see what was going on. "Lance is in the middle of a Mobile Surveillance Observation and Capture!"

Bo climbed into the EV and sat down in front. Both stared at the monitors. "Lance, what's going on?"

"The media turbocraft are coming in from all directions," he informed the two lieutenants. "I think they homed in on M-CAS, probably looking for some ground chase action to cover. I've got PNN, LAN, SCAN, SCAB, the 24-hour Live Chase Channel, the Police Chase Channel, the American Inquirer, about six regular networks and…HOLY MACKEREL!" Lance yelled. His face showed intense concentration. Beepers blared in his cockpit.

"What's happening?" The monitors answered Dolly's question. "Damn media."

"The High Speed Pursuit Channel," Lance yelled, resuming his verbal transmission, "just cut me off! That guy must be trying to win a prize for covering the most unimportant news event. He's got a better view of the M-SOC than I do! The doofus is blocking my flight path! Now I've got Speed and Crash, Mobile Surveillance, and FirstChase moving in tight!" The Cat-five shook from turbulence and thrust backwash.

"He's being crowded by the media!" Bo's face turned red.

Dolly looked at him. "Abort. Get out of there!"

"They're everywhere. I'm completely boxed in!" Lance spoke angrily. "There must be forty converging on me, swarming like hornets. The On-the-Run Network and CRUNCH are jockeying for position." He looked both troubled and nervous, checking in all directions: up, down, back to front, left and right. "They're nuts! They're crowding around trying to figure out which vehicle I'm following." More anger showed. "Instead of covering the news, we're all in danger of becoming the news! Everyone of them has disengaged his Midair Collision Avoidance System!"

Bo called Jim over. Lance continued. "We're flying too close together. They seem to be communicating with each other trying to figure out which car I'm chasing!" His vehicle bounced like a roller coaster, the kind of turbulence the pilots call Strap Stretchers. Not overly dangerous, Lance was experiencing hard reversals; first negative, then positive G-forces. Beepers were audible in his cockpit. Outside cameras showed just how close they were to each other, no more than fifty feet at some points. At such a slow speed, the turbocraft uses thrust to stay aloft.

"Lance, get out as soon as you can!" Dolly urged.

"Use ATMAT." Jim spoke calmly. He had been in similar situations, and knew how frustrating it was.

"I haven't taken ATMAT!" Lance shot back. "I'm only certified in Intermediate Media Avoidance Training!"

"Use it!" Jim urged.

All listened and watched the monitor for Lance's response. The views from the Cat-five shook from turbulence created by turbocraft in dangerous proximity; some neglecting any margin of safety. They were visible on the monitors, swarming like bees: above, below, in front, and behind. With the media looking for a juicy story, Lance attempted to disengage the M-SOC. Bo's face got redder than before. He looked at Dolly in sheer disbelief. "It's Sweeps Week! Lance, get out of there!"

Totally absorbed in the situation, he didn't hear. His vehicle was the center of attention. The two lieutenants watched as Lance tried to put some space between his Cat-five and three-dozen overzealous Cat-three media turbocraft. There was too much buffeting from turbulence. Buzzers were incessant. He was flying in the Egg Beater, a pilot-term for turbulent, unstable air.

"Lance," Jim spoke calmly, hoping his instructions might reach his brain. "Shut off M-CAS. Fly instinctively."

He disengaged the Midair Collision Avoidance System—its computer overloaded as the turbocraft darted back and forth to avoid a collision. The safety beepers and lights finally stopped their incessant demands on his concentration. Other media vehicles were now in the same predicament. A couple of the Cat-threes nearly hit each other, spun sideways in an airborne skid, then regained control and cleared. The young pilot finally spotted a risky escape route through the traffic jam.

The lieutenants said nothing. They knew Lance would not hear them. Two other Cat-threes near the outside of the swarm decided things were getting too dicey and pealed off. Lance was totally focused, seeing an opening if he acted quickly. He made his move!

A large grey object suddenly appeared on one of the monitors, taking up the entire screen in a blurry flash. The whole thing happened in less than a split second. It was the NewsFlash Channel, seeking a way out of the mess along with Lance. They had both seen the same opening. There was a grinding crash, then the sound of tearing metal. The Cat-five's forward, topside camera was crushed by the impact. The corresponding screen in the EV went blank. The comm. showed a jarring concussion on Lance's face. His head snapped violently sideways. After the collision, the two vehicles rolled off each other. Lance tried desperately to regain control but the front, starboard thruster of the Cat-five had been torn clear off his vehicle. It fell to the ground. He was now minus a thruster and totally unbalanced. The Cat-five went into an uncontrollable spin.

"MIDAIR!" Lance yelled as his turbocraft spiraled out of control. Speed increased dramatically, despite pulling back on the power. His ballistic parachute did not deploy.

FUTUREBUST

FUTUREBUST10.99

Lance wasn't killed instantly that day. The press believed he died on impact, but in fact was incinerated in the white-hot flames that engulfed his turbocraft. All the impact-resistant composites along with the best safety hardware available won't help if the Fire Suppression System fails. His skillful flying kept the out-of-control vehicle from slamming into a nearby playground where dozens of children were playing. After the initial 175-mile-per-hour impact with the ground, he slid across a four-lane highway, through a chain link fence, flipped end over end on the grass of a vacant lot, then rammed with bone-crushing force backwards into a twenty-inch-thick genetically engineered American Elm, deeply rooted in the soil. The twenty-two-year-old pilot was buried three days later, on a grey, drizzly Sunday afternoon in a ceremony televised across the southwestern United States. The mayor of Los Angeles delivered the eulogy.

Made in the USA